First paperback edition October 2024
Published by Ensemble Publishing

Cover design by Marija Džafo
Book design by Paper Rhino

ISBN 9781739724399 (paperback)
ISBN 9781739724375 (ebook)
ISBN 9781739724382 (hardback)

www.ensemblepublishing.org

MARLEY'S GHOSTS

by

JP Sheerin

ENSEMBLE
PUBLISHING

And did you get what

you wanted from this life, even so?

I did.

And what did you want?

To call myself beloved, to feel myself

beloved on the earth.

- *Late Fragment*, Raymond Carver

CHAPTER ONE

I was twelve years old before I met someone who read books for pleasure. His name was Edward Fraser and he was a semi-retired classics professor with a particular fondness for Jammie Dodgers and the works of Juvenal. Edward originally hailed from Aberdeen but had, by stages along the course of his life, moved as far south as he could manage without getting his feet wet, and by the time I met him back in the summer of 1972 had been calling Kent his home for many years. He and his wife Miriam lived the pleasant but vaguely melancholy life of the childless middle-aged and middle class, in a small three-bedroomed house within sight of the sea near Ramsgate. Being kindly and altruistic souls with time on their hands, Edward and Miriam had volunteered their home and a glimpse of their lives to the Children's Country Holiday Fund, a charity whose objective was to give the needy and impoverished children of inner London a two-week holiday away from the grime and grot of the nation's capital. The 'poor kids' holiday', as it was informally known in my part of the world. In this particular instance, the poor kids being me and my brother, James, who was three years younger.

One Saturday in August James and I, along with about thirty other children, were packed onto a train and sent off to spend two weeks with total strangers on the basis that sunshine and fresh air, while maybe not solving all the problems of our young lives, certainly couldn't make them any worse. James and I were assigned to the Fraser household.

Ramsgate was less than two hours from London but it was like a foreign country to us, a place that had light and colour, and where the natives seemed able to wrangle some small measure of happiness out of their lives. The Frasers met us on the platform at Ramsgate station and it was clear at first sight who had been the brains behind this charity scheme. As soon as she saw us on the platform, Miriam gave a short gasp and reflexively stepped towards us. I think she wanted to hug one or both of us, but it was a sudden and unexpected move and it produced our Pavlovian response. I stepped in front of James as he flinched behind me. This caused Miriam to pull up short. Edward stepped up behind her and put a hand gently on her shoulder. I could see a ripple of various emotions cross her face. Then she slowly and cautiously offered her hand to me.

"Daniel?" she said. "I'm Miriam and this is my husband Edward. We are so very pleased to meet you."

I croaked that it was nice to meet them too, then solemnly handed her a letter from our mother thanking them for their kindness in hosting us. I knew what it said because she had dictated it to me to write on her behalf. She had always struggled with writing and she'd had a broken wrist at the time. Miriam took the letter from me, shook my hand and crouched down to my eye level. She was older than my mother and her face was rounder, but her perfume smelled of flowers and I could see nothing but kindness looking back at me. I cautiously stepped out of the way. She offered her hand to James and said that he was a very handsome young man, that she was very pleased to meet him too, and she hoped they could be friends, as she needed someone to help her with baking a cake for dinner that evening. Specifically, cracking eggs into a bowl. James, who had fretted the whole train journey, tentatively allowed that this was something he might have some interest in. Miriam smiled at him with her whole face and James smiled back. With that smile I felt a weight fall away. James would be okay with this.

He would happily spend the next two weeks in Miriam's kitchen and garden, rarely leaving her side. He discovered that he liked cooking and baking, activities that back home, our father would have considered strictly the responsibility of women, but that James could indulge in here without fear of mockery or a sound beating. As for Miriam, she got a glimpse of motherhood, a role she clearly ached for, but that the fates had decreed she would never play.

All well and good for the two of them, but that left Edward and I to warily circle each other and attempt to come up with some form of accommodation. It was clear that Edward had absolutely no idea how to deal with a twelve-year-old boy from the back streets of Southwark, but he found his solution on our first night. When he showed us to the bedroom James and I were to share, there was a wall-to-wall, floor-to-ceiling bookshelf crammed with books. I stumbled to a halt in the doorway, staring at them, momentarily wonderstruck. I had seen books before. The Bible on the lectern on those rare occasions we were dragged to church. Multiple copies of the same textbook distributed around the classrooms at school, aged, cracked and held together with hope and sellotape. But a collection this size, multiple books on diverse subjects, of varying thickness, with different coloured spines carefully arranged row upon row, seemed to carry a weight and a power I had not considered or ever felt before.

The room was dark, quiet and warm, and though I did not have the vocabulary to articulate it at the time, what I imagine a gravity well might feel like, thicker and heavier than the space around it. A place where time might slow or even stop. And yet, at the same time, the spines of those books seemed to crackle with lightning. Like a rack of batteries – the promise of some unseen potential energy that only I could see.

"Have you read all of those?" I asked, amazed that a person might devote time and effort to such a task.

He glanced over at the bookshelf.

"Most of them, I think," he replied, his nonchalant tone indicating that if he had ever known this magic, he had forgotten, or it had become mundane to him. He went over and traced a finger along the spines, selected one and handed it to me, a hardback in black, red and gold. The picture on the cover showed a man in a large hat, holding a sword.

"*The Three Musketeers*," he said. "If you've not read it, you might enjoy it."

I had no idea what a musketeer was, but my mother had told me to be polite, so I thanked him and that night, after we went to bed, I gave it a try, partly out of curiosity, partly for fear that I was going to get quizzed on it in the morning. But mostly I wanted to know if the hint of promise I had seen at the first sight of all those books might be true.

That decision would change my life. Ramsgate was the furthest I had ever been from home, but that night, with James snoring gently beside me, and by the light of a bedside lamp, I found myself transported to seventeenth-century France and immersed in the political intrigue of the court of Louis XIII. I was lost the second I turned the hard cover onto the ornate gothic script of the title page. I read it until I fell asleep.

The next morning at breakfast Edward asked me how I was getting on with it and I said it was brilliant, and that Aramis was my favourite character.

"Not D'Artagnan?" asked Edward, sounding surprised.

"He's good," I said. "But Aramis is more interesting. He says one thing and does another. He does good things for bad reasons. He's…" I struggled for the right word.

"Complicated? Complex?" suggested Edward.

"Yes," I said. "All those. But mostly he just feels….real."

Edward nodded and smiled. I smiled back, feeling that I had somehow pleased him. It was only later that I considered that I might, in that moment, have reminded him what the magic felt like.

It gave me enough courage to lament that I would finish it that day then have nothing else to read. He smiled again, relieved at having found a solution as to how he could keep me entertained for the next fortnight.

"Oh I think we might be able to find another one or two to keep you going," he said.

By the middle of our first week we had found a rhythm. Every morning after breakfast, Miriam and James would bake some confection for dessert that evening. Edward and I would go on long clifftop walks with their dog Bilbo, then in the afternoon all four of us would go on some excursion together; net fishing in rock pools, watching the ships in the harbour, flying kites or playing cricket on the beach. All things we had never done before.

Although they tried, they didn't get everything right. One day they organised a trip to Kingsgate Bay to go swimming, an excursion that was abandoned with the discovery that James and I did not own swimming trunks. More germanely, neither of us could swim.

Another time in the back garden, Edward produced a football to have a quick kick around while Miriam was putting the finishing touches to dinner, the sight of which caused James to cry tears and run back to the safety of her kitchen. Edward looked a little hurt and embarrassed by this and asked if the other kids back in London had ever bullied James about his lack of football skills. I confirmed that they had, which was a lie, but the truth was too hard to explain.

Mostly our two weeks with the Frasers were a glimpse of an earthly paradise that would never be ours.

On our morning walks, Edward would tell me truncated versions of all the stories he was astounded and vaguely horrified to hear I had never even heard of, never mind read, by the age of twelve. That became my favourite part of the day, a time that was just for me. The coastal paths of Kent in August were a beautiful backdrop, having a dog for company was a previously unknown thrill, and Edward seemed genuinely interested in both my questions and my opinions, which was a novel experience. That someone was interested in my views and wanted to hear them. That the thoughts in my head might have some value. The double-edged sword was that there was a requirement to organise said thoughts before offering them up to someone for feedback. Edward didn't patronise. If he thought your thoughts were lazy or ill-considered, he told you, and told you why.

As we meandered the coastal paths Edward relayed the tales of Phileas Fogg's travels, wolves in the Yukon and rafting down the great Mississippi River. It was on one of these walks that he offered his opinion of what makes a good story. We were standing on a headland looking south and I was struggling in vain to make out the French coast in the distance, which Edward had assured me you could sometimes see on a clear day.

"A good story," he said, "is a true story."

"Was there really a Captain Nemo?" I asked excitedly, as *Twenty Thousand Leagues under the Sea* was my current pick of the tales I had recently been told.

Edward smiled kindly and elaborated that while it was not in the strictest sense true that an Indian prince had spent his years, his fortune and his engineering genius building a technologically advanced submarine with which to revenge himself on the British Empire, it was certainly true that a person might singularly apply their lives to the task of seeking revenge, or righting a great wrong. He turned to look at me.

"Life is random and messy and chaotic Daniel. I think you already know this. But people need order. For things to make sense. So they tell themselves stories. Religion is a story. Patriotism is a story. History is a story. Some of the stories people tell never happened. Some take the facts and bend them and shape them and twist them to give them meaning. Most of them are lies. But the ones that give meaning and remain true to human nature, to the way the world is – to my mind, those are the truth, and those are the really good stories."

I only met Edward that one summer – the next year the charity was discontinued, so no more poor kids' holiday for us – but he had a profound effect on my life.

James and Miriam were both crying when the Frasers left us at the station for our return trip to London. Neither of them had a problem with hugs this time. I think Edward and I would have hugged too, if either of us had known how to initiate it. Instead he offered me a handshake, his grip firm but gentle, his hand soft, the only physical contact with him I can remember for certain. Then he gave me a hard backed copy of *Lord of the Flies*. The inscription on the dust cover read:

'To my good friend Daniel Marley

– Edward Fraser August 1972.'

It was the first book I ever owned.

He then knelt down, looked me in the eye and said it was important to keep reading – that books made you stronger, made you smarter and made you better. "Life is a battle," he said. "Books are weapons."

I still have that gift and Edward's advice is something I have adhered to my whole life.

With every mile of the journey back to London I could feel its grey tones settling like a pall, but I couldn't dwell on that, since I had to make sure James was going to be okay. He had cried most of the way to Ramsgate and seemed intent on crying all of the way back.

Did he miss Miriam? Yes.
What part of the holiday had he liked the most? The smell of the kitchen in the morning when things were baking. And candyfloss.

What else? Playing with Bilbo on the beach.

Did he know I was always going to look out for him? Yes, he did. Was he going to be alright? Yes, he was.

Then he asked me what I would miss the most. The walks. And the stories.

We both agreed it was the best summer of our lives.

Less than three weeks later it would also become the worst summer of our lives, when my mother walked out on my father, James and me, never to be seen again.

My name is Daniel Jacob Marley.

This is the only story I have that really matters.

I have bent it and shaped it and twisted it.

But I believe it is the truth.

And I hope it has meaning.

CHAPTER TWO

There are many places I could start, but Salzburg is as good as any. Salzburg was not something I had planned, but as my father once said, every so often the universe sends you a sign. It was late August in 2013, nearly twenty months after Emery had left me to go wandering on the hills of Iowa, and for about half of them I had been living on the *Mary Ellen Carter*.

The *Mary Ellen Carter* was a seventy-foot wide beam barge that I had bought from Jimmy the Saint, a scruffy and cheerful veteran cruiser with a limp like a sniper's nightmare.

Living on a wide beam suited me for various reasons – it allowed me to rent out the three-bedroomed semi-detached house I had previously lived in, supplementing my police pension, and helping me avoid the constant prompting of memories that threatened to eat me alive like cancer.

There was also the benefit that a boat took a lot of maintenance – there was always some tank that needed emptying or filling, some bolt that needed loosening or tightening, or some surface that needed stripping or layering. Which in turn meant that there was nearly always something I had to drag myself out of bed for. Sometimes the hole is too big to be filled and you know it, but you've got to keep shovelling something in there, because the only other option is to climb in and pull the dirt over yourself.

The day started the same as most of my days. I got up at around 8.30am, checked the batteries and tanks, confirming that I had enough power and water to have a hot shower later, then went for a run with Fred. Fred was a rescue mutt from the Dogs Trust in Newbury. He mostly resembled a retriever, though he defied breed categorisation, seemingly the result of several generations of hasty and unregulated dog sex. But in personality he was pretty genial – and non-judgemental about those days when I just lay on the couch staring at the roof – so we got along okay. We followed our standard circular route, just over five miles in total. It was a pleasant morning and we managed to knock it out in just over forty minutes. By then the post office was open so I swung by to pick up my post, the paper, and a bacon roll for breakfast.

"Couple of tricky ones today – I'm stuck on about four," said Jean from behind her counter as she handed over my wares. She was referring to *The Times* cryptic crossword, of which we were both fans.

"You'd be more annoyed if it was too easy," I replied. "But I'll let you know how I get on."

Twenty minutes later Fred was fed, and I was showered, dressed and installed at the table on my large front deck with paper, bacon roll and mug of coffee. The mug itself was a dirty cream lopsided beaker with a twisted handle and two lumpy, unconvincing breasts on the front that interfered with every sip. Impractical, unsightly and totally irreplaceable. Jean was right about the crossword – there were a few stinkers in there. I kept chipping away at it and after about an hour, I had got all but two:

Damp fog hides nothing (5 letters ending in a T)

and

Bring Polish coin back to mediaeval European fort (8)

There are few things in life more annoying than leaving a crossword unfinished, but it was coming on for noon and I had things to do that day. The first thing on the list was some maintenance in the house I was renting out. A couple of fence panels that formed the perimeter of the back garden had gone over in a recent high storm and needed replacing.

I drove the three hundred metres to my house, took my toolbox from the boot of my car and walked around to the back garden which was brimming with late summer colour.

Through the exposed gap of the fallen fence, I could see Albert Lowenstein sitting in a lawn chair in his modest back garden, enjoying the late summer afternoon, eyes closed, clearly enraptured by whatever was spilling out of the oversized wireless headphones he was wearing. Albert was well into his eighties but still sprightly and independent. He had been our neighbour for the whole of our tenure in the house, and a good neighbour he had been too. He and I had got along fine but he had absolutely loved Emery, as indeed she had loved him.

Some sixth sense prompted him that he was being surveyed and he opened his eyes to look around. Seeing me, he smiled, waved and slowly dragged his long ancient frame out of his chair; it was like watching an arthritic clothes horse unfold itself.

He slid the headphones down to his neck and came over, offering his hand through the gap in the fence.

"Jakob," he said, as always pronouncing the first syllable like he was describing Himalayan cattle, his Germanic accent undimmed by his seventy years in Blighty, "it is good to see you again, my friend".

We shook.

"Good to see you too, Albert. You're looking well."

He snorted derisively and waved a dismissive hand.

"The three ages of man. Youth, middle age, and 'you are looking well'. Not much to recommend this time of life."

"Well it gives you the time to enjoy your music in the afternoon sun – and it's better than the alternative."

He offered me the headphones and I had a quick listen – something classical, dancing piano notes over a string section that put me in mind of a mountain stream falling over rocks.

"Bach?" I guessed.

He shook his head, disgusted at such a display of philistinism.

"Mozart. The Piano Concerto No. 21 in C Major. The Elvira Madigan. It is a source of pride still to me that a son of my hometown has made one of the greatest contributions to human culture. In this matter I might defer only to a native of Anchiano, Italy or Stratford-upon-Avon, England."

I knew Albert was Austrian but couldn't remember him ever telling me where he had grown up.

"You're from Salzburg originally?"

He nodded.

"For the first ten years of my life. Once, when I was a boy, my father took me to see Mozart played in the Hohensalzburg Fortress above the city. It was Christmas. I remember the powder snow on the ground, the smell of glühwein, holding his hand as we rode the FestungsBahn up to the castle. I think that might be one of the happiest memories of my youth." He paused and shrugged. "Of course, then came the Anschluss and it all went to shit."

I didn't know how to respond, so I handed the headphones back.

"Well, it is beautiful," I said. "You should have asked Emery."

He smiled at the mention of her name.

"I should." He hesitated then leaned forward conspiratorially, as though confessing a secret.

"Tomorrow is Friday. The evening of Sabbath. There is a psalm in Hebrew that is traditionally sung before breaking bread at this time."

"The Eshet Chayil," I said. "The Valour of Women."

He clapped his hands in delight.

"You are a strange man – does not know Mozart but does know the Eshet Chayil."

I smiled. "Just something I remember from when I was a child."

He paused. "I still say it for the women of my life. And when I do, Emery is one of those that I think of." He said it almost shyly, as if unsure of how I would react to his admission that he missed her too.

"I'm sure she would feel blessed to know that," I replied.

That evening, after completing the fence repairs and the few other minor tasks of the day, I strolled up to The Cross Keys for a couple of pints. Thursday night was pub quiz night and I usually wandered up to take part.

The Keys was a three-hundred-year-old building that sat at one corner of the High Street, with a whitewashed brick frontage and pretty flower boxes under its two bay windows, and matching hanging baskets on either side of the main oak door. I navigated around the crowd of smokers on the front steps and made my way inside. I could see my team ensconced in their traditional corner table. Peter caught my eye through the crowd and I made the universal 'You want a drink?' hand gesture.

He gave me a thumbs-up and I made my way to the bar. Tegs, the young barmaid with ambitions of joining the force and who would occasionally quiz me about various aspects of law enforcement, started my tab and I got the round in. Two real ales, a nice Sancerre, and my lager to lower the tone. I took two runs to get them from the bar to the table then sat down with my team. Peter was a retired army engineer and his wife, Helen, was a retired investment banker. The final member of our team was Jon, an assistant editor for the weekend supplement of one of the big daily newspapers in London. Not the kind of folks I would have known before moving to Wiltshire, but they'd had my back when it mattered, so I was grateful for their friendship.

They gave me their news headlines. Peter's topic was his latest village improvement project, getting enough money together to install a cinema system in the village hall. After a strong start, funding had stalled halfway to his twenty thousand pound target. Jon was bemoaning both the state of modern journalism and the reliability of the rail service to London. Helen was about to go on a painting weekend with some old school friends.

"Have you got any holidays planned?" she asked.

She had been suggesting for some time that a change of scenery would be good for me, and that reducing my world to a five mile radius from the deck of my boat – a boat which incidentally never went anywhere – was not necessarily good for my mental health. Helen was a firm believer that there was little in life that a week on a sunny beach couldn't fix. Initially I'd been dismissive, but the last time she'd brought it up I'd realised I had not left the village once in the three previous months. I'd reluctantly conceded that she might have a point, and started to give the notion some serious thought.

I shook my head. "Not yet, but I promise I'm thinking about it. Can't find anything to settle on. Something will sort itself out."

She let it go, but I could see her suspicion of being fobbed off.

The quiz started. Bruce, owner of The Keys, was behind the bar in all his ginger glory, and banged through the first few rounds with the brisk efficiency of a man who wanted to whizz through a tedious weekly chore and get on with the serious business of pouring alcohol down thirsty throats.

The first three rounds, current affairs, history and sport, we hammered out. The last round before the break was film.

Question four of the five was "Where was *The Sound of Music* filmed?"

"Hollywood?" suggested Peter.
Helen shook her head. "I don't think it's a trick question," she said. "It would have been on location in Europe"

"One of the Austrian ones," said Jon. "Vienna? Innsbruck?"

"Salzburg," I said.

Albert's hometown, I thought to myself.

"I think you're right," said Helen.

I nodded confidently. "One hundred percent sure."

The *Sound of Music* was Emery's favourite film. Every Christmas there had been a ritual of sitting through the entire three-hour orgy of mountains and goatherds and singing novices. I had groaned my way through it for two decades, but would currently have given an arm to experience that one more time.

The quiz carried on and we scraped a controversial one point victory. Jon suggested, as he did every time we won, that we donate our twenty pound winnings to the RNLI charity box on the bar.

Because he had a genuine affinity for that organisation, which had once plucked him out of the English Channel when a sailboat sank out from under him, we readily agreed.

The pub slowly emptied until by last orders, only the usual suspects were left propping up the bar. We talked amiably for a bit until Bruce politely suggested we finish up and bugger off home. I stumbled my way along the towpath in the dark, cursing myself for the umpteenth time for forgetting to bring a head torch. Once home, I did a quick forage. My options appeared to be cornflakes with water or the remains of a dodgy looking block of cheese. I went for the cheese, drank a pint of water to take the edge of the next morning's fuzzy head, and fell into bed.

Beer and cheese did not make for a great night's sleep and as I was tossing and turning, going over the day, I finally landed on my two missing crossword clues.

Damp fog hides nothing. Fog would be a mist. Nothing was zero which looks like an 'o' so if you unhide that, it made *moist*.

Which meant that *Bring Polish coin back to mediaeval European fort* (8) started with an 's'.

Polish coin was a zloty or ZL, so backwards it was LZ. Another word for a fort is a burg.

Salzburg.

Sometimes, as my father once said, the universe sends you a sign.

CHAPTER THREE

This is what I think I know about my father's early life. My paternal ancestors were Irish immigrants who, five generations before, at the advent of the Potato Famine, had fled Connemara moving first to Liverpool then eventually gravitating towards the sinkhole of the country that is London. My grandfather, by all accounts a sober and industrious man, fetched up in Silvertown on the north Bank of the Thames. There, having the stability of solid labour and more importantly regular – albeit low – pay, he had in quick succession secured the rental of a small terraced house on Gresham Road in 1920, and married my grandmother, a grocer's daughter, after a courtship that lasted precisely one month. Their only child, my father, was born a year later. They named him Daniel.

I have trouble reconciling the stories about the early part of my father's life with the man that I grew up with – of my father as a dashing patriotic hero or a debonair romantic leading man. Those stories may well have been true at one point, but they were not the experience that I had.

He was educated until the age of fourteen as was mandated by the Fisher Act, whereupon he left school and got a job working the docks as a stevedore. Although this paid better than a common dock worker

– therefore counting as an improvement on his own father's station in life – it was still tough and dangerous work, and so at the age of eighteen, in the spring of 1939, my father left the docks to join the army as a private, for the princely wage of two shillings a day.

With the benefit of hindsight, this was a spectacularly bad move, but by his own account – to drinking friends, not directly to me – the summer of 1939 was glorious. The pay was good, the basic training at Wellington Barracks was nothing you would break a sweat over by the standards of a stevedore, and pretty girls were always willing to flash a smile to a dashing young fellow in a uniform. That halcyon period lasted for exactly seven months, until Sunday 3rd September 1939, when, just after 11am, the glum voice of Neville Chamberlain announced to the country that the United Kingdom was now at war with Germany. My grandmother wept at the news, and it must have been around then that my father realised he had made a terrible career choice, especially as dock working was now listed as a reserved occupation, exempt from conscription. Too late by then to do anything about it.

On 9th September, he caught a train to Southampton and from there a troop transport to Cherbourg. One of the one hundred and fifty thousand men that made up the first wave of the British Expeditionary Force. He spent the next nine months digging a trench near Menin and developing a keen hatred of both shovels and French people, jaundiced views that would last the rest of his life.

When the German Army poured out of the Ardennes in May 1940, outflanking the Maginot Line, he was pulled back to Dunkirk, where he spent a gruelling seven days sitting on the beach waiting to get killed, captured or evacuated, whichever came first. His turn for evacuation finally came on the East Mole, and in the scramble to get men on board the smaller boat that was to ferry them out to the large transport, his left foot slipped off the ladder he was shimmying down and was crushed between the boat's hull and the dock. He'd lasted nine months in France without a single scratch and was undone in his last step. A permanent limp and a Modele 1892 revolver that he had taken from the corpse of a French lieutenant in Hazebrouck were the only mementos of his war that I ever saw with my own eyes.

Upon his return to England, that ruined ankle got my father rotated out of the army, but it also rendered him useless for stevedore work. In deference to his heroic war effort, his previous employers, Erskine and Scott Shipping Merchants, found him a clerk's job keeping track of the goods moving through their port. Although his education had been limited, my father wasn't stupid, and it didn't take him long to come to grips with a job which mostly involved counting crates and keeping paperwork organised in a chronological stack.

However, the combined armed forces of Germany were not yet done with the Marley family. In November of 1940 a direct hit from a Luftwaffe bomb reduced the family home, along with most of the street that it sat on, down to its constituent bricks, with both my grandparents still inside. My grandfather was bedridden with pneumonia and was unable to reach the air raid shelters, and my grandmother had refused to leave him.

The war was barely a year old and had already cost my father much of his mobility, his parents and his home. He spent a few weeks sleeping anywhere that he could find a place to rest his head – mostly underground tube stations – and I can only imagine that he must have been in a pretty low place when he finally managed to secure a room in a boarding house in Salmon Road. He was obliged to share a room with four of the eleven other people that were currently calling that hovel their home.

However, things were about to change for Dan Marley. Two of the men that he shared a room with were named Charlie Turner and Ronald Cook – men who later in life I would call Uncle Charlie and Uncle Ron.

They were business partners even before my father came on the scene, with Charlie covering the cerebral and conceptual parts of the operation, while Ron mostly dealt with smacking heads. It was Charlie who, over a pint of beer, told my father something that may well not have previously occurred to him. Namely that he was the point man at a bottleneck where a large number of extremely desirable goods were coming into a country under the effect of necessary but brutal rationing, and that such a position offered huge opportunities to a man whose integrity might be somewhat flexible. There was a chance for money – serious money – to be made and I can well imagine that to a man pretty much at rock bottom, as my father surely was, this must have seemed like a very attractive proposition.

Thus began his career as a black marketeer and petty criminal – side-lining the odd crate of butter here, cartons of cigarettes there, parcels of nylon stockings over yonder. Charlie already had some connections, my father was smart and adept enough at using the state of chaos the constantly bombed docks were operating under to avoid the authorities' radar. If there were ever any suspicions, I suspect his status as a Dunkirk war hero and his immediately intimidating physical presence kept any accusing fingers from being pointed.

Very quickly my father found himself with a lot of money to spare and a standing in the community that he had not previously been afforded. Black marketeers were mostly well regarded by the man on the street. All in it together might be a fine idea as a propaganda slogan but people still wanted sugar in their tea.

It only got better when the Yanks arrived in '42, the US army supply chain coming straight through the Royal Docks, offering a broad spectrum of consumable goods to purloin and pass on to his now inseparable business partners Charlie and Ron.

This was how he would spend the rest of the war, and the decade beyond.

Dan Marley. Dunkirk war hero. All round decent bloke, always money in his pocket, always willing to buy a man a drink, always ready to have a good time, always able to get you that much-desired item you just couldn't get a hold of anywhere else.

A story I heard more than once was that he would always pay for the fireworks for the children on the estate on Bonfire Night, an act of generosity that made him almost universally popular in his little corner of the world. I have one photo of my father from this period. He would have been about thirty, smiling at the camera while leaning against a lamppost in the Borough market somewhere. He was handsome back in the day, but it's the well-tailored suit he was wearing and the trilby hat cocked back at the jaunty angle that really made him stand out from the passers-by in their frumpy, ill-fitting make-do-and-mend attire.

Certainly, I can understand how dashing he must have looked to my mother, who he met a couple of years after that photo was taken, and how she could have been lured to fasten her ankle to this rock that would drag her down for as long as I knew her.

CHAPTER FOUR

It took me eight days to get to Salzburg, mostly because I used trains as my mode of transport, and when I got to Paris I turned left. I'd always hated flying, and given that I had fewer years ahead of me than behind, I figured this might be my last chance to tick a few outstanding items off the bucket list.

The late afternoon trip to Paris was quick and efficient. Upon reaching Gare Du Nord, I took a Metro to Montparnasse where I found a hotel to call home for the night.

The room was small but there was a bed and a lock on the door so that covered all my requirements. I got a good night's sleep and the next morning, set off early to try and get a feel for the mythical place that was gay Paree. I spent the morning ticking off a few of the big-name tourist attractions with varying degrees of satisfaction. Blew a pleasant thirty minutes mooching around the Shakespeare and Company bookshop where I purchased a pocket-sized translation of *My Mother's House* by Sidonie-Gabrielle Colette. Eventually I ended up at Père Lachaise Cemetery.

Within five minutes of passing through its main gates I decided it was the nicest graveyard I had ever seen. I meandered for a while, not bothering to consult a map, but still managing to find the final resting places of a few of its most famous inhabitants, including the aforementioned Mlle. Colette. Mostly, though, I just enjoyed the peace and stillness of its disordered cobbled avenues snaking between the tombs, and the warm sun dappling through the trees, the bustle of the city just a vague and pleasant thrum in the background.

I'd expected to find a flock of tourists at the grave of Jim Morrison but it was quiet. It was mid-afternoon so maybe all the debauched folk who might be inclined to seek out the Lizard King were still in their beds sleeping off all their debauchery from the night before. The only person there was a bored-looking gendarme, presumably tasked with guarding it. I could sympathise. I'd had some pretty naff gigs in my time in uniform, but making sure nobody vandalised the grave of a tubby rock star would be up there.

He assessed me as I approached and clearly decided I wasn't going to be causing him any hassle. The marker was a simple enough affair. A block of stone and a bronze plaque cast with his name, his lifespan and an epitaph:

KATA TON DAIMONA EAYTOY

True to the demon within. Or true to his own spirit, depending on which translation you wanted to go for. Personally, I liked the demon one better.

I left the gendarme to his watch and wandered on, passing a young couple cuddling on a bench, her head resting on his shoulder as he hugged her close. Looking at them filled me with rueful sadness. Around them was a prescient reminder that all roads led to darkness and dust, but there they sat, holding onto each other. Their surroundings proclaiming that the universe was callous and indifferent, their tableau suggesting that love is the only bullet that you have in your gun, the only armour that you can put on to go out and make your stand.

I could have stared at them all day but conscious that would have been weird and creepy I moved on, deciding to do my people watching from the more traditional location of a street-side café.

I found one just outside the cemetery, at a junction of five broad avenues. The waitress was a no-nonsense young woman of about twenty. I started to order in bumbling O-level French when she firmly held up a hand and made it clear that she would much rather conduct our business *en anglais* rather than hear me savage the language of Hugo and Molière. I was happy to accede. She brought my coffee with a small glass of water on the side.

I sat there watching the world go by at the going rate of one café-au-lait every twenty minutes or so for about an hour, reading and enjoying having nothing to do and nowhere to be, just experiencing the sights, sounds and smells of a strange city. I was just congratulating myself on how ridiculously urbane and sophisticated I was being when I clocked the pickpocket plying his trade across the road.

He was a thin nondescript man with cultivated facial growth somewhere beyond stubble but not quite a beard. A perfect face for committing crimes. Nothing to make it stand out. Your eyes just kind of slid over him. Were he in a line up you would hardly give him a second glance. He was wearing a rumpled suit and carrying a large satchel bag over his shoulder. Across the road from the café there was a plaza with a Metro entrance, steps leading down under the street. Next to it was a shop selling newspapers, cigarettes and postcards on a metal spinner. His modus operandi was to line up an unsuspecting mark at the postcard rack from about thirty metres away, then act like a pressed-for-time commuter hurrying for a train.

Picking a path that would allow him to accidentally collide with his mark at the top of the busy Metro steps, he would hold his hands up to apologise, then be on his way. The lift, when it came, was very fast. He bumped his mark, an American tourist wearing a USS Indianapolis baseball cap, foolishly carrying his wallet in his back pocket, something American men seem fond of, despite it exposing them to both theft and lower-back pain.

It took Monsieur Bland less than a second to relieve him of it and then he was gone, down the Metro steps. The guy in the baseball cap wouldn't know a thing about it until he next went to pay for something. I was across a busy street, too far away to do anything but grudgingly admire his speed and dexterity. I went back to my book and would have forgotten all about it, but then twenty minutes later he reappeared and did it again.

The second lift was another tourist, the victim carrying a large bag over her shoulder. Exactly the same: rushing for the steps, a small bump, almost a brush past, a brief murmur of apology and gone. Hard to tell from this distance, but I thought it looked like a mobile phone. From his first move to the bump took about fifteen seconds, then another five to get away. In all less than half a minute.

I considered this from a professional point of view. Most pickpockets move in packs, with the haul immediately passed to an accomplice, but that wasn't the case here, so he was clearly pretty confident he wasn't going to get caught in the act. Even if he did, the subway steps offered him about four pedestrian escape routes and a couple of Metro lines if he needed them. He must have known these well given that he was working the same patch over and over. That was a little out of the ordinary, but the nearby cemetery would be giving him a steady stream of marks to pick from. I should probably have let it go, but the second lift had annoyed me. Character and experience had taught me that there was no such thing as honour among thieves, but the vast majority of ne'er do wells I had encountered professionally had some kind of personal code, some line they would not cross. The second victim – the one who'd just lost her mobile phone – looked to me to be about ten years old.

At that moment my efficient waitress reappeared. "Encore un café, monsieur? Another coffee?"

I squinted up at her. "What do you think? Sit on the bench or get in the game?"

She frowned at me. "What game do you play with coffee?"

I looked over the road where I could see the ten-year-old now frantically searching through her bag for her missing phone, a crease of worry across her face. Then I checked my watch and started counting off twenty minutes.

"None, I suppose.. Le…." I mimed writing a bill.

She nodded. "L'addition? Bien sûr."

She was back two minutes later, setting my tab on the table next to my empty cup and weighing it down with the ashtray. I left thirty euros to cover coffees plus tip, then walked over the road to buy a postcard, and to see what would play out.

Monsieur Bland took about thirty minutes to return this time, which gave me plenty of opportunity to assess the environs and consider the vectors of motion. The ten-year-old, stifling snuffling sobs, had departed with her angry parents twenty minutes previously. The traffic, reasonably light but constant in the background. Light dappling through the trees on the wide boulevards. An ebb and flow of moving bodies in time with the arrival and departures of trains below our feet. This was not my city, but standing there motionless, I could feel myself becoming attuned to its rhythms.

I was leaning at the subway entrance on the opposite side of the road from the shop with the rack. A little twitchy, but mostly from my recent large dose of caffeine rather than any sense of anticipation. I decided I would give it another ten minutes before giving up when I spotted him standing under the line of trees that bisected Boulevard de Ménilmontant, his focus fixed on the postcard rack and the Metro entrance.

I glanced over at it. Currently there was no one there. It took another ten minutes but two middle aged women appeared and started browsing through the pictures of Paris, comparing their choices. It took about twenty seconds for him to resolve his internal 'go/no-go' logic then he started moving. Followed a second later by me.

I did a fast trot down the steps to the subway tunnel across the road, counting down from twenty in my head. I ignored the left turn that would take me to the Metro platforms and kept going straight, taking the steps up to the far side of the street two at a time. I timed it pretty well, emerging back into the sunlight at the top of the steps by the rack, just as M. Bland was about to start down.

Seeing that I was about to bump into him, I raised my hands in expectation of a collision. This looked like an instinctive response to an anticipated impact but was really just an excuse to get my two hands up from my side.

My right arm jabbed out across the small space between us, my fingers catching him in the brachial nerve cluster just right of his collarbone. It didn't hurt him that much but his entire right arm was now out of commission for the next ten minutes. Immediately following was my left which was a sucker punch with a closed fist straight into his liver below the ribcage. It wasn't lined up perfectly, but it got the job done. I could feel the ripple of the impact spread out across his lower torso.

That one would have hurt.

A lot.

A blunt-force trauma to the liver is not only massively painful but impacts breathing and circulation, lowers blood pressure and reduces heart rate. In short, it puts you down and keeps you there for a while.

Bland's face went white, his mouth opened emitting a wheezed gasp, almost a sigh, and he sagged at the knees. All of this happened in less than two seconds. To anyone watching it would have looked like two people had collided accidentally then one of them had collapsed.

I caught him as he fell and gently laid him out on the ground on his back, kneeling beside him.

"Doctor! Help!" I shouted in English.

I figured most urban French people spoke English well enough, even if they pretended not to, and a cry for help was pretty universal anyway. M. Bland was lying with one arm splayed out beside him and the other one waving weakly in the air looking for all the world like a stroke victim. The first passers-by gathered round us, the two women at the postcard rack who had just been robbed, another professional looking woman in a sharp business suit, and a bearded hipster in tight jeans and T-shirt.

There are two kinds of Good Samaritan laws. The first one exempts you from any litigious action if you attempt in good faith to help someone. The second makes it a crime not to attempt to render assistance to a stricken person. France had the latter so I was relying on that to overcome the curmudgeonly misanthropy of the average Parisian.

Sure enough within about twenty seconds a crowd of six or seven people gathered around Bland who was still lying on the street. I was crouched next to him. I figured I had about a minute left before he'd be able to speak again, so I grabbed his man bag, tipped its contents out onto the pavement beside him, and made to rest the empty bag under his head like a pillow, pretending not to notice what had fallen out of it.

Which was five wallets, two passports and four mobile phones. One of the women from the rack who was kneeling beside me gasped, clearly recognising her own possessions among that stash.

I stood up. At least two people were on their phones already, trying to summon medical assistance. The crowd was now about three deep. Then the woman from the rack said. "That's my passport. He stole it." Everyone looked at Bland on the ground and the booty lying next to him, suspicion coming off them in waves. Off to my right, about thirty metres away, I spotted the blue shirts of two gendarmes approaching at a fast trot: they had correctly assumed that a gathered crowd was worthy of their attention.

Once they'd arrived everything would be sorted, but I didn't want to be there when that happened.

I took one step back, then another, which got me to the edge of the crowd, then I turned and walked quickly down the underpass steps and away without looking back. I don't know if anyone saw me go, but if they did they were too slow to do anything about it. I continued down the tunnel, took a right into the Metro and two minutes later caught the first train that came along, a Line 3 heading west.

As I sat on the train heading back towards central Paris, it occurred to me that I had not hit another human being in over five years. It also occurred to me that Jim Morrison might not be the only one true to the demon within.

I got off the train at Sebastopol, six stops and about as many minutes later. I was still hyped up from all the adrenaline coursing through my system, so I sat on the nearest bench waiting for my levels to drop enough to stop my hands from shaking. Then I walked off the rest, tracing a path along the Seine past d'Orsay to the Eiffel Tower, looping back to the Latin quarter, as afternoon turned into evening, then night. I eventually settled in a cellar music club called Le Caveau des Oubliettes, having a beer at the end of the bar while a four piece group set up on a small stage, and then a second when they started throwing out some decent blues tunes.

As I sat nursing my drink, I looked at the pre-stamped postcard I'd bought. I bummed a pen from the waitress, with the intention of mailing it back to The Keys as an addition to Bruce's collection behind the bar. While I sat tapping the pen off my teeth, a group of six young Parisians – two men and four women – wedged themselves into the booth on my right. They appeared to have little interest in the music and a lot of interest in making out with each other. Initially I had them down as three distinct couples based on preliminary pecks and leg squeezes, but as it turned out it was one big group in pretty much every combination going. I did a quick mental calculation and came up with fifteen potential permutations, which they then blew out of the water by allowing more than two participants at any one time. Watching them, or rather trying very hard to ignore them, filled me with a strange melancholy, although I wasn't sure on whose behalf. I pushed the thought away and considered what to write on my card.

Dear Bruce and Sue – greetings from Paris. Saw the
Eiffel Tower, Notre Dame, and assaulted a pickpocket. Once
a fascist bully boy… Am currently trying to ignore six kids
having a monster snogfest to a soundtrack of some tight
Roy Buchanan covers.

PS. The Mona Lisa was a bit rubbish.

On reflection that seemed to be oversharing so I just slagged
off gingers and left it at that.

It was about then that I decided that I'd had enough of Paris for
one trip, so I drained my beer, and went back to my hotel. The next
morning I made for Gare du Nord and caught a train heading north,
forsaking the scenery out the window in favour of my book and the
company of Adèle Eugénie Landoy, Colette's impressive mother.

CHAPTER FIVE

However little I know about my father's early life, I know even less about my mother's. My father's stories were part of our family lore, told and retold over drinks, fine-tuned and revised over time to become legend. My mother's stories I had to work for. I gathered them up in bits and pieces. Very few of them were told directly to me. Instead I developed a talent for quietly fading into the background, overhearing her conversations with other women, unheeded but carefully recording. Some of the stories that women tell are not meant for children. And maybe some of the stories women tell are not meant for men at all.

She was born sometime in the summer of 1936. The exact date she never knew because she was found abandoned in a bus station in Camberwell one June afternoon, wrapped in a blanket inside a packing crate that originally held Bramley apples. Her parents were never found, and she was delivered to Barnardo's with a made-up name – Eve, and a made-up birthday of June 1st.

Barnardo's focus was heavily weighted to their physical and moral rather than emotional wellbeing of the children in their care. The staff tended to their charges with a brisk efficiency but there was little in the way of warmth or affection. The children were known by numbers. My mother's number was seven, and it was chain stitched into the few items of clothing she owned. She rarely spoke about her early life, so all I really know for sure is that at the start of the war, at the age of four, she was evacuated along with several hundred other girls to a large country house in East Anglia, where she would remain for the duration of the conflict. The local school was unable to cope with the large influx of evacuees and her education suffered as a result. By the time it was deemed safe to return to Bermondsey in 1945, my mother was nine and could barely read or write.

At the time, all of the children were steered towards certain careers. In the girls' case this was usually secretarial employment, but because of the lack of education in her formative years my mother was pushed instead towards domestic work. At the age of sixteen, she was sent on a transitional work placement with room and board at a tobacconist's shop where she worked for a pittance. Barnardo's did their best to vet these types of arrangements, but I guess the reality was that they were trying desperately to get older girls off their hands and beyond their responsibility. The tobacconist was a surly older man with an equally surly wife who viewed her husband's motives for my mother's employment with a suspicion that was not entirely unfounded.

I'm not sure how long she lasted there, but eventually the sideways lecherous looks crossed the boundary into the physical. One quiet afternoon when his wife was out, the shopkeeper made his move, coming up on her from behind grinding into her and reaching around to grope her breasts. She had jerked her head backwards catching him on the bridge of his nose and rocking him back. He staggered backwards, knocking off the shelf behind him. She spun around as he advanced on her again and she lashed out with her foot, catching him a perfect rugby punt in the kneecap. That was enough to put him down, cursing her name. With no road back, she popped the till, grabbed its contents and made for the door. She paused there, looked back and gave her parting shot.

"Follow me and I swear I'll kill you."

She fled leaving everything behind but the clothes she stood up in and what she had grabbed from the till.

Going back to Barnardo's was not an option even had she been so inclined. Thus, my mother found herself alone on the cold streets of London. A grimy, impoverished and dangerous bombed-out ruin of a landscape for a seventeen-year-old girl with about seven pounds to her name. For two days she just wandered, with no real plan. She nursed cups of tea in greasy spoon cafes. She rode the Circle Line, sleeping an endless loop under the city, until the stale air and the fumes drove her above ground again.

The first night she walked the streets until dawn, constant motion her only protection against the night walkers and ne'er do wells. The second night she did the same. On the third day, exhausted, she blew a shilling on a matinee in a cinema in Southwark. Back in those days they played films on an endless loop. If you came in halfway through the show, you just watched to the end then presumably watched the start until you got to where you came in then left if you so chose. My mother sat there in the dark and slept. One of the cleaners gently nudged her awake at some point late in the evening as the cinema was due to close.

The cleaning lady asked her if she had anywhere to go. My mother confessed that she did not. The lady gave her an address – the Charleston Music Hall one of the four places she worked at – and told her to come by the following day. That was the last night that my mother wandered the streets. The next day she turned up on time to find the cleaning lady and the manager waiting for her. The cleaning

lady was named Beatrice Callan and the manager was a man named
Lionel Costello. Beatrice had obviously had a word with Lionel
before my mother got there and, as my mother would later learn,
Lionel was a kindly man by nature. Over a cup of tea in his dingy and
cramped office, my mother gave an abridged version of her life story
– skipping over the twin felonies of assault and theft right at the end –
and in the end Lionel offered her a regular cleaning job.

The job paid thirty shillings a week, about a third of what she could
have made in a factory, but it was cash in hand. It came with a room
in the attic which she shared with two other girls, and the men kept
their hands to themselves. She was used to hard work from her time
at Barnardo's and she had the natural advantage of being pretty. Over
the course of a year she was moved to various other roles in the
music hall – managing admissions, coat check girl, working behind
the bar. Anywhere an extra hand or a pretty face was needed. One
of the pretty face jobs was that of a cigarette girl, wandering the floor
throughout the evening with a tray on a neck strap.

Because she didn't have a huge amount of disposable income, in
her spare time she tended to hang around the theatre and listen to
the big band practising. She became friendly with several of the
musicians. One afternoon as they were taking a five-minute smoke
break, they heard her softly singing the song they had just been
working on. The band leader was impressed enough to encourage her
to try out singing. It turned out my mother had a pretty decent voice
and that first time on stage she threw out a passable rendition of the
Kitty Kallen tune *Little Things Mean A Lot* with a big band behind her.
She was good enough that once in a while they let her perform that
song and another few numbers in front of an audience early on in the
evening. Lionel didn't mind this at all. Her voice wasn't going to scare

anyone away, and she was filling a half hour slot of entertainment on a cleaner's wages.

I think this was the happiest that my mother was in her entire life. Singing show tunes to strangers in a borrowed dress. Which is exactly what she was doing when my father arrived at the music hall for a night out with Charlie and Ron in 1956. After she had finished her short set and gone back to the less glamorous job of selling cigarettes from a tray, they called her over, ostensibly to buy some smokes. My father introduced himself and his friends, complimented her on her singing voice and apologised for having walked in halfway through her performance. She said she was going to perform five songs the following night but it would be very early in the evening. My father promised to turn up early to hear them all. This was one of the few promises he made to my mother that he kept, and the next night when she walked onstage at 7pm to sing, my father, Ron and Charlie were sitting in the half empty room. They applauded enthusiastically at the end of every number. She finished off the set with Rosemary Clooney's arrangement of *Come On A My House*, which my father chose to interpret as being specifically intended for him. When she finished, my mother came over to thank the three gentlemen for their support and my father asked her if she ever got a night off. She said that she did. And that was the start of that.

My father was fourteen years older than my mother, but he was handsome, well dressed and, with his cane, cut a rather dashing figure. My mother, at twenty-one, was little more than a child who lived in a box attic room above a music hall. He proposed after three months of courtship, offering her a diamond engagement ring that he had procured from some unspecified location. The ring was worth more money than she had ever made in her entire life up to that point.

They were married in a small church in the spring of 1957. Charlie was the best man and Lionel Costello walked my mother down the aisle. They spent their honeymoon in a Billy Butlin's hotel in Brighton. My father bought my mother a small green suitcase with solid brass buckles for the occasion and every personal item she had fit in it. The suitcase itself cost more than its contents.

Some months later, exploiting one of the advantages of being married, they applied for, secured and moved into a council house on an estate in Southwark. This sounds like the start of a love story that ends with a happy lifelong marriage, and I imagine there might have been a few good years for them at the start. But in 1960 two things would happen that would change the course of my parents' lives forever.

The first was the decline of the Royal Docks. The creation of containerised cargo required the use of much larger ships that could not navigate as far down the Thames, and new ports were created at Tilbury and Felixstowe. Less trade was now passing under my father's nose, which meant less opportunity to purloin certain items. New technology also meant better tracking of freight, which made it even harder to divert anything from these newly slimmed pickings. The decline of his empire would begin when he was laid off in March 1960.

The second was my birth in April that same year. My father's fortunes were suffering a downturn, just as he was thrust into parenthood, a role to which he would prove woefully unsuited.

In that time and place, communities lived closely together and wandered in and out of each other's houses to a degree that would be considered reckless and cavalier today. There was a Jewish family called the Abelmans who lived three doors down from us, and an older Caribbean couple, the Wedderburns, who lived directly opposite. The matriarchs of both these households took it upon themselves to act as surrogate grandparents to an inexperienced mother with her first child. I came home from the hospital – all seven pounds of burbling happy baby – with the name of Daniel, after my father. Mrs Abelman took one look at me and tutted.

"He looks like my brother Jacob." To this day, I have no idea if my mother knew the literary reference, but she liked the sound of it, so she snuck it in under the wire as a second name. Daniel Jacob Marley, born 20th April 1960. Even though my family and friends referred to me as Daniel or Danny, Mrs Abelman and indeed Mrs Wedderburn would always refer to me as Jacob, albeit with different stresses in the pronunciation.

Jacob.

He who will supplant.

He who will overthrow.

Looking back, Mrs Abelman might have called that one a little bit on the nose.

CHAPTER SIX

I made a whistle-stop at Brussels.

A whistle-stop? A whistle-stop stop?

I got off the train at Brussels for a brief diversion. None of the major attractions were of much interest to me, but there was one thing that I wanted to see since I was in the vicinity. It was less than ten minutes' walk from the central station. The trains to Amsterdam were running at the rate of about three an hour so it was a simple matter to get off one train then rejoin the next.

It was raining as I left the station, a steady vertical funeral dirge of a downpour that served to empty the streets of pedestrians. I didn't care. If anything, I was pleased to think that the universe might be offering a dissuading note of caution on my quest. That I had at least a small hurdle to overcome. Be careful what you seek. I found what I was looking for on Rue des Brasseurs, a narrow cobbled street a stone's throw from the Hotel Du Ville. Next to a boutique displaying lace goods under a garish pink neon sign, there was a subtle rectangular plaque denoting in French that something of import had previously occurred here.

As I stood there looking at it, I reflected that the incident it recorded had rippled down through the years to pivotally impact my own life. The plaque obviously didn't record that.

As I stood there, a tourist couple walked past, huddled under a large umbrella, clearly taking a short cut down a back street between one must-see attraction and the next. They saw me looking at the plaque and stopped to examine it too, wondering if they might have accidentally stumbled on something worth recording. The man took a quick picture of it with his phone and glanced over at me. When he spoke he had an Australian accent.

"Hey mate, you speak English? Do you know what that says?"

I knew the general gist of it.

"It says that at this location in July 1873 a poet got shot."

The man nodded sagely.

"Guess he was a pretty crap poet then."

I surprised myself by laughing. "I never rated him much myself."

I left them wondering why I was standing in the rain looking at a memorial to a poet I didn't much rate and walked back to the station, timing it perfectly to catch the next train. Total elapsed time in Brussels: less than one hour.

Whistle-stop.

I kept moving north until I got to Amsterdam. I dealt with that city in speedy tourist mode – Night Watch, Chet Baker, Anne Frank and canals, it's always interesting to compare another country's setup to your own – before turning south-east and heading for Germany. I pulled off a small but perfectly executed Operation Market Garden, crossing over the Rhine into the Ruhr valley just past Arnhem. I had no real plans other than travelling vaguely in the direction of Salzburg, and stopping wherever took my fancy, which turned out to be

Cologne, followed by Frankfurt, before finally stopping in Munich for a couple of days. I wanted to get to Salzburg with a clear mind, and there were two things that I wanted to resolve before I got there.

The first was a place. The Olympiapark München – home of the 1972 Olympic Games.

31 Connollystrasse OlympiaPark, the spot where I was standing, was where, forty years before, eleven Israeli athletes and one West German police officer were taken hostage by the Black September terrorist group and after two days, eventually murdered. The whole world had watched as this atrocity played out on their television screens. What the whole world didn't know was this was the same week that my mother walked out on my brother and me. Events totally unrelated anywhere other than inside my head, this the only memorial in the larger world to mark that private moment in time.

I couldn't articulate fully why I needed to be here after four decades, but I sat on a bench unable to think of a more fitting memorial to those murdered people than to sit in silence with my eyes closed and feel the warm sun on my face. To just feel. To just be alive.

I stayed there until the sun started to set. When I got up to leave, it was with a sense that I had done the right thing.

Then I went back to my business hotel, had a shower, and went down to the bar to complete my other annual ritual. As drinking holes went, the hotel bar was nicely laid out, if soulless. It was mostly empty – the only other people in there were two businesswomen at a corner table, each with a glass of red wine, keenly discussing in low voices whatever was on the laptop on the table between them. I perched on a barstool and the barman came over. 'Franz' according to the name badge on his waistcoat.

"Good evening sir. May I get you a drink?"

"I'll have a scotch. Single malt. Two ice cubes. Glenlivet if you have it. If not, whatever you think is closest."

"Certainly, sir."

As he fixed my drink, I checked my watch. Five past eight. One hour, I thought to myself. He gets one hour.

Franz set a beautifully presented Scotch on a paper coaster in front of me. I thanked him, knocked it straight back, then asked for another. There was a slight flicker of panic on Franz's face.

"Don't worry Franz," I said. "I'll take my time with this one. You won't have to carry me out, I promise."

Franz was clearly a barman with standards, as he insisted on starting the whole process again from scratch rather than just pouring a measure into my used glass.

"Enjoy," he said, setting it down in front of me.

"I don't particularly like Scotch," I replied, raising my glass. "This was my father's drink of choice. Today is the anniversary of his death. Normally I'd visit his grave then have this drink in London."

Franz nodded, as if he heard stories like this all the time. Let's face it, he was a barman, he probably did. "I'm sorry to hear that you didn't get to visit your father's grave this year. You have my condolences."

I thanked him for his sympathy and he wandered back down to the other end of the bar.

What I knew and Franz didn't was that the only reason I drank Scotch every year at this time was simply because I could and my father could not, and the only reason I visited his grave was to make sure that he was still dead.

CHAPTER SEVEN

The memories I have of my childhood are a fragmented jumble. While the lasting impressions of my early life are primarily poverty, hunger, cold and, later, violence, I can remember good times too, especially in the very early days. Holding my mother's hand as we went shopping in the East Lane market, or playing in the park as she pushed James along in a pram. I remember sitting by her on the stoop of our house as she sat chatting with the neighbours, peeling potatoes, or having a cup of tea.

I remember her hugging me by the fire, humming snatches of songs until I fell asleep. To this day I cannot hear more than a few bars of *Danny Boy* without feeling an aching hurt, that earliest memory of what it felt like to be warm and loved, to feel as well as hear the notes from my head resting on her sternum, the scratch of her oversized wool cardigan that she wrapped around both of us.

In all of those happy memories my father is absent. In that time and place, men were mostly truant from the business of raising children and it never occurred to me that this was in any way out of the ordinary. He would be gone for days, sometimes even weeks, at a time then one day turn up out of the blue, with Charlie and Ron in tow, for a brief pit stop before heading off again on his various business schemes and adventures.

Even then I was wary of my father, although I loved my 'uncles'. Charlie always brought a bunch of daffodils or some other flowers for my mother, and he would have a Texan or Milky Bar for James and me as a treat. Ron and I would playact a game where he pretended that I owed him money. He'd hold me upside down by my ankles and shake me as I laughed and the meagre contents of my shorts' pockets fell out on the floor. My dad would sit on one of the chairs by the kitchen table, smiling at this horseplay, smoking, and pouring celebratory glasses of Scotch for the adults, while my mother cooked a meal for them.

In those days, we might even have been well off by our neighbours' standards. The three men would sit up late into the night, sometimes with my mother, sometimes not. Occasionally, if she stayed up, I would hear snatches of her singing from my bed. Always the same old songs. Ron had a huge fondness for *When You Hear Big Ben*, Charlie always asked for a few verses of *Rags to Riches*. Invariably followed by a smattering of applause from her small audience. All of these sounds were familiar to me and, from the snug womb of my bed, were as comforting as raindrops against a windowpane. The next morning, I would wake to find my mother cooking back bacon in the heavy skillet with a warning to be quiet and not to disturb the men. By the time we got back from school, they would be gone again. On each of these visits home, my father would give my mother a handful of folded up banknotes for housekeeping. She kept this money in an old tin of Lipton's tea on the top shelf of the cupboard in the kitchen.

My father had not worked at the docks for many years, but over his twenty-year black-marketing career he had built up plenty of contacts, and had simply moved his activities into other murky waters of purloining and fencing stolen goods. He was known to the police. More than once they called at the house looking for him. Once or twice, they escorted him away. The mantra we learned as young boys was 'Say nothing and keep saying it.'

As far as I know he was never actually charged with anything, but he was certainly interviewed under caution several times and he was on their radar as one of the usual suspects any time something, somewhere, went missing or went down.

Then one day it all ended. To this day I have no idea what exactly happened but with the benefit of hindsight I can guess. The criminal underworld was changing in London in the 1960s and there were whole patches where the entire criminal element – drugs, prostitution, extortion, racketeering – was being consolidated under the purview of gangs, each with their own patch. My father had never worked for anyone but himself and his two friends, and I guess the gangs could not have lone wolf operators of any consequence operating without sanction or control. They might have let it go if he had remained small-time enough to fly under their radar, but I guess some enterprise or other they attempted made too much of a splash, made too much noise, got plod too riled up, and there were consequences.

One evening my father staggered home with Charlie, each of them holding the other upright, bleeding and bruised from the savage beating they had just taken. Of Ron there was no sign. No more would he hear Big Ben, having taken the brunt of the thrashing that had been delivered to the three men. Ron spent the rest of his short life in a permanent catatonic state in Lambeth Hospital, passing quietly in his sleep about six months later. That was the one warning. Enough now. If you don't work for us, you don't work. Not in this world. You're done. And just like that – they were.

My father could not, at this point, turn his hand to honest work, but he could no longer operate the way that he had. It galled him. He would still go out occasionally for days on end, but not at the same rate as before. One time he came back with twenty pairs of work boots that he piled in the corner of the living room and tried to sell to the local working men for a few shillings. He had gone from being the man who could get you anything you wanted, to the annoying bloke down the pub trying to flog you knock off rubbish that you didn't want.

When he was home he would sit, smoking furiously, at the kitchen table and picking endlessly and obsessively at the crease in his trousers. Trousers that were no longer replaced every three months and were becoming progressively more threadbare. More often than not, when he was home, he would either be drunk or getting there. The money for housekeeping got sparser, then stopped. Charlie still used to call around once in a while, but now there was a shiftiness to him, a realisation that the good times were no more. I remember him slipping my mother a few quid, and I do think that he genuinely cared for her, the young girl he had seen singing in a nightclub all those years ago. Maybe for James and I too, the closest thing he had to nephews, to family. But I think there might have been an element of guilt as well. He could see what my father was becoming and he knew he had a hand in stitching together the creature that was ominously lurching around our village.

I cannot remember the first time I saw my father hit my mother. I look back and it seemed all at once to happen all the time, that there had never been a time when it had not been. But once it started, anything would set him off. That there was no dinner waiting for him, that the house was untidy, that she was raising us soft. Then one day my mother had called me in from playing in the street and told me to run down to the corner shop to get some bread for tea. I had gone into the kitchen, pulled over a chair and climbed on it to get the Liptons tin. When I opened it, it was empty.

"Mum, where's the money for the bread?" I called.

She had come in from the back yard, and grabbed the tin out of my hand. She looked in the tin, twice, three times. There was no mistaking its lack of contents, but somehow she was having trouble believing what she was seeing, the line that had been crossed. She threw the tin across the room with enough force to put a dent in the kitchen wall and screamed "Bastard". The only time I have ever heard my mother curse. I stood there on a chair petrified as she leaned on the counter breathing heavily with her shoulders slumped. Then she turned and hugged me around the legs, while I hugged the top of her head.

"It's going to be okay Danny," she said.

I believed her simply because she was my mother and she made everything okay.

We had a mish-mash of scraps for tea that night. I remember that spam featured. I would come to know spam well.

When my father stumbled home at around nine, my mother flew at him, hitting him around the head and shoulders. He seemed genuinely shocked at her violence, but he gave as good as he got.

This time though, she would not back down.

"Dan Marley. Big man about town," she spat. "Stealing food from his own children's mouths to buy pints for the lads down the pub."

He couldn't look her in the eye, he turned around and walked past us, and out the front door. He didn't come back for a week.

That was how it was after that. My father continued to come and go as he pleased, but the housekeeping money he used to leave more or less ended. My mother would make money wherever she could, working the odd shift on stalls in the market, or in one of the shops on the high street, hiding anything she got from her husband. When he was home, he would beat her and us, if for no other reason than we were living testimonies to his failures in life. The rest of the time he would sit in the pub boring people with stories of his past glory days. It got worse when he lost his last ally. Charlie left London suddenly amidst rumours that he had fled to Liverpool, skipping out on some debt that he had with a local bookie.

But we soldiered on. My mother would send James and me down to the gates of the coal yards to pick up coal from the streets where it had fallen from the trucks as they left. More than once we had to hide behind the furniture when the rent collectors called. Our neighbours, who were well aware of our change in circumstances, looked out for us as best they could. I think my mother had been a good neighbour herself when times had been rough on other folks, so people were willing to help her out in turn.

Eventually things came to a head in the summer of 1972. James had always been good at football. He was a slight child but he understood the shape of the game and in a schoolyard of lumbering bruisers, he was deft and fast, almost balletic in his grace, with some genuinely good ball control. I liked that he was good at football – it was one of the few things that stopped the other kids from picking on him, and it was one of the few times that I could see him flying above the drudgery that always threatened to drag us down to drown. One day the PE teacher stopped my mother at the school gates and suggested she think about sending him to one of the football training academies in the summertime, confirming that he really might be that good. He did say that with his recommendation it would be free, but that James would need a decent pair of boots and some proper kit to play in.

My mother had asked James about it that evening over dinner, if he enjoyed playing it and if he might like to try out at the academy over the summer. Once he had confirmed that he would not have to stay overnight and could come home to us in the evenings, he was keen, so my mother said she would see what she could do.

That night she came into our room and gently shook me awake. I woke groggily but saw she was wearing her best dress and she smelled different from normal. More flowery. Her hair was different too, flowing down her shoulders, not tied up like it normally was.

She whispered to me so as not to wake James.

"Danny, I have to go out for a little bit."

"But it's dark outside," I said. We never went out after dark.

"I know," she said "but it's only for a little while. Really. I'll be back soon. I just need you to be brave and look after your brother for me. I promise it will be okay."

I nodded. "Okay, Mum."

She kissed me on the forehead. "You're my brave boy. I love you."

She left the house. I lay awake in the dark, not moving, not sleeping. Much later that night, I heard the front door open and close. I heard the creak of the stairs as my mother climbed them. I heard her sitting on the edge of her bed, then silence. I sat up in bed straining to hear more, but there was nothing. Our house creaked and groaned like an old ship at sea and it occurred to me that she must have been totally immobile to produce such an all-enveloping silence. I wanted to get up, see if she was okay, but something held me back. Somehow, I knew that seeing me would make something that was already bad, worse.

That weekend, my mum took James out shopping and when they came back, he had a new pair of football boots.

About a week after that my father came home. My father usually moved slowly, in part because of his dodgy foot, but also because of his alcohol intake. But this time he stormed straight into the kitchen and punched my mother in the face. He had slapped her before, but this was a closed fist that caught her on her cheek, just below her left eye. She went down. Then he started kicking her around the floor.

This was violence on a new level, and it was the first time I waded into the middle of it because I was genuinely terrified that he was going to kill her. I remember wrapping my arms around her torso and hugging her tight, my eyes shut, hearing James howling in the background, feeling the blows of my father's boots and fists on my back and sides as he tried to kick and punch his way around me, screaming incoherently the whole time. Forty years later, it's a blur of a memory, but the terror I felt, thinking that this was the end, that my mother and I were going to die, beaten to death on that greasy kitchen floor, is as clear as if it had happened yesterday. The assault only ended when my father slipped on the blood he had spilled and staggered against the table before sinking to the floor. The whole of the Marley family lay there, a tableau frozen in time for a few seconds, my father panting, my mother wheezing, James whimpering and me, silent.

I looked at my father then. Straight into his eyes. He stared back and waved a dismissive arm drunkenly at me with a mumbling growl. I continued to stare and he broke gaze first. That was my first realisation of something in our relationship that I had not considered before. That strength isn't always what you first think it is. That it didn't have to be this way.

He staggered to his feet and stormed out, calling James and I bastards, calling my mother a whore, leaving us lying there in battered silence. I got up painfully, limped down the hall and across the street to Mrs Wedderburn. Given the state I was in, I had no trouble convincing her she needed to come to our house straight away. She took one look at my mother and had her husband call an ambulance from the phone box at the end of the street. My mother was in the hospital for three days. The Wedderburns and the Abelmans looked after James and me. My father did not come back that whole time.

When my mother came home, social services came to see us. Nothing happened as a result. My mother might have feared my father, but I think in the end she feared institutions of the state more. Feared what might have happened to me and especially James growing up the way she had. James and I had learned well. We said nothing and kept saying it. James, who in many ways was much more intuitive than I was, figured out what had caused this outburst, even though I cannot recall ever hearing anything explicitly said. Whilst my mother was still in hospital, he made me take him over the road to our house, where he got his new football boots and solemnly placed them in the Abelmans' dustbin. That night as we lay in bed, he whispered that he didn't want to play football anymore, and that he thought it had made dad sad because he had a bad foot and couldn't play himself. He did not go to a football academy that summer, and as far as I know he has not kicked a football anytime in the last forty years. But my mother did sign us up for the Children's Country Holiday Fund and told James and me that we were going to have a nice holiday by the seaside.

It was a week after we got back from that holiday that my mother sat me down at the kitchen table.

"Danny," she said. "You remember when I had to go out and you looked after James?"

I didn't answer. I was only twelve but I instinctively knew there was nowhere good this conversation could go.

"I might have to do it again," she said. "Only this time for a bit longer."

I stiffened.

"It would only be for a few days," she said. "Then after that everything would be okay. And we'd never be apart again."

I knew the 'we' in this scenario did not include my father.

"How long?" I asked.

"Two days," she said. "Three at the most. You know where I keep the food money now, and Miriam and Mirlande would help if you needed anything. Your father might not even come home. Could you do that for me?"

Did I have a choice? I was her brave boy.

I nodded. "If you promise three days."

"I promise," she said and she hugged me so tightly I couldn't breathe.

Eventually my father came home. Broke and angry. He hung around for three days. Hit my mother twice. Me once. Then he left again. The next morning, as we were leaving for school, my mother said. "Miriam said to call around to her for tea tonight." I knew it was time.

She hugged James then me.

"Three days," I whispered so James would not hear.

"Three days," she confirmed.

Then I took James's hand and we left for school together.

I looked back from the top of the street and saw my mother standing in our doorway. She smiled and tucked a windblown strand of hair behind her ear. Waved and blew me a kiss. Then we turned the corner and she disappeared from our view. We never saw her again.

CHAPTER EIGHT

I got to Salzburg mid-morning on the 16th September, the high-speed train from Munich carving through the 90 miles in as many minutes. The city was divided into an *altstadt*, or old town, which was the bit all the tourists cared about, surrounded by a *neustadt*, or new town, which was presumably only of interest to the people who actually lived there. I had booked three nights in the Blue Goose Hotel located in the former and the Salzburg Hauptbahnhof train station was in the latter.

It was only about a mile away, it was a pleasant day and the whole setup seemed pretty amenable to pedestrians, so I walked it. The Salzburg altstadt looked like the backdrop of a fairy tale – built primarily in grey white stone, with narrow paved streets, and populated with horse drawn carriages, complete with the castle-like Hohensalzburg fortress towering high on a hill above it.

Crossing the Salzach river I found my hotel on Getreidegasse without too much trouble – the wrought iron guild sign of a large blue goose hanging over the door was a big clue. Technically I wasn't checking in until 3pm, but the young guy on reception was perfectly happy to let me drop my rucksack off so I could head off exploring. Now that I was finally here, I realised I had no real idea of what I was looking for, or what I expected to find. Some tiny spark of a magical made up world of pitch perfect naval captains, comic book Nazis and saboteur nuns? A notion of how happy Emery would be, were she here? I honestly had no idea, but I had come this far, so I was willing to keep looking.

Back out on the street, I turned and walked right, if only because I had come upon the hotel from the left. The street was the main tourist shopping thoroughfare of the Old Town and was busy enough to give it some atmosphere without being so rammed as to be annoying. Most every shop had seriously impressive guild signs overhanging the mediaeval street, and almost every building was flanked by a public passageway leading back to the river on my left and to a square on my right.

I passed Mozart's birthplace, an impressive looking building painted in a bold mustard yellow. I explored a few churches and cemeteries, cobbled back streets, market squares and about a hundred shops selling Mozartkugeln sweets, then swung back over the river. Wandering back in the direction of the train station, I passed another Mozart residence. This one was from his later years and looked more impressive than the first – so presumably Wolfgang was making some serious bank for his folks by that point in his life.

My wandering led me to the Mirabell Gardens, instantly recognisable to anyone who's been forced to endure multiple sittings of the Von Trapp children banging out the *Do-Re-Mi* song. I sat on a bench looking at the Pegasus fountain, the flowers and the passers-by, but I couldn't help feeling that something was missing. Possibly seven children and a novice prancing around singing show tunes, possibly someone to share the experience with. I grabbed a quick lunch of schnitzel and a beer in some generic tourist café. As I was leaving, I saw that the tourist information centre next door was advertising tickets for nightly Mozart Chamber Orchestra concerts in the Fortress Hohensalzburg. I figured if it was Albert's fondest childhood memory it had to be worth a punt. I got lucky with a ticket for that night, presumably because I was a Billy-no-mates and only after the one seat.

"Do you know if they're going to play the Elvira Madigan?" I asked the assistant as he handed me my ticket.

"The Concerto No. 21? I believe an excerpt from that is in the program, yes."

I thanked him and stepped back out on the street. I spent the rest of the afternoon aimlessly wandering around the main attractions of the city. Although impressive – I particularly liked the Sphaera sculpture in the Kapitelplatz – as the afternoon wore on I found myself getting increasingly vexed and frustrated. Mostly with myself. Salzburg was a beautiful and pleasant city, but no more so than any of the other cities I had wandered and explored over the course of the last week. The quest I had set myself had transpired to be a fool's errand. No great revelations had become manifest. The universe appeared not to have sent me a sign after all. Maybe, after all, that was just a throwaway comment made years ago by a violent drunk that my brain had somehow latched onto in some forlorn and desperate search for purpose or direction.

I went back to my hotel, with just enough time to grab a shower and a change of clothes before heading out again. I found the entrance to the FestungsBahn lower station, an old barracks house with a wide archway with modern automatic sliding glass doors, the imposing medieval fortress high above us. The car was a three-tiered modern affair with a glass roof. Even that annoyed me a little, as I had been hoping for something old and rattling in wood and brass, a relic from the time when six-year-old Albert Lowenstein had tightly held his father's hand, and made this same journey nearly eighty years before. There were twenty people in the car. By my guess, tourists outnumbered locals three to one, all of them better turned out than me. The journey took less than a minute and I turned to look at the fortress approaching. The rails ran through a circular arch in the walls, and I felt my sense of anticipation rise. It looked like an impressive threshold. Like Traitor's Gate at the Tower, or the Holy Door in St. Peter's Basilica. A portal you could not cross without a profound impact on the course of your life.

On reaching the top, however, I felt my anticipation drain away again. An usher expertly herded us through some stone corridors into an ante-room which already had about two hundred people waiting. There was wine on offer, and everyone milled around for a bit, murmuring conversations at a polite volume until another usher appeared through the double doors at the end and asked us – in three different languages – to please take our seats. It was hard to escape the feeling of efficient rote and repetition, a theme park ride that ran over and over. A tourist clip, a Disneyfied version of Augustan Neoclassical culture.

I filed through to the concert room with the crowd and found my seat at the end of a row near the door. The couple sitting next to me had splashed out on a concert program, and she offered it to me with a smile. I perused it quickly, just long enough not to be rude. I am sure there were a lot of interesting details in there about the historical context of Mozart's music and his place in the pantheon of great composers, but that kind of stuff has a strangely reductive effect on me. It's like someone reminding you the dawn chorus is really just birds trash-talking each other or that the bacon in your sandwich was once a friendly snuffly pig named Sir Oinksalot. I handed it back with a nod of thanks and at that moment ten musicians appeared out of a side door and took the stage to a polite smattering of applause. They were joined a moment later by the conductor who bowed to us. The lights dimmed a little, he turned to his orchestra, raised his baton. Then it began.

I know practically nothing about the technical elements of music. I never learned to play an instrument and I couldn't carry a tune in a bucket. For me it's simple arithmetic. I either had an emotional response to it or I didn't. You can put all the notes in the right order, but if it doesn't make my heart leap like salmon or at least make my feet start tapping, then I don't really get it. Every music critic in the world could stand in a line and take turns explaining to me why John Coltrane's *A Love Supreme* is the best jazz album ever, how it's a man laying his soul bare before his creator, and it would still sound to me like someone playing a saxophone solo that lasts about a week. I would absolutely concede that this was my failure, but I just wouldn't have missed it if it wasn't there.

Classical music was subjectively like that for me. Emery had played it constantly, and to me it had been the musical equivalent of wall paper. Not unpleasant, maybe added a little to the general atmosphere but easily ignored and forgotten about. The best thing I would have said about it was that if she was listening to classical at least it meant she wasn't listening to female singers with acoustic guitars banging out vowel-chewing country and western yodelling, another genre she heavily favoured.

For the first forty minutes I quite enjoyed it, despite my generally humpy mood. The music was being played live by professionals who knew what they were about. The acoustics of the curved solid stone walls were also excellent.

But then they got to the third piece, which hit me like a freight train, and that night in the Hohensalzburg Fortress I finally got it.

The first few bars were just a low bass phrase, then a woodwind instrument came in over the top. It put me in mind of the red kites over the fields of Wiltshire when they just hover, riding thermals, gliding on the currents. Then with a sudden jolt, I realised that I had heard this piece before.

It had been playing in our house, the night that I had come home late from work to find Emery struggling to prepare a three course meal for our friends.

That last perfect night.

The last night before it all fell apart.

I sat in that concert hall, enraptured as that single instrument was joined by others who took the basic musical phrase and turned it into something that washed over me like a river, carrying me down to a dark and deep ocean of lost time and memory.

The tiniest details of that last evening suddenly popping, fully recalled with crystal clarity, into my head – like Proust and his bastard madeleines – the smell of the beef Emery was in the process of burning to carbon, the waft of cold air from the fridge as I opened the door to pop a couple of bottles of white wine in to cool, the exasperated look that she had given me has she puffed a stray strand of hair out of her face, the errant splats of chocolate sauce she had managed to get on the walls.

It was like experiencing that whole evening again, the joy of it tempered with the sadness of hindsight. But that music remained, the last echo of an old life, reminding me that as long as I was here to remember, to have these emotions, then it was not yet fully gone.

Note after note washed over me, reaching into my chest, pulling at my heart. I am not a religious or particularly spiritual person, but when people speak of an out of body experience, maybe that is what they mean. I felt like I was soaring with that music, over myself, over the room, over the fortress, over the world.

I could almost feel myself moving backwards through time – back to that night, back even further, to my mother humming in our kitchen in Southwark, back to her singing with a big band behind her, things I had never witnessed, things that had happened before I was born. All of it condensed into one huge bolus of emotion.

All the highs and lows that had shaped my life carried on the note of a clarinet riding a musical phrase. It was like I was all the versions of myself that I had ever been all at one time. And all of the emotions that came with that.

It was only when we got to the intermission that I realised I was weeping. Which I think serves to say two things: One – that there really is no time machine known to man that is more effective than the right piece of music; and two – that emotionally, it took just a nudge to push me into a near collapse.

I left then, too overwhelmed to face a second half. Instead I took the long way back down the castle ramparts, and wandered without direction or purpose through the lamplit streets of the old city, their glow reflected on the recently jet-washed cobblestones. The alleys and squares that had been crowded with tourists earlier were now mostly empty apart from a few stragglers. Couples walking arm in arm, a few street cleaners, a man giving his dog the last walk of the night.

I walked until I came to the Makartsteg, a pedestrian footbridge that traversed the Salzach River, as it curved its way through the city. Fittingly for my mood it was covered in love locks, thousands of padlocks carrying the names of those that loved and were loved, adorned on its side, their keys dropped in the waters, tokens of endurance against time and fortune. I stopped halfway across and leaned on it a while looking at the dark curve of the river bisecting the city lights. Silent and cold, and inviting in its own dark way. One way or another, I had painted myself into this corner and I now needed to decide if I was going to stay here or try and plot a course out again. I was not so stupid that I didn't know that I was completely stalled. All I had been doing for the last two years was killing time until I got to a hole in the ground. My heartbeat had been reduced to nothing more than a ticking clock.

If I was honest with myself, this was what this trip had always been about, a tour around the perimeters of my past life. To try and draw a line under all of it, to take account of it, before trying to move on. Without acknowledging it to myself, I had travelled over a thousand miles to reach some kind of an end. To either accept or reject the belief that all of my best days were behind me. To put the past down or hold onto it even if I knew it was steadily killing me. Slowly for sure, but also for certain. Like it was nailing a bullet into my head.

I didn't want to go back to Wiltshire just yet, but I also knew I would find nothing more in Salzburg, beyond this moment, this revelation.

Somewhere else then. Although I didn't know where. I started walking back to the hotel and along the way met a busker with no audience but playing impressive acoustic arrangements of sixties classics. Somewhat fittingly as I passed he was banging out a passable cover of Blind Faith's *Can't Find My Way Home*. I stopped to listen, and when he finished I threw a note in his open guitar case.

He nodded at me.

"Danke. Thank you."

"No worries. Good to see Salzburg produced more than one

talented musician."

He grinned. "Thanks, but I come from Ehrwald. It's on the other side of the country."

"My mistake," I replied. "Good night"

I walked on.

The next morning, I checked out and caught a train across the length of the country to Ehrwald.

CHAPTER NINE

It took about six hours, three transfers and four traverses of the German-Austrian border to get me there, but it was a pleasant journey with the Tyrolean countryside rolling past. As soon as I stepped down from the train onto the platform at Ehrwald, I felt that I had made the right choice.

The railway station itself was little more than a raised platform but that was the only thing that was underwhelming. The scenery would have been spectacular at the best of times, but having been wandering through urban landscapes for the last ten days, I actually stopped for a moment, next to the train, in awe of the natural beauty that surrounded me. An ozone blue sky with a smattering of clouds for contrast, a huge limestone mountain range on every horizon, all sloping down into a broad treeline of straight pines and from there into gentle hills dotted with picturesque chalets. I would have expected such a landscape to make me feel small and insignificant, but it actually filled me with a strange sense of power. Like I had seen the face of God and lived. I stood there for a few moments just drinking in the scenery and filling my lungs with maybe the purest air I had ever tasted.

On the wall of the station's waiting room there was a large poster showing all the wildlife one might hope to find in the area. From the Eurasian lynx to the Alpine ibex, the peregrine falcon to the Eurasian eagle owls. The lions and tigers and bears, oh my. Next to it and more useful was a map of the local area with which to get my bearings. The town itself looked pretty small, about twice the size of my village back in Wiltshire, but laid out in a long crescent between the Zugspitze and Wetterstein mountain range and a wide flat valley about a kilometre above sea level.

About a dozen people got off the train with me. There were a few taxis in a rank outside, but it was a warm and pleasant day, the map suggested it would be a twenty minute walk so I took that option just so I could keep enjoying that fresh country air, and to stretch my legs after sitting down for most of the day.

Off to my left and just over the German border was the impressive lump of limestone rock that was the Zugspitze, off to my right was a bowling green flat oval basin of land called the Ehrwalder Becken – about two miles in diameter, crisscrossed with narrow roads that were little more than lanes, and dotted with old fashioned barns and farm buildings. There were three towns on the circumference of the basin at the three o'clock, seven o'clock and eleven o'clock positions. Lermoos, Biberwier and my destination, Ehrwald. The road I was following was a ring so I figured I couldn't get lost.

At least not until about two kilometres later when I got to a crossroads in the centre of Ehrwald and I was presented with a few choices. I stopped, hauled my rucksack off my shoulders and started searching through the outside pockets for the scrap of paper that had my hotel address.

As I was rummaging, a silver VW Golf with a red and blue go-faster stripe along the side pulled up next to me. The window rolled down and the occupant, a handsome blond guy, looked out, giving me the once over.

'Neumann', according to the name badge pinned to the left breast on his blue shirt. The local plod.

"Grüß Gott . Bist du verloren?" he said.

He sounded affable so I assumed that wasn't German for "All right let's be having you." But at the same time, I was aware that there was just a hint of wariness in his voice. I could understand that. I had been living out of a rucksack for a week and had not shaved that whole time. I probably looked less like your average tourist and more like a scruffy vagabond who had spent last night sleeping in a hedge.

"I'm sorry," I said. "I don't speak German."

"I was just asking if you were lost. If you need directions?"

"Thanks. I was just trying to find the address for my hotel. The Vorsehungberg."

He pointed over my shoulder.

"Just follow the road up the hill. About 225 metres. Take the right just past the church. Opposite the bank. It will be right in front of you."

I picked up my rucksack again.
"Thank you, Officer Neumann," I nodded towards the patch on his sleeve. "Apologies, I don't recognise your rank insignia."

He glanced down at his arm, then looked up again. "*Bezirkinspektor*. Equivalent to maybe a station sergeant in the UK. You are welcome. Enjoy your stay in Ehrwald. Tell Melanie I said hello."

He pulled away and I watched him go, then looked around at the chalets, mountains and pine trees. It didn't look like a high crime neighbourhood. He'd had an impressive-looking Glock pistol in a holster on his hip. As I followed his faultlessly accurate directions to the hotel, I wondered idly if he'd ever had to fire or even draw it in his career.

The Vorsehungberg was an inviting four-storey building, white with a brown chalet roof, flower boxes blooming on the balconies and a pleasant looking beer garden facing a public square. I found the door to the main reception around the side. The interior favoured a pine theme, simple but welcoming. There was a dining room off to my right, with a big gothic-looking bar beyond, and what appeared to be a large meeting area with oversized chairs around a large fireplace to my left past the reception desk. The split stairs leading up to the bedrooms were straight ahead of me. The woman on the reception desk looked up as I approached. I guessed she was early thirties. About five feet six inches tall. Blonde hair and a strong square face. In other words a formidable and professional front of house.

"Good afternoon, sir," she said.

"Good afternoon. Are you Melanie?"

She smiled a very professional smile, no doubt holding out until I explained why I wanted to know.

"Yes. I'm the hotel manager. May I help you?"

"Officer Neumann gave me directions from the train station and asked me to say hello to you."

She smiled again, this time more relaxed. "That was nice of him. Werner and I were in school together."

"You grew up around here?"

"Yes, although I've only recently moved back from Vienna. How may I help you today?"

"Sorry, yes. My name's Jacob Marley."

She nodded. "Ah yes, you are the late addition to the Morton's walking holiday group. I received an email this morning."

As she checked my passport and booking confirmation I assessed her. She was wearing a grey skirt suit with a white blouse. No jewellery at all. Assuming Melanie was as professional as she looked, and that working hospitality in Ehrwald was a backwards career step from Vienna, I wondered what had brought her back home. She returned to the desk and handed me my documents.

"Thank you very much Mr Marley. I'm afraid that all of the Morton's staff are out on walking tours with their other guests at the moment, but there is a meeting this evening at 6.30pm where they will plan their activities for the following day. You can meet everyone then. It will be in the reception area over there."

She pointed towards the open area by the fireplace.

"Thanks."

"I've put you in Room Number 7," she said. "First floor. Up the stairs and on the left. Any problems, please let me or any of the staff know. "

"Serendipity. That was my mother's name."

I could see her debating whether or not to ask what I meant, then deciding it wasn't worth the effort. Instead she handed me my key and wished me a pleasant stay.

As I crossed the lobby to the stairs, a petite gamine girl dressed all in black came out from the bar with a large frothy coffee on a tray. I paused so as not to force her to manoeuvre around me and she flashed me a nervous smile of thanks. A quicker, smaller smile than Melanie's but I suspected it was more genuine. She deposited the coffee at a table where a big guy sat hammering on a laptop keyboard. He looked to be deep into what he was doing, but he still took the time to look up and say thank you, so his stock went up a smidge on the Dow-Marley index. His laptop had a sticker on its lid – a cartoon Darth Vader and a caption that said "Protected by the Dark Side." Next to the laptop, there was a paperback copy of *Atlas Shrugged* by Ayn Rand, the bookmark indicating that he was about a third of the way through. Computer bloke didn't look like a natural adherent to Sithism or Objectivism, but since I was a living testament to not judging a book by its cover, I made no judgements.

With a few hours to kill before the evening reception I decided to go for a run. It had been over ten days since I had last got my heart rate above 100 beats a minute, and I had been nose-bagging beer and sausages pretty hard as I trekked across Europe so I was well overdue a trot around the park.

I got changed, tucked a twenty euro note in my sock, then wandered back down to reception.

Computer bloke looked up as I passed and gave me a smile and a thumbs up, which actually looked kind of sarcastic, but put his stock up another point or two. Still behind her desk, Melanie confirmed that it was perfectly fine to go for a run on the Ehrwalder Becken, gave me directions on how to get down to it, and also advised that locally it was just referred to as The Moos.

Three hundred metres down the road took me back to the spot where I had encountered Officer Neumann and another four hundred took me over the main road, down a slope between two buildings onto the flat, wide track that appeared to cross the Moos in the direction of Biberwier. I mentally calculated that if I followed the paths closest to the circumference I should come in at about the five-mile mark.

I was running for five minutes when I came upon six-point cross roads, and another jogger came into view about three hundred metres ahead of me, running diagonally across my view, left to right.

I assumed it was a she from the ponytail she was sporting, doing that mathematically weird horizontal oscillation based on vertical movements that never made any sense to my brain.

She was moving at a decent clip and I decided to use her as a pacemaker. I was empathic enough to realise that having a large unknown man suddenly change course and start chasing you around the farm lanes might well be a bit of a freak out for a single woman even in broad daylight, so I chose a lane that had us running in the same direction, roughly parallel but with about two hundred metres between our two paths. I could track the pace but still give her loads of space. Five minutes later, I realised that she was going to give me a spanking. I'd started about three hundred metres behind her and already I'd lost another hundred, which put me at least a half a kilometre off her pace. My lungs were wheezing like a broken concertina and my legs were already burning from anaerobic effort. I was genuinely shocked at how much my physical condition had deteriorated in a week, when it suddenly occurred to me that I had not factored in the one thousand metres above sea level.

Contrary to popular belief there is pretty much exactly the same oxygen at altitude as there is anywhere in the troposphere – just over 20%. But being less dense, the higher you get, the more air has to go through your lungs in order to get the same amount of oxygen to your muscles and brain. Basically, at maximum suck, I was not pulling in enough oxygen to get me the energy my leg muscles were currently asking for.

I struggled on for another ten minutes, gamely trying to keep up with the woman ahead. The Duracell bunny had not dropped her pace or steady rhythm one iota for the quarter of an hour I had been trying to match her pace. Either she was well acclimated to the height or had the lung capacity of a sperm whale.

Eventually I conceded defeat and groaned to a halt, my hands on my knees, sucking in air as fast as I could get, my heart beating like a jam jar full of bees. I watched her fade into the distance before I sheepishly sloped back to the hotel at a pace barely above a fast walk, stopping in the local chemists to pick up a disposable razor and a can of shaving foam.

Back in my room, I had a shave, followed by a long shower, then lay on my bed reading for a bit, wrapped in the fluffy bathrobe the hotel had provided. Just after 6pm I got dressed in the most presentable clothes I had, which wasn't saying much. I made a mental note to ask at the front desk about any form of a laundry service as I went down to the reception area to meet the other folks who had signed on for this mountain walking holiday.

I told myself it didn't matter if I liked them or not, I just had to meet them. To step outside my pre-existing borders just a little bit. After all, it was the reason why I had come here. I took a look at myself in the mirror on the back of the door just before I left the room. Scrubbed and freshly shaven, my face was older, and more weary, but still carried the bruises and scars both real and metaphorical, a reminder that life might play with you but sometimes it played hard. In my old life, I'd relied on Emery to give me a pass/fail mark on my appearance, but that I wasn't going to get so I figured it would have to do. I took a big deep breath, and went downstairs.

CHAPTER TEN

This time the reception area was full of people, sitting and standing in small groups, chatting in English. From my position just above them, at the first landing of the stairs, I counted ten guests with an average age of about fifty – the youngest barely out of her teens, the eldest somewhere in their mid sixties. The Morton's employees, easily identifiable from their logoed green fleeces and the lanyards hanging around their necks, were standing behind a large map of the area spread over a table and chatting to a couple of guests, pointing out various locations. Not a one of them was over the age of twenty-five, by my guess.

I walked down the five steps to the ground floor. The petite waitress from earlier was skilfully weaving her way through the room with a tray laden with various forms of alcohol. She had enough to deal with, so I went to the bar to get my own. The barman was over six feet tall, dressed in black like the waitress, with broad shoulders tapering down to a narrow waist, his entire torso like an inverted triangle. He had the face of a boxer, and a curling celtic tattoo circling his right bicep just below the short sleeve of his T-shirt. As he pulled my beer, I glanced down the bar. A tall man was perched on a barstool, looking intently at his phone. Chiselled features, close cropped brown hair with just a hint of pepper in the temples. He looked to be in decent physical shape. We made eye contact and he raised his eyebrows and gave a small nod as a greeting. Not unfriendly, but not exactly inviting a conversation either. I nodded back, then, armed with my beer, I went back to the reception area to introduce myself to the kids from Morton's.

There were three of them, one guy and two girls. The guy looked handsome and charming and gave the impression of being a natural leader, the sort of bloke a platoon might cheerfully follow over the top into a hail of hot lead. He introduced himself as Harry and gave me a firm two up two down handshake. After offering the standard 'Welcome to Austria' spiel, he gave a quick overview of the set up. Every evening the team planned excursions for the following day that guests could partake in if they so desired, but if you wanted to do your own thing, they were on hand to give advice about anything and everything from terrain and gradients to where you might locally source a packet of pickled onion crisps. The large and rather beautiful map laid out on the table in 1:50,000 scale showed the detail of every chair lift and gondola in the area, along with walking and cycling routes to and from the various peaks, lakes, mountain huts and restaurants, with some post it notes with added details. They had two excursions planned for the next day, which he stressed I was under no obligation to join: a twelve mile walk led by Penfold up to the Seebensee lake, which Harry helpfully pointed out on the map, while he and Vicky were taking a minibus fifteen miles or so across the German border to the Partnachklamm Gorge and waterfall, which he indicated with a wave of his hand as somewhere vaguely north of the map edge. I signed up for the former because it seemed like less hassle. Just turn up at the lobby at 10.30am the following morning with your walking boots on.

I asked Harry if my count of eleven guests including myself was accurate. He corrected it to twelve and advised the season was coming to an end – hence their diminished numbers. In the height of the summer or winter they could have as many as fifty guests a week, and as many as ten Morton's staff on site. They had twelve guests this week, and seven the week after, then that was it until the winter season started around mid-December when it all moved over to snow-based activities. Harry introduced the girl with flaming auburn hair standing next to him as Vicky, although I suspected within earshot of her parents, she might revert to Victoria, her received pronunciation suggesting the best elocution money could buy. That said, she seemed friendly, engaging and down to earth. The last member of the team was a sturdy-looking girl with an open, freckled face topped with what looked like an untameable mop of curls. She was in conversation with an older lady at the end of the table when Harry called over to her.

"Penfold, you've got another victim for your Bataan death march tomorrow. This is Mr Marley."

She smiled and waved to indicate I should come over and say hello, which I did.

"Penfold?" I asked.

"It's Penny," she replied in a heavy Scottish accent. "Harry just calls me Penfold as an in-joke. It's such an in-joke that he's the only person who gets it."

"Right, and the Bataan death march?"

She shook her head to dispel any fears, her curls still moving a good few seconds after her head had stopped.

"More of a Bataan death stroll really. Six miles there and six miles back. And there's strudel and coffee available halfway through."

She nodded at the woman she had been talking to. "Jane and her husband are doing it too. So you get to be in the cool kids gang, instead of hanging out with the losers on the waterfall bus."

Jane smiled cautiously at me and we shook hands. She was a tall woman, a little over six feet, and her height was accentuated by her thin, straight frame. She had long, grey hair that she wore in a loose low ponytail, and the thick-lensed glasses she wore made her eyes seem bigger, serving to make an already direct gaze a little more unnerving.

"I was just asking Penny if my husband and I could perhaps add another few miles onto the end of the walk to take in the Drachensee lake too."

"Which I suppose would elevate it to a Bataan death amble." added Penny helpfully

"Is your husband here?" I asked, looking around the room.

Jane indicated over to the fireplace where two men were in conversation – a balding man with a neatly trimmed beard nodding and listening intently to a scruffy looking younger man of maybe thirty five, his long hair gathered in a top knot at the top of his skull.

"George is the one on the left," she said with a smile. I smiled too, because there wasn't much doubt which of the two Jane was married to. The guy on the right was ludicrously handsome. Even that wasn't doing him justice. Despite being dressed like a beach bum – shirt open to halfway down his chest, yin-yang medallion around his neck – he looked like a pagan demigod walking the earth like a man.

"Jane was telling me yesterday that George once chased off a grizzly bear when they were hiking in upstate New York," added Penny in an earnest voice. I glanced at the entirely too innocent and deadpan look on her face then back at George. He looked as twitchy as a man who was scared of his own elbow, and certainly not someone I would have expected to be squaring off against ursine wildlife in the Adirondacks.

"It was a brown bear," said Jane with a smile. "And I know you're teasing. But that's all right. Everyone always underestimates George. Even me for a long time." That comment had a note of regret, a hint that huge swathes of years that had been squandered and thus I felt that it was probably aimed more at me than Penny. You can tell the young that time is a finite and precious resource, but they never believe you. And why should they?

I think Jane realised she had steered us dangerously close to maudlin philosophising, because she turned the conversation back to safe, small talk, telling me a little bit about her background and enquiring after my own. She was a retired librarian and seemed pleased when I told her that I still had fond memories of the librarian from Southwark back in my youth. Jane had been working in South London some forty odd years ago, around the same time. We both got very excited that we might actually have met at one point, but eventually concluded reluctantly that it had not happened. She and George were both retired to Somerset and rambling was their chief pastime these days, both abroad and back in England. She asked if I was here on my own. I confirmed that I was. She nodded. "There are a few other solo people. I mention it only because it's probably best not to go walking by yourself. Or at least not without telling someone where you're going. The routes aren't that challenging, but trouble can still find you pretty quickly if it wants to on a mountain pass."

Penny, who had checked out of the conversation when we had started reminiscing about London back in the day, checked back in to nod her agreement at this. "Sage advice, Mr Marley. If you're going to injure yourself, be a pal and do it on one of Harry's walks. No offence but you look a wee bit too big and strapping for me to be carrying you down off the hills."

I nodded. "I'll bear that in mind. Who are the other folks here by themselves?"

Jane nodded her head. "That chap that George is talking to, Mr Wall. Christopher, I believe. He's one. I don't think I've seen him on any group walks, so maybe he'd like a walking companion."

Penny frowned. "Not sure you'll have much luck with him. He turns up to the meeting every night, but hasn't signed on for anything yet. Never even asks advice about routes or paths. Bit of a loner it appears." She nodded to three women sitting around a table by the fire deep in conversation. "Abby is here alone too. She's the lady in the blue top."

Jane nodded agreement. "She's very nice. I think that she usually walks with Margaret and Bryce, the couple she's talking to. Bryce is American. Originally from North Carolina, Or maybe South Carolina. I've forgotten and now I'm too embarrassed to ask again."

"I can play the new guy card and work that into the conversation for you," I said.

"Thank you. I've always wanted to visit the American south, but my husband didn't have any interest so it never happened."

I studied the three women from a distance. From across a room Margaret was an angular, narrow faced woman wearing a tweed jacket. I guessed she was about my age, plus or minus a few years. She looked as English as cheddar cheese, and gave every appearance of having been created by Enid Blyton – apart from the fact that her partner was a striking black woman with amazing cheekbones and cornrow hair from one of the yet to be confirmed Carolinas. The lesbianism wouldn't necessarily have been a deal breaker as Blyton herself had once had a Sapphic fling with her children's nanny, but I suspected Bryce's skin would have triggered Blyton's ferocious racism. Even had I not been told, I could have guessed they were a couple – sitting next to each other, there was a palpable casualness, an ease of the other's presence in their space. Emery used to summarise this by saying you could always tell when people had seen each other naked.

The singleton of that group – Abby – had a strong face with shoulder length brunette hair and wore the kind of glasses a superhero might have sported to hide their secret identity. As I was looking she threw her head back laughing aloud at something Bryce had said and her hair swished across her shoulder. In that moment, I was suddenly sure that she was the woman I had encountered running on the Moos, and I felt a strange thrill of recognition – a moment of intimacy between us that only I was aware of. I looked away, feeling self conscious and voyeuristic about intently studying a woman from across a room. Especially since I suspected Jane had caught it.

"Who else is on their own?" I asked, casting my eyes around just to be looking somewhere else.

"Let's see," said Penny. "We have Mr Caulfield. At the bar looking at his phone. He's very polite. Bit posh, keeps mostly to his own company, but friendly enough when you're speaking to him. All about the bird watching though. Every morning, he sets off with his flask and his field glasses and we don't see him again until the evening. He might like some company, but I suspect you'd need to have – or fake – an interest in birds. And be very, very quiet."

Caulfield was the enigmatic guy I'd seen earlier as I was getting my beer, and the one I had not immediately pegged as part of the walking group. He didn't look any more approachable now then he had twenty minutes ago.

"Yeah, I know what you mean," said Penny, judging my expression correctly. "Hiding in a hedge with binoculars and twigs in my hat is not my idea of a good time either. So that brings us to Greg," she indicated to two men who appeared to be having an animated but good natured discussion on some topic they were passionate about. "He's the big lad talking to Mr Nicholls by the fireplace. Mr Nicholls is the other big lad talking to Greg by the fireplace. Let's just say that mountain walks are not really Greg's thing."

"Greg's the one on the right?" I asked. He was the coffee drinker from the lobby when I had first checked in.

"Yes," said Penny. "Good guess."

"He's not wearing a wedding ring," I explained. "The other guy is, so I guess there must be a Mrs Nicholls floating around somewhere."

"There is indeed," said a voice behind me. I turned around. Two women had wandered over to our group. One aged about forty five, the other maybe twenty. Mother and daughter from the look of them, assuming there was some merit to the science of genetics. It was the older one who had spoken. About five feet four I guessed, wearing jeans and a plain sweatshirt. Brown hair cut in an efficient bob. Her daughter looked to have mostly taken after her mother, although had obviously inherited her father's height and blue eyes, and she wore her hair longer.

"I'm Laura Nicholls," said the mother, smiling and offering her hand. "This is my daughter Christine. You'll be the late addition. The big galoot over there arguing about Gibson versus Fender guitars is my husband, Paul." I shook hands with Laura and nodded to Christine.

"Pleased to meet you both," I said. "Jake Marley."

"Jake?" asked Christine. "As in Jacob Marley? Like the ghost in Dickens? Really? "

"Carrying the chains I forged in life. It really is."

She smiled. "That's a cool name."

"Congrats, Mr Marley," said Laura. "You appear to have impressed my daughter. I didn't think that was actually possible for anyone over the age of thirty."

Laura rolled her eyes. "Mum…"

"That's embarrassing? You let your father argue about Gibsons for most of an hour without a peep. With added air guitar to make his key points. How does that get a pass?"

"He's beyond saving. You, there's occasionally some hope for."

Jane smiled at this exchange, then excused herself to go and 'rescue George', so I chatted to the Nicholls women for a while. Or more accurately, I chatted to Laura while her daughter listened, her head moving back and forth like a spectator in a tennis match. I gathered a little more information about them, whilst basically repeating what I had already told Jane. Here alone, travelled by train the long way around via Salzburg, which seemed to interest Christine who offered that trains were her favourite mode of transport and that she would love to do a similar tour of Europe herself one day. Laura was a hairdresser who ran her own business, Christine was a student doing second year in politics and economics at Leeds, and the husband Paul was an electrical engineer who worked for a Midlands power company.

The conversation moved on to tomorrow's activities. The Nicholls were going over the border to see the gorge and waterfall which Penny feigned outrage at, denouncing the Nicholls clan in its entirety as bus losers. It was at this point Melanie appeared in the reception area to announce that our evening meal was ready to be served, then started politely but efficiently herding the smaller subgroups into the dining area. The Morton's kids apparently did not eat with the guests, so Penny bade us a goodnight and went to help Harry and Vicky gather up their big map and various bits of paperwork. As we made our way from the reception area through the bar to the dining room. I saw the barman and the petite waitress standing behind the bar. She was cleaning glasses as he was pouring a drink and she casually nudged him in the side with a smile, causing a minor spillage of whisky. He smiled back and both her action and his reaction seemed to indicate a level of intimacy beyond the professional.

"Seen each other naked," said Emery's voice *sotto voce* in my head.

We sat down to dinner at one long table six to a side. I hung back, not wanting to hog anyone's place at the trough. Thus I ended up at the very end, sitting opposite the man Penny had identified as Mr Caulfield.

"Hi," I said. "Pleased to meet you. I'm Jake Marley."

He shook the offered hand, another firm two up two down.

"A fresh face? Richard Caulfield," he replied. "Likewise."

I looked down the table, mapping everyone's names and faces to get them all correct in my head.

George and Jane Smith sitting opposite each other at the far end.

Paul and Laura Nicholls next to them.

Christine Nicholls, their daughter, sitting opposite Abigail, the only woman travelling solo.

Margaret and Bryce, the gay couple sitting next to them.

Greg the computer guy sitting next to me and opposite the handsome guy with the top knot, whose name was Christopher Wall.

And finally Richard Caulfield and me.

Over the next ninety minutes and three courses of food, I added a few more details to my mental map. Richard Caulfield was not a big talker so I didn't learn much about his backstory, but sitting opposite him did allow me to listen to the conversation as it flowed, sometimes opening out to the whole table, sometimes contracting back into smaller groups, back and forth. Topics ranged from politics to economics, holiday destinations to music and books and I started to get a feel for the characters and profiles of the people sitting at the table with me.

Chris Wall worked in the Square Mile, although he was a little vague about what he did. From his appearance, I couldn't guess what job he might hold down in the city, aside from selling coke to the traders, but any gentle prodding was met with a pretty impressive stonewall. Greg Harvey was taking a break from the stresses of software coding. Bryce was from a small town named Hillsborough in North Carolina, had a doctorate in political economics and was spending a semester as a guest lecturer at the LSE. Paul Nicholls could play the Fender guitars he keenly advocated for, although not as well as he would like. The petite waitress was named Hanny, and the barman was named Bence. They were both from the same town in Hungary and were indeed a couple.

After dinner the group split in two – those who were heading back to the bar for a few after dinner drinks, and those who chose to call it a night. I was in the latter, electing to get a good night's sleep so as to be fresh and ready for my first full day.

As I lay on the left hand side of my big double bed, staring at the ceiling, trying to get comfortable in another strange room, I reflected that I had, for the most part, been lucky with my fellow guests. A nice, friendly, interesting and chatty bunch of people overall. Even if every single one of them, to one extent or another, had been lying to me.

CHAPTER ELEVEN

The thing about lying is that we all do it all the time. There was a study done once that suggested that any given person will lie on average 1.6 times a day. Whether by exaggeration, omission, equivocation, denial, minimisation or just flat out telling an untruth. At one end of the spectrum a lot of them are harmless – the inflated claims of your average CV, the size of the fish that got away, no your bum does not look big in that. At the other end they can have serious implications. Charlie Ponzi's stamp speculation scheme, Saddam has weapons of mass destruction, I saw Goody Proctor conspiring with the devil.

Because of my job I thought I had, over the years, developed a reasonably decent sense of when people were telling me porkies. Although all cops are convinced that they have a nose for this, statistically, some of us must be right. According to the training there are various physical markers for a person lying. These include changes in their vocal pitch, fidgeting or shifting, sudden stillness, subconscious movements towards their face or attempts to cover their mouth, inconsistent body language and elaborate explanations. The thing about all of this is that you need a baseline of normal discourse to support your assessment. Even a polygraph machine needs that. I had no such baseline as I was talking to my fellow vacationers, so my assessment was all just based on best guessing.

Starting with an easy one: 'Greg Harvey had come on a mountain walking holiday to relax'. I was sceptical about this for several reasons. For one thing I'd be willing to bet vital parts of my anatomy that he was going to top out on the scales somewhere north of three hundred pounds. When I had first met him on a glorious sunny day in said mountains, he was ensconced in the hotel bar on his laptop drinking frothy coffees. The twenty metre walk from the hotel bar to the dining area had been enough exertion to cause him to pant. Everyone has their natural habitat, and if I tried to picture his, it was down in a dark basement somewhere surrounded by the comforting hum of computer servers and bathed in the blue, cold glow of monitors. Not half way up a mountain surrounded by gortex-clad climbers with walking poles and cows with bells around their necks. Whatever reason he was here it certainly wasn't to relax.

The Nicholls? Paul sounded like an electrical engineer. He had managed to work the merits of metal film resistors versus wire wound resistors into a general chat over dinner, a feat of conversational gymnastics I had been quietly impressed with. More than that he sounded like an engineer. He had an intense ten minutes with Chris Wall on the sound quality of valve amps versus solid state amps and I got the impression that he lived in the left half of his brain and liked the things in his life quantified and qualified in neat and orderly lists. Laura was sporting a very impressive lob cut, so I had no reason to doubt she was a hairdresser who knew her way around a pair of scissors.

My suspicions revolved mostly around their daughter, Christine. She seemed like a nice, friendly girl, but I suspected this was an appearance that was an effort for her. As the conversation over dinner had progressed, she seemed to withdraw more and more from it, eventually lapsing into her own little cocoon of silence. Of course you could say that would be any teenager's reaction when trapped at a table with a bunch of people over the age of forty, but I got the impression that this was her default position regardless of what company she might find herself in. Undergrad in Economics and Politics at Leeds, I believed was probably true. But it was late September and as any Rod Stewart fan would tell you, she should have been back in school. Paul and Laura didn't seem like the kind of parents who would be cavalier with their child's education, so I was going to take a chance and say that Christine was having some kind of issue that was filling up her head and put her college life on hold for a bit. That this family holiday was the Nicholls either trying to give their daughter some space and time to get right with herself, or possibly removing her from an environment that was actively harming her.

The only time I saw any kind of emotion from her was when Chris Wall had thrown out the idea that human activity was not having any impact on global warming. That had caused her to briefly raise her eyes to stare intently at him for a few moments before returning to a keen inspection of the food on her plate. There was real fire in that gaze. From which I inferred it was a topic that she had strong opinions on but was unwilling, for whatever reason, to share them.

On the subject of Chris Wall, he seemed like a very charming guy. He was clearly intelligent, and engaged with his fellow guests on a range of subjects. In addition to discussing amps with Paul Nicholls, he had an interesting exchange with George about whether a lack of fuel had ultimately been Erwin Rommel's undoing in the Desert War, and a robust back and forth with Jane about the modern architecture in the City of London. These conversations were insightful and entertaining, but his scepticism about man-made climate change was not the only controversial view that he offered. Over the course of the evening he similarly opined – albeit in a self-deprecating and charming way – that social care was infantilizing, that free markets were ultimately a benefit to everyone in a society, that economic inequality was a natural state of all societies that drove people to achieve more in life, and that any notion of privilege was essentially just a social construct.

That last one was during an exchange with Margaret and Bryce which I thought was a bold gambit for a white, middle aged, presumably heterosexual male to be offering to a black lesbian from the American South. For her part, Bryce seemed to find this view wryly amusing, although I suspected it was only Margaret's sense of propriety that stopped her from smashing her gin tumbler off the side of the table and glassing him with it.

For the most part people were enjoying the debate, but I got the impression that this was his particular lie: he wasn't trolling people out of boredom, he wasn't just offering controversial opinions to play the devil's advocate or spark an interesting conversation over dinner – these were his genuinely held opinions and what he enjoyed was flaunting them so brazenly. As though he was mocking all of us, and getting away with it. That he could charm and con us all without us realising it. I suspect this was Margaret's opinion too. I thought I saw the mask slip once. The conversation had moved on to travel and places people had visited, and Bryce had mentioned that she was really enjoying Europe and that for a roughly equivalent landmass to the USA, there was so much diversity in peoples and cultures. How much of a difference she found between Rotterdam and Istanbul compared to the differences you might find between Portland and Boston.

"Agreed. Although Istanbul's mostly in Asia," replied Chris. "Only capital city to span two continents."

"Well it's the only city," said Jane. "But Ankara's the capital of Turkey."

George nodded agreement. "Lovely city Ankara. Wonderful museum of antiquities if you ever go."

Chris looked at them for a moment then smiled. "My bad. Ankara. Of course."

But for the rest of the evening, he kept glancing over at them with, I thought, a genuine fury at their transgression in pointing out the inaccuracies of his pronouncements. I got the distinct impression that Wall was a man who kept a list in his head, and the Smiths had just gone on it. There was a marked coolness in his interactions with them for the rest of the night. When Jane asked him what had brought him to the mountains he simply said "inspiration" then changed the subject as though elaborating would be as pointless as trying to explain algebra to a goose. It prompted me to wonder what exactly he was doing here. In the end I decided I didn't like him much. Partly it was his faux self-deprecation. Partly it was the man bun – which in my opinion you had no business sporting unless you were a samurai. But mostly it was just that his smile never reached his eyes, that beneath his charm there was something about him that suggested he would cheerfully unplug a ventilator to charge his iPhone.

Then we had the Smiths – George and Jane. When we had been chatting with Penny about which of the Carolinas Bryce hailed from, Jane had mentioned that she had always wanted to visit the American South, but that her husband had no interest so it had never happened. Later that same evening over dinner, George had mentioned to Bryce that he and Jane had always wanted to visit the American South, especially Savannah and its historic squares, after they had both read John Berendt's wonderfully evocative description of that city in his book *Midnight in the Garden of Good and Evil*. It was possible, of course, that he was only being polite, but if it was a falsehood it seemed strangely specific. It felt like the truth.

Later as I watched them over dinner I noticed that every so often, Jane would unconsciously reach out and squeeze George's hand as though either seeking or giving reassurance. I had no idea what any of that meant but I was willing to guess whatever other bits of the story came to light, they were absolutely not married. A bog standard infidelity seemed like the obvious deduction – even their surname Smith seemed a bit suspect in that regard – but that didn't seem to me to cover all the bases. There was something more to their story than that. I had no idea what that might be, but looking at Jane's face and remembering the comment she had made earlier, it seemed to me that she was aware that whatever transgression she might be committing, it was a lesser one in the eyes of the gods than the cardinal sin of wasting precious time.

Margaret struck me as one of those no-nonsense English women who might have spent the war driving a field ambulance or pushing small models of aeroplanes around a giant table map of the South Coast of England. Probably grew up on a farm and spent her teen years mucking out stables with the best of them. She had introduced herself as being a primary school teacher but I was sceptical. For one thing she didn't seem to have the personality fit for dealing with small children and again, she should have been back in school already. At the same time, I was trying to figure out why she would bother fibbing about it.

The only thing I could come up with was there was some job out there that gave a stuff about which way she swung, and that it had become an issue. What that might be in 2013, I could not guess, so in the end I just started filling in blanks for myself.

Teacher? She probably was. Tell a lie that's halfway to the truth.

Head teacher – given her demeanour and what appeared to be a strong personality.

Private school. Almost definitely.

All girls maybe? Possible with the Malory Towers Enid Blyton vibe I had picked up earlier.

Christian? That might work.

Would a private, Christian all-girls school care that their head teacher was gay and kicked her to the curb thus freeing up her time to go hill walking with her paramour? Since there was no burden of proof in a game played only in my head, and as that ticked all the boxes, I made that my final guess.

Then we came to Abby Guerin, who over dinner confirmed that she had indeed been the woman running on the Moos earlier that day and that she was here alone. According to the woman herself, this trip was a chance to clear her head after a long-term relationship had ended badly. I didn't press her on this, but given that she was English, and Guerin was a French surname, I wondered if it might be a married name she had not yet gotten around to giving up.

I didn't doubt that any of this was true, but I wondered if it was the full story. There were things about her appearance that were odd to me. I was fairly certain that her brunette hair was not natural. It certainly didn't match her eyebrows or the hairs on her forearm, both of which were a fine blonde. Nothing unusual in that, but as the evening wore on, I became fairly positive that there were no prescription lenses in her glasses. It was a subtle thing, but when I glanced sideways at her, there was no break in the line of her brow and cheek where it passed through her lens, something I probably would not have noticed had I not just witnessed the incredible distorting effect of the Coke bottle spectaculars Jane was sporting. It was almost as though she was trying to hide herself away, or at least needed psychological shields to face the world.

She had made light of that long-term relationship that ended, glossed over it, but I found myself wondering if had been abusive in some way. That her marriage had ended because of domestic violence, that this trip was an attempt to get out and face the world again. Listening to her talk to Bryce about having worked in Europe, there was a note of longing in her voice, like a desire to return to a simpler, better time, and I got the feeling that there was a level of hurt buried deep inside her, that she had carried around for years, but had learned to lock away, that she never let people see. In a lot of ways, she reminded me of myself.

Finally there was Richard Caulfield. When I first met him, he had been standing away from the group, observing the whole room at once. He put me in mind of a gunslinger who had instinctively learned to keep his back to the wall. He said that he was a management consultant for a software firm, which seemed plausible enough – he had that kind of aura that meant you could pick any career or role and see him doing it. I asked him if he had any luck spotting any Eurasian eagle owls, and he paused, then smiled and said 'not yet.' But for one tiny instant, I could see him working the question back in his head – Eurasian eagle owls to birds to bird watching to what he had told Penny – before giving his answer. It was less than two seconds, but in that small moment I could see the cogs working to come up with the correct answer. Which reminded me of countless conversations in interview rooms over the years. As though his bird watching was a total fabrication.

But the main reason he set off some alarm bells was on a more subliminal, primal level. There is a thing that I cannot help doing whenever I am introduced to another man – something in the handshake and the initial eye contact: an evaluation, a measuring up. Some throwback to an earlier part of my life as one of Maggie's stormtroopers cracking skulls for a living. Or maybe it's in all men, a hard coded genetic hangover from when we were all living in caves huddled around fires, fighting for food and breeding rights. Could I take this guy in a fight if I had to? If I got into it with this bloke in a stand-up, knockdown brawl, could I beat him? And the answer in the case of Richard Caulfield was an unequivocal no. I was pretty certain I would get crucified. It was hard to define. He was maybe mid-forties, solidly built, muscular and no superfluous fat. But more, it was something in the eyes – they missed nothing, and there was a certain hardness to them, like they had seen it all. They indicated that nothing would surprise him because he had seen what people could do to each other first hand. He had a kind of quiet centre in his bearing that exuded confidence – that there wasn't a bar or a neighbourhood anywhere in the world that he would hesitate to walk into for fear that he wouldn't be able to handle himself.

As the evening wore on I noticed something else too. Everyone had their own tics and tells. Abby tended to tuck her hair behind her ears. Christine Nicholls covering her mouth when she smiled. Jane regularly reaching out to squeeze George's hand. Margaret's nervous tapping of her index, middle and ring finger on the table top. My own, I knew, was a literal tic in my right eye when I was stressed or angry, or even just chasing a train of thought in my head. Richard Caulfield had nothing. Not a single one that I could see, and I was looking pretty hard for them by the end of that meal. A complete blank canvas. And everyone had a tell, unless they had trained very hard not to. Which I thought was a tell in itself.

As it happened I got accused of a couple of lies myself. Both accusations came from Bryce. When I first introduced myself to her she laughed as Christine Nicholls had done earlier and said "Jacob Marley, no you're lying, that isn't really your name is it?"

I had confirmed that Jacob Marley appeared on my birth certificate, which was half a lie since I skipped over the part that I had been named Daniel, after my father, and my relationship with him was such that I had rejected his name. The other accusation came when she asked how I had ended up in Ehrwald, and I said that since we were on the subject of ghosts, I had been chasing one through Europe across five countries and seven cities, and that eventually it had led me here.

She had smiled at that. "Now I know for sure you're lying," she said.

I smiled like I had been caught out and was conceding the point, even though that one was, of course, one hundred percent true.

CHAPTER TWELVE

I got a solid eight hours of sleep my first night in the Vorsehungberg and woke to find a glorious sunny day waiting for me. I got dressed and wandered down for breakfast which was a buffet affair. I ordered a coffee from Hanny who, as far as I could tell, worked every hour the hotel was open, and I started loading up on carbs in anticipation of some serious high level walking that day. The only other Morton's guest I could see was Greg Harvey, who was sitting out in the beer garden under an umbrella, as before, hammering away on his laptop. I wandered out there with my mug and a plate piled high with pastries.

"Hi mate, mind if I join you?" I asked, nodding at the chair opposite him. He looked up surprised then nodded.

"Help yourself."

I sat down.

"You signed on for either of today's expeditions?" I asked.

He shook his head. "I'll probably just get a bit of work done. Maybe read a bit."

I said nothing but my face must have betrayed my thoughts, because he sighed, shut the laptop lid and looked at me.

"Do you want to just ask the question?"

"What question is that?"

"What's someone my size doing on a walking holiday?"

"Well, I wouldn't have put it like that, and far be it for me to tell someone how to relax, but you don't seem to be in much of a rush to take advantage of your surroundings."

He nodded in agreement, took a packet of cigarettes out of his pocket, stuck one in his mouth and offered me the pack.

I shook my head. "No harm to you mate, but you're really tempting fate."

He shrugged. "Genetics is all a bit of a lottery isn't it. A big game of Russian roulette. All I'm really doing is shoving more bullets in the gun.'

It was at that moment I decided I liked Greg. It's probably a character flaw of mine – that I find fatalism and cynicism inherently attractive qualities.

"So, if you're not here for the walking, what's the story?" I asked.

He looked around to make sure there was no one within earshot then leaned in.

"You remember Chris Wall last night?"

"Point Break? With the topknot? Yeah, I remember him."

"How much would you say he's worth? At a guess."

I shrugged. "I don't know. Five, maybe ten quid?"

"What would you say if I told you it was somewhere in the mid seven figures?"

"I'd say he didn't spend any of it on his wardrobe."

"What did you make of him?"

"Honestly? I thought he was a bit of an arse. Mind you, I'm basing that on one dinner's worth of conversation. So best answer, I don't really know him well enough for my opinion to count for much."

"You're probably not wrong. But he's also one of the top five high-level artificial intelligence software developers alive today."

I considered this. "Is that a thing? Being a top five software developer?"

Greg nodded. "Absolutely it is. Not as famous as say being a premiership footballer, but just as lucrative."

"So, what does he do with all this coding talent?"

"Makes a ton of money. He runs a small contracting firm – a hired gun for financial houses in the Square Mile to give them an edge in the stock markets. Just him and a small hand-picked team. He comes up with the big ideas, gets the main code built then farms out some of the dev work to his associates. Sells it on to trading houses in the City for mega bucks."

The penny dropped.

"So, you found out where he was going on holiday and just happened to turn up in hopes of blagging a job off him?"

He nodded, a little sheepish. "It sounds kind of stupid when you say it like that, but yes. I know he comes here for a week every year so I thought I'd just turn up and see if we could meet, and I could hang out my shingle."

"You actually talked to him yet? About software."

He shook his head.

"Just general chit-chat. I'm picking my moment."

A thought occurred to me.

"Don't tell me. He's a big Ayn Rand fan."

Greg looked down, embarrassed. "Yeah. He said Atlas Shrugged is his favourite book in an interview a few years back. He's a big believer in objectivism apparently. I've been trying to read it, but to be honest, I'm finding the political philosophies a bit dodgy."

"I quit reading it about halfway through years ago with the same conclusion. I could see it being right up Chris Wall's street though." I checked my watch. "Anyway, mate, I have a few things to sort before this hike, I'd better shuffle. Hope it works out for you."

As I stood up two teenage girls were walking past on the pavement. One said something to the other in German, who laughed awkwardly and smacked her friend on the arm. Greg grinned.

"What?" I asked.

"First girl said you resemble a rather dishy teacher called Herr Hartmann that other girl is a bit keen on. Offence was taken, apparently because Mr Hartmann is 'not that old.'"

It was my turn to be embarrassed. I looked after them. "I bet there are days poor Mr Hartmann feels positively ancient. Take care mate. Speak later."

As it turned out, that was the last time I spoke to Greg Harvey.

After I left him I wandered across the road to the Sporting Goods Shop. I was not going to get any serious hiking done in my jeans and deck shoes, so if I was going to get the most out of this holiday, I needed to invest in some decent clobber. Twenty minutes later I walked out, three hundred euros lighter, but with a decent pair of lightweight, waterproof hiking boots, a couple of pairs of socks, a few cotton T-shirts, waterproof trousers and a jacket, and one of those tubular bandanas that you can supposedly twist into all sorts of different functions, but that I suspected would sit around my neck doing not much at all.

If nothing else, I would at least look the part. I got dressed in the changing room of the shop and shoved all my old clothes into a plastic bag, then went back to the hotel to dump them in my room. I crossed the lobby and took the stairs up to the second floor two at a time. As I was walking down the corridor to room number seven, I glanced into the open door of room number five as I went past.

Hanny was sitting on the edge of the bed. Presumably she was doing room service, but something about her body language gave me pause. Her shoulders were hunched, she was leaning forward and she was hugging a set of bath towels across her chest. She looked a combination of scared and angry. Like she was about to burst into tears. I hesitated then knocked softly on the door. She looked up. I didn't cross the threshold.

"Hanny". It seemed weirdly invasive to use her name. "Sorry," I said. "We've not properly met. I'm Jake. I just wanted to check, are you okay?"

She looked momentarily confused and as she was opening her mouth to answer, I actually saw her flinch. But then I realised she wasn't looking at me, but over my shoulder.

I looked behind me. Chris Wall had just walked past me in the hall, presumably heading from his room towards the lobby.

"Mr Marley," she said. Although her accent was very strong, she spoke English well. "Room number seven. I am fine."

"If you're sure," I said. "Didn't want to intrude."

"Thank you for asking. All is good." She stood up. "But room will not clean itself."

"Okay" I said and turned away. I walked quickly to my room, threw my clothes on the floor just inside the door then turned and went in search of Chris Wall.

By the time I got back to the lobby, Penny and all the other Seebensee walkers were loitering by the front door, and she called out to me.

"Jake? Are you ready?"

"You go on." I said. "I'll catch you up."

She nodded and they all set off.

I found Wall in the dining area, sitting with Caulfield in a table booth designed for six, and slid in next to them. I nodded at Caulfield then turned to Wall.

"I was just thinking this morning that I'd only ever met one other person called Chris," I said. "Guy called Chris Deacon. He was a mid-level lieutenant for an East End gangster named Tom Derby back in the late nineties."

"Okay," he said, uncertainly.

"Funny story," I said. "The last time I saw him we were pulling him out of a skip with a screwdriver in his ear. We never got the full story but whispers around the campfire were that he had put unwanted hands on a waitress that worked in one of Tom's clubs. A waitress that Tom was fond of. Apparently, she used to bake him muffins on his birthday and at Christmas." I shrugged. "You can see how a man who doesn't have much innocence in his life might be very protective of it."

Wall looked nonplussed.

"I don't know what to take from that story," he said.

"I know how you feel mate. I had to read *Madding Crowd* twice before I realised that Bathsheba Everdene's sheep weren't a metaphor for anything, they were just sheep. Guess the only thing you can take from it is that you should always treat people with respect because you never know who's got their back." I got up. "Anyway, you have a good day."

As I was leaving, I heard Caulfield getting up from the table a second before I felt his hand on my arm.

"What was that about?" he asked quietly.

"Nothing," I said, turning to face him, not sure if we were squaring off or not. "Just sharing boring cop stories from back in the day."

"I'm only asking because I'm saddled with him for the day."

"Really?" I replied. "He big into birdwatching too? Finally going to get that Eurasian eagle owl ticked off the list?"

He spotted the dig, he ignored it.

"We were chatting last night over a drink and ended up in a bit of a dick measuring contest. I said I was going to cycle out to the Heiterwanger See and back today. He said he could do it in about two and a half hours. I reckoned at least two forty-five for terrain. Somehow, we ended up with a gentleman's wager. Phallometrics."

I patted him on the shoulder. "Well, if you leave him in the dust, I'm buying all the beers tonight."

CHAPTER THIRTEEN

Once I got out of the hotel, I oriented myself with the local walkers map that Penny had given me, then double timing it down Ganghofer-strasse, catching up with the main party just as they arrived at the lower station of the Ehrwalder Almbahn cable car. Penny halted the troop there and offered the six of us a chance to ditch Shank's mare for the first two kilometres with the steepest incline in favour of catching the gondola to the top. I think all of us caught her undertone that this was supposed to be a walking holiday and that any use of a gondola would mean immediate expulsion from the cool kids gang. No one opted for the easy option, either because they were up for the walk, or for fear of losing the tacit approval of a frizzy-haired Scottish twenty-year-old.

Penny led the group up through on a long ascending gravel path that ran underneath the cable car, the shadow of a gondola passing silently overhead every minute or so, until we reached the top station about forty minutes later. Everyone had been chatty when we set off but conversation had dried up as the walk progressed and as we began to ration oxygen. Which was fine with me – in my opinion there is no picturesque landscape in the world that will be enhanced by a running commentary.

By the top station we had split into three distinct groups. Jane and Abby were the vanguard, Penny and Margaret in the middle and George, Bryce and me bringing up the rear. George kept periodically stopping to investigate some interesting piece of flora or fauna, Bryce would do the same to take a few landscape snaps with the oversized camera slung around her neck, and I had no excuse other than I was still struggling a bit with the altitude and was trying to break in a brand new pair of walking boots.

Though still in ascent, the path levelled off a little after the top cable car station, switchbacking on itself through pine forest flanked by limestone rocks, underneath clear blue skies. Finally, about two hours later, we came to the dark green waters of the Seebensee, an oval lake nestled in a bowl between several peaks. Once there, we sat down to eat the packed lunch that Morton's had provided. A ham and cheese roll, an energy bar and a bottle of water. Doesn't sound like much but after the Bataan death stroll, it went down well. At this point, Penny gave us a choice: Another climb to the Coburg hut, where your reward would be coffee and apple strudel, or an extra few kilometres to the Drachensee lake as per the Smiths' request, where our reward would be cold mountain swimming.

"Which will be cold," warned Penny sternly. "And remember, I'm Scottish, so when I say cold I mean Baltic. So no sneaky heart attacks."

Somewhat unsurprisingly, everyone bar the Smiths gave in to the lure of coffee and cake, agreeing to meet back up at this same spot in three hours. The addition to the expedition meant we'd have to take the cable car down the last stretch, which Penny allowed on the basis that it was going downhill anyway.

"Right," she said, pointing off to her left. "Official route to the Coburg is an extra two kilometres that way, clearly marked by the signs. Or you can just scramble up that cliff face over there, which is two hundred metres. I officially recommend that you take the longer route, but you've all signed release forms, you're under no obligation to take my advice. Please wait until I get out of sight so I have an alibi."

The Coburg Hut sat atop a mountain ridge another two hundred metres up, about a half kilometre away. We all opted for the unofficial route. The last section was more of a scrambling climb on all fours than a walk, pulling yourself up an uneven set of ledges and steps, shaped over time by countless travellers before us, mostly barren of plant life bar the odd spiny thistle which added an extra frisson to the challenge. Sweat in my eyes, backpack straps digging into my shoulders, boots pinching my feet. This was the first time on the walk that a stumble or slip might have been serious or even fatal, so the conversation that had resumed at the lakeside died again as we focussed all attention on the task at hand. Perversely, it was the bit of the walk I enjoyed the most, although I was quite relieved when we all made it to the top without incident.

The hut was a long timber single-story chalet building with a wide railed terrace along its front, set out with tables and chairs. We all ordered coffees, followed by apple pancakes, settling gratefully at a terrace table with a panoramic view of the valleys on either side of the ridge we were perched on. Seebensee on one side, Drachensee on the other. Off in the distance, I could just about make out Penny, George and Jane, wending their way down the path to the latter. Before we ate, Margaret raised her mug.

"Well done everyone, although I confess to thinking the losers' bus was looking like the smarter choice by the end."

"Never," said Abby. "Cool kids gang all the way."

We all clinked mugs and drank. As the caffeine hit burned down my throat, I was sure I must have had a nicer mug of coffee but I struggled to remember when.

It was nice to sit and chat with the three women, and I found myself warming to all of them. Margaret was a bit of a madam, but she was intelligent and had a refreshing briskness about her. Bryce appeared to have a genuine curiosity about life and all it had to offer, along with a dry and sardonic sense of humour, and Abby had a kindness and a quiet stoicism that I also liked.

"It was kind of you to talk to Mr Harvey today," she said. "I think he might be feeling a bit left out. The only person I've seen him speak to besides you is Mr Nicholls."

I shrugged. "It wasn't a hardship. He's a nice bloke once you talk to him. I'll drag him out on a walk yet."

"Who would bring a laptop on a mountain holiday then sit on it all day?" said Margaret. "It beggars belief."

I knew the answer to that question, but kept it to myself. I just shrugged again.

"Different strokes, I guess."

"Chris Wall has a laptop as well," said Abby. "I saw him working on it yesterday afternoon when I was going out for a run."

"Objectionable man," said Margaret. "Of the worst kind."

"What's the worst kind of objectionable man?" I asked, curious if her opinions of him matched with my own.

"Did you hear what he was saying to Bryce last night? About privilege?"

"I did," I replied, "but to be honest, I assumed he was just trolling for kicks."

"Exactly," said Bryce. "He's from a generation that grew up on internet chat rooms. Conversations are boring. Confrontation is cool.

It doesn't mean anything. I don't know why you let it annoy you. It's not like you lack the facts to win the argument."

Margaret looked at me, and something unspoken passed between us. If I had seen her face betray her thoughts on Chris Wall last night, so too, she had seen mine. Why wasn't I agreeing with her now? Partly because, by default, I tended to play my cards close to the chest, and partly because I suspected she and Bryce might have argued about this in private last night, and my endorsement of her position might have initiated round two.

"Do you have any opinions on the privilege argument?" she asked me archly.

"If you don't have to think about it, you probably have it," I said.

'That's interesting," said Bryce. "Care to elaborate a bit?"

"Not without the aid of alcohol," I grinned. "With all due respect, what am I going to tell a gay, woman of colour from North Carolina about the nature of privilege or lack thereof that could possibly be of any interest?"

Bryce smiled. "Why not let the gay, woman of colour from North Carolina be the judge of that? But if alcohol is the catalyst, the three of us had plans to go to dinner tonight. It's the one night where there's no hotel dinner or evening get together. Would you care to join us?"

"Sure," I said. "What were you thinking of?"

"Something with cutlery," said Margaret. "My only rule."

"Alphabet game for pizza," said Bryce. She looked at Abby and me.

"Can you suggest a topic?"
"Cities?" I suggested.

Abby nodded at Bryce's impressive looking camera on the table in front of her.

"Photographers," she said.

"That seems like a loaded deck," said Margaret.

Abby grinned. "What can I say, I like pizza."

"Okay," sighed Margaret. "Ansel Adams."

Bryce smiled.

"Henri Cartier Bresson."

"Robert Capa."

"Robert Doisneau."

After that I didn't recognise any of the names. Margaret fell on the letter K and it turned out we were all going for pizza.

After lunch Bryce insisted on taking some photographs. Having snapped the surrounding scenery with the forensic diligence of a crime-scene investigator she insisted on a few with subjects in the foreground. I took one of her and Margaret leaning on the guardrail with the lake and valley behind them then she demanded one of Abby and me in return. We swapped places and Abby and I stood there smiling sheepishly while Bryce frowned behind her lens.

"Come on guys, look like you know each other."

It was a surprise to feel Abby's arm cautiously snake around my waist. Not unwelcome but it did feel strange. I reciprocated by putting my arm over her shoulder and we inched a little closer to each other.

"Much better," said Bryce and she snapped a couple of efforts and promised to email them to us when she had the chance.

The delay for photographs meant we were twenty minutes late for our rendezvous with Penny and the Smiths, and we had to double time it back to the cable car station to catch the last run at 4pm, but as it was all downhill we made it with a healthy fifteen minutes to spare.

Another half an hour's walk at the bottom got us back to the hotel, by which time the sun had dipped below the mountain ridge, the sky was turning pink and the air was full of the smell of meadow as the dew fell. Penny congratulated the cool kids gang for a great walk, and gave us all a high five as we wearily tramped through the hotel's main doors in single file.

We invited the Smiths to dinner as well, but they cried off to do their own thing so the three women and I agreed to meet back in the main lobby at 6.30pm. After the twenty kilometre walk, I could actually feel my heartbeat in my feet, so when I got back to my room I kicked off my boots, before falling backwards onto my bed, groaning with the relief of letting my spine stretch out. I lay there for as long as I could, then had a quick shower and was back in the lobby by 6.15pm. I got a quick draft beer from Bence behind the bar while waiting for the ladies to arrive.

As I was sitting by the fire with a beer in my hand, I heard raised voices from the beer garden outside. Leaning forward in my chair, I could just peer around the edge of the curtain. Through the double doors, I could see three men and one woman: Paul Nicholls and Chris Wall facing each other and between them, Caulfield and Laura Nicholls. Paul looked incandescent with rage and was trying to advance on Wall, shouting something that was muffled by the double glazing, Caulfield holding him back by virtue of one hand firmly in the middle of his chest. Laura talked urgently to her husband, presumably trying to get him down from whatever ledge he was on. She looked like she was drowning in a sea of testosterone. Paul was not hearing her, shouting at Wall over the two bodies between them and pointing threateningly with a meaty paw.

Wall, for his part, just stood there with the same bemused look on his face that he'd worn with me that morning. As though he found the whole display somewhat diverting but not really worthy of any serious attention. I wondered if he would be wearing that same expression if Caulfield and Laura were not there to get between him and a man who looked like he genuinely wanted to tear him limb from limb with his bare hands. Eventually something Laura was whispering must have caught because Nicholls suddenly stopped pushing forward. He looked at her, as if seeing her for the first time, gave one last jab with his pointed finger in Wall's direction, then turned and stomped off. Laura, now that the immediate danger of violence had passed, turned to Wall. I didn't hear what she said but it was short and she positively spat it at Wall. Then she turned and followed her husband.

Caulfield watched them go, then turned and said his piece to Wall. Not quite as angry as either of the Nicholls, but clearly not offering his approval for whatever had just transpired. Wall caught sight of me through the window. The natural inclination when witnessing an embarrassing spectacle is to look away, but I held his gaze with a neutral expression on my face. Then he too walked off and the beer garden stage was empty – the one act drama complete. I took a moment to marvel at the fact that Wall appeared to have alienated a significant portion of his fellow walkers in less than forty-eight hours. I thought of Greg Harvey and his desire to hitch his wagon to Wall, and a line from somewhere occurred to me.

Have a long spoon if you're going to sup with the devil.

Chaucer, I thought. Or maybe Marlowe. I would have looked it up on my phone but it was at that moment, the three ladies arrived, so I stopped worrying about it and went out to dinner.

We ended up at Restaurant al Castagno, a cheerful and cosy little place, which seemed to be doing a lively trade with both tourists and locals, the latter always being a good barometer for food quality in my opinion. We were shown to a table for four, Bryce and Margaret sitting next to each other on the inside leaving Abby and me on the other. I had the strange vibe of being on a double date, and it occurred to me that Abby was having the same uncomfortable feeling, given the diligence with which she was studying the menu.

"Did you say last night that you lived on a boat, Jake?" asked Bryce.

"I do. A 70-foot-wide beam permanently moored in a village in Wiltshire. Plenty of space for one man and his dog."

Abby wanted to know what kind of dog Fred was and if I had a picture of him.

I said he looked like a happy simpleton and that I had no pictures of him.

"You have to," she said. "Parents have pictures of their kids. Owners have pictures of their pets. It's the law."

"Well then I've broken it." I replied. "One pet. No children. No pictures."

"You aren't married Mr Marley?" said Margaret indicating the platinum band I wore on my left hand.

"I was," I replied.

"But not anymore?" Refreshingly direct, like I said. "Where is she now?"

"Iowa," I replied.

"Wouldn't be my pick of the states," said Bryce. "Hell, wouldn't even be my pick of the 'I' states."

"I've never been," I said, "so I have no opinion on the matter."

Abby seemed to sense that this was not a subject I wanted to dwell on, so she changed the topic.

"What's it called?" she asked. "Your boat."

"The *Mary Ellen Carter.*"

"Who's Mary Ellen Carter?" asked Bryce.

"She's a fishing trawler in an old folk song. She sank off the coast of Nova Scotia in the 1960s."

"That doesn't bode well," said Margaret. 'Was the name Titanic already taken?"

"She was abandoned by her owners, but the crew that worked her realised that if they could re-float her, under salvage rights she would be theirs. So, they attempted just that."

"Did they succeed?" asked Abby.

"It never says," I replied. "The song's about just trying to face what life throws at you... 'like the Mary Ellen Carter, rise again.' But I like to think that they did."

Margaret smiled. "I've changed my mind. I think that is a fine name for a boat, Mr Marley."

"Do you think there is any chance you might call me Jake?"

"I can only promise to try."

We had a very pleasant meal with easy and wide-ranging conversation. The waiter brought us four glasses of schnapps on the house, with our coffee. Bryce and Abby declined theirs so Margaret and I had two each. She then surprised me by announcing she was going for a cigarette.

"I didn't take you for a smoker," I said.

"For the last thirty years, I've had one cigarette a day after an evening meal."

"One too many," said Bryce.

"No worse for you than the air quality of a major city," sniffed Margaret. She looked at me. "You're welcome to join me if you want."

"I think I might if you don't mind," I replied.

We went outside to the smoker's balcony.

It felt colder than it actually was after the cosy restaurant. Margaret drew her cardigan around herself with thin but muscular arms, before lighting her own cigarette then mine with a stainless-steel Zippo emblazoned with a Union Jack, a one-handed action that popped the lid and struck the flint wheel in a single, fluid snap.

"Nice move," I said, as I leaned the tip of my cancer stick into the flame.

"About the only thing my father ever taught me that was worth holding on to," she replied.

"You didn't get on?"

"Let's just say we each had a fundamental disagreement about what the other should be. To the point where I left home at the age of twenty two, never to return. He more or less cut me from the family and we never spoke again."

"Well in a way, that's impressive too. Forgive the observation, but I imagine it was a life of comfort and plenty that you walked away from."

She shrugged. "Principles only count if you stick by them. Otherwise they're platitudes."

We smoked in silence for a couple of drags, standing side by side, looking up at the night sky until she spoke again.

"The reason I don't like Mr Wall is that he reminds me of my father."

I glanced over at her.

"I'm assuming your father didn't have a man bun."

She smiled and looked back at me.

"There are people who are very cavalier about other people's lives. About who people are. Who deny them their agency, their nature, even their humanity. Over such trivial things as their race, their sexuality, their gender. Sometimes they stand on a platform and proclaim these views. They are evil and dangerous, but at least you see them coming. Then there are others. Who stand in the shadows like puppet masters. With money and power, extending influence that is hard to see but pervasive. My father was one of the shadow people. I suspect Mr Wall might be one of those people too. And I think those people are really dangerous. They have a philosophy, they pursue it, they divide and they conquer, they are accountable to no one, and you never see them coming."

She held up the lighter again.

"When my father died, this was the only thing of his that I took. It reminds me that even the tiniest little bit of him that I allow into my life poisons me slowly, drop by drop."

I didn't know how to respond to this but then she shook her head and smiled again.

"I'm not normally in a hurry to share this much. Clearly the schnapps talking. Still, more interesting than telling each other fibs and white lies, isn't it?" she said.

"Is that what we've been doing?" I asked.

"I'm pretty sure," she said, leaning forward. "For example, is your wife really in Iowa?"

I leaned forward too.

"Are you really a kindergarten teacher?"

She smiled and stubbed out her butt.

"Making my point for me, Mr Marley. I claim victory and depart the field."

CHAPTER FOURTEEN

The morning after, I went down to get breakfast just after eight on some pretty stiff legs. There was no one else around so I helped myself to some toast and scrambled eggs that I suspected had never seen the inside of a chicken and asked Hanny for a cafetiere of coffee. I was about to head out to the patio when I noticed Greg was in the same spot as he had been the day before, but this time he was not alone. It appeared he had finally got his chance to make a pitch to Chris Wall. The two of them were sitting at a table and looked to be having an in-depth conversation – Wall speaking animatedly with his hands and Greg nodding along. I didn't want to cramp Greg's pitch, nor did I aspire to Wall's company, so I turned back and sat down at a table. I was just finishing up when Caulfield came into the room. He looked around, saw me, hesitated then came over.

"Mind if I join you?" he asked.

I was a little surprised but nodded and he sat down opposite me. Just as he did, Abby entered the dining area, heading for the breakfast buffet.

"I was just wondering if you had any plans for the day," he said.

I shook my head. "No official walks, so I thought I might try and find a route to explore."

He nodded. "I was thinking of doing the Gartner Alm to Wolfratshauser to Grubig Hütte route. It's about fourteen miles, with a middle section across the peaks. The path looks laid out well enough on the map, though it's a little remote, so I thought I might try and press gang someone into joining me. Challenging, but the views should be great."

I smiled. "Penny been giving you an earful about wandering off solo?"

"Victoria actually. It's a brave man that will argue with a redhead. And objectively, it's not a bad point she was making."

I nodded. "I could be up for that. Fair warning though – I'm probably not as fast as you, and I don't want to slow you down."

"No worries. I still expect you'll be better company than Chris Wall."

"I saw that bust up last night with Paul Nicholls. What was that about?"

He grimaced. "Total madness. It turns out that Mr Wall is fond of the odd joint now and again and invited young Miss Nicholls to join him. Dad was none too happy when he found out about this and a frank exchange of views on the subject was had."

"He invited a teenage girl half his age to smoke weed with him? What reaction did he think he was going to get?"

"I'm not sure that self-awareness is Wall's strong suit. When Nicholls confronted him, his response was that his daughter was an adult in every sense of the word – emotionally, legally and biologically – which, needless to say, led to an escalation in tension. If the wife hadn't been around to calm her husband down, I think Mr

Wall might well have been searching his morning bowel movement for his teeth."

Over Caufield's shoulder, I saw Abby leaving the buffet counter with a tray. I smiled at her and indicated she should join us if she wanted.

"So how did it end?" I asked, as Abby sat down next to us.

"I told Wall if he had any sense at all to avoid the Nicholls clan for the duration of his stay. Asked him if he wanted to do the hut to hut just to keep an eye on the bugger, but he said that he was going to do his own thing today. 'Recentre himself' was how he put it."

"What does that involve?" I asked.

"Don't know. Don't care. Not my circus. Not my monkeys."

He shrugged, dismissing the entire thread of conversation and turned to Abby who had been quietly nibbling on the single croissant that appeared to be her breakfast.

"Mr Marley and I were just talking about walking a hut to hut trek across the peaks. Can we tempt you?"

She frowned. "I really wanted to try to get to the top of the Zugspitze today. I figured the rest day would be my best chance."

Caulfield nodded and checked his watch. "Fair enough. But I wouldn't leave it too long. I did it a few days ago and the cable car queues get stupid long, stupid fast, even at this time of year."

Abby nodded. "I'm going straight after breakfast. If the wait is too long, I'll just go for a walk."

"Okay. We're doing the Gartner to Wolfratshauser to Grubig route. It's circular so you might catch up with us, if the cable car doesn't work out."

She nodded. "Sounds like a back up plan."

Caulfield and I got up and left her to her calorie deficient breakfast.

"Maybe see you later," she said as we left.

Walking away, Caulfield leaned in. "Do you know, I suspect Ms Guerin is rather keen on you. The sideways glances are a bit of a giveaway. If she shows up today, I shall take that as a confirmation."

I had no response to that other than to say I needed fifteen minutes to get prepped and would meet him back in the lobby.

Caulfield duly turned up on time kitted out in walking gear and boots that looked worn and well maintained. He had a heavy duty canvas backpack which looked to be military in origin. We set off, walking half a kilometre down the road before turning right onto a barely visible single track path in the trees that began a steady ascent through the forest, Caulfield leading the way. After about a mile, we took another left, the rate of ascent increased again, and the path became more uneven. Where the walk yesterday was clearly a well-travelled and popular route, this one was a lot less defined, and a lot more challenging. Yesterday had been the tourist version, this one was the real deal. Once or twice, I had to lean on my own thighs to haul myself up the gradient. Because the pace he was setting wasn't leaving me much spare oxygen for small talk and we were in single file, we didn't actually speak much until we got to our first pit stop about ninety minutes into the hike. I was sure we were lost at one point, but Caulfield kept moving confidently onward and upward. Eventually the forest thinned out and we arrived at the Gartner Alm, a simple mountain hut with an impressive log pile stacked along its leading wall. We rewarded ourselves with a beer in the sunshine.

Caulfield went to get them, while I sat on the warm deck breathing in the pine scented air. The ascent had been tough, and although my body was protesting a bit, it felt good to be physically pushing myself for the first time in a while. The beer, when Caulfield handed it to me, was cold enough to have condensation beads on the glass. We clinked, and drank, the first swallow as refreshing as chalkstream water.

"You feeling okay?" he asked. "Not too much for you?"

"Not too bad," I replied. "But that's a pretty obscure path. How did you know it? You ever holidayed around here before?"

"No," he replied. "But I do know how to read a map."

"If you don't mind me asking, were you in the army?" I asked. Between the map reading and the solid pace he had been setting, that seemed like an obvious conclusion.

He smiled and shook his head. "Afraid not."

Which still left me wondering where he had learned to orienteer so well and double time it up a hill at a pace that would have impressed a sherpa.

The second leg was initially even tougher as we left Gartner, walking along the valley floor, before cutting left through the pine trees over the ridge, but just when my legs were ready to give up, we reached the top of the range, and the path levelled off. After that most of the challenge came from the uneven ground. Caulfield was right – the views were absolutely spectacular. The route opened out onto high mountain pastures with vast wide valleys on either side. It felt like this path had not been walked in an age of men – that we were the only two people left in the world, looking down on some unspoiled garden of Eden. That was the longest leg, but I don't think we said five words to each other. We just walked, occasionally stopping to drink from our water bottles and take in the vast canvas of the world as the sun moved slowly across the blue sky above our heads. It was vexing when we got closer to our second pitstop and the sight of other tourists broke the illusion.

Just as we were arriving at the Wolfratshauser hut, we bumped into the Smiths on the main path. They had come directly from Ehrwald, rather than the long circular route that Caulfield and I had taken. Since they were also stopping for lunch, it was only polite to invite them to join us. The Wolfratshauser was a bit busier than the Gartner Alm, with maybe thirty other tourists scattered around, but we managed to grab the last free table on the terrace. The Smiths had been planning to head straight back to Ehrwald but on hearing that we were heading on to Grubig, they asked if they could join us.

"I much prefer a circular route to a 'there and back'", said George. I hesitated, as this was Caulfield's expedition, but then he said that it was not a problem. If this request had annoyed him, as I had expected it might, he hid it well.

We were about half-way through lunch when Abby arrived on the deck, panting and out of breath.

She saw the four of us, waved and came over. Caulfield shot me a sly look which I ignored.

"You're still here," she said, still panting. "I was worried I might have missed you."

"Gave up on the Zugspitze then?" Caulfield asked innocently.

"You were right," she said. "Queues were insane. There were twenty tourist buses in the car park. I waited for about half an hour and decided to try and meet you here."

Rather than wait for Abby to order, I gave her the second half of my sandwich. We waited for her to finish it then the five of us wandered back down the hill in the direction of the Grubig hut, the last stop of the day. By now the route was mostly downhill. Easier on the lungs, harder on the knees. Because there were now five of us, the dynamic had shifted slightly. There wasn't a huge amount of conversation but even the odd comment here and there, an observation by George on some flower, a question from Abby on which official walking route we were trying to connect with, all made me feel that Caulfield preferred it being just the two of us. Which I probably had myself.

We made the final hut inside an hour, but didn't stop for anything longer than a toilet break for everyone, as we still had another ninety minutes back to the hotel.

About an hour into this final leg, just as we were coming out of the forest and onto the main street of Lermoos, we spotted Bryce and Margaret exiting the forest from a track about fifty metres down on the opposite side of the road, also heading back to the hotel. Cue another round of hellos, more muted, because at this point I think everyone was done with walking and just wanted to get back to civilization for a shower, a lie down and a drink. Not necessarily in that order. It was Bryce's birthday, and she and Margaret had spent the day having some alone time and a walk in each other's company. Fair enough – although as I was walking behind her, I spotted dried grass caught in Margaret's hair and dried mud on the back of her jacket, so I suspected their trek might have been punctuated with a little al fresco pair bonding, a thought I obviously kept to myself.

As we all slogged up the road to the hotel, I was weary but satisfied with the day's efforts. I was looking forward to dinner and a beer when I spotted a VW Golf parked outside. Silver. With red and blue go-faster stripes.

"Is that the law?" asked Caulfield.

"It is," I replied.

My initial assumption was if Neumann was here on official business as opposed to just finding some excuse to come and flirt with Melanie, that it would be something pretty pedestrian.

Counterfeit bank notes in local circulation, maybe a drunk and disorderly tourist hotel guest. I revised that pretty quickly as we walked through the main doors and into the reception.

Neumann was at the front desk talking in a low voice to Melanie and the three Morton kids, all of whom were listening intently to what he was saying. If the Morton's staff were involved, it was something to do with our group. A theft from the hotel rooms was my revised guess. They all looked up as we came in, then Harry came over and asked if we wouldn't mind going into the lobby. The police needed to talk to us.

We went into the bar and sat down. Paul Nicholls was already there, grimly attacking a beer. We all plopped into seats in a rough square around him.

Caulfield jerked his thumb over his shoulder towards the reception desk.

"Any idea what that's about?"

Nicholls took a long swallow of his beer.

"Chris Wall," he said.

"What about him?" I asked.

"He's dead," said Paul, bluntly.

Six different people, six different reactions, across the dark end of the spectrum of human emotions. From Jane's open mouthed gasp, through Bryce's wide eyes to Paul's own incredulity hearing himself say the words aloud. I wish I could say I took them all in, but mostly I was distracted by the spark of a long dormant curiosity deep within myself.

"How?" asked Bryce. "I mean, we only saw him at breakfast."

Nicholls grimaced. "Apparently he went out in the woods this morning. Tied a rope around a tree and…" he made a vague motion in the vicinity of his own neck, before returning for another pull on his beer.

Caulfield looked more shaken than I would have expected.

"Are they sure it was him?" he asked. "From the little I saw of the man, he just doesn't seem the type. Did someone ID the body?"

"I don't know," said Nicholls. "Christine spent the day white water rafting. Laura and I were just having lunch and mooching around the town, picking up tourist knick-knacks. We got back here about an hour ago, she went to have a nap before dinner, I came down to have a beer and heard that cop talking to the receptionist and the Morton kids. I think he was waiting for everyone to come back so he could talk to all of us."

Right on cue, Neumann came over with Melanie and the Morton's trio trailing behind him.

Melanie spoke first.

"Apologies everyone. This is Bezirksinspektor Werner Neumann, a local police officer, who would like to speak to you all."

Neumann stepped forward and looked around at us. He paused his scan at me, presumably remembering that we had already met.

"Hello everyone," he said. "Perhaps Mr Nicholls has already told you, but you should hear it officially."

He then told us that a witness had reported finding the body of a Caucasian male, aged approximately thirty-five years old, hanging from a ledge in the woods near the Blindsee Lake. Early indications were that it was a suicide and the individual in question was one Christian James Wall, UK citizen and resident of London.

"How did you identify him?' asked Caulfield.

"There was a wallet in his pocket that contained an ID that allowed for a preliminary identification. We will formally identify the body via dental records, but if any of you would be willing to view the body and confirm it's the man you knew as Chris Wall, I would be grateful."

"I should do that," said Harry, although he didn't look particularly thrilled at the prospect.

Caulfield looked at him.

"Have you ever seen the body of a hanged man?"

Harry looked pale and shook his head.

Caulfield sighed and looked at Neumann. "I was with him yesterday. I can do it if it's needed."

Neumann gave Harry an enquiring look.

"Mr Caulfield," Harry offered. Neumann looked back at Caulfield then down at his notes.

"You are Mr Richard Caulfield?"

"I am. Give me five minutes to go and change out of this walking gear and I'll be right with you."

"Thank you," said Werner and Harry simultaneously as Caufield got up and trooped off to his room. Werner looked around at those left. "I have already spoken to your walking company staff. I am very sorry that this tragedy has occurred, and I do not wish to interfere with your vacation plans any more than I need to, but I would be grateful if you could spare some time to allow me to build up a picture of Mr Wall's mental state before this tragedy. I believe that most of you are booked to stay here until the end of the week so, as much as possible I would ask you to please try and enjoy the remainder of your holiday as best you can."

He stopped suddenly and looked down at his notes then did a quick head count.

"I seem to be missing some people."

"My wife's having a nap in our room," said Paul. My daughter is white water rafting."

"Greg Harvey's not here either," said Penny.

Paul spoke up again. "I saw him heading towards his room just as Laura and I arrived back from town. About an hour ago."

"Before I arrived?" asked Neumann. "So, none of them yet know of this tragedy?"

"I guess not," said Paul. "Should we tell them all when we see them?"

"Thank you, yes please tell them," nodded Neumann. "But if you add that we would like to speak to them also as to Mr Wall's mental state."

"I saw them talking at breakfast," said Margaret. "Mr Harvey and Mr Wall."

I could see Neumann thinking about whether that constituted important information or not. Harvey may have been the last person to talk to Wall. But then someone had to be. He looked around as if considering climbing the stairs to speak with Harvey when Caulfield reappeared at the top of the landing wearing jeans, a T-shirt and jacket.

"We shall speak to Mr Harvey in good time," he said. "Thank you all. I will be in touch."

Neumann left with Caulfield in tow, and those of us that remained looked around at each other. Harry and Melanie shared a look, unsure as to whose job it was to deal with this skip fire. Both looked about to speak simultaneously when Margaret abruptly stood up and said that she was tired and sweaty and was going for a shower and a lie down. She would see us all in a few hours for dinner. She headed off in the direction of the stairs and a moment later Bryce followed. The rest of us took that as permission to disperse.

CHAPTER FIFTEEN

Dinner that evening was initially a subdued affair. The Morton's kids were back in the reception area with their big map, but it was clear that there was only one topic of conversation and it wasn't local scenic walking routes. I had a quick word with Harry who confirmed that he had been in touch with his bosses back in the UK, and that they were going to track down Wall's next of kin and start the ball rolling on getting his body back home for burial. Victoria tentatively asked me if I wanted to sign on to either of their planned excursions for the following day and I declined before even hearing what they were. Along with everyone else, as it turned out. I think the three kids were relieved when Melanie called us all into dinner and they could briefly give up the charade of business as usual, and quietly slink off to their accommodation. As we sat down, I noted that Greg had still not appeared. I wondered if he had heard about Wall, and decided to go home, given that Wall was the only reason he had come here in the first place.

Caulfield arrived back about halfway through dinner and confirmed that it was indeed Chris Wall lying in a drawer in the morgue. Everyone made the socially appropriate noises, although I noticed that their sympathy seemed to be inversely proportional to how much interaction they'd had with him. Paul Nicholls looked shaken and expressed a worry that their altercation the previous night might have somehow upset Wall enough to take his own life. Caulfield and Laura assured him this would not be the case. George quietly offered that his elder brother had attempted suicide once, and that people who outwardly appeared very confident and self-assured could in reality be really struggling underneath. Everyone nodded agreement at this and Jane gave his hand yet another reassuring squeeze. Margaret was quiet, and it occurred to me that she had nothing good to say, so was opting to say nothing. As for me, I had no emotions at all about Wall's death. Unless curiosity counted as an emotion. Something about it was niggling at me but I couldn't figure out what. That spark from earlier in the day, dormant since the days of Met Serious Crime, had not gone away.

After dinner everyone moved into the bar to continue their boozing and the evening segued into an impromptu wake, which I figured was the way of things since the first homo sapiens had stood up on two legs. Darkness and death comes calling, we huddle around a campfire and find strength in numbers. Wine was included with the evening meal and on previous nights Hanny had stopped serving it as soon as the mains were cleared. Tonight she came around and asked if anyone wanted another bottle or two. Clearly Melanie had settled on a strategy of letting us all get blasted and talk it out. Which was probably not a bad shout. The Smiths cried off and went to bed, but everyone else said yes. I wanted something a bit stronger so I went over to Bence at the bar to get my standard hard liquor upgrade.

"Hi mate," I said. "Could I get a Scotch with ice please? Glenlivet if you have it. If not, anything."

"Mate?" he asked. "This is English word?"

"Yes," I said. "It's like a friend or someone you like."

"Mate," he repeated, rolling the word around in his mouth, as he prepped my order.

"You are sad," he said as he set my drink down. "About your mate."

"He most definitely was not my mate," I said. "And I am more curious than sad."

Bence looked around to make sure no one else was in earshot.

"Me, I am also not sad." He leaned in. "Yesterday – you see Hanny. She is upset. She said you were kind. You ask if she was okay."

"I did. She said she was."

"What upset her. She is in room. Doing job. Changing bed sheets. He arrives back. Offer her money. One hundred euros. To take off shirt. To see the breasts."

"You're joking?" I said. "Who does that?"

"For sure serious," he replied. "He is *seggfej* who watch too much porn and treat my girl like *kurva*."

I had no idea what a seggfej was but onomatopoeically, I would have been willing to make a good guess. Bence held up his hands pacifically.

"I know, I know. Hanny always tells me, she is no one's girl but her own, but I cannot help it. In my head, she is my girl."

It occurred to me that for a guy who did not speak English very well, Bence seemed very capable of holding up both sides of a conversation.

He looked at me. "Hanny tell me later what he said, and I am angry and want to beat him like a dog, but Hanny says it is not worth losing job over. But I am for sure angry then I see you talking to *balfasz* Wall in breakfast room. Hanny say she did not tell you what he said, but I see you Mr Marley."

He pointed two fingers at his own eyes, then at mine.

"You smart guy. You see people. Figure things out. I not hear what you say, but Wall's face look like you promise him beating if he is bad to Hanny again, so you Mr Marley, you are my mate."

He offered me his hand over the bar and I shook it.

"Seriously," I said. "It was nothing."

Bence waved this away.

"You look out for Hanny. I am pleased. He is dead, I am not sorry. Maybe even happy. Man like him waste of life anyway."

Later, I bummed another cigarette from Margaret and went outside to the beer garden. I lit it, and exhaled loudly looking up at the stars, trying to tease out what was niggling at the back of my brain.

"You really shouldn't smoke, you know." said a voice behind me. I turned around. Christine Nicholls was sitting at one of the tables.

I looked at the cigarette in my hand. "I've heard the health warnings before," I said, "but good advice, duly noted."

She frowned. "I was thinking more of the waste of natural resources and environmental damage of the tobacco industry, but yeah the health thing too, if you like."

"Are you okay?" I asked.

She shrugged. "I'm fine. I don't much like groups of people," she said. "But I like the edges of groups, which I suppose is a bit of a contradiction."

"Do you want me to leave you alone?"

She smiled a small smile. "Are you worried about my dad?"

"Maybe a bit," I conceded, looking around. "The optics aren't great."

She smiled again. "Don't worry about it. I think my dad can tell the difference between a conversation and some creepy old lech trying it on. More to the point, so can I."

"Fair enough," I said. "There are however no circumstances under which I will offer you a drag of this cigarette."

She nodded, then looked up at the sky.
"So, Mr Wall..." she said.

"Mr Wall." I agreed. "You're not upset, I hope."

"No," she said. "I mean, I'm not happy he's dead, and he clearly had a lot of issues but..."

Nothing before the but counts, I thought to myself as I waited for her to continue.

"It's easy to pretend out here in the mountains," she said at last.

"Pretend what?" I asked.

"That the world is okay. That it's not all falling apart at a catastrophic rate. That the planet isn't warming, the seas aren't rising, the topsoil isn't degrading and that within the next fifty years humanity isn't going to reach a crisis point that it will probably not come back from."

As a fifty-three-year-old man, I didn't know how to react to this.

"I won't deny my generation has left yours with some big problems," I said. "Only excuse I have is that it was like this when I got here."

"Do you know what Mr Wall did for a living?"

"Something in the city I think. To do with computers maybe?"

She nodded. "Close enough. Data modelling. Or so he told me. Helping corporations squeeze as much money as they can out of an already exhausted capitalist system. Strip mining, heavy metal toxins, carcinogenic chemicals, water degradation, doesn't matter as long as it makes a profit." She sighed. "He was so proud of himself. His wealth.

His work. He thought it would impress me. And instead it made me feel sad for him. To live a life that shallow. And also angry. The lack of care. Lack of ambition. That you had access to the skill and the knowledge to genuinely make things better, and instead you just use it to get an advantage over all the other pigs snuffling at the trough."

She stood up.

"Do you know the trolley car ethics dilemma?" she asked.

I nodded.

"The baby Hitler question?" I said. "Would you kill one person to save millions?"

She nodded. "That's the one."

"So would you?" I asked.

She shook her head, impatient at my lack of understanding.

"No," she said. "I don't think killing Hitler would have made a difference. The world would still have gone that way. People would still have died needlessly. But..."

Again, nothing before the but matters. Again, I stayed quiet.

"...but…maybe you could have slowed it down. Maybe a few more people could have fled. Escaped. Maybe a few more people could have been saved. Maybe you could have bought them some time. To slam on the brakes for a moment. That's about all you could hope for. And the question is then – would that be worth it."

"And would it, do you think?"

"Sometimes, yes I think so," she said quietly. "And I find myself thinking that Mr Wall's death maybe slowed it down. Not by much and not for long, but maybe the future looks just a little brighter. Which is not a great epitaph for anyone."

I looked down at the cigarette in my hand, which had burned

itself out.

"It's funny," I said. "I pride myself on getting a good handle on people. Two days ago I thought you were a shy girl totally lacking in confidence, and really unsure of herself. I really got that one wrong, didn't I? This is by far the most interesting conversation I have had since I got here."

She looked at me crossly. "I don't like talking about guitars, or which airlines get you the best airmiles, or which restaurants in London you should eat in, or which books I should read. It's all just such a waste of time. I want to talk about things that are real. Do things that are real. Make a change that's real."

"I totally believe that you will do all those things," I said, smiling. But maybe you can waste ten minutes sometime to talk about trains."

She searched my face for mockery, and finding none, eventually smiled back.

"Yes," she said "I like trains. Good night, Mr Marley."

She went inside, leaving me alone at the edge of the group.

I decided to have one more drink before calling it a night. Bence was down at the other end of the bar, mixing cocktails for Caulfield, Margaret and Bryce, so I waited. As I was standing there, Abby sidled over and sat on the stool next to me, elbow on the bar, propping her chin with her hand.

"How are you?" I asked.

"A little drunk," she admitted.

"Understandable. You're in company tonight. I'm two past my limit myself. "

"I've got some Dutch courage though."

"For what?" I asked.

"I don't think I want to be alone "

She said it quietly but once it was out there, she seemed to gain a bit of confidence.

"Tonight," she added more forcefully, just in case I had misunderstood her meaning.

That made me pause, she saw it and misconstrued it.

"I'm sorry," she said, sliding off her barstool. "Forget I said anything."

"Abby, wait," I said.

She stopped and looked at me, cautiously

"Sorry," I said, tensing, sure that I would mess this up. "I want to say that you've had quite a bit to drink, and I don't want to take advantage of that, but honestly it's more that it's been a long time since I've been in that market, it wasn't something I was expecting and it caught me by surprise."

She nodded understandingly. "Me too, if I'm honest. I don't think that's even what I'm asking. I'm just very sad. And I really, really want a hug."

I could feel my shoulders relax as I exhaled a deep breath.

"Okay," I said. "That I think I can do."

She smiled. "Thank you."

She touched my hand briefly then turned and walked back to the main group, sitting on the big couches. Bence came down to my end of the bar and got me my last Scotch of the night. The one that I had intended sipping over the course of the next twenty minutes, but ended up downing in one.

She called it a night about ten minutes after that, bidding everyone a loud and obvious good night. I gave her five minutes then also made my excuses. Caulfield made eye contact as I was going, and

I knew no matter about anyone else, we had not fooled him for a second. We ended up back in her room. It was warm and smelled nicer than mine. Less like a locker room anyway. I kicked off my shoes and lay on the bed over the covers. She did the same, crawling over to lie beside me. She snuggled into the crook of my arm and we lay there in the dark. I could feel my heart hammering against my ribs and did not trust myself to say anything. Her body felt warm and her hair smelled of apple blossom. I could hear the sound of waves and a voice coming from her phone on the dresser.

"Is that the shipping forecast?' I asked.

I could feel her smile in the darkness.

"Yes," she said, "It's a sleep app. When I was a kid, I always found it soothing".

We listened for a while.

Rockall, Westerly to South Westerly five to seven. Rising.

She was right, it was soothing.

Then she spoke.

"Do you think it hurts?" she asked, softly. "To hang yourself."

"I don't think he would have suffered," I said. "From what Officer Neumann said, it sounded like he stepped off a ledge and fell straight down. I imagine it would have been instantaneous. Try not to think about it."

"I do though," she said. "You were a policeman. Did you ever have to deal with suicides?"

I had dealt with more than I could remember. People who'd sliced their own forearms in the bath, their blood floating like liver around their bodies, people who'd wedged their toes in the trigger guards of shotguns, the remains of their head a Jackson Pollock on the walls, people who'd swallowed the contents of their bathroom cabinets, or taped a plastic bag around their heads. Messy ones, tidy ones, some with notes, some without, the only common thread between them the belief that anything – or maybe even nothing – was better than what they were currently having to endure. That they were a burden they had to rid the world of.

"A few," I said. "Over the years".

"I always worry," she said. "that they change their mind. Right at the end. They rock a chair out from under themselves, their vision is going dark, and suddenly they frantically think 'No, wait, this isn't what I want.' Legs kicking out for support that isn't there. But it's too late to take it back."

I realised that as she was saying this, I had started stroking her hair.

"Try not to think about it."

She didn't say any more after that, but snuggled a bit closer. I continued to stroke her hair and somewhere around German Bight, Northerly four to five, her breathing became slow and even and I knew she was asleep.

CHAPTER SIXTEEN

When I woke up the next morning, Abby was already awake. I was laying on my side facing the middle of the bed and she was doing the same. Her brown eyes looked at me and she smiled.

"Only awkward if we let it be awkward."

"I don't feel awkward," I replied. Strangely I didn't.

"Did you have any plans for today?" she asked. "Have I messed them all up?"

"No plans beyond breakfast," I said. "Would you like to join me?"

"I'd like that," she said.

"Okay," I said, "this bit might be awkward. Where I get out of bed and look for my shoes."

She shut her eyes. "Does that make it any easier?"

I swung off the bed, found my shoes, made it to the door, opened it, paused and looked back at her.

She opened her eyes and gave a low sarcastic cheer. "Well done, you."

"Downstairs in half an hour?" I asked.

"Sold," she said. "And thank you for last night."

"It was my pleasure." I hesitated, wondering if I should say something else, and as the silence drew on, I realised I'd blown the opportunity to leave gracefully. Abby confirmed it by laughing.

"Yeah. Okay," I said. "Going."

It took me two minutes to get back to my room – I had to walk back to the main stairwell and cut over to the other corridor. I wasn't sure what to make of the night before. I wasn't stupid enough to read anything more into it than what it was – Abby had just wanted some human comfort after a brush with mortality. She was a nice person and I liked her, and I thought she might like me. On the other hand, I was well aware that I needed a team of porters to carry around all my baggage, and I didn't think that was very fair on her. Especially if she had just bounced out of a long-term relationship. I knew nothing about her background but had enough sense to realise that if she was after anything it was probably something a little casual and easy going. I also figured that she was more than ten years younger than me, which put me squarely in the dirty old man category.

I stopped and took a deep breath. All these thoughts were bouncing around my head like pinballs. Jesus Marley, I thought – have a word with yourself.

You like her. She likes you. Have a few drinks. Go out for dinner. Have a conversation. See where it goes. If not a plan, that at least sounded like an aspiration. Satisfied, I rummaged in my pockets for my room key and unlocked my door. Which was when my day started to get really complicated.

When entering my hotel room, immediately off to the right was the bathroom and a short corridor straight ahead that opened out into the bedroom proper. I took that immediate right, kicking off my shoes and jumping in the shower. Because I was in the market to impress a woman, I took a bit longer than normal with my personal grooming, and I was in my hotel room for a good twenty minutes before I saw that there was a book tossed carelessly on the bed. I could see the cover. Atlas Shrugged by Ayn Rand. A bookmark about a third of the way through.

The automatic reaction would have been to reach out to pick it up, but years of experience had bled that out of me. I approached it in the same manner as a Belfast native might have approached a ticking parcel. I had no idea what it was doing in my room, but it didn't bode anything good.

I dressed quickly, left my room, locking the door behind me, and went down to reception.

Melanie was on the front desk.

"Good morning," I said. "Have you seen Mr Harvey from room eight today?"

She hesitated, possibly trying to decide if she should give me that information.

"No," she said at last. "But I have only been on duty for about an hour"

"Could you call his room for me please?"

She hesitated again but then, prompted by my sense of urgency, picked up the phone.

As it rang she read something off her computer screen.

"No answer, but it says here that he requested a taxi for 6am this morning – to take him to the train station. I assume that would have been for the first train to Innsbruck, which is at 6.30am."

"Does it say when he made that request?"

"I was on until 8pm last night, and I didn't take it so it must have been sometime after that."

"Do you know if he caught it?" At 6am I assumed the front desk would have been unmanned.

"I can check," she said, tapping the cradle once to cut the line to room eight. She hit only one digit so I assumed they had a local cab company on speed dial.

It connected and she spoke quickly and efficiently in German for about two minutes before putting the phone down.

"No," she said. "The taxi driver arrived outside the hotel at 5.50am. The hotel door is locked from the outside until 7am so he had to wait for Mr Harvey to come out. He waited until 6.20am then gave up."

It was then that I knew there was no version of this that was going to turn out well.

"Can you come with me to Mr Harvey's room?"

She looked at me for a moment, and I could see her quick and accurate assessment of my rising dread, then she turned and grabbed the master key off a hook and we both went upstairs.

There was a 'Do Not Disturb' sign hanging on the door knob. Melanie knocked and, when there was no answer, cautiously opened the door with the master key. The door chain was latched from the inside. That took me a minute to get past, courtesy of a lace from my boot: Open the door a crack, slide your lace through a link of the chain bolt, close the door a little to give yourself some slack and pull the lace firmly away from the bolt. Gamekeepers know the ways of poachers.

We found him in the bathroom, which was as noisy, damp and warm as a rainforest, courtesy of the shower, which had clearly been running at full pelt for some time. He was lying on his back on the floor with his head at an awkward angle, wedged in a corner between the wall and the side of the bath. He was wearing a T-shirt and a pair of boxer shorts, his eyes open and unseeing. In his mouth and on his chin, I could see a dribble of toothpaste foam.

To her credit, apart from one initial jump upon seeing the body, Melanie held her cool. This wasn't my first body in a hotel room. Maybe it wasn't hers either. She hovered in the bathroom doorway as I slowly approached, being careful to touch nothing, and crouched beside his body. I cautiously reached out and touched Harvey's forehead with the back of my hand. I guessed about twenty degrees below mine, even with the warmth of the room. Working from the standard coroner's calculation, that put the time of death at about ten to twelve hours ago. Livor mortis, where without a heart to pump, blood starts to pool around the lowest gravitational parts of the body, had already begun. Rigor mortis had extended to his extremities.

Based on no medical training, but a lot of standing around observing people infinitely more qualified than me, my best guess was around 9pm last night. I stood up and looked around. There was water on the floor. There was an electric toothbrush lying next to him, and his mobile phone was sitting on the counter. The tap in the sink was running. It was easy to make a summary as to what had happened. Harvey had started running the water for a shower, had been brushing his teeth while waiting for it to warm up, slipped backwards on the wet tiled floor and executed an epic pratfall that had lined up with the side of the bath. And broken his neck.

Which made for two corpses with broken necks in as many days. It occurred to me that I had not organised travel insurance before I left Wiltshire.

It looked like the scene of an accidental death.

Except.

Except that didn't explain how his book had ended up in my room.

I stood up again and turned to look at Melanie.

"Is he dead?" she asked. Not a stupid question. He was deader than the ghost of my Dickensian namesake but officially he would remain alive until the relevant local authority called it.

"Yes," I replied. "You should call Officer Neumann".

CHAPTER SEVENTEEN

Less than three hours later, I found myself in an interview room in the local police station. Neumann had arrived within fifteen minutes of Melanie making the phone call. I was impressed with his efforts from a professional point of view. I imagined two corpses turning up, one on top of the other, was not a regular occurrence for him, but he was dealing with them efficiently. He arrived with a deputy in tow, a tubby guy whose name badge said 'Brandt'. He had a face like a human Labrador, suggesting the desire to please everyone tempered with a vague worry about where his next meal was coming from. Werner asked me to wait in the empty room across the hall, which was a mirror of my own. I said I was happy for us to go to my room, but he insisted. So I sat on the end of the bed and waited.

A medical team led by a woman somewhere in her thirties arrived. The coroner, or the Austrian equivalent. Once in a while Neumann would appear in the hallway to check that I was still where he left me, and every time I gave him a smile and a wave or small salute. About forty minutes after the medical officials had arrived, Neumann came back to me. He asked me ever so politely if I would mind accompanying him to the police station so he could get my statement.

"Am I being placed under arrest?" I asked.

"No. You are merely helping me to build a picture of what happened with the tragic death of Mr Harvey."

"If I'm not under suspicion, why did you ask me to wait in a corner where you could keep a close eye on me?"

He ignored that comment, instead stepping back and extending his arm towards the door with an ever so slight bow of his head.

"This way Mr Marley, if you please."

Abby was hovering around the lobby as Neumann and I came down the stairs, worry written all over her face.

"Jake, I don't understand what's happening. Are you in some kind of trouble?"

"I'm fine," I said. "I'm just going to help Officer Neumann for a few hours. Exchange a few notes professionally."

I hadn't convinced her, but there wasn't much either of us could do about it. As we got outside, Neumann opened the back door of his car for me – another sign that he had his suspicions. I settled in the back seat and he closed the door.

He walked around to the driver's side on the left, got in, then hesitated.

"You said exchange notes professionally? You are a policeman?"

"I was," I corrected. "Thirty years in the London Met. But hey, retired policemen can commit crimes too, can't they?"

He looked up to make eye contact with me via the rear-view mirror.

"Yes, they can."

Then he started the car, and we drove to the police station.

The police station wasn't in Ehrwald but in Lermoos, the next town over, and served the whole valley. Lermoos was much the same postcard-pretty mountain village as Ehrwald, but the police station was a modern glass and steel affair, sharing both a building and a car park out front with a local bank, which seemed to be getting the lion's share of activity. We walked up a flight of concrete stairs and Neumann deposited me in a room while he made an excuse to wander off and leave me to stew.

He was wasting his time – for making a prisoner sweat this was without a doubt the worst interview room I had ever been in. Across the table there was a large window which took up most of the wall, through which I had a panoramic vista of the hills, forest and the mountain peaks beyond. You could be staring at that view with your trousers on fire and not get stressed. Eventually he came back with two mugs of coffee, one of which he set down in front of me.

I looked around me.

"This is the nicest interview room I have ever been in. By which I mean it's the worst interview room I have ever been in. I thought you guys were supposed to be good at this stuff," I said.

Werner smiled thinly, set his coffee down and leaned forward his two forearms on the table in front of him.

"Mr Marley, you seem to be deliberately trying to provoke me by indulging in insulting cultural stereotypes. And Germanic ones at that. We are in Austria."

He pointed over my shoulder. "Germany is about nine kilometres that way."

Provoking him was exactly what I was trying to do, simply because I was curious as to how he would react, what kind of cop he would be. Not just calm, but insightful. So far I was impressed.

"Before we begin," said Werner in the same low measured tone. "I should tell you that you are not being charged with a crime, but you may still have your lawyer present if you so wish. I think the expression you might use is a 'person of interest.'"

I nodded, inwardly taking a moment to reflect on how I felt about being questioned regarding a suspicious death in a foreign country. No worry, no anger. Just a strange, heady thrill and a sense of purpose.

"Well, my lawyer's back in Hungerford, so shall we just crack on?"

Neumann nodded then leaned forward to start a tape recorder. He noted the date and the time and gave my full name, which he had presumably gleaned from my passport. He then spoke directly to me.

"I saw you and your walking companions yesterday at around 5pm to inform you of Mr Wall's death – can you tell me about your movements since then?"

"I went back to my room, had a shower, went back downstairs around 6.30pm, we all had dinner, then we all sat in the bar drinking and talking. I think everyone was processing the death as a group."

"Like a wake?"

I nodded. "Exactly that. Then I went to bed. A little after 10pm, I think. Definitely not any later than 10.30pm"

"Who else was with you?"

"The whole group, except for Mr Harvey. Christine Nicholls was not there for dinner, but I saw her later on the outside deck, when I went for a smoke. And Mr Caulfield was not there for the meal either, but that was when he was with you. I'm glad you didn't ask the Morton's kid to do it."

Werner nodded. "Mr Caulfield, I think, was more composed than the company reps would have been. I assume from his time in the military, it was not the first dead body he had seen."

I glanced up. "Caulfield said he was in the military?"

Werner nodded. "You are surprised? He never mentioned it?"

I shook my head. "No, he didn't."

Werner could see my confusion but after a moment, he let it go.

"And the others? What time did they leave?"

"I didn't see Christine Nicholls apart from the ten minutes on the smoking balcony. The Smiths went to bed first, around 9pm. The Nicholls parents went about ten minutes before I did. Let's say 10pm. Ms Guerin left around five minutes before me. 10.10pm. Then me at around 10.15pm. All those times are approximate. Caulfield, Bryce and Margaret were still there when I left, so I don't know when they called it a night."

"And what time did you wake this morning?"

"Not sure but I'd guess around 8am. Whatever time it was when Melanie phoned you – about forty five minutes to an hour before that."

Neumann nodded, then said nothing, just looked intently at me. But that was page one, chapter one of 'Interrogation Techniques for Dummies'. Let the suspect keep babbling and incriminate themselves. I had employed the same tactic myself many times. So I just sat there, saying nothing and waited for Neumann's next move.

Eventually he nodded, as though conceding he had not really expected me to fall for that one, but that it had been worth a try then asked, "And what made you go downstairs to ask after Mr Harvey?"

Which was a great question. Because it was the first time I could choose to be honest or start fibbing. I hesitated. We were both playing with our cards close to our chest and one of us was eventually going to have to tip our hand. It might as well be me.

"I found something in my room that I thought indicated that Harvey had been there the previous night. Something that I couldn't explain."

Neumann nodded, and reached into the leather satchel by his feet, and placed an object on the table between us. A large plastic evidence bag. Written up. The first link in a chain of custody. At the bottom of it was Harvey's book.

"Melanie recognised it as being the property of the late Mr Harvey. I was hoping you might be able to explain why it was found where it was."

"She's a clever girl. She did well when we found the body too. I can see why you like her."

He ignored this, so I conceded.

"Okay," I said. "That's the book that Greg Harvey was reading when I first met him. I found it this morning."

"You didn't touch it? Move it?"

I shook my head.

"Then I am curious as to how and when it got there. Who left it there?"

"I wondered that too. It seemed a bit strange. Which is why I asked Melanie to check on him."

"So what would you assume?"

"Well I would have assumed Harvey left it there himself"

"Why would he do that?"

It didn't matter to Greg anymore, so I told Werner everything I knew about him. How he had been hoping to meet Chris Wall, to talk himself into a job, how he had only been reading that book because Wall had said it was his favourite in an interview.

"So, the simplest explanation," I said, "Wall is dead, there is no reason for Harvey to hang around on a mountain walking holiday, so he decides to go home. Calls reception, books a taxi to the train station. He doesn't need to finish the book either if he was only reading it to impress Wall. I'd told him that I only ever made it about halfway through years ago. Maybe he left it as a parting gift. If Hanny was doing her turn down service, I'm sure there might have been a point where my room door was open. He could have just stepped inside for a second, lobbed it on the bed, and left."

Werner thought about this.

"But none of the tour group saw Mr Harvey last night?" he asked.

I shook my head. "No, he never came down."

"Then there is a problem with your theory," he said. "If he never spoke to any of you, then how would Mr Harvey have known that Mr Wall was dead? Also, the maid–"

"–Hanny," I said.

Werner checked his notes and nodded. "A preliminary guess to be confirmed is that this occurred at around 9pm last night. Hannah Szabo says she was doing the turn down service at around 9.30pm, and does not recall a book on your bed at that point. She said that she would have set it on the dresser. So the book was not there before at least 9.30pm. Which I imagine will be around the time that the coroner reports that Mr Harvey died. If he put it there himself, it is a very tight window."

"Do you actually suspect foul play?" I asked. He looked at me, impassively. Although his face betrayed nothing, I was confident he was doing an internal assessment both of what he knew and what he felt, trying to decide if he seriously considered me a suspect or not.

"I don't know," he said at last. "You saw the scene. It looked obvious what had happened. Mr Harvey turned on the water to have a shower. He brushed his teeth before getting into the shower. Water got on the floor. He slipped on it in his bare feet. Fell backwards with enough force to break his neck when he hit the side of the bath. It seems an obvious conclusion to draw."

"But you're not convinced?" I asked.

Neumann paused for a moment then gave a noncommittal shrug. "Maybe. Maybe not. It looks obvious, but maybe a little contrived. Arranged to look like an accident."

"Well that's a problem," I said. "If it was an accident, or set up to look like an accident, both of those scenarios will pretty much look the same. There might be tell-tale signs you could look for."

"Such as?"

I noted that question. It was the first one that Neumann had asked me, not as a suspect, but as a former policeman with some experience in the matters at hand.

"Usually the folds in the clothes. Suspicious debris from another environment on the body. Evidence that it was moved after death. In this case, I didn't see any. As far as I can tell, the only thing that is suspicious about Mr Harvey's death, is that it is the second in a fairly small group of people in as many days."

"And the book that was found in your room."

I nodded. "And the book that was found in my room."

Another thought occurred to me. "Do you still think Wall was a suicide or are you looking at that again?"

"They are both open cases. No conclusions have yet been drawn."

"Well, I have an alibi for both of them. When Wall died, I was having lunch with four other people in a mountain hut, five miles away. When Harvey died, I was…" I hesitated. For the first time since I'd sat down, I felt myself flush. It seemed implausible to me that this was the bit that threw me off track. I cast my eyes desperately out the window – bastard mountains no help to me now – around the room, mouth open, caught. Eventually Werner took pity on me and prompted my response.

"You were with Ms Guerin."

I blinked, as if breaking free from a spell.

"How did you come to that conclusion?"

"Your bed was made and the cover was turned down. It had not been slept in. You said you found the book that you had not touched on your bed this morning. So you were somewhere else last night. Ms Guerin appeared to have come concern for your wellbeing this morning. Which leads me to conclude you were in her company last night."

"You would have to ask her," I said.

"Oh, I will."

I nodded at Werner's file.

"Quite an interesting case you have to solve, Officer Neumann. Do you mind me asking if you have much experience with this kind of thing?"

"None at all," he replied. His frank honesty made me like him more.

"So, what's your next move?" I asked.

I wasn't sure if he would answer, but I was pretty sure by then that he had decided I was not a suspect. If anything my morbid and barely contained animation was probably giving him the most pause.

He sighed. "I am cautious of jumping to conclusions. Did you ever hear of Abraham Wald?"

"Afraid not. Was he a cop? The Austrian Lieutenant Colombo?"

Werner shook his head.

"He was a Jewish Hungarian mathematician. He fled to England in the 1930s when my great grandfather and his friends wanted to send him on a one-way train journey to Poland. He worked for your war department. One of his jobs was to figure out where best to place the armour on bombers. The patterns of bullet holes indicated that most of the damage occurred around the fuselage of the plane near the cockpit, so the manufacturers were inclined to place the armour there. Wald was the one to point out that they were making this decision based on planes which had made it safely back to England. The planes that were at the bottom of the English Channel were the ones that had bullet holes in their wings and engines. Simply put, he pointed out that making conclusions with incomplete datasets gives you the wrong answer. Accordingly, I shall try to avoid making this mistake. I will find my bombers at the bottom of the Channel."

"You don't talk like a policeman," I said.

"No? I studied engineering. I became a policeman only when I realised that I would be a very mediocre engineer."

"Potential homicides must be a change of pace for you."

"We have deaths here fairly regularly. People fall from the high mountain paths. Overweight tourists suffer heart attacks with the altitude. Things of this nature are known quantities. But these two deaths – they feel a little strange to me." He shrugged. "Maybe I am hearing the hoof beats and looking for zebras."

"Maybe," I said, "but then again, maybe not."

Abruptly he decided that the conversation was done, and stood up.

"Thank you for your time Mr Marley. I will confirm your movements last night with your fellow guests and be in touch if I need anything further."

He then noted the time, stated for the tape that the interview was over, and turned it off.

I stood up too.

"Best of luck Officer Neumann, I hope things work out."

"Do you want me to arrange a lift back to your hotel?"

"Thank you, but I think I'll walk."

He escorted me to the front door of the police station and left me standing there. I waited for him to go, then pulled the Morton's map out of my jacket pocket, oriented myself as to where I was then started walking in the direction of the Blindsee Lake where Chris Wall had taken his life.

CHAPTER EIGHTEEN

It took me about an hour to walk to the lake and about half way there, the rain that had been threatening all morning arrived, a steady misty drizzle. I walked the main road to Biberwier then took the forest path through the pines, passing the smaller Weissensee lake on my left. The miserable weather appeared to have scared away the tourists. I passed only one other person, an older man with an impressively waxed Daliesque moustache and a rolled-up towel under his arm, walking his dog. The forest had a clear, wide gravel path but between the rain and the darkness from the close-packed pines on either side, it was hard to shake an ominous feeling. When I reached the lake it spread out in front of me in a vague L shape with the longer length left to right in front of me curving around on my right-hand side. Side to side about three hundred metres across, the far shore maybe half that. I was facing west and there was a boat house and a jetty off to my left. In both directions the path appeared to hug the shore of the lake. The left path appeared to sit pretty much at water level, past the boat house and around the lake, about half way round the right hand path climbed up to a rocky outcrop that sat twenty-five feet or so above the water, and continuing along most of the northern shore.

Most people when presented with a choice tend to intuitively turn right, which was what I suspected Wall would have done for a few reasons. For one thing, that shore had more cover, and regardless of whether it was a genuine suicide or foul play, neither was an activity that would have invited spectators. Also, Wall had supposedly tied his noose to the base of a tree. He would have needed a drop. I turned right and started walking the path counter-clockwise.

I was walking slowly, partly because I didn't know exactly what I was looking for and partly because I had no idea how much physical evidence there would be of Wall's passing. As it turned out I found the spot easily. A little over a quarter of the way, I came across the remnants of red and white plastic barrier tape knotted around the base of two trees. The tape was now mostly gone, presumably removed by one of Werner's team once they had concluded their business, but there was still a knot of plastic around one trunk. I knelt down and carefully unknotted the strand and unfurled it. It had one word – POLIZEI – written on it.

Unless Werner had two incidents worthy of investigation on the same lakefront on the same day, this was where Wall had met his end. I stepped off the path to my left towards the water, and carefully picked my way about fifteen feet down a steep slope. It required the use of my hands to clamber down, but at the bottom it opened out onto a flattish rock that gave a clear, beautiful view of the lake, the forest on the far shore, and the peaks beyond. I crouched down and carefully looked around, starting with the tape still in my hand, trying to think of Neumann's mind set. He wasn't trained specifically in homicide investigation. While I thought he was an intelligent and conscientious copper, and would have followed the correct protocols when documenting the scene and obtaining any physical evidence, he might have fallen into the trap of confirmation bias.

Werner said he had a witness that allowed him to be fairly confident in the time of death at 3.30 pm. I checked my watch – that was almost 24 hours ago to the minute. Presumably that witness had contacted the police and said the word 'suicide.' The police had investigated what, to all intents and purposes, they already assumed was a suicide. The inclination of a homicide investigator is abject suspicion. You always think zebras: suicide is second last on the list after homicide, death by accident or misadventure, and just before death by natural causes.

I looked around the rock platform I was on. It was hard – so no footprints. Any other physical evidence would have been washed away in the rain. I got down on my belly and crawled to the edge to peer over. Twenty-five feet down to the surface. I could imagine local kids jumping from this spot into the turquoise water below. Right now, it looked grey and uninviting. I shimmied back from the edge and rolled over on my back. Directly behind me I could see three pine trees and some thick bushes that shielded this spot from a view of the path. I got up, pushed my way into the undergrowth and examined each one carefully. It was on the middle one that I found rope damage on the moss and lichen around the trunk. I stood up and turned in a slow circle, trying to construct the scene in my head. Chris Wall, thirty-five years old, a successful and financially secure coder, walks out into the woods one morning while on a week's vacation, ties a noose to a tree, puts it over his head then steps off a ledge to fall maybe ten feet, snapping his neck and killing himself. It was hard to come to any other conclusion. I guessed the witness had confirmed he had not seen anyone else with Wall. So far, so sad. Except something about it seemed off.

I looked away out over the water, shut my eyes, cleared my mind and counted to ten. Then I opened them and looked again. This time I saw it. I walked over to the edge near the narrow path I had climbed down. Some of the twigs and branches were broken and snapped about an inch from the cliff wall. Looking closer I could see a swathe of them, maybe a couple of feet across. Unreachable from the path itself. I examined them as much as I could from a distance and eventually, satisfied that some assumptions could stand up to preliminary scrutiny, I climbed back up to the main path.

It was then that I saw the figure on the far shore. He was hard to make out, nearly half a kilometre across the lake in the rain. He was standing perfectly still, wearing a grey rain slicker with a hood, but from the angle of his head, I got the impression he was looking at me. I waited for him to move, but he just stood there. Unnerving in his stillness. It was only when I started to move again that he did too, following the path around the side of the lake that would presumably put him on an intercept course.

I kept walking with my eyes down, figuring I had about ten minutes before I had to concern myself with the hooded figure approaching around the lake perimeter. The path I had already taken was the shortest direct route to the promontory that Wall had died on, but it didn't necessarily follow that it was the route he had taken. So I walked onwards, slowly and carefully casting my eyes about for anything that looked out of place or suspicious. Nothing. After five minutes, I abruptly stepped off the path and walked about fifteen metres back into the darkness of the trees, standing still and silent. About five minutes later, the figure in the grey rain slicker sloped past. A man, about six feet tall, his face hidden by his hood. Neither rushing nor dawdling. Methodical. If he was perturbed by my disappearance, he gave no indication of it. I waited another five minutes to be sure he was gone.

I was carefully picking my way down the slope back to the path under the dark canopy of the trees when an unnatural colour caught my eye. Off to my right, nestled against the trunk of one of the pines, as though casually discarded, was the oversized yin-yang pendant that I had last seen hanging around Chris Wall's neck. I bent down and picked it up. I had initially assumed when I first saw him wearing it that it was made of plastic, but it actually appeared to be of higher quality than appearance suggested. Two kinds of stone. Obsidian and quartz maybe. A black spiral with a white dot and a white spiral with a black dot. Technically the dots made it a *taijitu* – in Chinese philosophy a representation of dualism and the interconnectedness of opposing yet complementary forces. Or vague mystic hokum masquerading as character, if you're the kind of bloke who wore a top knot and wouldn't know the first principles of Taoism if somebody chanted them at you while beating you over the head with an Asian Chau Gong. It was about the size of a pocket watch, and attached to a length of black leather thong which was snapped just below a knot, as though it had been yanked off Wall's neck then discarded. Either by Wall himself or by someone else. If the former, then he had walked this way. If the latter, then someone else had definitely been involved at some point the previous day.

I got back on the path and slowly traced my way all the way around the lake, finding nothing else of interest, stopping only when I had made a complete revolution all the way back to where I had started, by the boat house and jetty. It had stopped raining and the sun had come out, which was a relief because I was soaking wet and cold. I paused one last time to look out at the lake. This was the last thing that Chris Wall had seen in this life. With the heat evaporating moisture off the forest at a rate of knots, it looked beautiful but ominous. Like something from a Gothic fairy tale. A snatch of a story by Jacob Grimm came to me.

You shall wed the ropemaker's daughter and the cawing of crows shall be your wedding song.

I shivered, mostly because of my wet clothes, then set off to find Neumann again.

It took me another hour to walk back to Lermoos, but that gave me enough time to work through my thoughts. I decided to keep the taijitu pendant to myself for the time being. I figured that while I had maybe just about convinced Werner that I was not a criminal suspect, rocking up with a victim's possessions on my person and a vague explanation of having randomly found it in the woods would only put me straight back in the frame again. The irony of trying to convince Werner that I was not a criminal by committing the criminal act of withholding evidence – for at least a little while – was not lost on me.

But disregarding the pendant, we still had a few things to discuss. As luck would have it, he was leaving the police station as I came squelching up the main street in Lermoos, presumably at the end of his shift. He was still in his uniform, although he had lost the sidearm, and was still carrying a leather rucksack that looked like an oversized school bag.

I called out to him

"Officer Neumann."

He stopped and turned.

"Mr Marley. I did not expect to see you again so soon. Did you get lost?"

"I had a few further thoughts since our conversation this morning, so I thought maybe we could have a follow up. "

"I am off duty now." He turned away. "Maybe tomorrow."

Undeterred, I came to a stop in front of him and nodded at the satchel in his hand. "Are those your case notes for Harvey and Wall?"

I was confident that they would be. I couldn't imagine there was much else on Werner's plate that warranted study in his personal time. He didn't answer.

"I used to do that too. Back in the day. Take files home and work through them for hours until something clicked. Sometimes it helped. Sometimes I used to sit and bounce ideas around with someone else on the case, just to see if that knocked anything loose."

He sighed. "But you are not someone on this case. You are a tourist, just like every other tourist, Mr Marley. Someone who has come to these mountains looking for something to make them feel better about life for a short time."

I nodded. "You're not wrong Werner. I'm not trying to fish in your pond but I went to look at the Blindsee Lake and have some observations if you want to hear them. If you do, I'll be in that bar over there."

He looked where I was pointing then after a long pause turned back to point over my shoulder behind me.

"I think you'd like that one better. I need five minutes."

CHAPTER NINETEEN

The five minutes was for Werner to change into civvies, refusing to go into the pub wearing his uniform. At his civilian car he unlocked the boot and dropped the satchel on the ground. Unselfconsciously, he undid the first two buttons of his uniform shirt and pulled it over his head, revealing a tanned and muscular torso below. He threw his shirt in the boot and swapped it out with a plain black T-shirt that he pulled on in one graceful fluid motion. He completed his ensemble with a cotton jacket, shut the boot and locked it. Re-slinging his leather satchel over his shoulder he held out his arm, as he had done in the hotel room earlier that day, and we walked to the pub.

It was called Lahme Ente. A wooden chalet type affair with a logo of a duck smoking a cigar. Inside was a simple room with a low wooden roof, a bar along the back wall and a couple of high tables. I ordered a stein of the local suds and a sparkling mineral water for Werner, at his request, then carried them back to the table where he sat waiting.

"Prost," I said, raising my glass and taking a sip.

He didn't respond

"OK," I said. "We're not off to a good start."

"It's considered bad luck to toast with water," he said. "I would literally be wishing death on you and your kin."

"Good cultural tip," I replied. "Noted for future reference."

He managed to smile and look impatient and vaguely irritated at the same time.

"Mr Marley, I'm really not sure why you asked me here."

I shrugged. "Mostly I wanted to ask you if I could look at the scene photos I assume you took when you recovered Mr Walls body yesterday..."

He opened his mouth to answer but I ploughed on.

"...but I figure your initial response to that is going to be 'not a chance in hell', so I'll work up to it. Instead let me ask you, were you initially suspicious of Wall's death? Before you discovered Greg – Mr Harvey – I mean."

For a moment I thought he wasn't going to answer.

"Initially, no. A local man who swims there every day reported that he had witnessed a suicide."

"I think I met him today. Old guy? About sixty? Mad Salvador Dali moustache and a dog?'

Werner neither confirmed nor denied this.

"He was drying himself on the jetty when he heard a noise. Shouting. One voice. He looked up and saw Mr Wall's body fall then swing over the water. He phoned us immediately. He waited there until we arrived. In his initial statement he reported that he did not see anyone else on the path."

I thought back. If he was on the jetty he would have had a pretty good view of the path in either direction of the promontory.

"OK, can you do me a favour? Can you take a look at the photos again and tell me if Wall had dirt on his hands and knees?"

"We checked his body for any external wounds. There were none."

"Not wounds – just dirt on his hands and knees. Oh, and if the rope around his neck had any grass stains on it."

Werner narrowed his eyes but reached into the satchel at his feet, and pulled out a file. Without showing it to me he flipped through some photos. Eventually he paused then looked over the top of the file.

"Yes, and yes. How did you know?"

He didn't sound suspicious, just curious. I took that as a good sign.

"Do you have a wide shot of the area? To the right of where the small path leads back to the main path."

"I'm not sure what you're describing."

"I could show you, but your rules, boss."

"Scheisse," said Werner, shutting the file and sliding it across the table to me.

I opened it and flipped through a couple of sheets typed out in German until I got to a whole stack of glossy photos. Chris Wall's corpse and the place it had been found from just about every conceivable angle. I noted that the photos followed Robinson's three rules of crime scene photography. Filled frames, maximum depth of field and level plane. This was good work.

I pulled out three to stack up my argument.

"See here," I said. "He has dirt on his hands and knees. And here there is grass and weeds caught around the rope. And here in this wide shot you can see that some grass and weeds have been scythed. Ripped away."

"Yes. I see that. So what does it say to you?"

"It's just a question really. How did all of that happen if Wall didn't try to get back up to the path from the ledge?"

I could see the lightbulb turn on in Werner's face, so I pressed on.

"Wall gets down to his little plateau on his ass – that's how I did it anyway. He ties a noose to a tree on the slope between the plateau and the path above and puts it around his neck. All he has to do then is take a couple of steps forward. Instead he turns and starts climbing back to the main path behind and to his right. Gets dirt on his hands and knees. Presumably jumps from there. Scythes out grass and weeds with the rope as he falls."

Another thought occurred to me.

"Your witness said swinging. Is that accurate? Not hanging. Swinging? Like a pendulum?"

Werner took the file back and flipped through the pages in German.

"Yes," he said eventually. "Swinging like a pendulum. Which would not have happened if he had stepped straight off the ledge as the rope was knotted to the tree directly behind him. He fell off-centre to where the rope was tethered to the anchor."

"Which seems a little odd. I mean, we could be overthinking it, maybe he was worried he didn't have enough of a drop, but it looks off to me."

Neumann nodded. "I agree."

"Leave that for a second and talk to me about Greg Harvey. Bit of a coincidence. Two dead computer geeks in twenty-four hours?"

Neumann pushed his water away and signalled the girl behind the bar.

"Noch zwei bier bitte."

Even with my rubbish German, I understood that. Talking shop over beers. I was surprised at myself how much I was enjoying feeling like a cop again. Werner waited for the barmaid to bring over our two steins, possibly collecting his thoughts. Then spoke.

"It seems obvious as to what happened. But it is annoying me…it seems..."

"Wrong. Somehow stage managed," I suggested.

"Yes," he said.

"Was it the phone?" I asked.

"What?"

I shrugged. "It's the only superfluous element at the scene. The only thing that didn't need to be there to explain the body. Everything else hints at the explanation. Harvey turns on shower to let the water heat up. Brushes teeth. Slips on wet floor. Neck broken. The phone doesn't add anything. So is that the thing that is sticking in your mind?"

"It was the toothbrush."

"What about it?"

Werner frowned. "An electric toothbrush found on the floor next to the body of a man who has died with toothpaste in his mouth. That makes sense. But when Brandt went to bag it, he hit the power button and it activated. If we assume that Mr Harvey was in the act of bruising his teeth when he slipped, then the toothbrush must have been on. If it stayed on, then presumably it must have stayed on for several hours until it ran out of power."

"It doesn't turn off automatically after a set amount of time?"

Werner shook his head. "I tested that this afternoon. So how did it turn off? Who turned it off?"

That had not occurred to me, and I acknowledged it.

"Good catch."

Werner shrugged. "It is, of course, possible that in the act of falling Mr Harvey turned off the brush himself, or even that the impact of hitting the floor caused it to power down, but it seems strange to me. A little odd." He returned my phrase to me, carefully.

"Anything else?"

He smiled thinly. "Again, just the book in your room."

"Again, I have an alibi."

"I know. Ms Guerin confirms your alibi – you were in the lobby with the other Morton's guests until about 10pm, then in her room with her until 9am the following morning."

"Nothing happened," I blurted out before I could stop myself.

He smiled again. "I am not your disapproving mother. I only care that she could confirm where you were, not what you were doing or not doing to pass the time."

"You check up on my past too?"

He nodded. "Thirty years service as a London Metropolitan Police Officer. Eighteen years experience as a detective working serious crime. Retired at the rank of Detective Inspector." He paused. "It seems at first glance to have been an above average career."

I smiled. "Jesus Werner, don't start gushing. I might blush."

"Okay, you can disregard the compliment, but you should understand that your record is the only reason we are talking right now."

I acknowledged the point, then continued. "So, let's break this down. You have two deaths in a single day. Chris Wall commits suicide. You have a witness who saw him fall and confirms that he was on his own. Later that same evening, you have what looks like a death by tragic accident, except for the fact that one of the victim's possessions is found in the room next door, with no explanation for how it got there. Hanny turned the sheets down at around 9.30pm and confirmed it was not there then."

"I can confirm that Mr Harvey died at 8.55pm also."

"That's accurate. Austrian pathologists nail their colours to the mast a lot more than English ones. I never got a time of an unwitnessed death that was narrower than an hour."

He smiled grimly. "The phone by the sink. The stopwatch on it had been activated. We think that Harvey used it as part of his tooth brushing routine. Thirty seconds in every quadrant of his mouth or some much. It was still running. Counting backwards, we established that he began brushing his teeth at 8.53pm exactly. And assume that he died somewhere in the next two minutes, which ties up with all the other physical evidence available."

"And when did he phone down to reception to book his taxi for the next morning?"

Werner checked his file notes again.

"Around 8.15pm"

"OK, so he's made the decision to leave. Presumably at that stage, he does not know that Wall is dead. He dies at five minutes to nine, while the Morton's guests are getting merry in the reception area downstairs. And sometime after 9.30pm, his book appears in my room. I went to bed at around ten past ten. When did the evening end?"

Werner checked his notes again.

"According to the barman, Bence Kovacs, the last guests were Mr Caulfield, Ms Lawson and Ms Dayton who retired at around 11.30pm. All somewhat intoxicated. The hotel doors were locked at midnight to non-guests. Key card confirms it was not used by any of the guests or staff until 7am the next morning. Do you think it's possible that Hanny simply missed the book?"

"It's possible, I guess," I said. "But once you start disregarding information that does not fit the narrative you're on a slippery slope."

Werner frowned. "At this point, we don't even know that any crimes have been committed. There are vague indicators of things that cannot be readily explained at both scenes, but it is hardly compelling evidence. And there is only the vaguest connection between the two men. It may all just be a coincidence."

"Lincoln's secretary was called Kennedy, Kennedy's secretary was called Lincoln. Always a possibility."

"It's funny," said Werner. "Policing around here is not very eventful. This is the first real detective work I have ever had to do. I would have expected that my motivation would be the solving of a potential serious crime, but if I am honest, I just want to solve the mystery. I just want to know the answer."

"I didn't like some scally thinking they were smarter than me. An equally ignoble driver."

We finished our beers. I insisted on paying. Werner said that he was expecting a full autopsy report on Wall the next day. He gave me his contact card and I said I would ping him if I thought of anything.

This time as we parted we shook hands.

He walked back up the road towards the police station and his car. As I headed in the other direction towards Ehrwald, it occurred to me that even if we weren't quite there yet, we had inched a little closer to being friends. I hiked back across the Moos. By this time the long twilight had tipped over into dark. My immediate plans extended no further than finding Abby and apologising for having been AWOL for the whole day. As I was approaching the hotel I saw Caulfield sitting in the beer garden. When he saw me he stood up. I slowed to a stop and we regarded each other like gunslingers in a Western.

"So," he eventually said. "You had a talk with Officer Neumann today?"

"Two, actually," I said evenly.

"He happen to mention my name?"

"That depends. Are you the Richard Caulfield that was in the army, or the one that wasn't?"

He sighed, looked around as if resolving an internal decision, then looked back at me. "Maybe it's time we had a proper chat."

With that he turned and walked off down the street, without waiting to see if I would follow him.

After a moment, I did. Werner was right. At the end of the day, you just have to know.

CHAPTER TWENTY

The years after my mother left were a gruelling slog. A steady litany of misery punctuated by occasional violence that just went on and on and on, wearisome and seemingly without end. It took my father two days to come home after my mother disappeared. On those two days, I had got up and dressed, taken a sniffling James to school, promising him that our mother would be waiting for us when we got home, and both times been proved a liar. I had made rudimentary meals from what I could scavenge in the near bare cupboards.

When I finally heard a key in the front door on the evening of the second day, I ran into the hall, sure that my mother had come back, keeping her promise to me.

Hope dashed will kill you quicker than anything.

It was my father, swaying slightly, not quite drunk, but definitely not sober. He walked past me into the kitchen, and having established that only James was there, turned to look at me.

Where was our mother?

I told him I didn't know.

He hit me on the side of the head to see if that jogged my memory.

It didn't.

He tried it again. Insanity by Einstein's definition. Expecting a different result from the same action.

I still didn't know.

James, sitting by the kitchen table, started crying. My father warned him to stop or he'd really have something to cry about. James dialled it down to a snotty whimper but failed to turn it off completely.

My father stormed upstairs. Our mother was not there, and neither were her few clothes or her small green suitcase with the brass buckles. He thundered down the stairs again, back out of the house and went on a tour of the neighbours, knocking on the doors most likely to yield him an answer.

The women of each house met him with folded arms and downturned lips. Where the men answered, he was met with a shrug.

Eventually he came back to us and told me to make something for us to eat. I fried some potatoes, onions and baked beans, the last of the food we had in the house, while he sat at the kitchen table smoking furiously, no doubt planning in some detail the beating he would visit on my mother for abandoning her post like this.

We ate in silence apart from the scraping of cutlery on our plates.

After dinner he told us to go to bed. It was quarter past seven in the evening. We went anyway. James cried, and I climbed into the bed next to him and hugged him for a long time, until he fell asleep.

Those were the early days. The days when I still had hope. She would come back. She had promised. But the three days became a week. The week became a month. My thirteenth birthday passed unremarked. Eventually, the months became a year, then another.

My father reconciled himself to the fact that my mother was gone and she was not coming back; that she had abandoned him with two useless, unwanted offspring. He made that reconciliation a lot faster than I did.

Things changed. When she left, I was twelve, James was nine. Even by my father's lax standards that was too young for children to be left without adult supervision. He would still go out during the day while James and I were at school – adding to his Supplementary Benefit Giro with whatever side earners and nixxers he could organise for himself. Sometimes, he'd have random items of food. A few potatoes or onions. Dented tins of beans or spaghetti. Sometimes the labels would be missing, and it would be a mystery what they contained. On one occasion that turned out to be dog food. We went to bed hungry that night. I sometimes remind myself that no matter how bad it got, we were never reduced to eating dog food.

Sometimes he gave us a pittance of money with which to source supplies. He'd come home most nights – sometimes he'd be back before we got home from school, but mostly he'd spill in after dark. If he managed to make it home sober he would finish the job in our living room, drinking cans in front of the black and white television, watching Colditz or Callan. Those nights we could deal with.

Other nights he would be itching to pick a fight. On some level, our mere presence made him angry. We were the two sons that fate and a faithless wife had saddled him with, the twin anchors holding him back from all the greatness that was out there in the world for him, if only he were free to pursue it.

He was particularly hard on James. I think this was partly because James was a gentle soul, softer and more fragile than me, bordering on effeminate. I think the thought of that infuriated my father, that people might think his son was a poofter or a nancy boy.

Partly I think it was because he looked like my mother – he could see her face in his, and in her absence, hitting him was the next best thing.

Mostly I think it was because he was a bully.

When he laid in to James, it was my job to get in his way. Used to be my mother's job, now mine.

This brought its own kind of tension to my relationship with my younger brother.

As an adult looking back, I can see how it might hamper the emotional development of a child – if violence was the only form of attention you can get from a parent, would you still want to it? I have never really reconciled this in my own mind. My father would start laying into James and I would step in and usually take the worst of it. Later James would be sullen and angry with me as I lay on my bed, bruised and sometimes bleeding from the beating I had taken for him. Maybe because, in a way, I was as bad as my father, assuming he was soft and couldn't take it, putting him in the role of someone that needed protection. Protection that he had not asked for.

Looking back, maybe he had a point. But I was twelve and my thinking was not that sophisticated. He was my younger brother, and it's hard, if not impossible, to stand by and watch those you love get hurt and not try to stop it. That being said, I would still get angry and frustrated at his seeming inability to stop acting in ways that were sure to set our father off. Unconsciously humming songs in the kitchen as our mother had done, leaving out scraps of food for a stray cat that hung around our street.

I feel shame as I remember having those thoughts. All I will say in my defence is that they never stopped me from stepping up again the next time our father kicked off.

As we got older, and I got further into my teens, my father slowly wandered back to his old habits, leaving the house for days at a time. I became more careful then. Working class London in the 1970s was a hard time and place to grow up in. I knew plenty of kids whose fathers regularly administered beatings to both their spouses and their offspring, so it took me a while to figure out that what was happening to me and James was in any way out of the ordinary. That the levels of privation and hardship we were enduring were at the top end of the bell curve.

But when I did figure it out, and added in the neglect of leaving a fifteen and a twelve-year-old alone for days at a time, I knew there was a real danger of the authorities getting involved. The powers and reach of social services had grown under the Wilson government of the mid-seventies but I had heard enough from my mother about her upbringing to want to avoid the system at all costs.

We made every attempt to fly under their radar. James and I attended school and kept our heads down when we were there, just trying to be ignored. We steered clear of our contemporaries, who were not above a bit of petty larceny or vandalism, and avoided any brushes with the law. My father still came into contact with police on a semi-regular basis, although by then I think he was mostly a figure of fun to them, the arc of his fall a source of cruel amusement.

I found a local library that stayed open until 5.30pm. We both went there every day after school. It was warm and dry and peaceful. James would sometimes flick through books, sometimes doodle in his copybook, sometimes sleep. Me, I read. Everything I could get my hands on. I started with all the books that Edward had recommended: Dumas, Verne and Twain. The librarian, a kindly young woman, on seeing these choices, suggested Dickens and Austen. I liked the former, the latter not so much, at least until I revisited them a few years later. I enjoyed Forsyth's *Day Of the Jackal*, loved Jack Higgins' *The Eagle Has Landed*, and read every Agatha Christie and Conan Doyle book I could get my hands on. Whenever I hit on something that I didn't understand, be it historical, geographical or in some cases, biological, I would find a reference book to fill in the blanks. If it was written down, I wanted to read it. Inside the pages of a book was the only place that I could go to escape the drudgery of my life and get out of the fugue state that was my emotional response to poverty and violence.

Luckily, we came from a part of the world where people still looked after their own, without the need to get outsiders involved. Extended families. Mr Grant at the end of the road would give me a pound note to run down to the corner to buy him two packets of Players Navy Cut, telling me to keep the change. Back then, forty cigarettes cost about fifty pence. Mr Grant, who would curse like the sailor he had once been, and used to ritually hack his phlegm and spit it in the gutter outside his front door, had his own surprisingly sophisticated social etiquette when it came to giving folks charity while allowing them to maintain some dignity about it. Other neighbours often supplied me with snatches of food to pull a meal together from. Over the years, food preparation became James' task, partly because by then I was working part time jobs, and partly because he was better at it than I was.

If my father was absent, the Abelmans would feed James and me. On Friday nights – the start of Shabbat – we would come around and all hold hands, and I would watch fascinated as they solemnly shared out challah and Mr Abelman sang his strange Hebrew prayers. All of the prayers fascinated me, but one especially became my favourite.

The *Eshet Chayil,* as I would learn over time.

The valour of women.

She whose value is above rubies. She who speaks with wisdom and has the teaching of kindness on her tongue.

I would watch and ache to be a part of something other than my broken, bleeding family. Two satellites spinning off into the darkness after things had fallen apart, after the centre had not held. The centre that was my mother. Long gone, now barely remembered – a hole at the core of our lives.

I did not hate her, but even though I could not articulate it then, I knew that my love for her was not unconditional. There were boundaries and I had found them. Being abandoned in the world whispers things to you, about your worth as a person, about your adequacy, about how much you can trust in other people – and none of the things it whispers are good.

We survived, in the sense that we stayed alive, but it was a cold hard existence for six long years. By then it was March 1978 and I was approaching my eighteenth birthday. I had done okay in my O-levels two years before, and the headmaster had convinced me to stay on and attempt A levels.

At the time I was working three nights a week in a boxing gym on the high street, and doing odd jobs on Saturdays at a garage down in Peckham. The UK was a grim place then. The economy had stalled for the last four years, there were power blackouts and fuel shortages, trade unions and the government seemed to be able to agree on nothing; but at the bottom of the pile, where we were, you barely noticed. It was the rest of the country that found itself suddenly cold and hungry, down in the hole we had been in, all this time.

The only reason I paid any attention to the news at all was because ITN had a newsreader named Anna Ford, who was the most beautiful thing I had ever seen. I would sit staring at her, not caring about the steady litany of misery – pit closures, unemployment, rising inflation – that she was relaying, just staring intently at the movements of her beautiful lips.

It was during one of Ms Ford's broadcasts late that month that I saw a report that the police had discovered the body of a woman in Manchester, recovered from a shallow grave on waste ground. Initially she was believed to be another victim of the so-called Yorkshire Ripper. At first, I didn't pay much attention. He had already killed Helen Rytka in January and Yvonne Pearson earlier that month, and I was removed from the horror of these crimes, so far away and foreign. But although the discovery of that new victim fell from the top of the news, there were a few follow up reports both on television and in the newspapers that caught my attention.

I knew nothing of Manchester. I knew nothing of the Ripper's other victims. But found near the body, they had recovered a small, empty green suitcase with solid brass buckles, which the police believed had belonged to the victim. And I did know about that.

CHAPTER TWENTY-ONE

Caulfield suggested a quick drink. We went to the bar of the Hotel Stern, because it was quiet and we could talk. He went to the bar, came back with two beers and sat down. I waited for him to speak.

"So, what do you know about Chris Wall?" he asked eventually.

"I thought you were going to tell me what you knew about Chris Wall. And Greg Harvey."

"I am going to tell you, but it would be helpful to know what you already know. So I can fill in the blanks." He shifted his beer slightly by adjusting the mat a half inch, but didn't lift it to his lips. I pictured it as a chess piece, he was working out whether he could trust me, what move to make. I didn't know nearly enough about him for comfort, but I felt I had more to gain than I had to lose.

"All I know about Chris Wall is that he was some kind of coder for hire, who made a solid living contracting out to financial firms in the Square Mile. From personal experience, he seemed to be a bit of a dick, especially around women, and, if current evidence is to be believed, he suffered from a deep-rooted depression that caused him to take his own life."

"You know more than I thought." He nodded slowly, still looking into the drink in front of him.

"So, what can you add?" I tried to keep my tone neutral, watching his face. After a pause he took a long breath and began.

"Chris Wall. Aged thirty-five. Got a double first in Computer Science and Mathematics at Cambridge. Moved to London. Briefly worked as a quantitative analyst for a financial house. After about a year, set up his own company, creating software in that field. About five years ago, he created a piece of martingale software, based on variables in the Levy Process, and he sold rights to that software to a hedge fund with an exclusivity clause for five years. Made a tidy sum from it too." He sounded annoyed.

"You're speaking English and I understand all the individual words, but I have no idea what you're telling me."

Caulfield's sigh was almost imperceptible. He scratched his eyebrow then started again.

"OK, do you know what a hedge fund is?"

"I know how to spell it."

He leaned back. "It's an investment fund that trades in liquid assets. Usually, they ignore standard trading transactions in favour of more complex models. Often a portfolio constructed with a broad range and higher risk management mitigation to improve investor return. Often using such morally dubious but perfectly legal methods such as short selling and derivatives."

He glanced up at my face. I nodded whilst frowning to indicate I was just about keeping up, so he summarised. "In layman's terms they get a pot of money from rich people, and they make that pot of money bigger, as fast as they can."

"I'm with you so far, comrade. Rich folk getting richer."

"Okay," he said, satisfied I was finally following. "So in order to build those portfolios, these hedge funds and investment banks use quantitative analysts. People who use complex mathematical models to price and trade securities."

"And Chris Wall was one of those guys? He created a good model?"

"By all accounts he came up with *the* model. About six years ago he built out a software program called Xanadu. It consistently produced incredibly accurate predictions. Even better than that, it could learn as it went. It didn't take factors in isolation but could blend them. He basically developed a holistic model that applied a numerical value to all the factors, chewed them all up then spat out numbers that proved remarkably accurate. And any time it got it wrong, it learned from itself and improved. Genuine machine learning." The lesson over, Caulfield seemed reluctantly impressed for a moment, but there was also a note of something else.

"And he sold that to a hedge fund?"

"Not the whole thing – he sold exclusive use of that product to a hedge fund."

"And that exclusivity was going to end?" I finally felt the significance of what he was trying to tell me.

"The five years is up next March. Under the contract, Wall was free to sell it to whomever he wanted. However, the hedge fund did have something written into the contract on their end." I raised my eyebrows at him. Now I got it, I wanted the punchline. He seemed to enjoy holding the pause.

"First refusal on exclusivity of the next generation. Wall didn't spend the last five years sitting in a jacuzzi lighting Cuban cigars with fifty pound notes. He and his team were working on an enhancement to his original model. He was about to release the first model to the wider market, and at the same time, sell the upgrade exclusively to his original firm. Keeping them ahead of the pack."

"Do you think this is the kind of money that people would consider killing for?" I knew the answer, of course.

"Christ, yes. I once saw a guy get shivved on a street in Freetown for ten dollars and the half pack of Marlboros in his shirt pocket."

"I assume this was when you were in the army?" I gave him a significant look but he smiled, and I felt a wall begin to crumble.

"I was a Marine – technically, I was in the Navy. But, to keep to the point, we're talking about the kind of money that could bankrupt small nation states. The hedge fund knew that Wall was on the home stretch with his new product but he wasn't over the line yet. He announces that he's swanning off to Austria for a couple of weeks to take in the mountains. To get inspired, to get his mind in the right place. So, they decide they want to have a presence on the ground, just to make sure that their asset is secure."

The penny dropped. "That's how you know all this."

"Yeah. I was the guy they sent to look after him."

I took a minute to process this. A lot of it made sense, except– "You left him on his tod to wander up the mountains and do his Spandau Ballet?"

Caulfield shrugged. "The acronym we used in the military was TARFU. The first three letters stand for Total and Royal. You can work out the rest. I was under strict instructions that Wall was not to know who I was, or who I represented. I figured I'd hang out with him when he was further afield. Yesterday he said he was staying close to the hotel, to meditate and do some work. I thought he'd be safe enough and I could spend one day not glued to his hip, so as to allay any suspicions he might have about me constantly hanging around." He hesitated, making a decision. "Also, if I'm honest, I was a bit suspicious of you. Late arrival to the group, who turned up out of the blue? And you'd issued a thinly veiled threat to my principal the day before. I wanted to check you out."

"What was the hot take?"

Caulfield eyeballed me directly. "Had some game back in the day. Been out of it for a while, but might still be able to bring the goods if push came to shove. Overall risk assessment, negligible."

I smiled. For the first time I felt that I had met the real Richard Caulfield and I decided I liked him. "Well in a reciprocal spirit of brutal honesty, that was a bit of a ball drop."

He sighed. "Tell me about it. In my defence, that's not the kind of security I offer. I'm the guy you send to spot that the grey-haired man with the scar hanging around the war memorial yesterday was the same guy who was in the market in Biberwier the day before. Not to figure out that someone is depressed and needs a hug because they put extra sugar on their cornflakes." He continued in a more reflective tone. "Security envelopes around a principal of up to a hundred metres, I can do. There is a litany of women in my past who will happily confirm I have the emotional intelligence of a breeze block. The square foot inside a man's skull is not my purview."

He shook his head suddenly, as if to clear it of maudlin introspection and continued. "Not that it will matter, but there is plenty of blame to go around."

"How so?" I asked.

"Have I talked enough to earn a question?" There was a plaintive note to that. I looked across the table at the man. He was still the same confident guy from the last two days, but there was no denying that he looked like someone who had taken a hit on the chin. That he was valiantly trying to get back on the front foot, and reluctantly found himself in the position of needing help. Most importantly I was confident that everything he had just told me was true. So I nodded.

"Ask away."

"Did Neumann say anything about Wall's autopsy?" He watched my face steadily.

"Only that he was expecting the results tomorrow. Why?"

"I think there is a good possibility that it's going to say Wall was out of his tree on LSD at the time of his death."

"Really?" I blinked, trying to understand the implications, if there were any. "This just gets better and better."

Caulfield nodded, then took a long gulp of the beer he had, thus far, neglected. Mine stayed untouched. I was already two beers up from my time with Werner, very tired, and trying to pay attention to what I was hearing. He set the stein down and continued. "I phoned in to say that Wall was dead. As you can imagine, not the most pleasant phone call I've ever had. It turns out that Wall was particularly fond of wandering out into the woods and sticking his head in a bucket of blotter acid."

"They didn't tell you that?" I was pissed off on his behalf.

"Apparently, having that information out in the open was considered a risk to their brand. The gazillionaires might not be so keen to hand over their dosh to a hedge fund running their modelling off a magic eight ball designed by some microdosing stoner. They had decided it was need-to-know, and that I didn't need to know."

"Stupid decision on their part," I said. His expression agreed emphatically but he shrugged.

"Steve Jobs partook too, so they say. So did Francis Crick. Paul Erdos, Richard Feynman. Quite popular amongst the mathematicians by all accounts. What do I know? Maybe it does free up your head, let you make weird spatial connections. I've never touched it, but I can barely manage long division." He took another drink.

"So where does that leave you now?" I was looking to wrap things up, it was all interesting stuff, but it wasn't lost on me that someone like Caulfield wouldn't be spilling his guts without an angle. He paused again. He had been open enough about the past, but it was a different ball game to let me in on plans still in play.

"Well that's an interesting question. Pragmatically, the hedge fund knows there's no point crying over spilled milk, and they didn't really care about Wall per se. They only cared about what was in his head. And since that's gone, they only care about how much of it he managed to get down in code. Which I guess is on his computer. I imagine the hotel handed his possessions over to the local authorities for safe keeping. The hedge fund can get involved in a legal battle with Wall's firm as to intellectual property. Just between you and me, if I'd had the chance, I might have gone into his room and lifted his laptop, because by the time the legal wrangling is done, you and I will probably be deep in the cold, cold ground. As it is, I'll probably have to get some official bona fides sent over and start the ball rolling with Neumann to try to take possession of it."

I thought back to the paperwork I had flipped through in the file a couple of hours earlier. There had been a couple of photos of Wall's stuff laid out on a stainless-steel table. Itemised. I was pretty sure I was right.

"You might have some problems with that," I said

He tensed and leaned forward. "How so?"

"Neumann let me have a sneak at his Wall folder. He wanted my professional opinion."

"And?"

"He'd taken photos of everything. Wall's body. Possessions Wall had on him and personal items taken from his hotel room."

"Nothing like a bit of Teutonic efficiency. What's the problem?"

It was my turn to take a moment. "I don't remember seeing a laptop in those photos. I'm not sure Neumann has it."

Shortly after that I made my excuses and left. With my brain firing off on all sorts of tangents, I was exhausted, I had not seen Abby all day and wanted to check how she was – where we were. I agreed with Caulfield that I would try to establish with Neumann whether he had Wall's laptop. If he did, Caulfield would have to start the painful legal process of who was entitled to what. If Neumann didn't have the laptop, then he definitely had a crime on his hands – either murder or theft. That could be tomorrow's problem.

When I walked into the hotel, Melanie was on the desk. She had obviously been waiting for me because she immediately walked around it and approached. At this point I had been up for fourteen hours, but had no choice but to stop as she explained, in very apologetic tones, that they had been obliged to seal my room off at the police's request. With a wary eye on my face, which I imagined was sagging with exhaustion, she explained that they have been able to move most of my belongings into a new room, and handed me the key. I thanked her. As I was turning back towards the stairs, she asked me if I felt like I needed any professional counselling. I politely declined, and she returned to the safety of her post.

I stood at the bottom of the stairs, one hand on the polished banister, one foot resting heavily on the bottom step. I thought of

Hanny diligently working the dark wooden surface to a bright shine, heaving an antiquated vacuum cleaner up each individual fold of richly coloured carpet bordered by more gleaming hardwood. Off to my right, through the double doors, I could see into the dining room. The room was lit by a low hanging chandelier of faux candles, glowing bulbs shaped like teardrops, pretending to be flames. The hall where I was standing suddenly felt very dark, and the room beyond seemed to hum with the warmth of the fire and the diners' sombre conversations. A few couples were visible at the smaller tables, and off to the left, drawing my gaze, was the Morton's guest table.

My memory went back to long afternoons in the library with James. This view of the four empty seats at a table set for twelve could have been taken straight from the Agatha Christies I'd devoured there. Caulfield was somewhere behind me, presumably drowning his sorrows. Harvey and Wall were in their respective drawers in the local morgue. I was standing in the lobby, on the edge, looking in on my fellow guests. I assumed that by now everyone knew about Greg. I remembered something Emery had whispered to me once, when we had been invited to the wedding of one of her work colleagues, and ended up on the odds and sods, losers table. "Party isn't going well if you can hear the scrape of cutlery on plates."

The body language had changed too. The first night, not only had the volume been louder, people had been more expansive and relaxed around each other. Now the mood was subdued, and they were leaning forward, offering what they had to say softly, murmuring beneath the hum of tension. I could only see the faces of four people – the three members of the Nicholls clan, and Abby. The Nicholls parents looked pale and wan. Laura had bags under her eyes, and she was holding the hand of her husband, who had developed a bit of a thousand-yard stare in the last forty-eight hours. Christine seemed the most animated, deeply engaged in a conversation with someone out of sight – probably Bryce or Margaret. Someone was talking to Abby, and she was responding, but I could tell from here that she was phoning it in, and that her thoughts were elsewhere. I couldn't go in there, pull up a chair and make small talk, make sense of platitudes, be polite, involved. No answers lay that way, at least not tonight. You can't see into the darkness if you're standing in the light.

I owed Abby a conversation, but whatever we needed to say could wait until the morning, when we both had the time, were alone and I could give it my full mental attention. I was just too tired.

I turned right at the top of the stairs and found room eleven. Stripped off and dropped everything on the floor. Standing in the shower, I realised I was cold to the bone, so I just stood there under the jet, cranking the heat to the point of scalding, the spray blasting me between the shoulder blades. I wrapped myself in the fluffy hotel bathrobe, which was easier than actually towelling myself dry. Lay on the bed, stared at the ceiling and waited for sleep. My brain twisted and turned the world like a puzzle. A riddle that might have no answer. My eyes felt sharper now that a long dormant and cobweb-strewn part of my brain had opened up again. Even though I was shattered, with all the thoughts bouncing around my head, sleep took a while to come.

CHAPTER TWENTY-TWO

O ver the last fifteen years of my police career, a term slowly snuck into our lexicon. 'Finding closure'. It became a new facet of what we did. We didn't just catch the guilty and punish them to make society safer or to mete out justice. We gave the victims closure.

Finality.

Acceptance of reality.

Let go of the pain that forlorn hope gave you. You can deal with your pain and your loss, provided you find closure.

Personally, I was always suspicious of the idea, and I tended to lump the term into the same category as I would words like 'unicorn' or 'Atlantis' – I understood the idea behind what the words described, but didn't believe it existed.

Grief or pain ebbs and flows, and it may diminish over time, but there is no silver bullet to bring it to an end, there is no road map or direction to get you there. And even if there was, people might not want it anyway.

If the pain of losing someone is the last little shred of them that is left in the world, you might be loath to let it go.

When we first saw the news reports in 1978, I had nothing like closure. All I did was exchange the pain of feeling abandoned by my mother with the pain of knowing that she was dead, and that her death had come violently at the hands of another.

It also raised a tidal wave of questions.

When exactly had she died?

What was she doing in Manchester?

Who had killed her?

James wanted to go to the police and report what we knew. That the victim was one Eve Marley, nee Smith, born 1936, late of London town, last seen by her husband and two sons six years ago in 1972.

My father disagreed. He had become less violent with us over the years. He was getting older, and I guess the exertion of hitting us took it out of him. We had slowly reached a set of guidelines that we could all operate under, while maintaining order. But the fury he directed at James for even suggesting we go to the police was a real return to past form, punctuating each of his arguments with another violent blow to the side of his younger son's head.

The plod had been after him for years.

They wouldn't waste this opportunity to stitch him up for a hard thirty on the back of this one.

You never involve the law, that's not our way.

James ducked some blows, blocked some, and ate the rest, but he wasn't backing down.

"If we don't tell them they won't know her name," he cried. "They won't know where to bury her. They'll just put her body in an unmarked grave and we won't know where to find her."

"She made that choice a long time ago, when she left. It's done."

There was a brief spike in my father's violence after that initial discovery. I think he was nervous that the police would somehow figure out whose body it was, and arrive at our front door to stitch him up, even though he was innocent – of that particular crime, anyway. He was nervous and drank more than usual, coming back from the pubs drunk and lashing out. Lashing out when there was no food in the house, lashing out that we were playing the radio too loud, lashing out at anything.

I think he was actually relieved when, on 16th May, the police discovered the body of Vera Millward at the Manchester Royal Infirmary, and found a new focus for their investigation.

The story, which had fallen from the news, resurfaced again briefly, but only as a postscript. The police were currently chasing a man they believed responsible for nine murders. The unidentified body of a woman discovered two months ago had been discounted as one of the Ripper's victims, due to modus operandi and the length of time the body had remained undiscovered.

During that month, I took beatings like I was walking around in a daze, not bothering to defend myself, not fighting back. Watching with clinical detachment, like it was happening to someone else. I deserved them. I had not held faith. I had forsaken my mother. Her memory. I had let myself believe she could turn her back on us. On the promise that she made. I was not worthy of love. I deserved everything I got.

Then one day, I was in my father's room. I needed a copy of my birth certificate, to apply for college funding after A-levels. My father, for all his faults, was a tidy man. I imagine it was a habit inherited from his time in the army. All paperwork and correspondence was kept in one of the shoeboxes on the top of his wardrobe. I stood on a chair to take them down. They contained his old army papers and the few pieces of genuine correspondence that he had received over the years – seaside postcards and a letter in an envelope, the corner with the return address removed.

I stared at the contents of that box for a long time.

There was something else in there too.

I realised then that this could be an end. But it would be an end that I would have to force, and it would more than likely be violent.

It was late May and I went and sat on the swings in the park, working out methodically what I was going to do, and the order I was going to do it in. From six years of part-time jobs, I had a post office account with a small amount of savings, whatever I had not needed to keep James and I fed. I told my various employers that I had to take a few days off for my exams. They were good with that and wished me luck.

I had enough in my account to catch a train to Manchester. Twelve pounds open return.

I left early in the morning, like I was going to school, some clothes shoved in my schoolbag. James would worry, but there was nothing I could do about that. I caught the tube to Euston and from there caught a three-hour train to Manchester Piccadilly. My second time out of London after our summer trip to the Frasers', only this time there was no friendly couple waiting for me. Just a cold empty platform under a Victorian train station. I stopped into a greasy spoon on the station concourse, ostensibly to buy a cup of tea, but also to find where the cemetery was.

"Which one?" asked the man behind the counter.

It had not occurred to me that there might be more than one.

"The biggest one. The one where they bury the people with no families."

He didn't know, but called over to another customer reading a paper at a table.

"Hey Fred, lad here wants to know where they bury the unknown folk."

Fred put down his paper and with a start I could see he was wearing a policeman's uniform.

"Southern Cemetery," he said and looked at me. "You from London, lad? Why would you want to know that?"

"I think I might have some family there." The honesty of that answer must have shown in my face, because after a moment he nodded.

"Largest municipal cemetery in the country," he added with a hint of civic pride. "My own mam's resting there. Nice spot she has too. Anyway, plenty of room in there. That's where they put the poor unclaimed souls."

"How do you get there?" I asked. "If you were walking."

"Oh, it's a fair bit away," he said. "Follow Princess Road all the way out – about five miles I'd say. Bus 101 to Wythenshawe would get you there in about half an hour. Just outside the station."

I thanked him and left. Managed to find the right bus stop. Went to the newsagents next door and bought some flowers. I gave the conductor my destination and asked him to tell me when we got there. Half an hour later, he told me this was my stop.

I wandered the cemetery for over an hour. But where Père Lachaise thirty-five years later was peaceful and pleasant, this place on a cold day under a grey and overcast sky, felt like a sad memorial garden to the poor and anonymous, a collection of small monuments to forlorn little lives under constant threat of being consumed by the city surrounding them. It filled me with desolation and sadness.

Eventually I found a section of graves marked by nothing more than small wooden uniform crosses. Maybe a hundred or more. I picked what I thought was the nicest plot at the end of a row with a few wild primroses growing at its perimeter. I sat down next to it, laid my flowers gently at the base of the cross, and rested my palm in the uneven grass in the centre of the plot. As well here as anywhere.

"Hello mum," I said.

I sat there for a long time.

When I got home the next evening, James was in the kitchen frying liver and onions, a heady odour of sugar and burnt rubber filling the house. He looked up when I came in and I thought he was going to burst into tears with relief. Instead he ran forward and grabbed me in a massive bear hug. I hugged him back.

"Where were you?" he cried. "I thought you'd left for good."

I patted the back of his head.

"I wouldn't leave you behind Jimmy," I whispered. "I'd never do that."

"Where did you go?"

I gently disentangled myself from his grip.

"Let me take over and I'll tell you."

He sat down and I swapped places with him at the sizzling pan. It was a big solid single piece of metal and James had wrapped an old cloth around the handle to keep from burning his hands.

I gave it a perfunctory shake.

"So?" he asked

"I went to Manchester," I replied.

I could see his mouth opening to ask a litany of follow up questions but at that moment, the key in the front door turned. My father.

He saw me from the hallway and stumbled forward. To my right I could see James shrink in his chair. I guessed my absence had infuriated the old man, and he could anticipate what was coming. I was amazed at how calm I felt. My father stopped, swaying in the doorway.

"Where the bloody hell were you?"

"Manchester," I said again. "I caught the train to Manchester."

"Manchester….what the fu….?" he began, then stopped. I could see the wheels turning in his head.

"You stupid little bastard. Did you talk to Old Bill up there? Did you? You bloody did?" He was clenching and unclenching his fists. Primed for action. He was older now and flabby, but there was still a solid core of muscle under all that fat.

I thought of Fred, reading his paper in the greasy spoon café. It wasn't even a lie. But this was it. The Rubicon flowing before me, daring me to cross.

"Yes," I said. "I did."

He roared an incoherent syllable of rage and leapt towards me, crossing the tiny kitchen in two steps, his left arm up to rain violence down on my head. I swung the skillet as hard as I could in a wide arc at the end of my arm, sending hot fried onions and liver flying across the room to splat a messy crescent on the kitchen wall. My father's own momentum carried him straight into the path of that swing, and the corner of the pan caught him high on the forehead, the force enough to bounce him left, his legs smacking the table, his head hitting the wall, the rebound putting his whole body on the floor.

The collision knocked James off his chair and he ended up on the floor too, where he gave a single yelp, more shock than terror then went silent, his face a mask of open mouthed, bug-eyed horror.

He backed himself into the corner, hugging his own knees up to his chest. Aghast, but unable to take his eyes off the terrible scene playing out in front of him.

My father was bleeding from his scalp and he slowly rolled onto his front, groggily pushed himself up onto his hands and knees, one arm reaching blindly up for the counter to give him some purchase.

I swung again as James screamed at me to stop, that I would kill him.

It was a vicious overhead blow, the flat of the frying pan base catching him on the top of the crown, with a clang that was almost cartoon comical, putting him all the way back on the floor on his belly.

Silent tears were streaming down James' cheeks now. My father was barely conscious, and I dropped the pan and rolled him over.

His eyes were rolled back in his head, only his whites showing, and he was mumbling incoherently. I waited for him to come back. To see me.

Eventually his eyes focussed again. He looked at me and groaned.

"Bashthard" he slurred, one arm reaching up to me.

I leaned in close, gripping his coat lapel with one hand.

"Look at me," I said, then I took his Modele 1892 revolver out of the pocket of my parka. I held it out at arm's length, the muzzle making contact with the centre of his forehead. I cocked the hammer back, the click as it locked incredibly loud. His eyes were wide with fear and he dropped his two hands to the floor.

"Look at me," I said again. "Touch us again and I will kill you. Believe me, I will. You can stay here, but you don't touch us, you don't speak to us, you don't even look at us. Just stay out of our way, get drunk, sleep it off, until you die. Or it ends right now. You understand?"

My father was silent for a moment then let out a long keening wail, sobbing a hot mess of tears and snot down his face that was creased, lined and bloodshot by years of hard living. Not out of guilt for what he had done to James and me, or for pushing us to this denouement. He was crying for the destruction of the last tiny corner of a world where he had once been a king. Look on my works, ye mighty and despair. It scares me to remember how black and hard my heart was at that moment.

I stood up and stepped back, leaving him mewling on the floor. I slowly eased the hammer back down on the gun and put it back in my pocket and turned to look at my brother.

"It's okay James," I said. "It's going to be okay."

I reached out my hand to him but he only looked at it, then at my face, and gave a small but resolute shake of his head.

I knew at that moment that I had killed something between James and me. We would get past this and move on with our lives, but there would be a distance now. A distance that I had put there. James had witnessed in me the same thing that was in my father – something I had instinctively always known was there. A potential for savagery, for violence. The potential to hurt. That was not something he wanted in his life. I was not something he wanted in his life. Looking into his eyes, all of that passed between us in an instant. In that moment I understood what he felt and that he was not wrong.

I left them both there and climbed the stairs to our room. I pulled the curtains and lay there in the yellow gloom from the streetlight outside my window. I waited. If there was going to be a counter-offensive, it would be tonight. Eventually I heard a slow and methodical creak as my father hauled his heavy frame up to bed. There was a pause at the top of the stairs. He would either walk down the hall to get to me, or go straight to his own room. He chose the latter.

I heard the creak of bed springs as he laid his battered body down and waited for another thirty minutes until I heard low and rhythmic snoring. James had still not come to our shared room by the time I risked falling asleep two hours later.

We lived like that for six months. The three of us shared the same space, but that was about all we had in common now. James still spoke to me, but I could feel the distance between us that had not been there before. My father came and went, but he now drank in his room. Occasionally if he was sitting watching the TV, I would make him a cup of tea when I got in from work. That was as close to a rapprochement as we ever got.

My father died suddenly in September that year. He was down in the pub, had just finished a drink, stubbed out a smoke. He was waving his pint to get the barman's attention, when he fell off his bar stool. He was dead before he hit the floor. When we saw his body, there was a bruise on his head where he had hit the bar counter on the way down. The doctor told me he hadn't even felt that one. Massive heart attack. There were six people at his funeral, including James and me. It was a better ending than he deserved.

Less than three months after that, James moved out to work full time in a pub bistro and attend catering college. Two months after that I went to Hendon MPC to become a policeman.

CHAPTER TWENTY-THREE

The day after my tour of the lake and Caulfield's revelations, I woke early, hammered through my morning routine and was downstairs by 8.10am. All the Morton's guests bar Abby and Caulfield were scattered around the room in their various subgroups. I grabbed a coffee and a croissant and went outside to the patio to get some privacy for a text and a phone call. As I sat down at the outside table I saw Caulfield pacing up and down by the war memorial, mobile phone to his ear. Even from here, I could tell it wasn't a pleasant call.

I rummaged in my wallet, added the mobile number from the contact card Neumann had given me into my phone, and fired off a quick text.

Hi Werner. Quick question. Do you have an itemised list of Wall's possessions that are in custody? If so, does it contain a laptop? If not, we should talk. Signal dependent, you can reach me on this number. Later. Jake Marley.

Then I scrolled through my contacts, found Jon and hit call.

He answered after four rings.

"Hi Jake," he said. "You back in Blighty yet?"

"Still on the continent. Just phoning to see if you have time to do me a quick favour. Unless you're busy rummaging through the bins of some Z-list celebrity?"

"Don't be daft, Z-list celebrity bin-rummaging is on a Tuesday. What's up?"

"Could you see what you can dig up on a guy called Chris Wall?"

"Hang on," I could hear him typing in the background. "I have a neurosurgeon, a horse trainer and a computer coder."

"The last one," I said.

"What's your interest?" he asked.

"He was part of our holiday group," I said. "He killed himself out in the woods a few days ago. I was just curious about his background. I think he was a Cambridge grad so maybe you have a few contacts you could hit up."

"Any kind of urgency on this?" I appreciated Jon. He was a mate who would lend you a shovel and give you directions to the most secluded spot in the woods without any pesky questions.

"Not really. Whatever you can rustle up in the next day or so."

"Yeah, sure, leave it with me. I'll give you a buzz back tomorrow at the latest. That all you need?" He was also the sort who would then ask if you needed to borrow any plastic sheeting for the boot of your car.

I looked through the glass door to the breakfast room, through which I could see Margaret and Bryce. My brain cross-referenced the dirt on Wall's hands and knees with the dirt on the back of Margaret's jacket and the twigs in her hair when we encountered them on the day of Wall's death.

"Margaret Lawson," I said. "About fifty years old. Possibly a schoolteacher, although I wouldn't swear to it. Specifically, I'm interested in her family background."

"One second." More typing. "Nothing showing up on LexisNexis. You got anything more to work with?"

"Not really. What about her partner? Bryce Boseman?"

"Bryce Boseman, the author?"

"I don't know. Is she?" She'd kept that quiet.

"Black woman? Amazing cheekbones?"

"Sounds right. She wrote a book?"

"Yeah, she's an economics professor. Wrote a non-fiction thing that had a bit of a breakout. We ran a piece on her a few months back in the literary review section."

"She never mentioned it." Was that impressive or suspicious?

"A stark warning on the growing danger of unchecked AI and its potential negative impact on society at large. Social unrest, economic and political upheaval, your basic post-apocalyptic nightmare. I read a few chapters and decided to quit before I diverted my entire pension pot into canned goods and shotguns."

I kept my voice neutral, although my grip tightened on my phone. "Interesting. If you could do a bit more digging, I'd appreciate it."

"No worries. I'll find out what I can and buzz you back."

"Good man."

"You back next week? We got robbed on the quiz last Thursday. Lost by a point. What was Mr Darcy's first name?"

"Fitzwilliam," I said automatically.

"You see. Peter said you were just ballast, but I knew you had your uses."

"Twenty-four hours?" I confirmed.

"Consider the clock running," he said, and rang off, leaving me with a lot to think about.

Caulfield had finished his call. I waved and he came to sit down opposite me.

"Any change in the operational situation since last night?" he asked.

I handed him my phone, with the text I had sent Neumann onscreen.

He read it, nodded slowly, then handed it back.

"Right. So either Neumann has Wall's laptop, in which case I need to touch base with my hedge fund overlords and get them to start the process of getting their grubby mitts on their intellectual property."

"And if he doesn't have it…" I felt a genuine interest in his life, I couldn't picture him being deferential to a bunch of men in expensive suits.

"Then I need to try to find it. Which I guess Neumann will be doing too. If that's the way it plays out, I'd appreciate you keeping me off his radar, for the time being. Might give me a bit more operational wiggle room." My face must have revealed some level of discomfort with this, because he added "I'm not asking you to lie for me. You were a copper, you know where the line is. Don't cross it on my account. In my world, everything is on a need-to-know basis. Odds are, Wall took his own life and his laptop is either in Neumann's possession, or hidden under his hotel bed. But if you're correct that it's in the wind, then I'll need to do some serious reassessing. " He looked deflated at the prospect.

"Fair enough," I agreed. "But if Neumann sees that he doesn't have a laptop that I just told him he should have and that he can't find, he's going to be confident that he's dealing with a crime. Theft at the bottom end of the scale, premeditated homicide at the top."

Caulfield thought for a moment. "If the laptop is missing, there's always the possibility that it's at the bottom of Blindsee Lake. That Wall flung it over the side before he flung himself over the side."

"Why would he do that?"

"No idea. Fit of pique? Existential crisis? Some Oppenheimer thing? I'm just throwing out possibilities here."

"It's possible. Why don't we wait and see what Neumann comes back with." His turn to look less than comfortable.

"OK, I'll wait for the word." He pocketed the impatience he clearly felt. "What do you make of him? Local bumpkin plod, or has he got some juice?"

"By his own admission, he's not got much experience. But he's not stupid, and he seems methodical and up for the grunt work. If you're asking for an opinion, that will get you over the line most times."

He nodded. "So, what's your plan for today?"

I looked back inside. Abby had arrived and was now sitting with Margaret and Bryce. The full complement of Morton's guests, all gathered together.

"Let me ask you a hypothetical," I said, turning back to look at him. "If you thought one of the guests was in some way involved with Wall's death, who would you go for?"

He scoffed. "You're not serious."

"Probably not. Just call it an exercise in eliminating lines of enquiry. If you had to pick one." I let the sentence hang.

"Honestly? You."

I nodded. "Feeling's mutual."

"Okay, I'll indulge you." He looked to the sky and counted on his fingers. "We're each other's alibis. We can also rule out Abby and the Smiths. Based on the timeline, the only people unaccounted for are the Nicholls clan. Daughter white-water rafting. Parents shopping in Biberwier."

I shook my head. "Margaret and Bryce. We only caught up with them at about 4.30pm. They have a window too. Narrow, but it's there." I realised I was showing too much enthusiasm. "As long as we're indulging in hypotheticals."

Caulfield thought about this, then shook his head. "Sorry, but I just don't see it. Occam's Razor would say that Wall took his own life, and that Harvey is just an unfortunate coincidence. Until I hear that Neumann doesn't have Wall's laptop in his possession, that's what I'm going with." He hesitated. "Not to be a buzzkill, but have you considered that you maybe want it to be suspicious? That you just want a crime to investigate?"

"I thought you said you weren't any good at the psychological stuff," I accused. "But there's some truth in that. As long as we're talking about the old days, there was a feeling I used to get working cases, when things felt a bit sketchy. A bit off. Which usually turned out to be correct."

"And you're feeling that now?"

"A little bit, yeah. I can't quite put my finger on it, and it's not anything I could give to Neumann as hard evidence, but something about all of this is just not adding up for me."

"Is he treating this as suspicious?" There was an significance to his tone.

"Not as far as I'm aware. At least as of last night." I felt the need to remind him I wasn't officially involved, or to remind myself. He must have understood the look on my face because there was the lightest of pauses.

"What about you?" His voice was lighter, but his eyes didn't leave my face.

I gave him a self deprecating grin. "Just out here trying to conjure meaning and purpose, Doctor Freud."

Caulfield sighed. "No harm in having a hobby, I suppose, although I think you're wasting your time. Let me know as soon as Neumann says anything about the laptop."

We went back inside and caught up with the other Morton's guests. Margaret, Bryce and Abby were heading off to see the waterfalls, whilst the Smiths and the Nicholls were walking the high mountain pass on the Gatterl-Knorrhutte route. I had a quick word with Harry and added Caulfield and myself to that expedition. Abby looked a bit disappointed that I wasn't in her party, but when everyone else had wandered off to get ready, I managed to find a quiet moment alone with her in the lobby. She was looking out of the small square windows that framed the doorway to the building, her face restful and her eyes unfocussed, unseeing. She seemed to wake as I approached, and turned to me.

"I'm sorry I didn't see you yesterday." I said, softly. "Speaking to Officer Neumann took longer than I thought."

"Is everything okay?" she asked, giving me a searching look. "It was awful to hear about poor Mr Harvey. Especially after Wall. Was it a heart attack?"

"I don't think they'll know for sure until they do an autopsy."

"So you're not in any trouble?" Her wide, unframed eyes looked concerned.

"No, he just wanted a statement because I found the body." I tried to change tack. "Look, it would be great to have a proper conversation, would you like to have dinner with me tonight? Just the two of us. I'll book somewhere. If you want me to, I mean."

She smiled. "I would really like that. Thank you."

"Great. I'll aim for, say, 8pm, if I can. Meet you back in the lobby at 7.30 tonight?"

"Sounds perfect," she said, then leaned up and gave me a kiss on the cheek.

"See you later."

I went back to my room to gather my gear, the sensation of that peck lingering on my cheek.

I met Caulfield outside the hotel with the Smiths and the Nicholls clan. As we were heading off, I glanced across the road. A large guy with a crewcut was sitting on the bench by the war memorial, silently watching our group plod out of the village over the top of his newspaper. He was dressed in jeans and a green combat jacket. We made eye contact, and after a moment, he stood up and walked away. I was watching him slope off when Caulfield caught up with me.

"Something the matter?" he asked.

I considered. A guy sitting on a bench, watching a group of walkers go past. On reflection, not worth getting excited about.

"Probably nothing," I said. "Can you recommend somewhere decent to eat around here?"

He grinned. "Does someone have a hot date? If you need any seduction advice, just let me know."

My suggestion for what he could do with his seduction advice, had he complied, would have made his eyes water.

"Das Walters in Biberwier," he suggested. "I had lunch there the first day. Quiet, cosy, good wine selection. Bit overpriced maybe, but I can get their details if you want".

"Perfect," I said.

He did a brief search on his phone then dialled.

The phone connected, and he gave my requirements in a rat-a-tat of accentless German.

After a minute, he disconnected. "Sorted. 8pm, name of Marley. I asked for a quiet corner spot. Smart casual."

"Thanks, mate."

"No problem. Personally I think it's a better use of your time than playing Jessica Fletcher, so happy to help."

We wandered up the Liegen path, a route through Alpine meadows that slowly ascended into the peaks beyond, the cool breeze carrying an almost absurdly perfect scent of wildflowers and distant snow. As we walked, I considered what Caulfield had said – there was more than a good possibility that he was correct. Once, when on a camping trip, Emery had protested that there was no way that the Ursa Major constellation looked like anything other than a big saucepan, and that anyone who managed to get a bear out of that collection of dots in the sky was clearly smoking some industrial strength weed. I smiled at the memory. Here I was, trying to turn a saucepan into a bear. But that niggling sense of something off would not leave me be, and given that I had started down that road, I might as well continue for a bit. I had Jon looking into Bryce and Margaret, that left the Nicholls as the only other folks not in my presence when Wall had died. I decided to focus on them for the day.

Given that Paul was the strongest of the three, and had demonstrated that he was capable of near-berserker levels of rage, he was my main party of interest. But he seemed determined to stay by his daughter's side, and the narrower paths forced us into pairs. I found myself plodding along with Caulfield, studying Paul from behind. I hadn't really considered him before this, other than to note his height and width around the chest. His legs seemed disproportionately short compared to his long arms and torso, not helped by his cropped holiday cargo pants. Apart from the general sag of encroaching middle age, he wasn't fat. He looked like a professional rugby player maybe five years out of the game. Watching him walk ahead of us with the slight frame of his daughter beside him, both silhouetted by the glare of the morning sun, put me in mind of Winnie the Pooh and Christopher Robin – if Pooh had been a ten foot snarling grizzly instead of a short, tubby yellow teddy. But that was as far as my observations got.

We stopped for lunch at the *Tirolerhaus*, a large three-story pine building ringed with a wide balcony, with picnic tables arranged in two rows along the back wall and against the balcony guardrail. A thoroughfare for tourists ran between them. There was a food fair underway, with a collection of stalls selling various forms of Austrian cuisine, schnitzel, wurst, käsespätzle and tafelspitz. A few other stalls sold knick-knacks and tourist tat. Most of us settled for wurst and beer in the warm sun. A few metres away, a man was giving a demonstration of sculpting with a chainsaw, carving an impressive totem pole out of a large upright tree trunk pounded into the ground. That attracted most of the group's attention, although the Nicholls father and daughter opted instead to play a variation of horseshoes, with wicker rings painted in primary colours on a basic pitch. It was clear from the amount of brinksmanship, player interference and outright cheating going on that they were not taking it seriously. I only realised that I was smiling when Laura Nicholls sat down at the picnic table next to me and pointed it out. I looked at her, embarrassed to have been caught staring intently at her family.

"Sorry," I said. "It's a nice image."

"You don't have children?" she asked.

"No," I said. "My wife always wanted them, but I worried that I wouldn't be any good at the job. Maybe it's for the best, given the way things turned out with us."

Laura nodded. "Paul felt the same way before Christine was born. That he wasn't wired to love someone he had never met."

I looked at the two of them, him trying to throw a ring while his daughter waved her hands in front of his face. "I'm guessing that turned out to be unfounded."

She smiled, but I detected a note of sadness in it. "You can't fight a billion years of evolution. He loved that girl from the very second he laid eyes on her. Absolutely, totally and unconditionally."

I decided to push my luck a bit. "You're saying that like it's not a good thing."

She looked at me, impressed by my powers of perception or annoyed at my impertinence, I couldn't tell. "No," she said at last. "But it's just that sometimes you can feel like a bit of a spare wheel. Don't get me wrong, I love my husband and my daughter, but sometimes I get the feeling that there is this connection between them, some wavelength that I cannot tune into, and it makes me feel sad. Like an interloper."

"Like an unspoken understanding."

She shook her head. "No, it's not that. Half the time he doesn't understand her. This strange, angry child of his. But he doesn't have to. He just loves her with every fibre of his being. It's separate from anything else. Out there by itself, attached to nothing. It just was, is and always will be."

"I guess that explains the other night." I suggested.

She looked confused for a second then caught up.

"Chris Wall? Yes, safe to say that he was not happy about that."

"I suppose all fathers buy alsatians and shotguns when their daughters are born?" I tried to joke.

I could see instantly that this annoyed her, because she put down her coffee cup and looked directly at me. "You don't have kids, so I can see why you would think that. But the truth is, my husband and I know that part of your child's development is that they will grow up to live a full life. That she is a young woman, that she will meet people and they will be intimate. Some of them will hurt her, some of them she will hurt. That's just part of growing up. It's not our job to interfere in that."

"I'm sorry, I'm missing the point. Like you said, I'm not a parent." It had been a while since I had been upbraided so thoroughly and the apology was honestly meant. She seemed to see my genuine contrition and continued in a more forbearing tone.

"The point is that people can hurt each other even when they don't mean to. That's just life. But then there are predators. People who take. And use. And those people you put through a wall. Those people you would bury to protect your child."

"Your husband thought that's who Wall was? A predator?"

"Never mind my husband," she said. "If I thought that he was a predator, that he might hurt my child, they could have buried what little they found of him in a matchbox."

With that she stood up and walked off. I knew the conversation had vexed her, and had not actually added to my store of knowledge in any meaningful way, but it did make me like her and her husband more.

After watching her go, I happened to glance up at the second-story balcony. A man was leaning on the railing. From his vantage point, he had a good view of the Morton's guests – the large group admiring the chainsaw artist, the Nicholls family, and, to a lesser extent myself, now sitting alone on my bench. It was the man from the war memorial earlier. Crew cut, jacket. However out-of-place he had looked before, he looked even more so here. Twice in one day was too much of a coincidence, even if he hadn't appeared to be so obviously shadowing our group.

I looked around. There was a side door to the Tirolerhaus that appeared to be exclusively for staff use. I stood up and stretched casually, watching the observer from the corner of my eye. As soon as the angle of his head indicated that he was looking away, I ducked through the side door. I found myself in a noisy, bustling kitchen, full of the sounds and smells of various foodstuffs frying and boiling. A chef in kitchen whites, chopping onions at the work counter nearest the door, looked up at me and shouted something in German. I held my hands up in apology, and before he could say anything more, marched quickly through the main swing doors to the restaurant interior. From the restaurant floor, I went up the main stairs to the second floor balcony. Crew cut was still there, leaning on the railing, with his back to me. I looked around. There were twenty or so tourists at picnic tables on this level. I was pretty sure nothing was going to kick off in front of that many witnesses. So I walked over and addressed his back in a loud voice.

"Dr Livingstone, I presume?"

I don't know exactly what reaction I was expecting, but the one I got surprised me.

He spun around and, on seeing me, paled, and straightened up, his arms coming up like he was ready for a fight, then dropping again, as if realising that wasn't an option.

"Nein, ich spreche kein Englisch," he said loudly, looking around in a panic.

I stepped forward and offered my hand. "Don't sprechen much Deutsch myself mate, but good to meet you."

He shied away from my hand like it was radioactive, and backed up. Not looking where he was going, he tripped over an empty picnic bench and landed heavily square on his back on the deck.

I took a step forward. "Seriously mate, who are you?"

He clambered to his feet. "Nein," he said again. "Kein Englisch". Then he turned and fled, at a pace just shy of a run, to the stairs and away.

I didn't follow him, but instead went to the balcony and watched as he beat a hasty retreat back down the hill towards Ehrwald.

What our exchange meant I had no idea, but it did firmly convince me that I was right and Caulfield was wrong. There was something going on here that was sketchy as hell.

An hour after lunch, just as we had reached the high point of our single-track mountain path and were heading down the far side, my phone pinged. It was a text from Werner.

> No laptop for Mr Wall. No laptop for Mr Harvey either and I understand from Melanie he was never seen without it. Scope of investigation is now changing. Please contact me as soon as possible. Regards, Neumann.

I was last in our single file troop, with Caulfield just ahead of me. I tapped his shoulder and showed him the text. He read it and looked at me. In that look, I could see that I was no longer the mad conspiracy theorist that I had been at nine o'clock that morning. He silently mouthed a word that had *Lady Chatterley's Lover* banned for thirty years, handed the phone back and we continued winding our way down the mountainside.

CHAPTER TWENTY-FOUR

We didn't get a chance to catch up until we got back to the hotel that evening. I had about an hour before I had to meet Abby, so we went for a stroll and ended up sitting on the bench just by the war memorial, the same bench our strange observer had been sitting on that morning. I gave Caulfield a quick update of that encounter just to get him up to speed, and we sat in silence as he processed it.

Then he said, "I think this might be the most interesting war memorial I've ever seen."

I considered this. It was a statue on a plinth but the figure was that of a woman, kneeling and weeping in anguish. It had a plaque underneath the statue. *Unseren Helden die heimat.*

"What's the translation?" I asked.

"Our heroes are home," he said. "A nice sentiment but not sure I'd agree. They probably weren't all heroes, and they are definitely not home. They're dead and gone, their remains scattered on some anonymous foreign plain."

"I figured you for a cynical guy, but that's the first time you've confirmed it." I said.

His laugh was more like a humourless bark.

"You have no idea," he replied. "You know, the day I was offered the Chris Wall job, I bumped into a guy I used to serve with. Nick Carrow. Sergeant in 7th Armoured. Desert Rat. Good man, solid soldier. Lads used to call him Mr. Bojangles because he'd never give over talking about this dog he had when he was a kid."

"Nice to catch up?" I asked.

Caulfield grimaced. "He was sprawled outside Liverpool Street station, out of his mind on meths, with a cardboard sign and a begging bowl. I tried to talk to him, but he was just a babbling mess. Didn't recognise me. I ended up just giving him the eighty quid I had in my wallet and leaving him there in a pool of his own sick." His eyes didn't leave the statue, his voice was bitter.

"Do you know what happened to him?" I asked quietly, after a moment.

"In the war?"

I nodded.

"He was crewing an armoured personnel carrier. One of the old FV432s. They took a hit from an anti tank mine. Not some improvised IED made from fertiliser and bleach, a Soviet TM-62, proper flesh shredder. Turned the inside of that APC into a food blender. Killed nine people instantly. I heard they had to scrape one guy's face off the bulkhead. By some miracle Carrow was the one who made it. Walked away with minor lacerations." He shook his head but kept his gaze forward. His voice was hollow now. "But that was just his body. Something in his mind broke that day. Broke and never got fixed. I guess he just fell and kept falling because there was no one there to break it for him. Take it from me, he was not the only one that got chewed up and spat out."

I had no idea how to respond to that, so in the end I just reached out and patted him on the shoulder. It felt appropriate and awkward as hell at the same time.

He sighed. "I won't end like that. That's why I ended up in close protection. You might be working for the undeserving, but the pay is considerably better. Make enough to retire, bugger off to the south of France somewhere, buy a house on the beach, live in peace and swim in the sea every day." I could picture it. "That's not too much to ask, is it?" He was really asking me.

"I don't think so," I said, gently.

Caulfield nodded. "Okay, well none of that is happening without salvaging something out of this mess. So back to the matter at hand."

He wanted a way out of his thoughts and I was happy to provide it. "Okay, first thing: Wall's habit of coming to the mountains, going out into the woods and getting high. Was that well known?"

Caulfield shrugged. "Well the overlords told me it was need to know, but at the same time, probably nothing is as secret as you think. I imagine anyone with a keen interest in Wall could have found it out."

"OK, so not common knowledge, but maybe some key people know. So maybe one day he goes out, he gets stoned, and he gets bumped off. They put a noose around his neck and throw him over the side. He struggles a bit, musses up the grass, but he goes over in the end. Exit pursued by a bear. The laptop is now in play."

"An eyewitness said he was on his tod." He cautioned.

"Skip that for a second. Neumann gets the call. He identifies Wall as English. He has to phone around the various hotels in the neighbourhood to figure out where Wall was staying. I'm going to bet that certain nationalities favour certain hotels, and it didn't take him long to get to the Vorsehungberg."

"OK, then what?"

"The phone rings. Melanie answers it." I gestured to him to and Caulfield mimed picking up the phone holding his thumb and little finger to his head. I knew he was mocking me but I ignored it.

"Hello?"

"It's Neumann," I said. "Do you have a guest named Chris Wall currently staying there?"

"We do."

"He's dead."

"Mr Wall is dead?" Emphasising each word loudly and flatly, like a six-year-old in a Nativity play. "I can't believe it. How did it happen?"

"He committed suicide. Hanged himself."

"No. How awful." Caulfield put his mime phone down. "Plausible, but what's the point?"

"I'm guessing Greg was perched in his traditional spot in the lobby. Banging away on his laptop, drinking his frothy lattes. And he overheard." I shrugged, satisfied with the account of events.

"They're two Austrians. They're not going to speak English for his benefit."

Feeling low-key smug, I said, "Harvey spoke German. I'd bet Melanie didn't know that, which was why she would have been okay having the conversation in front of him in the first place."

Caulfield nodded slowly. "So if you're right, Melanie confirms that Wall is a guest, and Neumann says I'll be over as soon as I get his corpse slung in the back of the *kübelwagen*."

"Yes," I said. "And Harvey has only heard half a conversation but it's enough to know that Wall won't be needing his laptop anymore. And he knows he has a small window to commit a crime of opportunity."

"But he ends up dead." He sounded like a Hollywood producer listening to a movie pitch.

"So, this is the question." Despite myself, I could feel the old thrill returning. This was fun. "What if someone bumped off Wall just to get their hands on his work, only to get beaten to the punch by Greg Harvey? How long do you think it would take them to figure out who it was?"

Caulfield considered this. "Well if your theory is correct, it took them less than six hours. But if they have it, then they're long gone. Wall is dead, brief wobble if Harvey gets in the way, but he's disposed of as well. Laptop recovered. Job done. No need for your man to be watching us."

He was right, of course.

The light around us had faded enough that the world appeared in greyscale and the streetlights were powering up. It wasn't cold, but there was a change in the quality of the air, as the day's warmth slowly bled away.

"Okay, well maybe they still don't have it. Maybe Harvey hid it somewhere. Somewhere they couldn't find it." I could feel my momentum fade and I was floundering again.

Caulfield shook his head. "Sorry, I'm still not buying it. It's too messy and full of risk. You want to kill someone, you put one behind the ear. You want to do it quietly, you drag him into the woods off the beaten path and do it. His body wouldn't be found for months, after the wildlife had used it as a tasty snack."

I wasn't convinced. "I wouldn't be sure that industrial spies are that professional. You ever read all the details of Watergate? Total skip fire of ineptitude from start to finish." He gave me a look which I accepted and turned away. "But okay, let's say for the sake of argument, no one killed Wall. Maybe someone was just hanging around, just waiting for an opportunity to execute a theft and Wall actually does take his own life. Gods and fate just throws them a golden opportunity. Only Harvey gets there first. They dispose of him. But then they discover he doesn't have it on him. He's hidden it somewhere and they're now looking for it."

"You think that was what that guy was doing today? Looking for Wall's laptop? In someone's rucksack? Up a mountain? Again, that doesn't stand up to any kind of scrutiny." Caulfield was trying and failing to keep incredulity out of his voice.

"Maybe not the laptop itself. Maybe some clue as to where it was hidden." In the dusk I couldn't see his face but I was avoiding his eye anyway.

"A treasure map? X marks the spot?"

"Neumann doesn't have the laptop. So there are four options. One, Wall got rid of it. Bottom of the lake. Two, the laptop was taken by person or persons unknown. They have it and are long gone. Three, Harvey stole it, either as part of a conspiracy or not. They took it from him after killing him, and are long gone. Four, Harvey took it, they killed him to recover it, but failed to do so. So they're obliged to stay and try to find it."

Perhaps it was the tenor of my voice, but Caulfield gave me a moment before speaking again, and when he did, it was kinder. "But Harvey died at 9pm. We were all sitting in the lounge drinking until midnight, more or less. That guy today was nowhere in sight. I would have remembered seeing him. So would you. After midnight the hotel doors are locked to the outside . No one got in or out after that."

He was right, again, but I couldn't leave it there just yet.

"There must be a side door to the hotel somewhere. It's not impossible that he got in that way. And maybe someone else was involved."

Caulfield looked sideways at me. "Are you back to someone in the hotel?"

"Honestly, I don't know." I hadn't realised the strength of my dissatisfaction until I heard it in my voice. "If Wall was murdered, the people we were with have alibis. Abby and the Smiths. The people we weren't with – what are their motives? That Wall was letching on their daughter or girlfriend? That he held unsavoury opinions? That his work posed an existential threat to the world as we know it? Pretty weak sauce. Especially when you stack it against industrial theft. Simple financial gain is an easier sell. It would explain Harvey's death and missing laptop too. Can you really see anyone here capable of premeditated homicide?"

Caulfield paused, giving it some serious thought, then slowly shook his head. "No. Probably not. It's not as easy as you'd think." There was a heavy silence. "You don't need to know, but let's just say that there is a reason that I long for a quiet life in the south of France, where I can swim every day and live in peace."

"Understood." After a minute I leaned back. "Tomorrow, I'll go and talk to Neumann. I'll leave you out of it if you still want to fly under the radar. I'll let him know about the guy today, and see if he's got any updates on the laptop. Maybe he's managed to find it since we told him he should be looking for it. I'm also due an update from a friend back in England on a few things."

Caulfield nodded. "Sounds like a plan." He checked his watch. "I need to drink scotch and ponder the ruins of my career in security. You need to go get ready for your hot date. Hope it goes well. I'd ask you for the gory details tomorrow, but I'd assume you're not the kind of chap who'd kiss and tell or brag about the number of women he's bagged."

I stood up from the bench.

"On the contrary, I'm exactly that kind of guy."

Caulfield squinted up at me, surprised. "Somewhat disappointing, but I'll bite. What's the number?"

"One."

CHAPTER TWENTY-FIVE

I'd never gotten around to asking Melanie about a laundry service. I'd scrubbed my jeans in the sink then laid them under the mattress I was sleeping on to press them. I'd read a thriller once where the hero had done this to get an extra few days out of his trousers, so decided to give it a go. The results turned out better than I expected. I found an unworn navy shirt in the bottom of my rucksack, then really pushed the boat out by having a shave. I was looking not-too-shabby as I checked the results in the full-length mirror inside my wardrobe. I wandered down to the lobby feeling pretty good about myself, until Abby appeared.

She looked amazing. Made all the worse by the sense that she hadn't made much of an effort, just throwing on the first thing she found in the drawer. She was wearing blue jeans, a simple blouse and black blazer jacket. Her hair, which she normally wore down, was in some kind of complicated Gordian updo, held together with what looked like a pair of wooden chopsticks, showing off her cheekbones. No jewellery apart from a simple chain and sapphire pendant that sat at the base of her throat and made her eyes seem even more dark and sultry. In a millisecond I realised how massively above my weight I was punching, but by then she had seen me and it was too late to beat a cowardly retreat.

She walked down the stairs to me and smiled.

"Hi," she said. "I didn't know where we were going so I played it down the middle. Hope it's okay."

I didn't trust myself to give voice to the thoughts banging around my head. "You look great," I said weakly. I had always been rubbish at this kind of thing.

She leaned in and whispered, "I think everyone is trying not to see us."

I glanced sideways, trying to be surreptitious. All our fellow guests, plus the three Morton's kids, were sitting or standing around the reception area having their evening drink and planning activities. Every single one of them was studiously not looking in our direction. Apart from Bence at the bar, who grinned the wicked grin of one hound dog to another, and gave me a big thumbs up.

"Do you want to get out of here?" I asked.

"I would love to," she replied.

It was a pleasant twenty-minute walk along the perimeter of the Moos. There was a direct route by road, but we both agreed it was worth adding an extra half-mile for the lack of traffic and additional pine trees. From the outside, Das Walters looked pretty low-key, a single-story building with cream plaster walls. There was a long wooden bench outside with upturned logs and lanterns on top, serving as tables.

My opinion picked up once we got indoors. The acoustics managed to turn the combined conversation of about fifty people into a pleasant background murmur. The décor was heavy on the wood, with pine panelling on the walls matching the pine floor.

Somewhat incongruously, a large red deli meat-slicer was parked in the middle of the room.

The friendly waitress escorted us to our table. Abby caught a couple of glances as we threaded our way to the corner, and I could see people comparing the two of us and wondering if I had maybe won her in a competition. As Caulfield had promised, we were in a secluded spot in the corner and the waitress went off to get our respective choices in Dutch courage. The menu was in German. Abby was planning on having the schnitzel and I had faith in my near-supernatural ability to find steak on any menu in any language.

The waitress came back with our drinks. Abby picked up her gin and looked me in the eyes. "If I'm being honest, I'm kind of nervous about tonight. The last time I was on a first date, Tony Blair was PM."

I smiled. "The last time I was on a first date, Margaret Thatcher was PM."

"So we're both nervous. How about this? It's not a first date. It's just a chance to have a nice meal and a conversation. Shall we run with that idea and see how we get on?"

"Works for me," I said.

So that's what we did.

We spent starters in generic small talk, talking about the high points of our holidays, the people we'd met, studiously avoiding either of the fatalities. Abby said that she had really enjoyed the company of Margaret and Bryce and that she was going to try and stay in touch with them when she got home. "I know how everyone says that after a holiday, but I might really try," she said.

I didn't know if I fell in the category of people to be kept in touch with or not, so instead I asked her for more details of what she did for a living. She gave me a brief summary. Everything from organising events to making sure paychecks went out on time. Basically keeping all the plates spinning behind the scenes at one of the Oxford colleges. That, of course, led on to what I did for a living, which these days amounted to bugger all, punctuated by dog walks and pub quizzes.

"Retired by fifty-three? You lucky sod." She teased. "I'm like Ben Hur – chained to the oar that I'll be forced to row until I die."

Our main courses arrived. Abby got her schnitzel and was suitably impressed when a sizzling rib-eye was set down in front of me. I didn't want to get into the whole conversation of how having nothing to fill up your days was a bit of a double-edged sword, so I asked her, if she didn't much like her job, was there something that she would rather do?

She shrugged and said that there was a time when she had a promising diplomatic career in Strasbourg, but that events had overtaken her.

I got the impression this was a big thing in her life, so I offered the 'you don't have to talk about it if you don't want to' line.

She took a drink of the very nice red she had selected, steeled herself, and said "No, it's okay. My family died in a car crash a few years back. My parents and my sister." She smiled sadly. 'I was in my flat in Strasbourg when I got the phone call. I remember, I was watching the news, which had just broken the Clinton-Lewinsky story – I'd met him once and was just thinking to myself that I wasn't at all surprised – when the phone call came. Funny the stuff that sticks in your head, isn't it?"

I too remembered that date, as it was the same day as I had been promoted to Detective Inspector. Emery and I had celebrated by going to The Ivy, but I didn't volunteer this information, I didn't want to derail Abby's tragic story with my pointless trivia.

She shook her head as if to clear it.

"Anyway, we were a very close family, and after that I lost the run of myself for a bit. Quit my job. Lost drive and focus. Got a bit self-destructive. Drank too much. By the time I'd picked myself up, a few of my boats had sailed."

"I'm really sorry to hear that". I really was.

"Thank you," she said. "It was just bad luck. They were driving in bad weather. They hit a patch of black ice, and the car slid across the road into the path of a truck coming the other way. Killed instantly. The truck driver was okay. Physically, anyway. He was clearly traumatised at the inquest."

I thought it said a lot about her character that she could find some sympathy for the guy in those circumstances, but I kept that thought to myself.

I thought I should meet this emotional soul bearing with some of my own. After all, if someone is willing to show you the places where life broke them, it seems only fair to reciprocate. I gave her a brief and potted history of my life. My mother's disappearance, my father, how our relationship had ended, everything up until I joined the police.

"Was your mother's killer ever caught?"

I shook my head. "No. No one was ever arrested or charged. In fairness, I think the police had their hands full at the time with Peter Sutcliffe, and the longer a case goes on, the colder it gets. As far as I know, it's still open, but after forty years, I'm not holding my breath."

"Is that why you became a policeman?"

I smiled. "That would be an easy out, but probably not. I always said what appealed to me was a steady paycheck and the chance to do something more exciting than oil changes on cars. I think I was just angry at the chaos that had been my life, and I saw it as a way to put some order back into the world. To have some control. Maybe a chance to fit in somewhere. Be a part of something. It didn't really work out though. Not for a long time. I was too broken. I didn't fit in and, looking back, maybe I didn't want to."

She smiled. "52 Hertz."

"Is that a science thing? I don't know what it means."

"I read an article once a while back. Back in the early 80s, the Woods Hole Oceanographic Institute detected a whale song and got very excited because it was at 52 Hertz. The reason they were excited was because nothing previously recorded sings at that frequency. Too low for a fin whale, too high for a blue whale. There was some initial hope that they might have discovered a brand-new species of marine mammal. But after the initial excitement they all calmed down and realised that it was very unlikely that there was a new, previously unknown species of whale. They determined that it was much more likely that it was from some existing species that had either been born with some kind of birth defect, or was possibly deaf. Which was why it was singing in the wrong key."

"Great. Now I want to start sad-drinking on behalf of some poor whale."

"It gets worse," she said. "Because when it sings, nothing answers. The other whales don't recognise the noises as whalesong, so don't respond. It's been swimming out there somewhere in the Pacific between Southern California and the Kodiak Islands for forty years, calling out and getting nothing but silence in return."

"And you think that I'm the whale?"

"Maybe," she said. "Was that you? Way back when? Singing and not being heard?"

"Well, you're not a million miles away," I said. "But back then, I wasn't even singing."

It was dark by the time we'd finished our meal, but the moon was practically full, and the sky was clear. We decided to walk off our meal, retracing our steps across the Moos. Abby reached out to take my hand to steady herself as we cautiously picked our way down the sloped track to the flat path, but once safely down, she didn't let it go. It felt nice to have had a real conversation about real things with someone, and I offered as much. Abby replied that she felt the same, then hugged herself into my arm.

I was just trying to remember how you worked up to kissing someone, second-guessing how much the rules might have changed in all the time I had been off the market, when I became aware of someone walking behind us. That in itself wasn't necessarily cause for alarm, but the thing that set off a warning light was that our pace was slow, more of a lazy meander, as we enjoyed the moonlit, crisp night air. He should have overtaken us, but he didn't. He was keeping pace. It felt like we were being flanked. I glanced back and tensed. I couldn't be sure, but I was almost certain it was the same guy I'd seen at Tirolerhaus that afternoon.

Abby hadn't noticed him. I was just about to stop and see how he reacted, when I became aware of someone approaching the other way. That would do, I thought. Potential muggers don't like witnesses.

As he saw us, the guy coming towards us held a hand up to flag us down.

"Excuse me" he said, changing course slightly to intercept us. "Do you have a light?"

At that moment I saw that his hair was grey and he had a long thin scar running down his right cheek. The description that Caulfield had mentioned in passing of a man he had seen more than once in the last few days. And with that, the warning lights went red across the board.

"How do you know we speak English?" I asked.

He smiled thinly, reminding me of a younger Christopher Lee.

"You look English." He held up his cigarette. "No light?"

"Sorry. Neither of us smoke."

Lee tutted. "You were smoking two nights ago with the other lady."

Abby gasped and I saw that in the hand not holding the cigarette, he had an automatic pistol that was now pointing directly at me.

Police advice for how to respond if you are getting mugged at weapon point is to run, if that is an option. If not, try and remain calm, try not to exacerbate the situation, follow all instructions and try to memorise as many details of your assailant as you can for the police report that you hopefully get to file later. Abby was there and I didn't want to needlessly put her in danger. I also wanted to see what they wanted. I raised my two hands up to my shoulders. Same thing as with the pick-pocket in Paris – it looked like a natural response, but it also closed the distance between my hands and the gun.

The guy behind us had stopped too. Close enough that when I glanced behind me, I could confirm it was the same guy with the crew cut who had been shadowing us that afternoon. Lee was about five feet in front of us, with the gun pointing from the elbow.

Abby and I were standing side by side a foot apart, and crewcut was about ten feet behind us.

Lee looked at Abby. "Bag," he said. Then he turned to me. "Empty your pockets"

"Okay," I said, not taking my eyes off him. "There's no need for anyone to get hurt. I'm going to very slowly reach into my pocket for my wallet and phone. Abby, take your bag off your shoulder."

She did. I had my wallet and phone in my hand.

"Okay," I said. "What now?"

"Put them down on the ground and step back."

I set my items carefully on the ground and a moment later Abby followed suit.

Lee then turned to her and said, "Necklace too."

I had been expecting Lee to relax a bit with his prize in sight, and figured that if I was going to make a counter move, this would be the time. But then Abby beat me to it. She took a step back and shook her head.

"No."

Lee took a step forward towards Abby, raising the gun away from me to point it in her face. I took a step sideways and forward at the same time. He saw me coming and went to swing the barrel back towards me. It was in his right hand, so if he fired the recoil was going to pull up and to his right, my left. I feinted slightly right as I stepped forward until I was inside the range of his arm. I figured he wasn't going to fire with his partner standing behind me, but even if he did, the bullet would miss me. I reached out with my right arm and clamped a firm grip around his wrist just below his gun hand. Pushed, so that he was now pointing out across the flat empty landscape of the Moos, then I twisted forward savagely like a motorcyclist cranking the throttle. He grunted through clenched teeth but didn't cry out.

More importantly, he didn't drop the gun. That made the next bit dangerous. He was on my left and still gripping his wrist with my right hand, I twisted my entire body around in an awkward pirouette, the barrel of the gun drifting within range of Abby's face. I spun my left elbow, aiming for his neck, but catching his left ear. That was enough to put him on the ground. His right arm twisted as he fell and I heard something crack. The gun went limp in his hand but he didn't fall to the ground, his finger still inside the loop of the trigger. I grabbed it with my left hand, yanking it off his fingers, not caring that I was scraping the skin.

All of this happened in about five seconds. By the start of the sixth second, he was down and I had the gun. I was ninety percent sure he was out for the count, but I took the time to heel-stomp his head. I had enough control to hold back a bit, I wanted him unconscious, not dead. Although I wasn't too worried if he would be able to remember the names of all his grandchildren in the morning.

By now his partner had figured out that things were going badly awry and was running forward. He looked about as bright as Greenland in December and I figured he would not be too much of a problem. He turned out to be easier than I imagined. I had backed up two steps to give myself some room, and as he passed Abby, he suddenly screamed and raised his hands to his eyes, still barrelling forward, but now blinded. Abby had maced him in the face, with a can of deodorant grabbed from her bag. Pepper spray may be illegal in the UK, but there's no law against carrying anti-perspirant. He was still stumbling when I swung a haymaker, holding the barrel of the gun, the butt catching him squarely on the temple. His momentum carried him forward even though, by then, he had parted company with consciousness. I side-stepped as he face-planted on the ground. His shirt had ridden up and I could see a black ink Gothic tattoo across his lower back, a grinning skull over a single word, Noricum. I could also see a pair of dog tags that had popped out of his collar, lying on the ground next to his head. I reached down and yanked them over his head, jammed them and the gun in my pocket and turned.

Abby was breathing heavily, mouth open. I bent and reclaimed my phone and wallet, grabbed her hand, and said "Run."

We didn't stop until we got back to her hotel room. Jammed the snip on the door and hit the lock. She had lost one of her chopsticks and her updo had lost structural integrity, a long strand of her brown hair hanging down one side of her face. We both leaned on opposite walls of her hallway, panting, looking at each other, then she leaned forward, grabbed both sides of my face with her hands and kissed me. A split second later, I started kissing her back.

After that, we found a way to burn off all the adrenaline flooding our bodies.

CHAPTER TWENTY-SIX

It was a cold, miserable Monday evening in February 1985. By then I had been a policeman for six years. Most of my early years as a bobby were spent doing mundane jobs: patrolling streets in the rain, dealing with petty burglaries and shoplifters, giving talks to school children about not getting into cars with strangers, writing reports. But there were times when I found myself on the front lines of various fights that Mrs Thatcher was not going to back down on.

One of Maggie's Boot Boys, as they called us in the pit villages of the North and the Welsh valleys; Babylon to the Rastafarians in Brixton; Nazis to the more excitable CND protestors; and plain old-fashioned pigs to the crews on the terraces, the ones we were currently babysitting to stop them murdering each other. I treated all of them more or less the same. At that point in my life, I had a near-constant, simmering anger that was always threatening to surface, which meant there wasn't a fight I was going to retreat from. Everyone we faced had their own ideas and philosophies, but once the bottles and bricks started flying it all tended to boil down to one idea in my head – if you kick out at the world, don't act surprised if the world kicks back.

I was standing south pitchside at Stamford Bridge listening to Harry J Allstars *Liquidator* being massacred over the tinny tannoy as the home team jogged onto the pitch. Chelsea versus Millwall at home. FA Cup fourth round. Normally there was about one policeman for every hundred fans, but we'd doubled that to one for every fifty, as both teams had some serious crews wearing their colours. The Head Hunters on the Chelsea side, the notorious Bushwhackers firm for Millwall. Chelsea had already played Millwall twice that season winning the first one 3-1, pulling a draw over at The Den.

This one was at home, and the Pensioners were expected to win it, but Millwall were playing well. I was trying to keep my eyes on the crowd. I was down at the Shed End, and by half time Millwall were one ahead, Steve Lovell scoring an early goal. The Millwall fans were jubilant. Despite only making up about a third of the twenty-five thousand crowd, they were making most of the noise. There was a ten-foot metal barrier coming down from the back of the stadium to the pitch, and on the far side of it I could see some Millwall fans starting to jeer across the border, and the Chelsea fans in turn suggesting that Millwall supporters knew their own mothers, their sisters and various barnyard animals rather well. I could see the odd blunt object being lobbed over the barrier, could feel the charge building. They were summoning a demon that would not be dismissed without blood.

My minimal interest in football had died with James's a decade before, but I heard enough about it from lads at the station house to at least know the London teams, and I hoped that Chelsea sorted it out in the second half. A draw was probably our best chance that nothing would kick off. The Pensioners came back well, Spackman and Canoville scoring two within five minutes of each other about ten minutes into the second half, and the Shed End was jubilant. But Millwall dug in, and John Fashanu put them level again. The same Millwall fans who would throw bananas at him next week were currently cheering his name.

I could feel the tension building again – for a brief span, it felt like the right kind of tension. Edge-of-your-seat football from two teams and their loyal fan following. Then about twenty minutes from the end, Lovell scored his second for Millwall, and that was the last goal of the match.

Final score – Millwall: 3, Chelsea: 2.

As soon as the ref blew his whistle the Millwall fans erupted into rapturous jeers. I could see within ten seconds of that whistle that we were going to have trouble. We'd successfully kept the Bushwhackers out of the Shed End, but there were too many of them just on the far side of that barrier.

I had been on the lookout for skinheads in Doc Martens: a mistake that I resolved not to make again. The blokes on the Millwall side, doing the interpretive dance of 'come on if you think you're hard enough' at the Chelsea section, were wearing V-necks and half-zips. The new breed of yob. You could give them Ford Cortinas and satellite dishes and tell them they were middle-class, but they still had an emptiness in their lives, the need to be a part of something. These artificial tribes were their solution. Bushwhackers lobbed bottles over the barrier, provoking as best they could, and the Headhunters wanted blood. There was nothing on the pitch that could not be fixed in the stands.

Some people were already moving for the exits but a section of the crowd around the barrier, pitch-side, began to ebb and flow like a tide, pushing forward then falling back, only to push again even harder, moments later. It was impossible to source its origin in that heave of maybe four hundred bodies, and to me it suddenly felt like one great animal, with many parts but with only one consciousness, that no one had to take responsibility for. A beast that was angry and stupid and hungry.

Ebb and flow, over and over, each time the push just a little bit harder. I cast a look around. Off to my left, I could see a group of uniforms beating a hasty path over, realising that trouble was brewing. Off to my right there was one single copper, a twenty-year veteran called Alfred Hayes. He didn't wait for me but marched over to the gate in the barrier, drawing his truncheon.

"Enough" he roared, loud enough to cut across the white noise of the terrace, rattling his billy club across the metal barrier. "Enough of this shit now."

Those at the front instinctively pushed back from his show of aggression as the wave behind them pushed forward, and it was momentarily neutralised. For a brief giddy moment, I thought Alfie had actually managed to subdue a mob just by sheer force of will. I distinctly remember thinking "He-Man's got nothing on you Alfie, you utter legend."

Then the crowd suddenly burst forward as one and the wave restarted. It flowed and ebbed once more, then again. But this time a guy at the front in stonewashed denim aimed a well-timed kick at the padlock. It held for a second, then the weight of the wave hit it.

The whole gate groaned and bulged, then the padlock snapped and the gate fell towards them. A couple of men at the front spilled awkwardly onto the pitch, pushed by the weight of bodies behind them, narrowly avoiding being trampled and crushed by the mob coming up behind them.

They completely overran Alfie, who went down under their charge, and looped back towards the barrier separating them from Millwall supporters, some attempting to climb over it even as others were trying to pull it down. For their part, the Millwall supporters were doing the same. I left them to it, focussing only on getting Alfie off the ground before he was trampled to death. I drew my truncheon and waded in swinging.

They were still spilling out of the stands onto the pitch, but most swerved around me like river water around a rock, staying out of the arc of my truncheon. I had just managed to get to Alfie up on his feet when a large blow landed on the side of my head, knocking my constable's helmet off. I fell sideways, taking Alfie with me. I could feel blood running down the side of my face. The crowd was still flowing around me, but one guy stood over me with two of his mates backing him up. About fifty years old. Certainly too old for this nonsense. Looking for bragging rights – the night he gave Old Bill a good kicking.

"Come on," he screamed in an absolute rapture of blood lust. "Come on you bastard." I had a flashback of my father in our kitchen the night after Manchester.

"Come on," he screamed again.

So I did.

I launched myself at him, catching him in a rugby tackle around his chest, easily ducking under his slow swing. He fell backwards and I landed on top of him. I put my left fist right into the middle of his face. It was over right then, for the bargain price of a couple of his teeth. But just to be sure, I hit him again. Then again. Somewhere in the middle I might have blacked out for a bit. I kept going until another copper pulled me off his limp body and dragged me to the edge of the fracas. I could see his mate had managed to grab Alfie. The copper who had dragged me off pushed me away, told me to take Alfie and find some medical help. I was breathing heavily, but I could read the subtext in his face. Too far mate. Step back before you kill someone.

I was going to protest, but as suddenly as it had arrived, the anger left me. Dead battery. Spent charge. I just nodded, lifted the still wobbly Alfie up by his arms, and did as I was bid. Just another night of policing in old London town in the mid 1980s.

An hour later I found myself in the A&E at the Chelsea and Westminster Hospital. Alfie was deemed okay, with nothing more serious than a few dings and some bruised ribs, but whatever my opponent had hit me with had opened up a nasty gash on my forehead about an inch across, bleeding at a rate of knots. There was a medical officer at my section house back in Paddington, but the site officer in charge, a sergeant, had opined that it probably needed stitching and got a panda to drop me off at the nearest A&E. They offered to come in with me just in case any Headhunters turned up with their own injuries, but I told them I was fine, so they left me to it, telling me to radio in if I needed a lift afterwards.

I had lost my bobby's helmet, but was still wearing my uniform, which I hoped might bump me up the waiting list. Having given my name and my medical complaint at reception I sat down to wait in a hard plastic bucket chair.

It was about 11pm on a Monday night, but there were five other people ahead of me in the queue. Some with obvious ailments, like the young guy with the grazed and bleeding leg who looked like he'd had a spill of a pushbike; some not so obvious, such as the old black lady who appeared to be having some difficulty breathing. All avoided making eye contact as I sat there holding a bandage to the side of my head. After about ten minutes, the old lady was taken through the double doors and at the same time, I saw a red-haired woman wearing an oversized parka jacket exit with a large bag, decorated with beads, slung over her shoulder. She went to reception; presumably a nurse ending her shift. She had a few words with the receptionist, and I saw the woman behind the desk nod in my direction. Redhead looked over. I saw her body language slouch in frustrated resignation, then she walked over to me. She stopped in front of me. I looked up at her – I could see her nurse's blues under her green coat. She had an oval face with a pixie chin and kind brown eyes.

"PC Marley?" she asked. Her accent was strange, almost like she was singing.

"Present, ma'am," I replied.

She reached out and gently pushed my hand away from the wound, examining it carefully.

"Pretty nasty," she said.

"You should see the other guy."

That's the kind of thing you would say in the police canteen, but I realised instantly it was a mistake from the reaction on her face.

"I probably will," she said drily. I elected not to make it any worse and kept quiet.

"Come on," she said at last, "Let's get you sorted out."

I followed her to the A&E ward and she parked me on a gurney, behind some drawn curtains. She threw her coat on the chair, her oversized bag on top of it and left me. I glanced over at the bag. Through the opening at its top, I could see the spine of a paperback book. The collected poems of Rimbaud.

She returned a few minutes later with a stainless-steel wheeled trolley laden with gauze, bandages, tape, various antiseptic unguents and a stainless-steel bowl filled with water.

"I'm just going to clean the wound. We might get away with just taping you up. Save you having to wait to get stitches and having to come back to get them out again."

"You're the expert. Whatever you think best," I replied.

She set to work, gently mopping the dried blood from around the gash on my head.

I glanced over at her bag again and she followed my gaze.

"Not my choice of light reading." she said. "I'm in a book club. We each take a turn to pick what to read and discuss. Marjorie picked that one. She always chooses obscure intellectual stuff. I think she gets her jollies from making the rest of us look like thickos. Her last one was by Kafka. Someone turns into a bug. The only thing I could think to say I liked about that one was that it was short."

"Short and someone turns into a bug. Sounds like a classic," I said.

"Yes," she said gently applying a tape strip to my head, "it's still better than this one. Not sure I have anything good to say about Rimbaud's love poetry. Mind you, I heard that he shot his lover, so I'm not sure I should pay any mind to what he has to say about it."

"Other way around," I said.

She looked down at the gauze strip in her hand, and established that she was holding it correctly.

"Sorry?" she said.

"Verlaine shot Rimbaud, not the other way around," I replied.

She stepped back to look at me, and I imagined how I looked to her – my uniform torn, stained with mud and grass, an open wound on my head, my knuckles grazed and covered with another man's blood, offering corrections on the biographies of French symbolist poets.

"Are you sure?" she said.

"In a hotel in Brussels. Sometime in the early 1870s. Pretty sure," I said. "And it's not against the law to think he's wildly overrated, no matter what Marjorie thinks. Or thinks she should think."

She cocked her head to one side. "What would you tell Marjorie?"

"If she asked me, I'd say that he's arrogant and it shows. He assumes his own miserable outlook is universal, and anything he says about the human condition is highly suspect. Basically, he's not half as wise or insightful as he thinks he is. There are a few decent bits in *A Season In Hell*, a couple of solid efforts in *Illuminations* – 'Childhood' isn't too bad, 'Departures' is pretty decent, but overall, I'd give him a C minus. If she wants a Frenchman who writes a decent love poem, I'd go for Baudelaire or Hugo every time."

She looked at me for a long moment then smiled. "I'm stealing all of that," she said.

"If it gets you out of reading Rimbaud, please do." I replied.

She finished patching up my head, gave me an antiseptic salve and a stern warning to take it easy for a few days. Then she put on her jacket, grabbed her bag and walked out with me. We stopped at the sliding doors outside the A&E, under the awning. It had started to rain. I offered to escort her home, but she said it was fine, she was only a ten-minute walk away.

"Thanks for the patch up," I said. "Hope your book club goes okay."

"I can't wait," she replied. "Thanks for the crib notes, PC Marley."

"Daniel," I said, offering my hand.

After a moment, she hitched her beaded bag up on her shoulder, reached out and shook firmly, looking me in the eyes.

"Daniel," she said. "Pleased to meet you. I'm Emery."

CHAPTER TWENTY-SEVEN

Abby was already up by the time I awoke the next morning. Dressed and sipping a coffee in the window alcove of her room. I was awake for about a minute before she noticed, and I could tell from the furrows on her brow that she was trying to process a lot of stuff from the night before. I could no longer remember what the correct etiquette was for this social interaction, so I yawned and made a big show of waking up. She smiled at me.

"Good morning," she said. "Sorry, I didn't want to wake you. I've been up for a while."

"How are you?" I asked gently.

"Surprisingly good," she said, then frowned. "A little bit freaked out about last night to be honest."

I sat up in bed and waited patiently with a neutral expression until she spoke again.

"I've never had a gun pointed at me before," she said. "That was horrifying. But then you stopped them."

"You helped."

"Yes, but you hurt them. And seeing that, knowing you could do that, was terrifying. And when we got back to the room. How I felt looking at you. That might have been the scariest thing of all."

"I'm sorry," I said, "if you felt like I took advantage of you."

"Please," she said. "Let's not rewrite history. I kissed you. A girl could grow old and die waiting for you to make a move. It's more how I felt. Scared at first. Angry at those men for scaring me. Angry at myself for risking our lives over a stupid necklace just because my sister gave it to me. Then feeling powerful that we fought back. That this was an option. And the realisation that I didn't care that you hurt them. That I had wanted to hurt them myself. Then wondering if that was really the kind of person I am."

She hesitated. "That's about as well as I can explain it. It's all a bit of a mess in my head."

"It's how everyone is," I said. "It's primal. Everyone wants to be in charge of their own life. Have their own agency. When someone tries to take that from you, it's okay to say no. It's what you should say. Are you worried that you'll see them again?"

She considered this.

"No," she said at last. "I'm not worried about them at all. Should I be?"

"I don't think so," I said. "I'll go and see Neumann today and tell him what happened. I think the kind of people who try to mug tourists in the dark are not going to be a problem in broad daylight."

She nodded.

"You want to talk about the rest of last night?" I asked. Needy or what?

She smiled. "I overshot again, didn't I?" she said. "That's twice now."

"If you think I'm feeling used right now, trust me, it's not the case."

"You say that now, but I'm about to scurry out the door." She held up her phone. "Text from Bryce reminding me that I promised to do the summit with them today. Vicky's taking a group up there. I can duck out of it if you want me to."

"No, it's good," I said. "I have a few things to do today anyway."

She looked at me. "Do you know what you want this to be?"

I figured I owed her an honest answer. "I'm not sure."

She nodded. "Neither am I. I think this might be the strangest relationship I've ever had."

"I guess one of them had to be."

She smiled. "I guess so."

"Look," I said. "Go hang out with Margaret and Bryce. See the summit. You've been trying to do it for a week. Maybe go for a walk by yourself on the Moos afterwards. I'll stay out of your way. You have a think about what you want, and if you figure it out, come and tell me. I'll do the same. Before we leave Ehrwald, we can talk again."

She thought about this then nodded agreement.

"I'll do that. Are you okay if I go downstairs by myself? I'm already running late and I don't want to have to face everyone if we come down together."

"That's fine. I'll just sit here and weep into my pillow. Well, your pillow, but you know what I mean."

She smiled then stood up, came over and kissed me gently on the forehead.

"Take care of yourself," she said. Then she left.

As soon as she left I got up, dressed, and went back to my room. I unlocked the door and let myself in, then paused. As I stood there, any lingering idea that last night's attempted mugging had been random disappeared. Someone had been in here and searched the place. I could feel it on a primal level, as though the molecules were swirling in different patterns because bodies had passed through them.

Whoever it was had been careful, but not careful enough. Things had been picked up, then put back down, but not in the same position. The toothbrush leaning on the wrong side of the glass, Hanny's turned-down bed, which would normally pass military inspection, looking a little scruffy. Strangely this made me angrier than the attempted mugging. This was an invasion of territory, coming at me where I slept. I established that nothing had actually been taken, then went to find Caulfield.

He was in the breakfast bar by himself. I got the impression he was waiting for me.

I grabbed a coffee and a croissant and slid into the booth beside him.

"I just saw Abby leaving with the sisterhood," he said. "Don't tell me your date went so badly that you've driven a woman to bat for the other side."

"I wouldn't say badly, but certainly interesting."

"That's a word that covers a multitude of scenarios," he said.

I gave him a quick update on the events of last night. The walk home, the attempted mugging, our escape. The fact that one of the blokes involved was armed, and that we had both seen one of them – Caulfield, the grey-haired bloke with the scar, me the younger skinhead with the tattoos.

"Fair play," he said. "You've still got some moves."

"More luck than anything else," I said. "Could just as easily have gone the other way. But I have a name for you." I threw the dog tags across the table.

He picked them up and read them.

"Herman De Cherusker?" He looked at me. "These aren't official, they're just vanity jewellery."

"Yeah, I didn't get the impression that Herman had ever served. But it's still a name."

"Why do you think they have anything to do with Wall? It could have just been a random robbery."

I told him that I was almost certain my room had been searched, and added, "Something about last night felt off. Like they were waiting for us, like they singled us out. I think they thought I had the laptops."

"That makes no sense," said Caulfield. "Even if you did, they're too big for you to carry around."

"Maybe, but they sure as hell weren't after my Tesco clubcard."

Caulfield sounded exasperated. "If they think you have the laptop, that means that they don't have it, either. In which case, where the hell is it?" He was silent for a moment, thinking hard and then said "Okay, talk me through your current theory again."

I did.

Industrial spies were out here, scoping Wall. Keeping an eye on him from a distance, waiting for an opportunity to steal his work. Presumably, without his knowledge. They witnessed his suicide, and realised this was a golden opportunity to nick his laptop, but by the time they got back to the hotel, Harvey had beaten them to it.

They killed him, then couldn't find where he stashed his and Wall's computers. They had seen me talking to Harvey, or possibly seen Neumman interviewing me following his death. Either way, they think I might know where the laptops are.

Caulfield thought this through, then nodded slowly.

"Few assumptions in there, but mostly stands up. Most importantly it means in this scenario the laptop is still in play." He handed the dog tags back. "Any idea where Herman is now?"

"If he's not still lying on the Moos, bleeding from his head, I have no idea. But he does stand out in a crowd, so if you go looking for him, I don't think you'll be in any doubt if you see him. The other guy I think you've already seen. Tall, thin, grey hair, scar on his face."

"In that case, I might patrol the three villages, to see if they pop up. What about you?"

"I'm going to see Neumann."

I walked to the police station in Lermoos. I swung out of my way while crossing the Moos to return to the scene of the crime from the night before. I stopped roughly where I thought we had been accosted but could see no evidence of anything having happened. I was about to continue on my way when the phone rang.

It was Jon, and I answered.

"Mr Wares," I said. "What's the news that's fit to print?"

"Not much. I just wanted to update you. Your computer guy, I assume you know the basics. Christopher Eric Wall, thirty-five years old. Grew up in Berkshire, father an electrical engineer, mother a schoolteacher. She died of breast cancer when he was ten. Showed an aptitude for maths at an early age. Got a place at Cambridge reading Mathematics, then convinced them to let him do Computer Science as well. Wrote his thesis on variables on the Levy Process and probability studies. Got a double first, moved to London, got a job in the Square Mile working for an investment house. About seven years ago, set up his own company; soon after started making serious money. Incidentally, no word on the wire yet that he has shuffled off the mortal coil, so you're closer to the fire than me on that one. That's the official bio. But it turns out a friend of Hilary was at Churchill at the same time as Wall, reading Natural Sciences. I gave her a ring on the off chance that she might have crossed paths with him. Turns out that they were on the periphery of each other's circles and she was only too happy to dish what dirt there was."

"What dirt was there?" I asked.

"Well nothing too serious, but the general impression she gave was that he was a bit of a pill."

"I don't think he improved much with age."

"Well as Wordsworth said, the child is father to the man. He was known to some by the nickname Christ Wallmighty, which probably tells you all you need to know about his demeanour. Swanned around like he owned the place. Gave off a bit of an elitist vibe. Which, in Cambridge, is a parapet that's hard to stick your head above. She hesitated to say supremacist, but said it wasn't far off. She also heard a few rumours of him shamelessly nicking other people's work."

"Plagiarism?"

"Clare said that was probably a bit strong. He wasn't ripping off people's work verbatim and passing it off as his own. More like standing on the shoulders of giants without bothering to ask the giants if they minded. Taking other people's work and expanding on it, without acknowledging the leg-up."

"Any truth to that, or just bad feeling?"

"She honestly didn't know. She was quick to point out that history is littered with multiple discoveries and simultaneous invention. Discovery of oxygen, development of calculus, the telephone or the theory of natural selection. But at the end of the day, history records a name. Everyone knows who Charles Darwin is; most people have never heard of Alfred Wallace. She had no doubt that he was an extremely intelligent and talented guy. In her words, he just didn't have to be such a dick about it."

"As dirt goes, that's pretty tame."

"She also said that he was a bit of a creep. Which again, at Cambridge, is a challenging field to stand out in."

"Anything specific to that? Did he ever get pulled up on anything?"

"She picked her words very carefully. She said she never heard anything on the campus grapevine about him actually crossing the line into assault or rape, he just made some women feel very uncomfortable. To use her words, not the kind of bloke you'd feel comfortable eating a banana in front of. As far as I could find out, he was never in any serious trouble with the law up there. One caution for being drunk and incapable in RAG week, and he was interviewed when a fellow undergrad committed suicide. But then so was everyone else in her class. Sorry, it's not much."

"No worries mate – it's all useful stuff."

"Good to hear. Your other query was more interesting."

"Go on."

I could hear him flipping through notes.

"Let's see. Margaret Lawson. Fifty years old. Was headmistress at St Mary's Christian girls' school in Surrey. Currently on indefinite leave. There appears to be some legal shenanigans going on. Apparently, she went on medical leave when she got rear-ended in a traffic accident a few years back. Somehow that has morphed into being removed from her post, with an unfair-dismissal case about an affair with a female colleague. School claims that any relationship between a head and staff is not kosher, she claims it's because the relationship was homosexual in nature."

I ran a small victory lap on the spot with my arms in the air. Still got some game, Marley, I thought to myself. Hit a bullseye and guessed right on complete conjecture.

"But here's the interesting part," said Jon. "Her father was Trevor Lawson. Successful businessman who dabbled on the fringes of politics back in the long ago. A man of some strong beliefs, it appears. Keep Britain white. Bring back hanging. Remember the good old days when the poor knew their place. Financial contributor to Enoch Powell, and threw a few quid in John Tyndall's direction too. Doubt he was too impressed with having gay offspring."

"I think we can safely assume not."

"But anyway, if I was to ask you which mainstream politician was currently the heir apparent to Mr Powell's particular brand of political toxicity, who would you say?"

I could think of three off the top of my head. I guessed one, if only because he was our local MP. Jon confirmed my guess.

"What does that have to do with the price of beer?" I asked.

"Well it turns out the hedge fund he's a majority owner of is the same one that Chris Wall has been exclusively working for these past five years. Also, Mr Wall has made a few significant donations to his various political campaigns in the same period."

"So a right-wing coder in the employ of a right-wing politician meets a woman who, it's safe to say, despises right-wing philosophy with every fibre of her being," I said. "And has a girlfriend who believes that the work of said coder might potentially bring about the end of the world as we know it. Not sure if it points to anything, but very interesting all the same. Nice work mate."

"No worries. But from here, it sounds like your tour of Europe has gone a bit off-piste."

"That's a thought that is not entirely without merit. For example, last night my dinner with a nice young woman descended into MMA with a side-order of firearms."

"So many questions, starting with 'you were on a date'? Can I tell Helen?"

"If you must, but it was just dinner with a woman from the holiday group I'm with."

"And she pulled a gun on you?"

"No."

"You pulled a gun on her?"

"It's a long story. I'll tell you about it over a pint sometime."

"Well if nothing else, it will probably go down as the most memorable first date you've ever been on."

"Not even close mate," I replied.

I hung up and went to see Neumann.

CHAPTER TWENTY-EIGHT

B ack in 1985, I was living in the section house above Paddington Green police station, a large concrete block that looked like it might have been conceived in John Betjeman's worst nightmares and built by a Soviet Bloc planning committee. Along with ninety other single officers, I had been allocated a room to call home, where I had been living for three years. Though it was pretty spartan – a ten by thirty-foot space with a single bed, a desk and a sink, shared toilets, showers at the end of the hall and a twenty-four-hour canteen on one of the lower floors – the stability it offered after living with my father was like a tiny corner of heaven. I had no desire to up sticks to anywhere else.

It was the Thursday evening after the Stamford Bridge match. I was off shift and lying on my bed reading when a call went out over the tannoy. "Telephone call PC Marley. PC Marley telephone please."

I looked up. There was a payphone for outgoing calls, but people could dial in on the phone by the canteen and they would put out a call for you. The only person who had ever called me here was James. A perfunctory but regular update of the bullet-point headlines of his life. He'd call once a month, and rarely exceeded a five-minute window. We weren't due to catch up for another two weeks, which made me think something was wrong.

I put the book down and hustled to the end of the corridor, then down two flights of stairs to the phone. The duty officer saw me and nodded to the phone hanging on the wall bracket next to his desk. I picked it up and there was a click as the call connected.

"James?" I said.

"Hi," said a female voice. "Is that Daniel Marley?"

"Speaking," I said. "Who is this?"

"Emery Driscoll. We met last Monday night. I bandaged your head. We chatted about French poets."

Unbidden, my hand touched the taped wound on my forehead. "Is there a problem?"

"With your head? No. Not that I know of. I was just…" she hesitated, and I got the impression she had not fully committed to her course of action. Then I heard her clear her throat and she started again with more resolve in her voice. "I was just phoning to see if you were working this weekend. I'm off Saturday until Monday and I was wondering if you fancied meeting for a drink."

My heart did a lazy flutter. "I'm free Saturday evening," I heard myself say. "On shift until five but free after that."

"Is that a yes then?" she asked.

"If you want to."

"Yes. Great," she said. "Do you want to meet at The Lord Chancellor? Say half past seven?"

I assumed she knew the Lord Chancellor – known in my nick as Paddy's Palace – was a copper's pub. Almost guaranteed to have at least a few off-duty lads in there at any time of day or night. On a Saturday night it would be rammed with them.

"Do you want to pick somewhere closer to where you live?" I asked.

"Okay," she said. "How about St Stephens? On Parliament Street. Do you know it?"

"I'll find it," I said.

"Good. So, 7.30 on Saturday? I'll see you there. Bye."

"Thank you," I said, but she had already rung off.

I slowly set the handset back on its cradle and walked back to my room.

Saturday night came and the lads who were off on my floor were heading down the Palace as expected. They invited me along, but I cried off, saying I had other plans. They would have been more surprised if I had accepted. They asked out of a sense of obligation, and I always politely declined, knowing that they were only asking because they felt they should and that they didn't really want me there. I wore the uniform, but beyond that, I was not one of them. I was too much of an oddball in their eyes, my presence made them feel uncomfortable, my silent observation from the sidelines like a judgement. This was the first time I wasn't lying about having other plans.

Having plans was probably overstating it, since I had no idea what I was doing. I was nearly twenty-five and this was the first official date I had ever been on with a woman. An actual live member of the opposite sex. The plan as far as it went was to turn up wearing the best clothes I owned, having absolutely marinated myself in Old Spice, and hope for the best.

It was raining a light drizzle as I walked down Edgware Road to catch the tube to Westminster. The journey took about twenty-five minutes, so the fact that I had given myself an hour to cover for emergencies meant that I had to kill thirty minutes once I got there.

I checked the pub to make sure that Emery had not got there even earlier than me, then went and stood back outside. Five minutes later, it occurred to me that she might have been in the loo, so I went inside and checked again. Still, no Emery, so back out to the pub door. Thirty whole minutes to either stand in the rain, or do laps of the pub, to make sure I had not somehow missed her. Thirty whole minutes where I came close to convincing myself that the whole thing was an elaborate wind-up and she wasn't going to show.

But arrive she did, exactly on time. I saw her coming down the road, under an umbrella, wearing a pair of jeans and an off-shoulder baggy jumper under her green army parka. She looked beautiful and the sight of a black bra-strap revealed by her choice of top made me ache with a dull longing. She saw me standing outside and quickened her pace to reach me.

"Oh my God," she said. "have you been waiting long?"

"Just a couple of minutes," I lied.

"You should have gone inside," she said. "I would have found you."

"I didn't think you'd like going into a crowded pub on your own," I said. "So I waited for you. It wasn't bad. There was some shelter." I pointed at the pub entrance.

She looked about to say something, then changed her mind. "Shall we go in?" she said.

The pub interior was oak and red leather with high ceilings. It was reasonably busy. In two hours' time it would be jammed to the rafters but we managed to get a couple of drinks at the ornate curving bar and a table for two by the frosted front window.

Having got us to a table with a couple of drinks, I found myself completely at the edge of the map of my known world, and had to wait for Emery to start the conversation proper.

She leaned forward and inspected the cut on my head.

"That's healing nicely," she said. "You've been staying out of trouble?"

"Light duty for a week," I replied. "How did your poetry group go?"

"Oh, I didn't say," she perked up. "It went great. I repeated almost verbatim what you said and it was like I had opened floodgates. Everyone pretty much unloaded on Rimbaud and how much they hated him. We came this close to banning Marjorie from book selection privileges. She was none too impressed and flounced off in a bit of a huff. So thank you."

"You're welcome," I said.

She paused. "That's partly why I called to see if you fancied a drink."

"Because I know a bit about Rimbaud? What's next on the reading list?"

"No. Not like that."

"Like what?"

"You know. I mean, not like when I was ten and showed Billy Travis my knickers behind the climbing frame so he'd let me cog maths homework off him. More like…"

I could see pink rising in her cheeks. She stopped, realising she was babbling a bit. It dawned on me that she was as nervous about this date as I was. That went some way to calming my own nerves.

"Let me start again," she tried. "When did you read Rimbaud?"

"Technically, I haven't," I said. "I can't read or speak French. I read a translation by a man called Fowlie. It was a bit dry…" Now it was my turn to stop, embarrassed at how much of a pedantic arse I sounded, so I just answered the question I had been asked. "I don't know. Maybe two or three years ago."

"Okay," she said. "And after you read it, before last Monday, had you ever spoken to anyone else about Rimbaud? Ever?"

"No," I said, smiling at the idea that anyone I knew would give the slightest damn about the literary ramblings of a gay, French alcoholic.

"So why did you read it?" She watched me as she took a drink.

"I read everything." I said, shrugging. "A friend of mine told me a long time ago that life was a fight and that books were ammunition. I decided he was right."

She continued to peer at me. "I've met the boys in uniform who hang around the A&E trying to pick up nurses, sneaking them past the duty sergeant into the section house. None of them are quoting Rimbaud. And I found myself thinking about you and wondering who you talk to? If you have all these thoughts in your head that never see the light of day? Never get a voice. When I phoned you last Thursday it took you about five minutes to come to the phone. Were you in your room reading? By yourself? I bet you were."

I was somewhat awed at how well she had sussed me out after one meeting of less than half an hour.

"Yes," I said.

"Right, so anyway, after you left I could not get this thought out of my head. Of you going back to your little room in the section house, and reading your books. And it was starting to haunt me that you might be thinking all these things and have no one to talk to about them. And how lonely it might make you feel. And that's why I called you. To see if you wanted someone to talk to. About books. Or anything really."

I went to protest that she was wrong, that I was fine, but then realised that she wasn't wrong. I had never considered the possibility that I might be lonely before. It was just the way I was. The way I had always been. But Emery giving voice to the idea required an acknowledgment that, once made, was hard to deny. But instead of saying any of that, I just said "Yes."

We talked all night, starting with *The Unbearable Lightness of Being*, the book she was currently half-way through, one that I had finished about six months before. About how she liked some bits of it, and hated others, how Emery knew doctors who were just like Tomasz, about whether the characters were real, or just sketches to throw angst and philosophies on top of. I can barely remember what we talked about after that. I was so enraptured by the idea that someone so pretty, so alive, was sitting opposite me, I would become so distracted by her attentive face that a couple of times I just stumbled and stalled into silence, and she had to give me a prompt to get me to the end of my sentence. If that sounds like the worst first date ever, bear in mind that it was the first discussion with another person about anything that I felt had meaning since standing on a cliff trying to see France in the distance.

After the second round of drinks, she pointed out that the rain had stopped, the pub was getting busy and noisy, and did I want to go for a walk? So we did, moving down Birdcage Walk, past Buckingham Palace and up Constitution Hill towards Hyde Park.

Emery told me a little bit about her life. Her father was a mechanical engineer from County Cork, who had moved to Merthyr Tydfil for work, where he met Emery's mother and they presumably decided to get married and have a child with a really strange accent.

She told me her parents were both dyed-in-the-wool lefties who had given her stern warnings about policemen being nothing but brownshirts of the state, about how she became a nurse, her ambitions in life, and how she wanted to end her days in a red brick country farmhouse making scones surrounded by animals that she would rescue from the local pounds. "The really rubbish ones that no one else will take," she said.

We kept walking and talking, and somewhere between the Achilles Statue and the Serpentine she reached out and took my hand as though it were the most natural thing in the world. This was the first contact of affection I had experienced since my mother had kissed my forehead over a decade before, and it made me feel faint. Eventually she stopped and suggested we sit on a bench because she had something she wanted to say.

I sat there upright looking at her face in profile as she stared off into the park, trying to compose her thoughts.

Eventually she turned to look at me.

"Okay," she said. "Let me get through this before you say anything."

I had no idea what she was going to say, so I just nodded agreement. She reached out and took my hand in hers.

"I've been thinking about you since we met last Monday," she said. "I can say that because I know already that you're not the kind of guy who's going to go back and brag to all his mates about how some nurse is well into him. It's not that you're handsome, it's that you just make me feel like there's this amazing person walking around trapped inside someone who's bruised and angry and hurt. That you have a soul that wants to be gentle and appreciate beauty and love and kindness and poetry. But then you end the day trying to rinse bloodstains out of your shirt. And I don't know what happened to you, but I know you are carrying it around with you. And I don't mean that like a metaphor. I mean that you are carrying it around with you like physical weight. And I just wanted to say that you don't have to. That you can put it down. That it's okay to put it down. If you want to."

I sat silently through all of this, too full to speak. When she was done for one angry instant I wanted to tell her she was totally wrong, that she should just leave me alone and mind her own business but then I looked into her eyes. They were brown and earnest and I saw no judgement in them at all, just kindness, and a need to help if she could. And I realised that this was one of the big moments of my life. Maybe the moment of my life. That she might make it okay if I let her. That I too could be worthy of love. If I just reached out and asked for it. If I just took a chance on her, on a different life, chose a different path than the one I was on.

And there on that bench, just down from the Serpentine in Hyde Park on a cold night in February 1985, I did.

I told her everything. About growing up poor and hungry, about my mother abandoning James and me to our father's violence, about my anger towards my younger brother for being weak and unable to defend himself. About the discovery of her body in Manchester, about my pilgrimage to a grave I would never truly find, about my return home, about beating my father to within an inch of his life, about how that drove my brother away from me, and how we barely spoke now. In short, I told her how I had ended up angry and lost and alone.

When I finished she just sat there and looked at me for a long moment, processing everything I had said. I was sure she was going to just get up and walk away into the darkness, that I would never see her again. I knew this with absolute certainty. But instead she slowly reached out a hand and gently cupped my cheek.

Those brown eyes still held nothing but understanding and she told me it was okay.

I cried then. I don't mean a little trickle down my cheek. I mean I cried out two decades of hurt, full on floods of sobbing, my shoulder heaving, my breathing ragged, snot streaming from my nose and I buried my head on her bare shoulder as she held the back of my head and gently stroked my hair and whispered that it was all going to be all right.

We were rarely apart after that night. I spent every moment that I could with her, and every moment that I wasn't with her thinking about when I could next be with her. I could feel myself changing because of her. I became less angry, less pessimistic, and discovered the strange sensation of optimism for the future.

She had her own scars. Her best friend had died at the age of six in the Aberfan disaster. She had been sexually assaulted at the age of twelve by a local scout leader who was now serving a life sentence in prison. But she absolutely would not let these painful things define her, she remained firmly in charge of her own life, no matter what it threw at her. I used to call her Rocky, teasing her that the indomitable spirit she displayed reminded me of the film character. Refusing to lie down and die no matter what kind of a beating you were taking. Over the years that got shortened to Rock. She called me Jake, because as she explained, Daniel was my father's name and I was not my father. Except when she was super angry at me, when she would call me Marley. Thus Jake became the name I went by.

Emery was the best thing that ever happened to me and if I live another fifty years, I don't expect I would have a different answer at the end of it.

We went out for meals, for drinks, we held hands for walks in the park, we looked at house listings in estate agents' windows for properties we would never be able to afford, enjoying the dream. She discovered I had a sense of humour. "It's rubbish," said Emery, "but at least it's there." I discovered that she could speak both Welsh and Irish, would occasionally drop phrases from either into her conversation, and that she had truly terrible taste in music and films.

In short, we did everything that young lovers do. It was in Wembley Stadium in July 1985, just after Elvis Costello had just finished singing his old Northern English folk song, that she proposed to me.

Because as she said later, she really did believe that all you need is love.

I said yes.

Four months later we were married.

CHAPTER TWENTY-NINE

Brandt was on the front desk at Lermoos station, cheerfully organising his files and no doubt dreaming of lunch. He looked genuinely happy to see me and toddled off unbidden to find Neumann. Through the glass partition I could see him tap his gaffer on the shoulder and nod in my direction. Neumann strode out at a storming pace. "Where have you been?" he asked. "I must have left you five messages since yesterday."

I checked my phone.

"Six, I think. I've been on my holidays. Ehrwald. You ever been? It's lovely this time of year."

He made an exasperated translingual noise that simultaneously expressed frustration and conceded that I was not on his payroll, and had no actual responsibilities in his investigation whatsoever. He held open the door to his rubbish interrogation room with the fantastic view of the mountains. I sat down in the nearest chair. He left briefly and when he came back, he had two cups of coffee and under his arm was the same manila folder as he'd had in the bar, which I noted was considerably thicker than the last time. He sat down in the opposite chair.

I went first.

"I spoke to a friend of mine back in England. He's a journalist and did some digging for me as a favour. I assume you have some more information since yesterday, so do you want to tell me what you have and I'll add in any detail if I can?"

He nodded and flipped open the file.

"These incidents are now being treated as a crime. Theft and at least one suspicious death. Possibly two."

I nodded and added what I knew as best I could without really understanding what it is that Wall did. "And what about Harvey's laptop?" asked Neumann. "I don't see where it fits in."

"Like I said, Harvey was only here because Wall was here. He knew of Wall's reputation as a lucrative coder and wanted to try and ride his shirt tails a bit. Talk himself into a job. I don't know if Wall took him up on the offer, or farmed out a bit of development work to him as an interview test, but it's possible that there was some information on his laptop as well. Or at least enough of a connection that someone thought it was worth stealing too."

"So we have two laptops with potentially valuable information on them," said Werner. "Both belong to men who are now dead. Both now missing. So a crime of theft. Now we move onto the possible crime of murder." He held up a sheet of paper from his folder. "These are the preliminary findings of Mr Wall's autopsy. She is preparing a more detailed response but initial findings are that his neck was broken at two specific places in the C2 vertebrae and once on the C3 vertebrae. Her impression is that it was an attempt at a clinical hanging. An attempt to replicate the" – he made bunny ears with his fingers – "'humane' type of long-drop hanging used in capital punishment. In a formal execution the neck is broken at the C2 in two places. This appears to be what was attempted here, although due to circumstances – the rough terrain, the angle of the fall – the end result was clumsier, albeit still fatal."

He paused, flipping through his file. "There was something else too. I asked her to run a full blood toxicology screening."

He slid another piece of paper across the table to me.

I nodded at it.

"Does it say that he was high as a kite on acid at the time?"

Werner's brows twitched inward and an almost imperceptible line formed above his nose. Was it surprise or irritation?

"Not in those words, but yes. The body contained high quantities of LysergSäureDiethylamid. She has forwarded the results to a reference laboratory for further analysis as this is not something that they specialise in, but her impression is that it would have been enough to seriously impair Mr Wall's judgement. How did you know that?" It was irritation.

"Wall had a history of recreational drug use, particularly LSD. He liked periodically going out into nature and getting high. Thought it helped get his mind in the right space to allow him to do his work."

"Really?" Now Neumann sounded surprised.

"Apparently so. It's not clear how well known it was among the general population, but certainly his employers knew about it. I think they turned a blind eye as long as he kept producing the goods. But presumably if they knew, then some of his competitors did too."

"So he took the acid himself?"

"Yes, but that doesn't necessarily mean that he put a noose around his own neck."

Werner thought about this.

"As a method of murder, this is too prone to chance. I mean, someone puts a rope around his neck, then pushes him off the ledge, when he is incapable of resistance or protest. But an eye-witness will swear under oath that he was on his own. I spoke to him. He heard the noise of Wall falling and saw him swinging." His face cleared, a picture of concentration, his eyes narrowed slightly and I saw them move from side to side as if reviewing an image of the location in his mind. "If anyone else had been there, they would have been seen. You can see the path and ledge clearly from that jetty. The alternative is that they put the rope around his neck then left him. He either accidentally falls or he sits there quietly with a rope around his neck staring at the sun and the sky until he regains his senses. No guarantee that he will be dead at the end of it."

I thought about it, then nodded. "I think you're probably right. Which makes me think that it wasn't a crime. He did it to himself. Which means that the theft was opportunistic. Which brings us to Mr Harvey. Let me ask you a question. How did you initially identify Wall?"

"He had a UK driver's licence. Tourists stay either in personal rented accommodation or one of the hotels in the area. I phoned the hotels first."

"And when you phoned the Vorsehungberg, Melanie answered the phone?"

"It might not necessarily have been Melanie," he bristled.

"But it was?"

"Yes," he conceded.

"I'm not having a dig mate, I'm just saying that you're friends with her, so you might have been a little informal. There is a point. Think back to that conversation. Melanie confirmed that Wall was a guest. Did you tell her why you were asking?"

I talked him through the scenario I had suggested to Caulfield the night before. Werner thought hard. "Yes," he said at last. "She asked what we were going to do with Mr Wall's body. Any German speaker overhearing would have been able to deduce that he was dead."

He pulled his mobile out of his pocket. "Easy theory to test."

"If you're phoning the hotel, I think Melanie is off today."

"It's her personal mobile," he answered smoothly.

I smiled and said nothing.

"Don't be a child," he snapped, just as Melanie answered.

Possibly because I was there, the conversation was brief and presumably to the point. Three or four back-and-forths, less than two minutes and he hung up. He avoided my eye as he put the phone away.

"Melanie confirmed that Mr Harvey was working on his laptop in the reception area when I phoned. She left the reception area to inform the Morton's employees and when she returned about five minutes later, Mr Harvey was gone."

"Is she sure about that?" I asked.

Neumann nodded. "She's always had a good memory. I'm confident in her version of events."

"So far so good. How long did it take you to get to the hotel from the lake?"

Werner rummaged through his file. "Left the lake at 4.25. Arrived at the hotel just before 5pm. 35 minutes."

"OK, so that gave Greg plenty of time to get upstairs, gain access to Wall's room and make off with his laptop. Safely back in his own room with his spoils before you arrive."

Neumann shut his eyes for a moment, replaying events in his mind.

"I arrive, I check Wall's room with Melanie, but it is only a cursory inspection. Mostly to see if there is a suicide note or obviously anything unusual. I made no plans to take possession of the room's contents until we had a formal identification. We did that the following day after Mr Caulfield confirmed that the body was recognised by him to be Chris Wall. After leaving the room, we lock the door, return to the lobby to advise the Morton's employees that one of their guests has died. Mr Nicholls overhears us, and asks what has happened. I inform him that regrettably it appears that Mr Wall has taken his own life. I briefly speak to Mr Nicholls about Mr Wall's state of mind. He admits that he had a confrontation with Mr Wall the previous day about offering his daughter drugs in which Mr Caulfield intervened. Then shortly afterwards the large group, of which you were a part, returned." He passed me the narrative.

"OK," I said. "So at this point we think there might be one potential crime. Harvey has stolen Wall's laptop."

"Yes, and Melanie also advised that he later booked a taxi for the next morning. It was to the station, so she assumed he was catching the early morning train to Innsbruck."

"But he doesn't make it," I said. "He slips and falls in his bathroom. Breaking his neck on the side of the bath. Did your coroner offer any thoughts on that?"

"She has not performed a full examination, but she did say that to break a neck would require a significant amount of downward force.

Although, given that Mr Harvey was an overweight man, it was not at all beyond the realms of plausibility."

He took a sip of his coffee before continuing. "There are two possibilities that I can think of. One is that Harvey had hidden the laptops in his room or somewhere else, for safekeeping. I was only gathering up his items, not looking for secret compartments. Or two is that someone else stole the laptops from him and killed him in the process. I think the latter because of the book found in your room." I was nodding.

"I think they tried and failed, but talk me through your timeline," I said, pleased to hear that he was independently working his way to a theory that roughly tallied with mine.

"Someone breaks into Harvey's room at around 8.50pm. Breaks his neck. Makes it look like an accident. Both the coroners report and the phone support this time of death. They chain lock the door from the inside. They take the two computers, shove them in his laptop bag. They climb from Harvey's balcony to yours – there is only a partition separating them. Gain access to your room through the balcony door. At this point they leave the book on your bed." He broke from his monologue briefly to interject. "– This I don't understand. Maybe misdirection on their part. To make you a suspect? – Leave your room and pull the door behind them. You did not return until the next morning, having spent the night with Ms Guerin. How much time would that take?"

I thought about it. Sneak in quietly, kill someone, arrange the body, gather laptops, lock door, final check that you're not leaving any evidence, exit by the balcony door, climb over to my room, pick my balcony window lock, leave my room.

"I'd say twenty minutes. Maybe fifteen if you were a ninja. At this point the entire group was downstairs drinking together."

"And everyone was there the whole time?" Neumann asked, leaning forward in his chair.

I looked at his crime folder then at his face. "Do you think someone in our group was involved?"

"It's just a question," he replied evenly.

"Occasional runs to the bar, to the toilet, to the smoking balcony. I'd say no one was gone for more than five minutes. Certainly not enough time to commit a murder."

"What about the Nicholls girl?" I was surprised, but it was true that she had not been there.

"Apart from the ten minutes when I went for a cigarette, no, I didn't see her."

I looked at Neumann with what I imagine was the same look of incredulity Caulfield had been periodically giving me over the last few days. "You suspect the kid?"

Neumann shrugged. "She was involved in an incident of assault and battery, which caused her to be suspended from her college for a year."

"Assault and battery?" It sounded wrong, but I remembered her fierce, confident disdain, and suddenly her animated face was lighting up the sombre dinner table after Greg's body had been discovered.

"Yes. At a debate about global warming that took place in her college, she and two other students threw a bucket of red paint over a Mr Nicholas Robinson. I understand he is a UK journalist and media personality? He generally advocates that climate change is a natural phenomenon."

"I caught that in the papers a while back. That was Christine Nicholls?" Under my breath, I added, "Good for her."

"You approve?" asked Neumann, looking surprised.

"He's a hack who lies for money, so that's probably the least he has coming to him. But there's a big difference between throwing some paint at someone and committing a murder. Plus Harvey weighed three times what she did, I doubt she'd have the strength to put him down."

"I agree, but she is the only one with a criminal record and without a solid alibi."

He paused again.

"What about the Smiths?" he asked.

"Seriously?" I said.

"You previously said they went to bed around 9pm, but that this timing was approximate."

I looked at him. "What aren't you telling me?"

He paused, looking uncomfortable.

"They're not married, and their names aren't Smith. I already guessed that much," I prompted.

He relented. "Their names are Smith, but you are correct, they are not married. Jane Smith is married to George Smith's brother, Henry. Henry Smith has been in a... wachkoma, sorry –" he checked his notes "– persistent vegetative state for the last three years, following a failed suicide attempt. They claim they were not in a relationship before this. They have been together since George was diagnosed with cancer."

Now that I finally had that answer, I rather wished I didn't.

"Which means what, in terms of the matter at hand?"
I asked instead.

Werner shrugged. "Henry Smith attempted suicide after suffering severe financial losses in a possibly manipulated stock speculation. I am chasing a trail of paperwork which is incredibly complex, a Russian doll of companies within companies, but it appears that there may be a connection between that speculation and the hedge fund that Mr Wall worked for. It is a possibility until it is not, although I agree it is unlikely."

Everyone always underestimates George, I thought to myself. Instead, I said, "I think it might have been an outside party."

"No one accessed the hotel after the doors were locked and no suspicious parties were reported by either guests or staff before then," he said, matter-of-factly.

"It's a hotel, not Fort Knox. I'm sure there must be a way to get in undetected. "

"You have further information that makes you believe in an outside party?" He was challenging me, but I could tell he didn't expect anything.

I nodded. "The day I walked out to the lake. I was standing on the ledge where Wall died. There was a tall man standing on the far shore. Not walking. He might have been admiring the view, but I got the distinct impression he was looking at me. We didn't interact but Caulfield mentioned in passing he'd seen a man with grey hair and a scar on his cheek a couple of times over the last few days."

Neumann straightened up looking excited at the prospect of an honest to god suspect. "It was the same man?"

"I was standing half a kilometre away across the lake in the rain, so I can't say for sure but maybe. But I definitely saw him last night. A tall man with grey hair and a scar along his cheek, along with an associate, tried to rob Ms Guerin and I at gunpoint as we were walking back across the Moos from Das Walters. I'd seen the associate earlier that day tracking our walking group."

Werner was definitely irritated now. "What? What happened?"

"One came up from in front, one from behind. The tall man in front pulled a gun and tried to steal our wallets, phones and bags."

"Why are you only telling me this now? You should have reported it last night," he said angrily.

"I was busy last night. I'm reporting it now." I remained steady but he had every right to be annoyed.

"Is Ms Guerin okay?" He relented.

"She's fine. They tried to rob us, but we fought them off and ran. But the point is they weren't just mugging random tourists. They seem too interested in our group. I think they were targeting Wall. His suicide was an opportunity to steal work they were planning to steal anyway. Harvey beats them to it, like you suggested. They kill him. They take the laptop bags, and drop the book, again like you said. But I don't think they have the laptops. Or they have the laptops, but not the hard drives or something." I hazarded. "Otherwise they'd be gone by now. When I got back to my room this morning, it felt like it had been searched. Like someone had been looking for something. They think that I have the laptops or know where they are hidden. Which is why they targeted me."

Werner rubbed his face with his hands wearily. "Do you have any idea who they were?"

"The tall skinny guy, no idea. I got the impression he was the brains, he literally did all the talking. Native English speaker. The other guy was big. Crew cut. Tattooed. Muscled – looked like a steroid juicer. Local heavy I would say. He definitely spoke German when I accosted him yesterday afternoon."

"You'd seen him before?" He interjected, before throwing up his hands and allowing me to finish.

"He did have identification on him. Does the name Herman Der Cherusker mean anything to you?"

"Yes," said Werner. "Why?"

I handed him the dog tags. He looked at them and gave a short laugh.

"You said he had tattoos. The number eighteen? Noricum? Blud Und Boden?"

"The middle one," I said. "Have I just said something stupid?"

"Herman Der Cherusker is the Germanic name of Arminius, who led the German Alliance in the Battle of Teutoburg and drove the Romans from Germany." He threw the tags onto the desk with disgust. "He's an icon of the far right and neo-Nazi movements. Noricum was the part of Austria occupied by Celtic tribes before the Romans. It is also a totem of the Neo-Nazi movement. Whoever this Herman is, I would agree with you that he is local muscle and certainly not an industrial spy." He turned away from me to the scenery beyond, no doubt testing my theory as to how much stress one view can salve.

I reached over for the file and had a random flick through it. Not really looking for anything but just to see if something caught my eye. Photos of the body. Photos of the scene. Photos of Wall's possessions. Clothes. Hotel key. Wallet. Smartphone. iPod. Swiss Army Knife. Watch. Notepad. Pen. Absolutely nothing out of the ordinary. Pages of typed notes in German. Werner really was very methodical.

"What's your next move?" I asked.

"I am awaiting the results from Mr Harvey's autopsy. I am also following up on the details of Mr Wall's business affairs. If you can give me a full description of the two men who tried to rob you, I will advise my colleagues to be on the lookout for them. Although I suspect they are lying low or gone. What about you?" He sounded weary.

I checked my watch. "I'm going to play the tethered goat. Stand in plain sight and see if they come to me. But as it's lunchtime, I might simultaneously get something to eat."

CHAPTER THIRTY

Emery and I were married in November 1985. The ceremony took place in Saint Mary's Catholic Church in Chelsea. Emery referred to herself as an 'above-the-waist Catholic.' Having moved to London two years ago, St. Mary's was the church she attended once in a while so that she could truthfully tell her parents that she was going to mass, then hastily change the subject if there were any follow up questions about the regularity with which this event occurred. Lying to your parents, she informed me with mock solemnity, made baby Jesus cry. I worked hard with said parents but I could tell they didn't really approve of the union of their only child to one of Thatcher's stormtroopers.

Sin mar a bhfuil se, as Emery said philosophically. That's just how it is.

James was there but politely declined to be my best man. On our second date Emery had said she wanted to meet him, and despite my stalling she kept pushing. She knew our relationship was distant and she knew the reasons why, but at the same time he was the only real family I had left in the world. Even without my delaying tactics, getting the schedules of a police officer, a nurse and a chef de partie to align was its own logistical challenge, but eventually my future wife met my brother at a nice Michelin Star restaurant that James wangled because the sommelier was a friend who owed him a favour. I warned Emery not to expect too much from it. By this point all James and I had in common was DNA and a shared childhood that neither of us were in a particular hurry to remember or relive. It wasn't as bad as I expected, but probably not all that Emery hoped for either. James and Emery got on well, he was friendly to me, but I knew that while we might close some of the distance that now existed between us, we would never remove it completely.

At the end of the evening, as we stood out on the street about to go our separate ways and waiting for Emery to come back from the loo, James had said to me, "I think she's good for you. I hope it works out."

Other than James and the disapproving in-laws, there were about forty people at our nuptials. My side of the aisle accounted for five. The Abelmans and Mrs Wedderburn came, along with two friends from the force that I wanted to be there. Our first dance was to *All You Need Is Love* – Elvis Costello's old Northern English folk song.

We spent a week in Cornwall for our honeymoon then came home to the three-bedroomed house that we had just bought in Islington. The house was structurally sound, but inside was a wreck – the only reason we could afford it. We set about getting it exactly the way we wanted, a process which would take years, and require me to learn all sorts of DIY skills, but we had time. I would stand there with nails in my mouth, hammer in my hand, and feel what it was like to build something, to make the world a little better than I had found it.

The first thing Emery did once she was free of a landlord was to run out to the animal shelter to pick out the most unwanted animal they had – the one that had no chance of ever being adopted. She came back with a three-legged, one-eyed street cat. Unnamed, unwanted and unloved. She called it Claus Van Stauffenberg or Stauffy for short. The first of a litany of wounded and broken animals that she welcomed into our home. Or possibly the second, depending on your point of view.

Emery encouraged me to take detective exams, partly, I think, because she thought I'd be good at the job, partly for the salary increase, but mostly I think because she liked the idea of me out of uniform. The exams were a slog, but I got through them, and slowly I started advancing a career which for its first six years had been stalled at the bottom rung. It took me twelve years, but I eventually made it to the rank of DCI, in charge of a team working serious crime. Caught a few good wins in there, and the ones that I lost, well, I just went home to Emery and the cat.

James moved to New York in 1994, landing a job at some posh midtown Manhattan eatery. Although he was not really a part of our lives, I was sorry that the distance between us was now geographical as well as emotional. We kept threatening to visit but somehow it never happened.

We developed rituals – Friday night takeaway. Rubbish rom-coms from Blockbuster. Long walks in one of the London parks on the weekend. Sharing a bottle of wine over a game of backgammon. If she was working a late shift, I would sometimes go to the hospital and sit in the waiting room with a book for hours, just for the chance of ten minutes she could spare to have a cup of tea.

Because we had no children, we threw any spare money into getting shot of the mortgage. The rate spiked out at about 15% about five years into our home ownership. We'd fight about money, something we'd never done before, and little things would cause us to snap at each other. But looking back, that was just window dressing. Our foundation was rock solid. We hung on, sometimes by our fingertips, cutting back, working overtime and occasional second jobs, and eventually we got free of it in November 2000.

Stauffy died in 1996 of old age. We both cried real tears as we buried him in the back garden. Three months later we got another cat, which Emery named Hodge Podge. She took up pottery. She was splendidly bad at it, but she enjoyed it, and I enjoyed her enjoyment. Her best effort was to produce a set of six irregular coffee mugs, one of which had the dimensions of a test tube and three of which featured impressive pairs of breasts. It would have been praiseworthy had she actually been attempting that design. Over the years they got broken and lost, and now only one boob mug remains, which I still have and guard like treasure.

She took up scuba diving in the local swimming pool.

She took up photography.

She took Spanish language lessons.

She filled her life to the brim, and dragged me along with her.

We worked, we earned money, we paid bills, we ate, we slept, we enjoyed each other's company. That was the life we built together, and it was more than I could have ever believed was possible for me. I would lie there in the dark with my arm across her, warm and sleeping, and there were times I could not hug her close enough.

Emery's mother died suddenly from breast cancer in 2004. Both she and her father were heartbroken and he followed her into the ground soon after. His death certificate said that he died of heart failure, but honestly, I think he just gave up on life. I knew her well enough not to smother her with platitudes, knew that she would deal with it in her own way and her own time. She did, but she was never quite the same after that. Some things, you can't put down, you just have to carry. As she said herself, there's no age limit on being an orphan. We had never been close, but I had liked her parents – after all they had in my opinion, between them, produced the best thing there ever was.

We celebrated our 20th anniversary by going to Malaysia. Emery scuba dived and took photos of fish. For all I know she spoke Spanish to them too. I hid from the sun under a large umbrella and worked my way through Stephenson's Baroque Cycle.

One night after dinner we walked down to the beach to discover bioluminescent plankton washing up in waves on the shore. We swam in that sea naked as newborns, and I remember watching her beautiful face, framed by her wet and tousled red hair, lit by the blue glow of the water under the strange stars of the southern hemisphere, feeling such an overwhelming sense of awe and love. The vastness of the universe, and yet most everything I cared about in an infinity of space and time was contained within the tiny body of the woman swimming next to me.

By then we were coming up on fifty and vaguely wondering where the last two and a half decades had gone. We started thinking about the future.

I had done my thirty years in the Met, finishing my career with a satisfactory result on a double homicide. Although we had not really planned on it, we ended up moving to the country. Emery had been offered a job running the medical unit at a retirement village in Berkshire. We discussed it over dinner, and decided that maybe it was time for a new chapter in our lives. We sold our house in Islington, for an amount of money that I still have trouble comprehending, and bought a cosy three-bedroomed house in a small village on the border of Berkshire and Wiltshire. We met the old boy next door, who took an instant liking to Emery and would flirt shamelessly with her every chance that he got, whether I was there or not.

Although I had lived my entire life as a London boy, I liked Wiltshire: It felt older than other places I knew. We were only a few miles from the Savernake Forest, where Henry VIII had hunted deer with the Seymour family. There were oak trees there that were over a thousand years old, that had been there before William the Conqueror's boot had even touched the sand of Pevensey Bay. Ancient trees talking of pagan things, as Chesterton would have said.

I got a job as a PIP1 investigator with Wiltshire Police to top up my pension and keep me busy until Emery retired, which she had decided would be at fifty-five.

I gave fishing a go. Hated it. Tried mountain biking. Not much better. Eventually I went back to running. One Saturday afternoon, we went down to the Dogs Trust. I wasn't sure about getting a dog, but Emery suggested we just go and talk to them. We came back home with Fred, big of heart, small of brain. It's not like I didn't see that one coming.

Emery joined the village Bridge club. I declined to join on the basis that Bridge was just Whist with notions about itself. Instead I wandered up to the pub on the night Emery was playing and got press-ganged into a pub quiz team. Over time we became good friends with the team members and their spouses.

Somehow, we ended up having regular dinner parties. It started when Peter got a warning from his doctor that his cholesterol count was alarmingly high. He pointed out that this was exactly the problem that cholesterol pills had been invented to solve, but Helen decided that on balance she'd like him around for at least a bit longer, and immediately put him on a diet that consisted mostly of vegetables poached in misery. The only loophole Peter could find was to periodically invite friends around for dinner. Naturally they felt obliged to return the favour, so Peter got a regular fix of steak and red wine and we ended up in a loop of hosting or attending dinner parties about once every six weeks.

One Saturday night it was our turn. I was at work that day, but Emery texted me a list of required ingredients that she had forgotten to add to the shopping list. It occurred to me that it was a pretty long list. I got home to find her figuratively and indeed almost literally spinning plates. Something classical was playing loudly on the stereo.

Loud music was usually a sign that things were not going to plan – Emery turned the volume up to hide her swearing. I found her in the kitchen, tongue sticking out of the corner of her mouth, frowning in concentration as she attempted to make a three-course meal with about half the ingredients and a third of the required time.

It had started badly, then gone south from there. By the time Bruce and Sue arrived, she had accidentally added the gravy to the chocolate sauce, realised that she had forgotten to turn on the second oven to roast potatoes, and made a total arse of the beef wellington. I entertained the guests for about half an hour, all of us trying to ignore the sounds of chaos in the kitchen, before she appeared, her face dusted in flour, holding a large glass of white wine in one hand, and an Indian takeaway menu in the other.

We ordered far too much curry and got nicely drunk trying to eat it all. That was a good night. Everyone went home past one in the morning with a nice buzz on and we went to bed, ignoring the mess in the kitchen.

The next morning, as I was making breakfast and tidying up, Emery fell over in the shower.

CHAPTER THIRTY-ONE

Werner was only halfway through his shift, and didn't have time for lunch, but he took a twenty-minute break to grab a quick coffee. Given that we'd spent the last hour talking about Wall and Harvey, we ended up chatting about other things. I told him about Emery and married life, and he told me about growing up in Ehrwald with teenage dreams of escaping to a big city, but lasting only about five years before being desperate to return home to the mountains.

"I grew up in a city," I said. "I'd take your mountains any day of the week."

He nodded. "I don't regret it, but the realisation that you belong to a certain place, sometimes feels like an admission of failure. Especially when all the friends you grew up with appear to have gone on to bigger and better things."

"If that's how you feel, it must have been nice when Melanie showed up again," I said.

He glanced at my face, to establish I wasn't having a sly dig. I could see him making a decision about how much he was willing to share.

Eventually he said, "Melanie had a good career in Vienna. She only took the job here because her mother developed early onset dementia and it had progressed to a stage where her father could not deal with it by himself. It has become progressively worse over the last eighteen months."

"I'm sorry to hear that," I said. "That must be a hard road to walk."

"It's terrible," said Werner simply. "A long, slow, painful, end. She was such a formidable woman when we were children. Strong, fierce, funny. Now she is like a child, sometimes wandering the streets in confused agitation, until we find her."

"Does that happen a lot?"

He nodded with a grimace.

"More regularly now. Once every few weeks, instead of every few months. Often it takes some effort to calm her down, and allow us to take her home. Brandt is especially good at that."

"Have you talked to Melanie about it?"

He nodded without looking at me. "The last time we found her was in a rainstorm, late at night on the Biberwier road. She was wearing only a nightdress and was near hypothermia. After that, I told Melanie that she was at the point where a care facility was her only real option. She was angry with me and we fought about it."

I shook my head. "She's not angry with you, she's angry at the situation. She's a smart woman, she knows you're right, and that you've got her mother's best interests at heart. You did her a favour. Saying it out loud, just gives her permission to consider that option. Deep down she knows that. Sometimes being there for someone is telling them what they don't want to hear."

He nodded slowly. "You may be right."

I paused. "Have you talked to anyone about this?"

He glanced at me again. "No. And maybe I am only telling you because I know you will be gone in a few days."

"Doesn't matter," I said. "It's good to talk."

He nodded. "It is, but at the same time I would be grateful if you could keep this between us."

"That goes without saying, mate," I replied.

We finished our coffees, and this time as we shook and parted, I reflected that our conversation over coffee had not once touched on Chris Wall, Greg Harvey or the case at hand, and that Neumann, standing a somewhat lonely guard over his little corner of the world, bore a closer resemblance to me at that age than I had first realised.

When Neumann went back to work, I looked up the number of Cambridgeshire Police and gave them a ring. I got passed around their IVR phone system for a bit but eventually managed to get a hold of a live body with some authority. I explained that I was hoping to speak to the lead officer regarding a suicide they had investigated ten years ago – the only time that Chris Wall had apparently had a brush with the law. The voice on the other end of the phone was very disinclined to help me, so I gave my name and muster out rank, which had the desired effect of getting them to take the request seriously. The disembodied voice took my number, the scant details I had, and said they would find the relevant officer and ask them to give me a call.

With nothing better to do, I walked back to Ehrwald, the long way around via Biberwier, a complete circuit of the Moos, keeping an eye out for Hermann or Lee. Which I assumed was the same thing Caulfield and Neumann were both doing. All told, the route took about four hours at my dawdling pace. I didn't see either of them, which wasn't entirely surprising. After the failure of their attempted heist last night, I guessed they'd chosen a tactical retreat to lick their wounds and plot their next move. Of course, there was always the possibility that they'd given up and gone home, but I thought it was unlikely. If they had already murdered at least one person to get their hands on Wall's code, a couple of smacked heads was unlikely to persuade them to call it quits.

As I came to the T-junction in Biberwier, I saw the Morton's minibus turning right on Ehrwalder strasse, heading back to the hotel having completed one of today's excursions, which I remembered had been a trip to the Alpine coaster near Innsbruck. Harry was driving, with Penny in the passenger seat. Behind them were the Smiths and the Nicholls. I followed the same route as the bus had taken. An hour later, as I was coming up to the T-junction where I had first met Neumann, five days before, I saw Margaret and Bryce crossing the square, heading back to the hotel from the direction of Obermoos, the bottom end of the cable car station to the Zugspitze summit. Abby was not with them. I assumed she had taken my advice to go for a solitary walk and figure out where her head was at. I checked my watch, and saw that it had just gone 5pm.

In an hour's time, the Morton's kids would be having their nightly reception, planning the last round of excursions for tomorrow, our last full day in Ehrwald. The last day before we all went our separate ways. On an impulse, I turned away from the hotel and sat on a bench to look at the church opposite, a welcoming building with an onion-dome roof and plastered walls that appeared almost pink in the early evening light. There was a large mural on the outside wall. Almost childlike in its execution, but vibrant and strangely compelling. The crowned Messiah in the centre surrounded by adoring angels.

Christ Wallmighty, I thought to myself. And all those who surrounded him. Logically, I agreed with Werner that it was likely that Wall had taken his own life, but at the same time, I marvelled at how he sat at the centre of the web of people I had met here.

Greg Harvey, whose encounter with Wall might have cost him his life.

Richard Caulfield, whose professional reputation was now severely damaged, because of Wall.

Paul Nicholls, who had threatened to kill him for creepy overtures towards his beloved daughter.

His wife Laura, who despite not being as demonstrative as her husband, seemed equally committed to the protection of her child.

The child herself, Christine, who viewed Wall's death, in cold and pragmatic terms, as a net positive for the world, due to his contribution to rapacious capitalism.

A view shared by Bryce Boseman, albeit for his work developing a technology she considered an existential threat to humanity.

And by her partner Margaret Lawson, for his subscription to and support of political positions she had opposed for her whole adult life.

Bence the barman, who took exception to Wall treating his partner like a prostitute.

George and Jane Smith, with a husband and brother now dwelling in a shadow world halfway between life and death, possibly as a result of financial machinations that Wall had been party to.

And finally, Daniel Jacob Marley, using his death to search for something undefined that might give him a purpose, bring him back to the world. Which, so far, was going swimmingly. As I sat there, I thought of all those people.

Two old souls trying to find some measure of happiness in what time they had left.

Loving parents prepared to defend to the death a child they could not fully understand.

A couple whose relationship had cost at least one of them dearly.

A woman who carried around a huge burden of loss.

Then I thought of myself, scratching around the edges of their lives, finding their secrets and their pain for my own selfish reasons, and it made me feel an emotion somewhere close to shame. I decided I didn't want to face them for dinner, that I just would not be able to put on a face. I stayed on the bench until it got dark, then snuck up to my room. I glanced into the dining hall as I crossed the lobby, as I had done just two nights before. Everyone bar Abby was there. Possibly because she had expected that I would be. I went to my room and lay on my bed, fully clothed, staring at the roof, turning over all the questions I had, all the information I had thus far accumulated. I came up with nothing.

If I'm being honest, I was also waiting for a call or text from Abby. But none came. I guessed that, along with her avoidance of dinner, was an answer to one of the questions that were bouncing around my head.

CHAPTER THIRTY-TWO

There were a few days when Emery's slip in the shower was a source of some amusement in our house. A moment of goofball slapstick, with no side effects apart from a momentary loss of dignity and a bruise on her backside that was a remarkably accurate outline representation of the island of Sicily.

Then, after a week, she confessed that she was experiencing tremors in her right arm and she was having trouble gripping things in that hand. She went to the local surgery to get it checked out and came back with the worrying diagnosis that she might be suffering the after-effects of a mini-stroke.

She was booked in for an MRI scan at Great Western Hospital in Swindon to make sure, and I drove her over there. The four days between booking that MRI and actually getting the test results were nerve-wracking, but there would come a time when we would look back on them as the good old days – when a stroke was all we had to worry about.

We were called back in three days later, where a nice Asian doctor informed us that Emery had been diagnosed with a brain tumour. Our reaction was about what you would expect. If anything, Emery took it better than I did. I managed the first three stages, Denial,

Anger and Bargaining, in that first twenty-minute meeting. In the end Emery had to comfort me while at the same time asking pertinent questions.

Overall Dr Patel was quite upbeat and optimistic. She said that it was an astrocytoma and that as brain tumours went, that was one of the best kinds to have. Or to quote her accurately 'one of the least bad ones' to have. She said that Emery had probably had it for most of her adult life, they were more common in women than men and usually they were slow-growing.

Apparently the weakness on one side of Emery's body meant it had bumped up against something important in her grey matter. She spoke of ten-year survival rates being around the 75 per cent mark. Emery asked if it would require brain surgery and Dr Patel confirmed that total removal of the tumour was the best chance of ensuring the cancer would not return.

In the car on the way home I was numb, but Emery was practical and focussed on the positive. High survival rates, cut the whole thing out, draw a line under it.

"They talk about survival in terms of ten years," I said. "That's only sixty."

"Jesus, Marley," she snapped. "You could trip and break your neck jogging this afternoon. Tomorrow is promised to no one."

I shut up then, knowing she was right. I was gripped by the paralysing realisation that life could give you more than you ever dreamed possible, but it could take it away too.

Emery's surgery took place in the National Neurology Hospital in Queens Square. She was conscious throughout. This sounded barbaric to me, but as the surgeon explained, there were no pain receptors in the brain and they needed her awake, reciting the alphabet, the days of the week, counting backwards from ten and other simple mental tasks, so they didn't accidentally hack out anything important when they were trying to remove the tumour.

The whole procedure took about six hours and I waited in a small room, alternating between pacing a furrow in the carpet and climbing the walls.

Eventually the surgeon came out and told me it had gone well. By now I was finely attuned to medical bullshit and I knew that 'gone well' was not the same thing as an outstanding success.

They let me in to see her. She looked exhausted and they had shaved off her red hair.

I told her that in all the years we had been married, I had never realised what a nice-shaped skull she had and she cried.

She was released home a week later. A week after that, we were called back to Swindon.

Dr Patel was still all smiles, but I could tell that my pessimism was no longer as unfounded as it had been. I was no longer John the Baptist howling in the wilderness. She informed us that while the surgery had, on the whole, been successful, they had not managed to remove the entire tumour, as some of it was lodged a little too closely to the stuff that made Emery Emery. Experimental prodding at the last straggly stray ends had caused her to lapse into dysarthria. Slurred speech to you and me. Consequently, they had removed as much as they could without permanent brain damage, and they were hoping to zap the rest with radiotherapy.

So began that phase of her treatment. Six days a week every two weeks. Visiting time was kept to a minimum during the treatments. Eventually, after a fortnight, they let her go home.

They had to wheel her to the car. I gently put her in the passenger seat. I went around to the driver's side. She was fumbling to get her seatbelt fastened. I leaned over, took it from her and gently clicked it shut.

"I hope you kept your receipt from twenty-five years ago," she said, smiling weakly. "I think I might ask for my money back."

"Burnt it years ago," I said, and gave her a peck on the cheek.

On the drive home, I glanced over at her. She was leaning against the window on her side.

Her eyes were closed, possibly sleeping, more likely trying to control the queasiness she suffered from the sessions. Sunlight through the passing trees dappling her forehead.

I found myself thinking of the night that I had first met her all those years ago. Strangely, it was not meeting her in the hospital that my brain kept zeroing in on, but earlier that night, watching the gate in the Stamford Bridge stadium bulge against the force of the weight being applied to it by the mob.

I kept dragging my mind back to Emery walking across the floor of the A&E in her green parka and her CND badge and her oversized bag. But no matter how much I tried to move away from it, my brain kept circling back around to that gate in the fence.

It was around about Chieveley, when we were joining the M4, that I finally figured it out.

That moment.

The gate bulging against the swell of the crowd.

The loss of structural integrity, the lack of containment.

It was then that I had my damascene epiphany.

Which was this: The treatment was not going to work and my wife was going to die.

For a month I grimly ignored this thought. Emery was bald, had lost a lot of weight – her appetite was shot to buggery – but she was still herself. We went for a drive to Lacock and sat in the house gardens eating ice creams we'd bought from the Mr Whippy van. I'd suggested we eat it on the bench next to the van, but Emery insisted that we go into the grounds in case she threw up and scared away his potential customers. That night we went home and even though it was only February, we watched *The Sound of Music*. I still mocked it, because I knew she expected me to, and had I not, she might have realised the thought that would not leave my head. That this was the last time.

Eventually, after two long weeks, Dr Patel called us back in again. As soon as I saw her face I knew the news was not good. But it was Emery's news to deal with, not mine, so I waited. Sure enough, Dr Patel confirmed that the treatment was not going as well as we had hoped, that the tumour was proving more aggressive than had been expected, and there was now a definite subtext that we shouldn't be buying any green bananas. She suggested continuing the treatment, but for the first time mentioned palliative care.

Emery processed all of this in silence, then thanked her and said she would be in touch. I wanted to hit someone, but I kept a lid on it.

We drove home in silence. Emery said Fred needed a walk. She said she wanted some time to herself. I acceded to this request and took Fred out for an hour. I wasn't sure this was long enough for Emery to be alone so I stopped into the Keys for a pint.

It was 7pm on a Monday night, so I was literally the only customer. They had a new lager on draught. There was a time in my life when this would have been the big news item of the week. Where had those days gone?

I asked for a pint. Bruce set it in front of me and asked me how things were going. I had sympathy for the line he was trying to walk. We had not told anyone about Emery's illness, but at the same time, it was a small village and word would be out. If nothing else, Emery had lost about twenty pounds and had gone from looking like Botticelli's Venus to Sinead O'Connor.

He knew she was ill, I knew he knew she was ill, but at the same time, since he didn't officially know, he couldn't officially offer any help or words of sympathy. At least not until I told him myself.

Which I didn't. I told him everything was fine and said the new beer was not at all bad.

When I got home, Emery was sitting at the kitchen table listening to some country music. Acoustic guitar and a nice female vocal.

"That's not the worst thing you've ever played," I said, kissing her on the forehead.

"I've not heard it in years," she replied, "but I was thinking about it today so I dug it out."

"You want a cuppa?" I asked, sticking on the kettle.

"You should sit down," she said. "We need to talk."

I sat down opposite her as I had done many times before.

"What's up, Rock?" I said, forcing nonchalance.

"I'm going to stop the treatment," she said.

And there it was. Dashed hope will kill you quicker than anything.

We fought. I told her she was giving up on life, that she was being selfish and that it could be okay and she said that she wasn't, and she wasn't, and yes it could. But I would have to promise her that. I reached out my hands across the table and took hers.

I begged. I literally begged her, but she just squeezed my hands and smiled.

"When I'm gone –" she began.

"I can't hear that..." I said, pathetically.

"Shh," she said softly. "It will be okay. I know you don't believe me, but it will, I promise."

I went around the table and hugged her, this moment bookending that one all those years ago in Hyde Park.

"There's a reason I was listening to this song," she said. "I know you don't believe that there's anything after this. That this is it. And I know that the thought of me going in the ground is killing you. But I don't want you to pretend or lie to yourself that I'm in heaven. That's what made me think of you. There's a line in this song about wandering in Iowa, and I thought you can just say that. I'm not dead. I'm not in heaven. I'm just wandering out on the hills of Iowa. And when you feel sad, you can just think that."

"You think that will help?" I asked, incredulously.

"It might," she said kindly. "You can find out for me."

We hugged for a while longer. She said she was tired and asked if I would take her to bed. I did and we lay there, me pulling her to me as tightly as I dared, worried that I might crush her bones that now felt as delicate as a sparrow's. She gently patted my hand with her own, until eventually she fell asleep.

I lay there in the darkness still holding her, struggling to accept the fact that there was no getting out of this, there was nothing to do that could turn this around. The only sounds were the ticking of the alarm clock, and her soft breathing, which sounded like grains of sand running through the neck of an hourglass.

I'm not going to talk about the end, except to say it got bad. You'd hit a point and think that's it, that's the nadir, the lowest it can be, and then something else would come along and force you to revise what you thought rock bottom looked like.

She had to go into palliative care about three weeks after that night. Whatever bit of her mind the cancer didn't eat, the pain meds took care of. She slept most of the time, and when she was conscious she rarely said anything that wasn't gibberish. She would compose a shopping list aloud, interspersed with snatches of the Owl and the Pussycat. She talked about homework she needed to do, recited sections of the carbon cycle. Eventually she stopped making any sounds that could be recognised as words. I stayed with her, going home only to change clothes, have a shower, and come straight back.

Because if you make a vow you should try and keep it. And because I had nowhere else to go.

Then one night at four in the morning as I lay asleep in a chair, a nurse gently shook me awake.

"I think it's time," she said, kindly.

I lay by the bed and gripped her hands, crying but trying to hold it back, not wanting that to be the last thing she heard in this world.

But I couldn't help myself. I know what people mean now when they talk about their life flashing before their eyes. It's like your brain is searching through all it knows, all it has ever experienced, trying desperately to find some way to stop the inevitable. That's what my brain was doing, anyway. But there was nothing to be done. All I could do was sit there and hold her hand, choking back sobs. The last thing I ever said to her was pathetic and selfish but I couldn't help it.

"Please," I begged, as her breathing became more ragged. "Please don't leave me here alone."

She didn't reply. I'm not sure she even knew I was there. Her eyes were wide open, looking up at the Styrofoam-squared grid of the ceiling, but unfocussed and I don't know what she could see, if she could see anything at all.

Then she drew in a long, laboured breath and somehow, I knew that was the last and this was it. The person who had given my life meaning.

The person who had understood me, and accepted me, and taken me as I was.

My only love.

And suddenly she smiled. Her skin was little more than a wet sheet stretched across the bones of her face, but with that smile she looked beautiful again, and I could see her–

Walking across the A&E floor to me.

Swimming with bioluminescent plankton in her hair.

Hugging a three-legged cat in our first home.

Full of life.

Full of joy.

And she said something. At least I think she did. It may have just been the last exhalation of breath scraping across her vocal cords, but to me it sounded like a single word driven by an emotion somewhere close to rapture.

"Iowa."

And then she died. She was forty-nine years old.

There's not much to say after that. There was a service in a crematorium near Newbury followed by a few drinks and three-cornered sandwiches in the pub. There was a good turnout. People shook my hand and told me how sorry they were. At about six o'clock in the evening, I went home. Peter and Helen came with me. Helen produced a shepherd's pie from somewhere and put it in the oven for me.

"Half an hour at one eighty," she said. Then they left, telling me to call them if I needed anything, anything at all. The only thing I needed was not in anyone else's power to gift.

I distinctly remember sitting there in that kitchen by myself, unmoving, for two hours, thinking that I had no idea what I was going to do now.

I bought an oak tree sapling. I walked deep into the forest on the hill above the village, well off the beaten path and buried her ashes there, planting the sapling on top. With a bit of luck, it might still be there in a thousand years.

There's a weird thing that happens when someone you love dies. You think that they die once, but they keep dying on you over and over again. You open a drawer and see the clothes they wore, you get the last lingering smell of their hair on a pillow, you hear a song they loved on the radio.

On her side of the bed, I found a paperback called *House Rules* with a bookmark fifty pages from the end. I read the whole thing, then walked into the woods to tell her how it finished. I caught the train into Paddington and spent the day touring the perimeters of our life. The old Wembley stadium was gone, as was the restaurant where Emery had met James, but a few markers of where we had passed remained.

I considered drinking myself to death, and indeed I gave it a serious try for about a week. But my heart wasn't really in it, and I felt like I was virtue-signalling my own grief. I also knew it would have pissed Emery off. That it was an insult to the time of which she had been robbed, to waste mine in such a fashion.

I also knew that the graveyard in the local church was filled with tombstones now illegible with age, of people long forgotten, their mark on the world faded to dust in the wind.

That was the fate of us all, I supposed, but Emery was alive, as long as anyone who remembered even a piece of her was alive. One by one those lights would flicker and burn out, and the last of her would go. In the meantime, here was me, carrying the precious cargo of the memory of her around in my head.

So I resolved to live.

That was about the extent of my ambition, so I bumbled around and killed time.

I set myself small goals.

Get out of bed.

Make a cup of coffee.

Make a cup of coffee the way you actually like your coffee, and make the effort to buy milk and sugar and put it in the boob mug.

I got up and shuffled around, and filled my days as best I could, little more than a stumbling ghost.

Then one night I was up in the pub, staring into my pint, and I overheard from one of the regulars that a boater named Jimmy the Saint was moving off the cut to set up house with his partner, and his wide beam, the *Mary Ellen Carter*, was up for sale.

CHAPTER THIRTY-THREE

I was awoken early the next morning by my phone ringing, trying to vibrate itself from the bedside table onto the floor. A UK number I didn't recognise.

I answered. "Hello?"

"Hello, is that Dan Marley?"

I was about to correct them, when I remembered I had given that name to Cambridgeshire Police, as it was the one on my official records.

"Speaking."

"This is DI Collins," he said. "Cambridgeshire police. I understand you were trying to get a hold of me."

I swung my legs onto the floor and sat on the edge of the bed rubbing the sleep out of my eyes.

"I think so. Thanks for calling me back."

"As I understand it, you were phoning about a suicide in one of the colleges about fifteen years ago. Marianne Tate?" The voice sounded terse and irritated, which made sense. Cops hate getting their homework marked, especially by other cops.

"I don't know the name, but if it's the one you interviewed Chris Wall about, then yes."

"What's your interest, if you don't mind me asking? I looked you up before I called. You were Met. Retired five years ago. How did this get on your radar?"

"Not much to tell really. I'm on a mountain holiday. Wall was on it too. He killed himself. He seemed like a mentally together guy, so I was just doing a bit of digging. Mostly for my own curiosity."

"Fair enough, but I don't think I've got anything for you. There's nothing much to report really. A girl committed suicide and we interviewed classmates, tutors and colleagues to establish her state of mind at the time. Standard procedure, and by the book. We get a fair few suicides in the colleges, so we know what we're doing."

My brain heard that as 'we didn't kill ourselves with work', but I didn't give that thought a voice, as Collins carried on.

"Wall was one of the people that we interviewed. There were some rumours that he and the girl had a thing going on. When I talked to him, he confirmed that he had gone out with her a few times, four or five months before, but it hadn't really been much more than that. He said he hadn't spoken to her for at least ten weeks before she died."

"When was this?"

"Let's see – I spoke to Wall on January 24th 1998."

I felt a bolt of electricity shoot through my entire system.

I gripped the phone tighter.

"January 1998," I repeated. "Are you sure?"

"I'm looking at my notes right now."

Somewhere inside my brain a lock tumbler moved slightly, and I swear I heard a click.

"What was the student's name again? The girl who died."

"Marianne Tate."

"And you didn't like Wall for any involvement?"

"I didn't like anyone for any involvement. Everyone we talked to reported the girl as being a very highly-strung individual with a history of mental problems. She'd briefly been sectioned the year before by the Transport Police."

"The Transport Police?"

"Yeah, she was walking along the train tracks in her underwear. Somewhere between Eddington and Cambridge. She spent a couple of days in observation at the local psych hospital after that escapade."

"The 24th was the date that you interviewed Wall. Presumably she died a few days before. Was it the 17th?"

I could hear him flipping through his notes.

"Close," he said at last. "The 16th. She was found on the 17th, but the autopsy confirmed that she would have died the day before. Does that date mean something to you?"

"Only that it's the date I got promoted to DI."

"Well done you, but hardly relevant is it?"

"Not a bit," I said. "Anything else you think is worth knowing?"

"Like I said, it was pretty much cut and dried. They found her in her room. Door locked, empty bottle of red wine, the needle riding the label of a record on a turntable."

Another tumbler turned over in my head.

"I don't suppose you made a note of what the record was, did you?"

"One second… it was a scratchy forty-five of Edith Piaf singing *Hymne A L'amour.*

"OK, one last question," I said. "True or false. Marianne Tate committed suicide by hanging. Lashed a noose to a beam, put her head in it then rocked the chair she was standing on out from under herself."

"I'd say a good guess but I assume it wasn't a guess."

"Not really," I said.

Her vision going dark, frantically thinking 'This isn't what I want'.

Her legs kicking trying to find support that was not there.

"DI Collins, that's really good stuff and it helps a lot, but I've really got to go." I'd swung my legs off the bed and had started looking for clothing.

"Hang on," he said. "Not so fast. I have a few questions of my own. I worked that case and it's closed, but now I'm thinking I missed something. I told you I was looking at my notes from fifteen years ago. It's not a coincidence that I had them to hand. You're the second person who called me about Marianne Tate in the last forty-eight hours. Some German cop phoned me the day before yesterday asking about it."

"Werner," I thought to myself. I felt strangely proud of him. Like my positive assessment had been justified. Grunt work beats flash every time.

"He was an Austrian cop," I said. "Germany is nine kilometres away. I was helping him out – we must have got our wires crossed about who was chasing which thread. And you didn't miss anything. I think it was a suicide. If I find out any different, I promise I'll let you know. Nothing official that can come back and bite you."

"Fair enough, I guess," he said. "Hope it was some help. Stay safe out there, DI Marley."

"Same to you, DI Collins."

And with that he rang off.

I got dressed in a hurry and went downstairs. There was no one in reception, but as luck would have it a taxi was dropping a couple off at the hotel down the road, so I grabbed it for a short hop to Lermoos. Got out at the police station, threw the driver the first note I found in my wallet, shot through the double doors, and took the stairs two at a time.

Brandt was behind the desk and looked up at me with his big goofy face. Behind him the office looked empty.

"Werner?" I asked.

He shook his head.

"No Werner," he said apologetically. "Werner away."

I cursed and dug out my phone. Texted him.

At your office. Where are you?

I paced up and down the reception. After ten minutes he still hadn't replied, so I went back up to the desk.

Brandt looked up again, ever eager to help. Through a combination of pidgin German, mime and interpretive dance, I indicated that I wanted to come behind the desk. Brandt looked at me with real concern, possibly worried that I was having some kind of episode. I tried hard not to get frustrated, then dug out my phone to translate.

"Chris Wall Besitztumer?" I asked.

My German accent was obviously not helping, so I showed him the screen and finally a light bulb went off. He nodded, came around to the door and let me through. He led me down a corridor and stopped at a door, unlocked it and let me in. Inside was a small storage room, maybe ten feet by eight feet, with shelving units covering three walls. They were mostly empty. Brandt pointed to two boxes. I stepped forward and Brandt held out a cautionary arm, blocking my way. He waggled his fingers in my face and I nodded that I understood. You can look but you better not touch. At least not without gloves. I cautiously approached the two boxes. Inside were Chris Wall's possessions, sealed in evidence bags of various sizes. His wallet, his phone. I looked in the first box and found what I was looking for. I pointed and Brandt produced a pair of blue latex gloves from a box on the shelf and handed them to me.

I cautiously rummaged through the box then picked out the plastic bag containing his iPod. I pressed the centre button through the plastic and after a few moments the Apple logo appeared on screen. Brandt was leaning over my shoulder, so I turned slightly to show it to him as well. Even though he had no idea what was going on, it was still more his investigation than mine. The main menu appeared.

I selected playlists. There was only one. It contained about thirty songs. That in itself was a flag. You could fit maybe two thousand songs on the device if you steered clear of the more self-indulgent Pink Floyd efforts. Thirty seemed like a waste of effort. I started scrolling through the list of songs. My heart was beating faster with the thrill of a potential breakthrough, of solving the riddle. But there was also a part of me that was praying that I was wrong.

I wasn't, though. After about twenty pieces that I didn't recognise, I found it.

Hymne A L'amour by Edith Piaf. I pressed play, and the progress bar showed it had started. Four minutes and thirty seconds. I couldn't hear it but I didn't need to.

I powered down the iPod and put it carefully back in the box. I turned to Brandt, who was smiling cautiously, clearly sensing that there had been some kind of a breakthrough, and at the same time hoping he had not massively screwed up by letting me in here without Werner's express approval.

Although the expression on my face must have been kind of grim, I gave him a thumbs up.

I pointed at him.

"Werner" – I held a mime telephone with my thumb and little finger to my head and pointed at myself. "Phone me."

He nodded. "Weisen sie Werner an, sie am telefon anzurufen. Ich verstehe."

I nodded, patted him on the upper arm then left the police station at a pace just shy of a run.

As soon as I got onto the street, I dug out my phone and dialled Abby's number. It rang to voicemail. I disconnected without leaving a message and hit redial, walking at pace back towards the hotel. By now I was certain about two things. Lee and Hermann had specifically targeted Abby and me not because they thought I had the laptops, but because they thought she did. If I had not seen her since the afternoon before, then it wasn't because she was avoiding me, it was because she was in serious trouble. I tried her phone a third time, just as I reached the flat oval of the Moos, and to my surprise, this time she answered.

"Abby?" I said. "Where are you?"

"Jake," she sounded angry and stressed. "I can't talk to you now."

"Where are you?" I asked. "We really need to talk. I was wrong about the two men. I think you might be in danger, so I need to know…"

"No," she said sharply, cutting me off. "I can't talk to you. I don't want to talk to you. You need to leave me alone."

And with that, she hung up. I stopped walking, looked at the disconnected phone in my hand then around at the basin surrounding me. I had no way to track her, and no idea where she might be right now. Except as I thought about it, I realised that I probably did. I shoved the phone back in my jacket pocket, then turned right heading towards Biberwier and the start of the hiking trail that led to Blindsee Lake, where Chris Wall had died and all of this had started.

It took me about ninety minutes to walk the seven kilometres, reaching the lake around noon. Werner called once as I was walking, no doubt following up on Brandt's instructions, but I ignored it. Past the boathouse and jetty. No hesitation this time, I turned right and started walking the lake perimeter along the shore, to where the path rose above the water. Past the plateau, the last few straggly strands of police perimeter line tape still fluttering in the breeze. Then I saw her, dressed in her outdoor gear, walking slowly along the path with her back to me, shoulders hunched, eyes down.

I stopped and said her name, loudly, but gently.

"Abby."

She jumped and spun around, her face white. I could almost smell the adrenaline, her body language screaming fight or flight.

When she saw it was me, I saw her face relax the smallest amount, but her posture remained unchanged.

"I told you," she said. "I don't want to talk to you. You need to leave me alone."

"It's okay," I said. "I can help."

"I don't want it," she replied. "I don't need it."

"Okay," I said. "Just answer one question, then I'll leave you alone if you want me to."

She looked uncertain but nodded.

"Can you tell me how you killed Chris Wall?"

She started at the accusation, but she didn't deny it.

At last she said, "It's not the how, but the why."

There was a length of felled tree trunk lying by the path, halfway between us. I nodded over at it.

"Let's sit there for a bit."

After another moment, she nodded again, then slowly walked forwards and sat down on the tree trunk. She looked exhausted. I sat down beside her.

She was silent for a long while, not looking at me but into the depth of the forest.

At last she said, "I honestly don't know where to begin."

I spoke as gently as I knew how.

"Take your time," I said. "It'll come."

There was another long pause, then at last she started speaking.

"I was five years old when my sister Marianne was born…"

CHAPTER THIRTY-FOUR

Abby was five years old when her sister Marianne was born. That was a reasonably significant gap between siblings, and though it was never spoken about, in later life Abby would always assume that her parents had trouble conceiving. Because she had spent the first five years of her life as a precocious and somewhat indulged only child, there had been some early concerns that she would not react well to a sibling and jealously regard her as an interloper. This fear turned out to be groundless. Abby loved her baby sister from the very first moment she saw her, an eight-pound bundle of chubby human with fat rings around her wrists, looking out at the world through large brown curious eyes.

Abby forsook all her other activities to spend time with her younger sister, telling her about everything that she had to look forward to when she grew up, all the fun things they could do together. Playing with dolls, riding bicycles through the woods, paddling in the streams. Ice cream was nice. Chocolate cake was better. Boys were mean and smelly and to be avoided, kittens were the cutest and horses were a bit scary but nice. Marianne, or Polly as she very quickly became known in the Tate household, listened to all of this, lying on her back, waving her arms and legs in the air, and burbling happily. She developed well, able to take a few faltering steps and speak a few words by her first birthday.

Her first word was Abba, which was understood to mean Abby, to the mild chagrin of their parents. These developmental steps were a little to the top end of the bell curve but nothing to stop the press over. The visiting nurse made a comment whilst watching her play with blocks that it was unusual for a child of that age to remain focussed on a singular task for such a long time, but that was about it.

As she grew to be a toddler, becoming a person in her own right, a few more foibles became manifest, but again little to be overly concerned about. The sound of the whistle on a boiling kettle caused her to weep hysterically and clap her hands over her ears, to the point where her parents had to stop using it. She would spend hours staring intently at technical blueprints that their mother brought home from work, or studying the contours of maps in a large hardback family atlas, without making a sound. She proved able to pick out any tune she heard with relative ease on the family's upright piano, and her parents started to teach her how to play even though she was only three years old.

When she grew old enough to attend school she seemed to integrate well with the other children, and her teacher reported all was well. She did seem to have a problem with boundaries and a tendency to give her thoughts a voice without running it through a propriety filter – telling one fellow student that she needed to lose weight and a teacher that she had halitosis. But then many children said the damnedest things, so it was not a cause for concern.

Polly reported to her family over the first few months that she liked painting and music and geography and stories from history but maths was boooorrrrrrrinnnnnngggg. Abby smiled as she recalled how Polly had always said it like that as a child. It was not until about six months into her first year at school that Polly's secret was revealed.

Abby had been given as homework a fun learning game that she dragooned her mother into playing with her. A story where every so often there was a mathematical formula, which when entered into a calculator and viewed upside down, gave you the missing word. We were being chased by blank. You did the sum. You looked at the answer – 5338 – upside down and you confirmed that you were in fact being chased by bees.

It was a simple story whose only real narrative drive was to get you to encounter as many things as could be spelled on a calculator. As Abby and her mother were working through the story, they were asked to multiply forty by five times twenty-five, then by seven then add six. This was to tell you what the farmer gave you to take home from the farm.

Even as they were tapping the numbers into their calculator, Polly, just shy of her fifth birthday, and who had been sitting quietly at the other end of the table, filling in a colouring book with crayons, had asked, "When we get our goose, can it live in my room?"

A good ten seconds later, Abby and her mother, with the aid of the calculator, arrived at the solution of 35006, which when viewed upside down spelled the word 'goose'.

The reason why Polly found maths so tedious was revealed. For her it was as boring as being forced to paddle about in a rock pool while being told to ignore the vast horizon of the blue ocean. Teachers got very excited about having a gifted child, and did their best to convince Polly and Abby's parents that this talent should be nurtured. They cautiously allowed tests to evaluate Polly's abilities. It appeared Polly had a brain that could instinctively grasp complex mathematical ideas, spatial relationships and intuit visualisations of complex mathematical concepts. That was the upside.

The downside was that her brain was also hardwired without a trip switch and she could not drop a problem until it had been solved. Early in her exploration of this brave new world Polly came across a currently unsolved maths problem called the Collatz Conjecture and became obsessed with finding a solution. This was a problem that experts had been working on for nearly a century with no joy. It consumed her for a week, to the point of doing nothing else, neglecting sleep, food and human company, hiding in her room. Eventually their parents had pulled the plug on this behaviour for the sake of her mental health, forcibly removing all the maths books and notes from the house. Polly's response was initially to have a crying fit, then to go catatonic for the best part of a week.

This obsessive behaviour occasionally manifested in milder forms. Once, at the age of seven, attempting to learn a particularly challenging Chopin piece, she woke the entire family by getting up in the middle of the night to work on it.

The Tate parents decided that they did not need to test the limits of their daughter's brain to destruction in order to figure out its capacity, and as much as possible steered her towards a normal level of academia and social interaction.

They also had her tested to see if she was autistic. The results were inconclusive. The doctors reported that while Polly did appear to have some difficulty in social interactions, with a little help there was no reason at all that she could not live a happy, independent and normal life. Abby felt that they had not needed a doctor to tell them this, because around her Polly was always happy and at her best. She would laugh at jokes, engage in conversations and respond appropriately to most situations. As far as Abby was concerned

Polly was just her smart, beautiful, occasionally annoying baby sister. Although there was five years between them, they were very close, and spent most weekends involved in some activity together, be it swimming, cycling in the woods near their home, or dancing in their bedroom to scratchy 45 singles.

For Abby there was a joy to being around Polly that she could never adequately explain – it was just there. Like gravity or sunshine. An unforced and unspoken bond. They knew each other in a way that no one else could. There was a part of Polly that Abby knew only she could see, and she knew it was precious and delicate and fragile and had to be guarded fiercely from the world, up to and including, on occasion, their own parents.

Even when boys appeared on the scene for Abby, previous opinions of smelliness and meanness having been somewhat revised over the years, there was always room in her life for her younger sister. More than one suitor had to reconcile himself to the fact that the planned excursion to the cinema was going to have an eleven-year-old chaperone, and one promising relationship with a young gentleman ended rather abruptly when he dared to opine that her kid sister was a bit weird, wasn't she?

After their parents' decision to back away somewhat from the limitless horizons of mathematics and let her education continue as normally as possible, Polly went to the local secondary school just as Abby was about to leave it and go to college. With some help she improved in her social interactions, although she never really fit in anywhere. She was the squarest of pegs in a world of round holes, so most cliques tended to just pretend that she didn't exist. The 'never-was-a-noceros' as Polly laughingly referred to herself, a reference to a book in their shared childhood, that only Abby really understood.

It took her some time, but she did make some friends, all of them to some extent in the borderlands themselves. Polite, bookish, quiet children, whose interests tended towards the intellectual. Two girls and a boy, who were the only friends of Polly's that Abby or their parents ever met. Abby was grateful for these friends of her sister's, because they cared not a fig for the social landmines that Polly occasionally stepped on, accepting her for herself. At the same time, Polly was mostly happy with her own company, either reading, studying or mastering Chopin on the piano, playing note-perfect renditions, though she thumped the piano keys like they owed her money.

Abby went to college, studying Economics and Geography at the LSE and living in student accommodation that had roughly the dimensions of a large wardrobe. She came home to Oxfordshire at least once a month, but a lot of the fears she had for her sister had abated. Polly had transitioned into secondary school and was continuing to excel in maths. She was taking extracurricular classes in the subject under her parents' careful supervision, and her teachers had indicated that if she wanted to, she should consider taking her A-Levels early.

Polly wanted to do this, having been quite taken with the university experience when she visited Abby in London. As she said, 'home didn't feel the same without Abby around.' Plus, she pointed out, there were only a few prestigious places where she wanted to study mathematics, and taking advanced A-levels two years early was a good way to get on their radar.

Abby was initially hesitant, but seeing that Polly was a happy and confident young woman, and conscious that her family could occasionally be over-protective, eventually shifted her position to think that if Polly was up for it, she should do it. After all, though she might be two years younger than other undergraduates in her class, Polly might have more in common with those people. Her parents reluctantly agreed.

At the age of sixteen Polly Tate took her A-levels and absolutely smashed Mathematics, Advanced Level Mathematics, and Computer Science. She was accepted to study Computer Science at Trinity College, Cambridge, and in 1996 started there as an undergraduate six months shy of her 17th birthday.

By this stage, Abby had graduated college and was moving on with her own life. She had successfully applied for a job at the EU headquarters in Strasbourg and was living the life of a cosmopolitan and sophisticated single woman in a culturally significant European city. She had been seeing a young engineer named Marc Guerin and it was starting to get serious. When she phoned home, reports were that things were okay. Better than okay. The Tate parents were incredibly proud of their two daughters and life was good.

But slowly Abby began to notice changes in Polly. In the beginning Polly had phoned to excitedly report on every new thing she discovered about Cambridge – punting on the Cam, drinking illegal wine spritzers in the Eagle courtesy of a fake ID, the Newnham lamppost where she joked she had half hoped to catch sight of Mr Tumnus. But over time her phone calls became sporadic and when they came she talked incessantly about the work she was developing with the Levy Process, and how she was close to a breakthrough that she believed would be of significant mathematical importance.

Abby spoke to her parents and they confessed to feeling the same way – that Polly was becoming hyper-focussed on her work, possibly making herself unwell, both physically and mentally. Like Chopin and the Collatz Conjecture before it, they knew where this might end. They agreed that Abby would book a holiday at half term and come home so the family could spend some time together. As well as the concern over Polly, Abby had some news for everyone.

Before that happened, however, their parents got a phone call from the police. Polly had been arrested and detained under Section 136 of the 1983 Mental Health Act for her own safety, after being found walking along the railway line in her underwear. Abby rushed home on the first flight and went straight to Cambridge, where she met her parents and they all went to see Polly in the psychiatric ward of the Fulbourn Hospital.

The doctors reported that when she was found, in addition to being semi-naked, she was also exhausted and dehydrated. They had sedated her and were onboarding fluids to give her body the best chance of recovery. After twenty-four hours, the doctors decided she was well enough to receive visitors. Polly was upset and embarrassed, but when she explained what happened she managed to make it seem perfectly logical.

She had missed her train. She was late for a lecture. Clearly the train tracks would take her to town so if she followed those she would get to where she wanted to go. So she walked that way. It was hot walking along railway tracks, so she decided to take some clothes off. In hindsight this was clearly a huge mistake, but at the time it had seemed perfectly rational in her mind. Tearfully she explained that although she was really enjoying the work, and being challenged for the first time, it was also a new experience to encounter other people equally adept at maths driving her onwards. She had allowed it to get on top of her. Eventually the decision was made that she would take a break for the last three weeks of the Lent term, go home with her family to recuperate and come back fresh after the Easter break. After that, Abby's big news was a bit of an afterthought. Marc had proposed and she had said yes.

Abby managed to organise working from home and the Tate family closed protective ranks around their youngest member. During that month, any mathematics more complicated than calculating a Scrabble word score was strictly forbidden. Polly slowly recovered, getting back to being her bright and slightly weird self. There was some trepidation when she went back to Cambridge after Easter, but the college had been informed of the 'incident', as they euphemistically referred to it, and had found her accommodation nearer the Porters' Lodge. Tutors had been advised, so there were some guard rails in place to try and ensure nothing like that happened again.

Abby went back to Strasbourg, and Polly resumed phoning regularly. She was self-deprecating about the incident and resolved not to do anything that stupid again. She was enjoying her work but taking pains to ensure it did not take over her life. As the term went on, Polly actually seemed brighter and there was even a coquettish element to her conversation now. Abby, who was very finely attuned to Polly's moods, had the strange sensation that she had a secret. But a good secret. Abby wondered if Polly might have met someone, but she felt sure that Polly would tell her in her own good time, if so.

And then one Friday Polly had not phoned. Abby tried to call her, but got no answer other than a text saying that Polly was a bit caught up in something and would phone later in the week, maybe the weekend. Abby had texted back asking if everything was okay, and got a curt and rather hurtful reply saying that she was an adult and she didn't need her sister to sort out all her problems.

That Friday evening, Abby met Marc for dinner. She walked down the three flights of stairs from her flat to the street and as she pulled the front door behind her, she realised she had left her phone charging on the nightstand. She checked her watch and, already running late, figured she could survive fifteen hours without it.

It has been remarked that if the sun suddenly burned out, no one would know about it for eight minutes, as that is how long it takes the light to travel the ninety-three million miles of space from its surface to the earth.

Abby would later reflect that the evening she spent with Mark was the eight minutes. Not because the darkness was coming, because the darkness was already there and she just didn't know it yet.

Abby got home around noon on Saturday following a lazy morning in Marc's super king-sized bed and a waffle breakfast at a local café, picking out potential honeymoon destinations from the weekend supplements.

When she got back, there were four missed calls from Polly and twelve from her parents. On her house phone were two messages. The first one was from her sister – a long incoherent, garbled and sobbing message left at 7.30pm the previous evening. Something about lies and betrayal. She sounded drunk, and Polly rarely drank to excess. There was one more from her father at 10am, his composure not hiding that he sounded shocked beyond all reason, asking her to please phone as soon as she picked up the message. She tried her sister first. There was no reply.

She tried both her parents' mobiles and the house phone. No reply.

Eventually, running out of options, she phoned the bursar at the college, gave her name and said that she had received a phone message from her sister the night before, and that she appeared to be in some distress. She asked if there was anyone who could please check on her. The bursar asked her to hold. The line went silent for a couple of minutes and then another voice came on the phone. Older, male, authoritative. He asked Abby for her name and asked her to confirm Polly's name and their relationship. Abby did so with mounting panic and the voice informed her that he was very sorry to say that her sister had been found dead in her room that morning, apparently as the result of a suicide. The police had been informed, as had their parents, who were already on their way to the college, and he was really dreadfully sorry to be the bearer of such awful, awful news.

Abby, in a daze, heard practically none of what he said after the word 'dead'. She didn't even stop to pack a bag, just grabbed her passport and caught a taxi to the airport. In the back of the cab she kept trying to phone her parents. Her mother first, figuring her father would be driving, then her father when that failed. There was no reply from either. She made it all the way to the airport, bought a ticket from Strasbourg to Paris for a connection to London. She was sitting at a gate in Charles De Gaulle, crying her way through a forty-five-minute layover, when her phone rang again. She answered it and was asked to confirm her name. She did, and the voice on the other end of the phone identified themselves as a liaison officer with the Hertfordshire Police. They regretted to inform her that both her parents had been involved in a fatal road traffic accident just off the M25 earlier that morning.

Abby had no real recollection of the flight from Paris to London, or how she made it to Cambridge. She had no real recollection of the next few weeks of her life. She identified first the body of her sister, then her parents, and provided enough information to the police to build up a picture that they were satisfied with. Her sister, who had a history of mental problems, had taken her own life. Her parents, on being informed, had made an ill-advised trip in bad weather on treacherous roads. In their haste and shock, her father had hit a patch of black ice and slid their car into the path of an articulated lorry.

The inquest found nothing other than a multi-faceted tragedy. There was no note. More than once she caught people on her periphery, in huddled conversations, casting glances in her direction. The poor wretch who had been struck by lightning twice in as many days. She stumbled through inquests and funeral preparations in a daze. A ceremony was held for all three of them and they were buried in a plot in the graveyard in the Fairmile Cemetery. After the last guest had gone, she thought "What the hell do I do now?"

In her case, not much. Marc was there to comfort her, and still wanted to marry her. Even as she was repeating the words in the registry office, she knew it was a mistake. It didn't last. He wanted to help her to move on with her life; she couldn't do it. Actively resisted any attempts to force her to do so. She was actually relieved when he said he felt there was no room for him in her life and he thought they should separate. She quit her job in Strasbourg and moved back to the family home. Abby did not know why it felt important to be at home. It gave her no comfort, but she felt like a guardian of their small and random marks on the world. Her mother's thumbprint on a lump of blue tack on the wall, the pencil lines marking her and Polly's height over the course of their lives. It wasn't a house so much as a museum, a memorial to a family that had been reduced to one shell of a person, mooching around in pyjamas and a tatty dressing gown.

A friend of her mother's came to visit and offered her a job. She refused at first, but she periodically repeated the offer every few months and eventually Abby accepted. It killed time if nothing else. She would work all week, stop off at the off-licence on the way home on Friday, buy two bottles of vodka, steadily work her way through them over the weekend, then get up and do it all again. Five years would pass like this.

Then one Saturday morning in 2007, there was a knock on her front door. It was a young Polish man named Bartek Drew. He told her apologetically that he was a building contractor in Cambridge. Abby cautiously offered him a cup of tea. Sitting in the back garden, Bartek explained that he was currently in the process of renovating student accommodation in Trinity College. She had a cold feeling of recognition from long ago, from a life now gone.

"Your sister's name was Polly?" asked Bartek

"Marianne – we called her Polly," croaked Abby. "How did you know that?"

In answer, Bartek reached into a bag, and produced a large blue hardbacked notebook. Abby pulled it slowly towards her and opened it. The front page read *Personal diary of Polly Tate*. Below it was the college address and the address of the family house in Sutton Courtenay. Bartek explained that he had been lifting floorboards to replace them, and found a hidden compartment that contained this book.

"I only looked at the front page," he said. "I asked around and found out it was the girl who died. I'm sorry if it pains you, but I thought you might want it."

"Thank you," croaked Abby.

Bartek left shortly after, and Abby stared at the book for over an hour before she turned the first page.

She read it all straight through in less than an hour. Then she went into the kitchen and screamed until she thought her vocal cords would shred. She went back outside and read it again. Because her life now had a purpose: revenge on a man she had never heard mention of before that day, named Chris Wall.

CHAPTER THIRTY-FIVE

It took Abby an hour to tell me that much, sitting on a tree trunk by the side of the path above Blindsee Lake.

"How did they meet?" I asked.

"He just walked up to her one day in the cafeteria and introduced himself," said Abby. "He said they shared some of the same classes and he would be interested in sharing some thoughts with her about the Levy Process. She knew who he was, of course. He walked around the campus like an Adonis, he had a reputation as a bit of a ladies man, and it was a thrill to have a handsome man talking to her, and about maths to boot. She wrote he was funny and charming and smart, and he seemed genuinely interested in her. After that first meeting, he asked her if she wanted to go out for a drink or dinner some time. And she did. Within a week they were a couple. They kept it quiet because he was twenty-two and she was still only seventeen."

Abby sighed and looked away.

"Polly was so very smart in some ways but totally naïve in others. She was such a genuine person in herself, she really struggled to see that people could be duplicitous or underhanded. I read that diary and it was so heartfelt and honest from her point of view, all her fragile hopes of where a real relationship might go, and all I could see in the subtext was a step-by-step plan of emotional and psychological manipulation."

"I'll take your word for it," I said.

"One page he wasn't there, the next page he was everywhere. It was just Chris, Chris, Chris, all the time. Sharing his life story. Expecting her to do the same. Playing up his own problems and diminishing hers. Finding weak spots to exploit. Slowly cutting her off from her few friends. Telling her that he didn't think they liked him, or approved of them as a couple.

"Creating 'us against them' scenarios. I initially thought he might just have been a self-absorbed jerk, but the more I read, the more I thought – 'No, this is a sociopath. This is someone who knows exactly what he is doing.'

"Polly didn't see any of that of course. She wrote about how happy he made her feel, about their first night together, which was her first night with anyone. She wrote about how afterwards they lay there in bed listening to *Hymne A L'amour*, on her old record player. How it became their song. That was hard reading. It was an invasion of her privacy but it also made me so sad and angry that she put so much faith in a lie.

"He talked to her about objectivism and Taoism, philosophies he was interested in. She read a little of them, liked the latter but not the former. He seemed a bit hurt and suggested that maybe she didn't understand it. Because she thought she had upset him, she bought him a yin-yang medallion as a birthday present. He had kissed her and said it was perfect, because they were complementary parts of the one whole."

"There's more, isn't there?" I prompted.

Abby sighed again.

"Polly was working on variables of the Levy process and he was working on Schwartz distributions. When Polly showed him her work, he got excited about the practical applications. Really excited. He suggested they could combine their efforts and produce predictive modelling that could change the world and make them a fortune in the process. I think he was surprised when she said no, that she wasn't interested. That someone might not be interested in money, or maybe that his control wasn't as absolute as he had perceived.

"She tried to explain to him, maths was pure and beautiful and shouldn't be prostituted, and further, wealth was already unevenly distributed throughout the world and she had no desire to make that situation worse. Chris was disappointed in her decision but said he understood. All was well for another two weeks. They continued seeing each other, went to dinner, walked hand in hand from Cambridge to Grantchester along the river blah, blah, blah. Polly forgot all about the argument and considered that it was over.

"Then one day he just stopped calling. He didn't reply to her phone calls or texts. She called around to his accommodation and was told that he had moved off campus with no forwarding address. He stopped turning up to lectures. She was worried that something had happened to him or that she had done something wrong. Eventually one day, by chance, she happened to see him walking across the quad and ran to intercept him.

"He was cool, even cold towards her. He said that he had been very busy and was close to a breakthrough with his work and that he had been focussing on that, that maybe things between them had gotten a little too intense too fast, and it was time to take a break. That was when she stopped phoning me.

"Polly was heartbroken by this, but it got worse. A month later, the maths department was afire with news that Chris had submitted a paper that was being developed for publication in an academic journal.

"When Polly got a look at it, she instantly recognised that a good portion of the work was her own, work that she had sweated herself to a nervous breakdown for, now stolen and claimed by another. She had to work to find Chris, sitting on a bench on the quad in the freezing cold for hours until he eventually showed up. She accused him of stealing her work and threatened to go to the university authorities. He denied that he had, said that she did not have a monopoly on developments in the Levy Process, and that she was welcome to try, but who did she think they would believe? Their star player, or the weirdo with a history of mental illness?

"It's hard to guess which hurt her the most. The cruelty of those words or the realisation that he was probably right. She walked home in the snow, crying. When she got there she drank a whole bottle of wine. Took all of her meds at once. Tried in vain to phone me. Then our parents. Then, in a despair of loneliness and rejection, she tied a dressing gown cord around a beam in her room. Put on a record, and climbed on a chair."

She sniffed and a tear fell down her face.

"And that was that."

She exhaled deeply, and I could tell that this had been a huge effort for her to get through.

She wiped the tear away and her voice became stronger and harder.

"I became obsessed with Chris Wall. He had destroyed everyone I ever loved and I couldn't live with that. Every article I read about his success was an insult to their memory. So I studied and planned and waited. I had only one purpose and it consumed me. I engineered meetings with his friends and acquaintances, I tracked down disgruntled ex-colleagues. I found every single detail about his life that I could. That he came here every year. About the acid and his bullshit philosophies. Everything I learned about him made me hate him more. Last year I came here and tracked his movements from a distance. Twice he went out into the woods to the same place and got stoned. I still had Polly's last message on my phone. It haunted me. It hurt to listen to but I did when I got drunk. Like a scab I couldn't stop picking at. I wanted it to haunt him too. I spliced it into the middle of their song. I added it to a playlist. I learned about the dark web, got hold of the strongest acid I could find. Took some myself to make sure. Came to nine hours later, covered in my own vomit on the kitchen floor feeling like I had just crawled through hell. Then I came here. To finally meet him in person."

"You were wearing glasses when we first met," I said. "Not now. You don't need them?"

She nodded.

"Just in case he would recognise Polly in me." She scoffed. "He didn't look twice. Then last Tuesday, I followed him out here with a water bottle full of dissolved acid. He was sitting on a ledge when I found him. He smiled when he saw me and said hello.

"He said 'I think I know you.'

"I said 'I know you too.'

"He was already high, but he drank the water when I offered it to him. It was that simple. I had expected it to be more difficult, but he had no hesitation. Maybe he was just so confident, so invincible, nothing could hurt him. But that was it, I offered, he took it and drank. I sat down next to him, and we just looked out across the water in silence. About twenty minutes later he was totally out of it, just staring at the sunlight with a dumb look on his face. I tied up a noose from a rope in my rucksack and put it around his neck. As I was doing that I noticed the medallion. The same one Polly had given him all those years ago. That made me angry – so I yanked it off his neck. He didn't notice. Then I put an iPod in his pocket, put the buds in his ears and pressed play. I'd given myself forty-five minutes of random music to get away. Before he got to Polly and their song.

"Then I climbed back up onto the path, and ran cross country to get to the Grubig hut where I met you all that day. I figured it was all in the lap of the gods now. I was giving him a chance. Fate would decide. And Edith Piaf."

There's no time machine like the right piece of music, I thought to myself.

"You wanted to meet all of us so you had an alibi."

"Yes," she said, "but at the same time, I didn't care. When we got back to the hotel, and I heard he was dead, that he had come to the same end as he drove my sister to, I felt such a strange mix of emotions. Like I had come to the end of a long hard journey, that I had crossed an ocean and there was no going back. I felt a sense of vengeance, but mostly I just felt free of everything I had been carrying around for so long. I was quiet that night, thinking it all through in my head. I was sure I made a mistake somewhere, that I would get found out, get caught. But then I realised I didn't care about that. Mostly I was just very sad, because I knew that even then, nothing was going to bring Polly or my parents back." She smiled sadly. "I really needed that hug."

"So what happened?" I asked. "Why are we out here now?"

She shivered.

"Yesterday afternoon. I caught the cable car to the summit with Margaret and Bryce. When we got back down I took your advice. Took a walk to be alone. To think about what I wanted to do now."

"What happened?"

"I decided to walk to the Häselgehr Waterfall, just to have a destination. Plus the route was busy with walkers and cyclists, which I thought was a sensible precaution after last night. Along the way, I came across a small church – the Chapel of Saint Anna. So I went and sat there for a while." She shrugged. "I'm not religious, but the silence and peace was a blessing. I was just thinking, I could happily sit there and never move again. Then…"

I could guess the next part. "Then they came?"

She nodded. "The two men from the Moos that tried to rob us. They just came in and sat at either end of the pew I was on."

"What happened?"

"I froze. I was terrified, but there were a few other people in the church, an old woman praying and a father and child lighting a candle, so I thought at least they can't do anything to me in front of witnesses."

"And did they do anything?"

She shook her head. "No – the older one, the one that had the gun, he just spoke quietly to me. He said that they knew what I had done and that I had something they wanted and that I needed to give it to them."

"What did they want?" I tried to keep my voice even.

"Chris Wall's pendant. The one with the Chinese symbol."

"Why do they want that?"

She shook her head again. "They didn't say. I told them I didn't have it. That I only took it from Wall in a fit of anger. But then I realised that having it on me was linking me to his death, so I threw it away. I didn't want it, I just didn't want him to have it."

"What was their reaction?"

"He told me that I needed to find it. They told me to meet them on the Coburg Path tonight at 11.30pm with it. Or else, they would start hurting people I cared about. Bryce, Margaret, you. People back home. Then they got up and left."

"They tried hurting people already. It didn't work out well for them." I was trying to reassure her but she turned to me, eyes wide.

"I was still terrified. I went straight back out to the lake to search for it. I spent the whole day crawling up and down where I thought I had thrown it, then a couple of hundred metres either side. But I couldn't find it. I tried again today, but still no joy. It's gone." She turned back to the view, defeated.

"So what's your plan now?" I asked.

She shrugged. "I'm going to have to confront them. Explain that I don't have it. That it's gone."

"They're not going to accept that. They might kill you."

"I don't know what else to do."

"I could go instead of you."

She frowned. "I can't ask you to do that. And why would that be any better?"

"Well partly because they won't be expecting me, partly because I have more experience in dealing with armed antagonists. But mostly because I have the medallion in my pocket right now."

327

CHAPTER THIRTY-SIX

A bby wanted to take the pendant and organise the exchange herself, but I refused to hand it over, eventually resorting to 'finders keepers' when every other argument of logic and reason in my arsenal had failed. I told her to go back to the hotel and get her passport and plane ticket, then walk to either Biberwier or Lermoos. Go into a restaurant, order a meal, linger over it, and when done, somehow slip out the back door.

I had no idea if she was being followed at a distance or not, but it seemed like a sensible precaution to take. Once she had executed that move, just find a room for the night, pay cash for it, and lock the door. Text me the details of where she was and I would come and find her if I was successful. If she had not heard from me by the morning, run for the airport. Make it back to England. After that she could hand herself in to the authorities, if she thought that would make her safe. Personally, I thought it was a bluff on their part, and if she called it they wouldn't follow through, but I didn't bother arguing the toss. If this scenario played out, then I was already dead, and would not care either way. But if I went up the mountain, I planned on coming back down. Because I had an ace up my sleeve. And as luck would have it, he called just as I was watching Abby walk back across the Moos, towards the hotel.

I met Caulfield in the Caledonian Irish bar, grabbed a quiet table in the back by the dartboard, ordered a couple of coffees and got him up to speed as quickly as I could on the bits that were pertinent to him. I left Abby out of it, just saying I had been approached by the two men who wanted Wall's medallion. More importantly, I told him about the meeting due to take place up the mountain in eight hours' time.

"So where is this medallion now?" he asked

"Currently hanging around my neck." I pulled it over my head and we looked at it. I had not given it more than a cursory glance since picking it up at the lake. Clearly it had more significance than I had previously afforded it.

Caulfield was clearly having the same thought.

"That's it?" he asked. "They went to all that effort to get a hold of this?"

"Hang on," I said, tracing my fingers around the surface. I had just realised that it wasn't perfectly smooth. There was a small groove in the white dot on one side. I pressed into it. Nothing happened. Then I discovered that there was a similar button in the black dot on the other side. I pressed both at the same time and the pendant came apart neatly along the curve of the black white line. Inside was a USB stick.

"What do you think?" I asked. "I mean, clearly it's a USB stick, but does that mean that Wall had all his work stored on this thing, and the laptops were a red herring the whole time.

Caulfield considered this. "I don't think so," he said at last. "I think that Wall has some kind of encryption or bit locker on his hard drive.

The key is on this. Something that ensures you can only access data if you have this jacked into a port on the side."

"That makes sense. They already have the laptops, but without this, they're useless. Which is why they're going to so much trouble to get it." I slotted the two pieces back together with a soft click.

"Indeed. So both teams currently have half the spoils. We turn up tonight. They expect us to hand this over. We will convince them of the alternative scenario, in which they give us the laptops instead."

"That might be easier said than done."

"Oh, I wouldn't worry," he said grimly. "I can be very persuasive when I have to be."

We laid a map of the area out on the table in front of us and agreed on a plan. I would leave the hotel at 9pm. Caulfield would leave separately before me, just in case I was being watched. We would rendezvous at the cable car station at 9.30pm. It would not be running at that time, and should be deserted. From there it would take ninety minutes to get to the Coburg ridge. In the last half mile, Caulfield would break off the main path and cut through the pine trees over the top of the ridge. He would then shimmy along the far side for about three quarters of a mile, then come down behind them. That way we could pincer around our opponents.

"How many do you reckon?" he asked

"I've only seen two. Grey haired bloke and Herman. That's not to say there won't be more, maybe three, but I can't see there being any more than that. They're expecting one unarmed person. They've not got anything heavy to transport down. It's a narrow path – they'd just get in each other's way. What would be the point?"

"I think I agree. Okay, that makes our job easier." He raised his hand to attract the barman's attention and called out.

"Ich hätte gerne zwei Pilsner bitte. Barmanns Wahl. Danke."

The barman nodded and started to pull a couple of drafts.

"You think drinking beer is a good idea?" I asked.

He shrugged. "Call it Dutch courage if you want. I don't know what you're planning, but I'm going to have this beer then sleep for five hours. Did you mention me to Werner?" he asked, after the barman had brought our two beers. I shook my head.

He looked pleased.

"That's good, because I suspect I'm going to need that operational latitude after all. There's a chance this is going to get messy," he said. "You could always leave me to sort it out by myself."

I shook my head.

"I don't like the idea of just farming it out to you. I need to see this through to the end. And I feel I owe it to Harvey. I liked him, he didn't deserve what he got, and I'd like to see some justice for him."

Caulfield sighed. "He stole something that wasn't his. If he got his neck broken with dreams of fortune in his head and the taste of Colgate in his mouth, that's kind of on him."

"Bit of a harsh punishment for an opportunistic theft," I replied.

Caulfield nodded. "I'm just saying, if you start trying to fix all the world's problems, that's a bridge you'll never finish painting." He raised his glass.

"Nemo Me Impune Lacessit."

"Not one I know."

"Motto of the Scots Guard. Rough translation – no one screws with me and gets away with it."

"Amen," I said. We clinked glasses and drank our courage.

Caulfield and I parted company in the lobby of the hotel, and I was halfway to my room when a significant thought occurred to me.

I stopped and played it through in my head carefully. Satisfied with my own logic, I turned on my heel and went back down to the lobby, looking for Bence. I found him in the storage area behind the bar, stacking empty beer bottles into crates. He stopped working as I approached and straightened up, looking genuinely pleased to see me.

"Mr Jake," he said, "how are you, mate?" Bence clearly liked the addition of the word 'mate' to his lexicon.

"Good thanks," I said. "How about you?"

He indicated the beer bottles. "Hanny has big plan that we will save up money and open small hotel back in Hungary. I promise myself that this job I pay some kid to do. What is up?"

"I just wanted to ask a favour. Do you have a tool box I could borrow?"

"You have problem in room?" he asked. "I come fix when I am done here."

"No, it's okay," I said. "I just want to borrow a screwdriver."

He shrugged. "Sure. Is in storeroom by the bar. Black box. Yellow handle. Take what you need, leave back when done."

I dug out my wallet, pulled out a fifty euro note and handed it to him. He shook his head.

"No need for tip."

"I'm giving it to you because I might be taking a screwdriver off you that you're not going to get back."

He shrugged philosophically and pocketed the offered note.

He lit a cigarette and offered me one. Screw it, I thought, condemned man. Last one, either way. He lit us both, and we stood there puffing away in comfortable silence.

"I did not ask," he said suddenly. "Your hot date. You have good time?" He nudged me in the ribs. "Do baszni? Boom boom?"

I smiled. "You know in the UK, a question like that might be considered rude?"

He shrugged again. Bence had a great repertoire of expressive shrugs. "In Hungary too. But hey, Mrs Abby, she's a good looking woman. Nice too. Too old for me, but when I am your age, I sleep next to a woman that nice, I think to myself, 'Bence, you are lucky man'".

"You're sleeping next to Hanny, you are a lucky man," I replied.

"I am," he said. "She is too good for me."

"They're all too good for us mate," I said, dropping my butt and stepping on it. "Pretty much every single one of them."

CHAPTER THIRTY-SEVEN

I grabbed the tool box, exactly where Bence had said it would be, and hauled it up to my room. Once there, I opened it up and found a screwdriver that would suit. Spent about half an hour working it to my purpose.

After that there was nothing much to do apart from lie on the bed, try to get some rest, and wait for the clock to roll around to 9pm.

I'd set the alarm clock for 8.30 and was awoken by its insistent and steady beeping. As I went to turn it off, I saw that I had a text from Abby.

MyTirol Hotel. Room 204. Stay safe.

I texted back. 'You too.' Then I deleted her message and my reply, got up, splashed water on my face and dressed in my walking gear.

I shoved the gun I had taken from Lee into one pocket, and the screwdriver shiv I had fashioned in the other. Made sure I had the pendant around my neck, and hauled my rucksack over my shoulders.

That was it. No more stalling.

I left my room at 8.55, walked along the hall and down the stairs.

As I was crossing the lobby I glanced left. The entire Morton's crew and guests were there. Last night of the holidays, and they appeared to be going for it. No one saw me apart from Bence. He waved, then paused, no doubt noticing I was wearing walking gear and a solemn expression.

I smiled and pointed my index and forefinger at my own eyes, then at him.

I see you.

He smiled and did the same.

I see you too.

Then I left, unsure if we would ever see each other again.

It was a clear and cold night as I made my way down the streets to the Moos. Once there I was clear of the reach of streetlights, but the fully waxed supermoon meant I didn't actually need the torch I had brought with me. I hammered through the walk as much to get my core temperature up as anything, and made it to the cable car base station with ten minutes to spare. I skulked in the shadows under its jutting terminal loop and waited for Caulfield to show up.

He did, exactly on time, suddenly stepping out of the shadows at 9.30pm. Though I had been on high alert looking out for him, I still didn't see him until he appeared next to me. I guessed he'd had years of training and experience to hone that skill.

He was dressed all in black, including a black beanie hat covering his hair and black war paint in smears across his face.

"You don't think the mascara's a bit much?" I asked.

"I don't think so. Moon's a lot brighter than I'd like."

"You know I can still see you, right?"

He shook his head. "It's not meant to hide you. The human brain is very good at picking out faces in the dark. All this does is break up the lines a bit, make a face harder so spot. Realistically it might only buy you maybe ten seconds, but they could be a vital ten seconds. Did anyone see you leave?"

"Bence," I said, "but we didn't speak. Hopefully he thinks I'm taking a last stroll around the mountains before we all go home."

"Well, shall we do exactly that?"

I extended my arm, inviting him to lead the way.

The gravel path underneath the cable car pylons was even and smooth and we made good time despite the gradient. We didn't speak. There wasn't anything to say.

An hour brought us to the top of the peak where the path turned right through the trees, the curve of the peak off to our left cutting through the pines. We followed this along, still ascending, but at a slower pace, and eventually Caulfield paused. We crouched down. He produced a map inside a plastic protective cover and a small torch.

"Okay," he whispered. "This is where you and I part company. I break left here, up through those trees. Over the ridge, stick parallel with you on the far side, past the meeting spot by about three hundred metres, then shimmy back over and down, and come back to meet you. You go straight up the path and follow it around the mountain ridge. Give me a five-minute head start, then go. Try to keep them talking for as long as possible. Talk loudly to cover my approach. There's nowhere to go to your right but a sheer drop down, so if it's going south, run back along the path and hope for the best. If they start shooting at you, just stay low."

"Have you got anything in the way of weapons?" I asked.

"Steak knife I pinched from the hotel kitchen. You?"

"A shiv I fashioned from a screwdriver. And this." I said, producing the gun from my pocket.

He stared at it. "Where did you get that?"

"From Lee – the guy with the scar," I said. "You want it?"

"You don't?"

"I've never had firearms training," I said. "I'd probably take my own foot off if I tried to use it."

"Did you test fire it to make sure it works okay?"

"Yeah, I popped a couple of rounds into the side of a barn on the Moos this afternoon, just to be sure. Of course I haven't bloody fired it. He was prepared to shoot me with it, so I assume it's in working nick."

I handed it to Caulfield by the barrel. He took it off me, hit the magazine release and slid it out of the butt, and seeing that it was full, and jammed it back into place. He pulled the slide back and confirmed that he had a round in the chamber.

He grinned. "Well that's a bonus," he said. "Odds moved slightly more in our favour." He made sure the safety was on, jammed the gun in his pocket and zipped it up.

"OK," he said. "I'm good if you are."

"Good as I'll ever be," I replied.

"Right. In that case, see you on the other side."

With that he turned and scampered off into the trees. Within three seconds I couldn't see him, within ten I couldn't hear him.

Left on my own, I stood up again and looked at my watch, counting off his five-minute head start. It seemed to take a lot longer than five minutes, and I was fighting a near overwhelming urge to just turn around and double-time it back down the hill as fast as I could. But the time passed, and I was still where I was supposed to be. Taking one last deep breath, I forced myself to move forward.

Two hundred metres brought me clear of the trees and the path levelled off. As Caufield had said, there was now nothing but a sheer drop to my right, while to my left was a loose shale slope angling up to the top of the ridge, maybe fifty metres above me. The path itself was only about a metre wide. To my right, on the far side of the gorge, I could see the lights from the Coburg hut, maybe half a kilometre away and roughly level with me. For one second I thought I saw someone walk past one of the lit windows and I found it absurdly comforting. Then I forced myself to look down and in front of me before moving again. Despite the visibility of the moon, I trod carefully, as there was every possibility that one wrong step would pitch me over the side. I had only about three hundred metres left to cover, but due to a combination of fear and caution, I calculated I was only covering about fifty metres a minute.

I was about halfway there when I saw the figure appear on the path before me. Tall and shadowy, impossible to make out in any detail at this distance. I figured this was who I was going to rendezvous with. Who else would be stupid enough to be up here in the dark? A few seconds later, I could see a change in their body language and realised they had seen me too. They took a few steps forward, then stopped, obviously deciding to stay put and let me navigate the treacherous narrow path to them. As I inched forward, I realised it was Herman, and he had a look of grim satisfaction on his face. Whatever was going to happen, he was clearly planning on enjoying it.

Two things were now immediately apparent to me. The first was that there were plenty of deserted places you could have picked for a midnight clandestine meeting that were a lot easier to get to than this. And the second, was that there was absolutely no way he intended to let me walk off this mountain alive.

What else could I do but keep going forward? About ten metres away from him there was a large boulder that jutted out from the cliff wall into the path, narrowing down to about a half a metre. I shimmied cautiously around that, my heart thumping, and made it safely to the other side where the path widened out again. Abruptly, I decided that was far enough. I stopped. I couldn't think of what you were supposed to say in a situation like this so I just called out.

"How's your head, mate?"

Herman held out his hand and indicated I should approach him.

I had no desire to be within arm's reach of him, but I forced myself a little closer.

Then suddenly Caulfield appeared silently behind him, stepping out of the darkness. Herman heard him and turned, then Caulfield used the energy of his spin to shove him clean off the path. I could see his arms flail as he disappeared over the side, reaching desperately for some non-existent purchase, then he disappeared. He didn't even have a chance to scream. About four seconds later I heard a sickening noise as his body hit the hard rocks below.

"Jesus Christ," I gasped. That had not been part of the plan. Caulfield peered cautiously over the side and, presumably, visually confirmed what his ears had told him.

Then he turned. I could see he had the gun I had just given to him in his hand.

"Sorry old chap," he said apologetically, as he raised it and pointed it at me.

CHAPTER THIRTY-EIGHT

I felt my knees go weak and wobbly and start to sag. Then they went entirely and I plonked down hard on the boulder behind me. Caulfield seemed happy to give me time to get myself under control, watching my face carefully as I worked through the details in my head. Eventually I shook my head to clear it and looked at him.

"I should have seen that one coming, shouldn't I?"

Caulfield smiled. "Don't be so hard on yourself, Marley. It all got very messy towards the end. You know what they say – no plan survives first contact with the enemy."

I looked at him. "So are you just going to shoot me?"

He nodded, looking glum but determined. "I really didn't want it to come to this, but we are where we are."

"You killed Wall?" I asked.

He tutted. "Come on. We've mostly been honest with each other, more or less. Let's not stop now. Abby Tate killed Wall. You know that."

I had a stab of panic that I had been royally duped by Abby, and I replayed her story over in my mind, trying to see where Caulfield might have been standing in the background. "Yeah, okay but then how did you figure the angles – I mean, you weren't in on it with her, were you?"

"Well that's the thing. I really did get hired by the hedge fund people to look after Wall when he was off tripping balls up the mountains. But while the pay for that work is better than her majesty's forces, it's still just crumbs from the big table. I saw a chance for a real payday. So I organised a little side deal for myself with the hedge fund's competitors. They were only too happy to cough up for what they could make on the back of Wall's new code, should they get their hands on it. Easily enough set me up for a long and happy retirement."

"Nice beach house, south of France?" My voice sounded forlorn in the dark stillness of the mountain.

"I'm thinking Cote D'Azur," he confirmed. "So either way, Chris Wall was going to have an accident on the mountains. But I'd done my homework when I got the deal. Researched Wall's past life and flagged up anyone who might have a grudge against him, might want to do him harm. That was quite a long list, by the way. I recognised Abby Tate from the first minute I saw her. Signed in under her divorced husband's name? I knew she was planning to make her own move. I thought to myself – well, this might make my life a lot easier. I'll just give her a minute and see how she plays this one out. That first night when you introduced yourself, I was actually looking at her, trying to figure out if she had the spine for it. I had just decided that she did when you said hello. Serves me right for trying to dodge my own dirty work."

I kept talking, all the time keeping my eye on the gun and evaluating the distance between us. I focussed, holding my voice steady, but the back half of my brain was replaying that wet crunch of bones in the valley below, and my stomach was doing lazy flip-flops.

"So we're all out walking. We come back and Werner tells us Wall is dead. What was the plan then?"

"Pretty simple really. I'm silently applauding Abby for a good job well done. Impressive how she covered her tracks. Werner asks us if we can identify the body. I know he won't take possession of Wall's stuff until that happens. I say I'll go. Just give me a minute to change out of my walking gear. I went upstairs, figured it would take me less than three minutes to pick the lock to Wall's room and lift the hard-drive from his laptop. But it's not there. I didn't figure on Tubster making his opportunistic play. I had the whole way to the morgue and back to figure that one out. There were not that many people in the frame. Then I get to the morgue and see that Wall's stupid yin-yang decoder is not where it's supposed to be. Things are well and truly getting out of hand now. You can see why I was kicking myself for not just doing the deed myself. Would have been so much simpler in the long run."

"So then you killed Greg?" And anger crept into my voice for the first time. "For money?"

"What do you think I was doing in the army?" he spat. "My entire career was killing people for money. It makes no difference that it was sanctioned by the powers that be, the end result is the same. Only difference here is the pay cheque I get."

I took a breath. Let my shoulders relax. "But when did you do it? I mean, as near as I can figure, it must have taken you twenty minutes at least."

"To kill him? No, it took less than four." He mirrored my own release of tension. There was no venom in his tone, instead he talked as he had done before, in the pub, or over breakfast. Just men at arms, sharing stories. "When we were all drinking at that impromptu wake.

We were there, but people were running in and out. Margaret and you going out for a smoke. People heading to the bar. Popping off for a pee. I went to get a big round of drinks. Ordered it. Told Bence I was nipping to the toilet while he got it sorted. Ran up the backstairs from the bar. Into the room quietly, one minute. Find him in the bathroom brushing his teeth, put him down, another minute. Leave and pull the door behind me, leaving the Do Not Disturb sign on the handle, back downstairs, pay Bence, arrive back at the table with the round as ordered. Three minutes, forty-two seconds. I actually had to wait for Bence to finish making Bryce's margarita. Done and dusted."

I don't know if he noted my look of impotent rage that I had no doubt had crept across my face, and added, even with some softness, "It was quick and he didn't see it coming, if that's any consolation."

"You killed him, then came back down and spent the next two hours cheerfully drinking?"

Caulfield shrugged. "I just needed his time of death to be sometime when I had an alibi. Everyone, including you, would swear on a bible that I was downstairs at the time, because I was. No one is going to attach any significance to the amount of time it takes to get a round in. Then later, after we'd all gone to bed, I snuck back down let myself back in, took my time, set the shower running so it would look like he'd slipped on the wet floor, locked the door with the chain to make the scene even more secure, gathered up the laptop bag and both laptops. Then went out the balcony doors, pulled them behind me, and shimmied over the balcony to your room. You and Abby weren't subtle about leaving together so I knew the coast was clear."

"But you dropped the book on the bed?" My rage began to turn inward, hating that I had so many questions still to ask, but I knew that questions were the only thing between me and a trigger pull.

"I didn't drop it," said Caulfield. "I tripped over the sodding rucksack you left lying in the middle of the floor. The book fell out of the laptop bag as I went over, and I didn't hear it hit the bed."

"So now you have the laptop? Only problem now is the bit-locker key."

"Yes, but not insurmountable. I had to call in the reinforcements for that one." He remained motionless.

"Lee and Herman?" I prompted.

"Well Lee, as you call him, is a man I used to serve with. He wasn't averse to a bit of wet work back in the day. I trusted him, and our favourite queen's pension not being what it once was, he was up for a slice of the Wall pie. He was living in Munich so it was a short car ride for him. He brought Herman as some local muscle. At this stage we thought Abby had the necklace. I'd already searched your room and her room and couldn't find it, so I figured she had to have it on her. Couldn't figure out why, but didn't really care. We figured a simple mugging and we'd be done."

"Didn't work out as planned though."

He smiled, happy to grant me my small moment of mockery.

"That woman can be an awful pain in the arse when she wants to be. They would have let you go. All of this would have been unnecessary. Even back in the bar today, I really tried to talk you into letting me come up here alone. You didn't need to be here. This is your doing as much as mine."

"What was it you said earlier? No one screws with me and gets away with it. Doesn't just apply to the Scots Guards."

"Yeah, fair point. My colleague is very pissed off with you, by the way. You're lucky I didn't let him come up this mountain – you'd already be dead."

I shrugged. "None of us like to be reminded we're getting old. Are you planning on killing him too?"

Caulfield shook his head.

"He's earned his share and money doesn't cover what I owe him." He nodded over the side. "Between the dog tags and the tattoos, he'd have been too easy to trace, a risk best not to take. Besides, I don't like racists."

"But now the holiday's coming to an end and you're running out of time. You thought Abby had the pendant. You sent the goon squad to threaten her. But it turns out, I had the medallion. And here we are."

"Here we are," he agreed.

I stood up. Caulfield immediately gave up the pretence of a relaxed conversation and pointed the gun at my centre mass, even though there was a good five metres between us.

I slowly reached under my collar and removed the pendant. Offered it out to Caulfield.

"Look," I said, "just take the sodding thing. We don't care. Rich get richer. Always have, always will. What do we care which rich person it is?"

"I'm sorry old boy, but that's not going to work out. You'd never let it go. Jesus Christ, you're supposed to be on holiday and you spent most of your time doing Neumann's job for him. Even if you said you would, you're lying to yourself. And secretly you know that."

I knew he was right, but that wasn't what I cared most about.

"Just let Abby go."

"That boat has sailed. I like the woman and I have sympathy. With what Wall did to her and her family, she was deserving of her revenge. But I can't trust what she will do when you turn up dead." He looked at me with real vexation. "You have no idea the hoops I jumped through to try to resolve this without unnecessary bloodshed, but you beaked your way in and fouled it all up."

"You don't know where she is." I tried.

"I'll find her. It will be quick. If I can do it without scaring her, I will. But we're done now." He looked at me with what I perceived as genuine regret. "It's over. I'm sorry it's come to this, but we are where we are." He straightened up and pointed the gun at me. "Can I convince you to just step off the ledge? They say you pass out on the way down."

"I've got a mate who's a skydiver. He'd call bobbins on that. Besides, you're not going to shoot me. I assume Neumann's supposed to mark me down as a walking accident statistic. A bullet hole will mess with that theory."

Caulfield shook his head. "I'll toss the gun over after you. Neumann will figure it was Herman's."

So that was it. Game over.

"Was any of what you told me true?" I asked.

For one second, he lowered the gun. If it wasn't absurd given the circumstances I would have called his expression incredulous, indignant. "Are you asking were we really friends? The walk? The beer in the sun? Everything I told you about myself. Yes, all of it was true. Yes, you were my friend. And for what it's worth, I really regret this."

Then he raised the gun again. The muzzle looked as big as the Channel Tunnel.

"Don't," I said quietly.

"Sorry, old man," he said sadly.

And pulled the trigger.

There was a flash. I felt something hit me on the forehead just above my eye and it was only as I fell backwards, that I heard the loud bang of the bullet that was going to kill me.

CHAPTER THIRTY-NINE

This is what happens when you pull the trigger on a firearm loaded with live ammunition. The trigger pull activates a spring mechanism that hammers the firing pin into the back end of the cartridge like a nail into a wall. This ignites an explosive charge in the primer of the cartridge. The primer then ignites the propellant – the main charge that takes up most of a cartridge's volume. The propellant chemicals burn at an extremely high speed – an explosion – and this in turn generates an expansion of gases very quickly. The sudden generation of gas splits the bullet from the edge of the cartridge and sends it rocketing down the gun barrel at extremely high speed, the grooves gyroscoping it as it goes. In a handgun, the chemicals are designed to start burning slowly, in a process called deflagration, so the bullet starts moving smoothly. They burn faster as the bullet moves down the barrel, gaining maximum velocity just as it reaches the end. In a handgun, the bullet might be somewhere in the three-hundred-metre-per-second range by the time it exits the muzzle. After that it's just a case of seeing if you hit where you aim. End to end, that's what happens when you fire a gun.

That's assuming, of course, that no one has taken a hacksaw and cut a length of a stainless-steel screwdriver shank, then wedged it tightly about halfway down the barrel, ramming it home with a mallet. When you fire a gun under those circumstances, something completely different happens.

CHAPTER FORTY

I must have passed out, if only because I came to looking straight up at the night sky. I was lying on my back with my right arm hanging over the edge of the path and my left leg perched on the boulder. I shimmied left and backwards, and sat up with a grunt. Something was running into my left eye, partially blinding me, and touching my hand to my forehead revealed it to be blood. I pulled the gaiter from around my neck up to my forehead to use as a bandana, and wiped the excess blood from my eye. It helped a bit.

I tried to stand and realised that in addition to my head wound, I had twisted my left knee, and that something had shredded through my jacket and grazed an impressive looking laceration along my ribs on the right-hand side. Other than that I appeared to be alive and relatively unscathed. I cautiously shimmied over the boulder and limped forward to see how Caulfield had fared.

He was a mess. He was sitting on the path, his back slouched against the sloping ridge of shale. His right hand, the one that had been holding the gun, was completely gone, and with his forearm cradled in his lap, I could see a nub of bone sticking out where his wrist should have been. He had several bleeding wounds in his torso, at least one of which looked serious, and the whole right side of his face from his cheek to his hairline looked like mincemeat. If there was an eye left in that mess, I couldn't see it. He was wheezing heavily, and I guessed he was losing his grip on life at a pace only slightly slower than he was losing blood.

I wasn't sure he was conscious, but then he turned his head towards me, rolling it against the rock support behind him.

I think he was trying to smile, but the end result was lopsided and ghoulish.

"Good move," he said, his voice raspy and slightly slurring. "Didn't see that one coming. How did you know?"

"In the Caledonia today, you said that Harvey died with the taste of Colgate in his mouth. Werner never told you that he was brushing his teeth. Neither did I."

He thought this through, then nodded philosophically, conceding his own foul up.

"So what now?"

"Even if I tried to help you, I don't think you'd make it down this hill alive. I could try to call Werner and get the local mountain rescue involved, but I think the end result will be the same."

He shut his eyes and grimaced. He must have been in a staggering amount of pain. "OK, so maybe let's just sit here awhile."

I nodded and sat down on the boulder. My left knee had frozen solid, I couldn't get it to bend, so I had to keep that leg out in front of me.

We sat there in silence for a minute or two, just listening to the night sounds of the mountain.

At last he turned towards me and said, "I'm sorry. I just really wanted that beach house on the French coast."

"I know you did, mate. Don't worry about it."

That was the last thing he said. He went back to looking down into the valley below, and a minute or two later, his chest stopped rising and falling, and his wheezing breath tapered into silence. I waited another few minutes after that, just to be sure, then I limped over to his body. I found his room key in his trouser pocket, along with a wallet. It had a driver's licence in the name of Richard Caulfield, and two bank cards, one in the name of Brian Crosbie and the other in the name of Stephen Keller. There was also a picture of a woman with a small boy on her lap. Sitting on a blanket on a beach somewhere. A nice sunny day. Both smiling and happy. I put the picture carefully back in the wallet, then slid it back into his pocket.

"I wish you'd told me that story," I said to whatever was left of him.

Then I stood up, took a deep breath and heaved his body over the side.

I didn't hear it hit the bottom.

I sent Abby a text that said, 'You're safe now,' and turned around and started limping my way slowly back down the mountain.

CHAPTER FORTY-ONE

Even though gravity was on my side, it took me about four hours to walk down the mountain, due in part to my inching steps, and partly because I had to stop periodically to give myself recovery breaks. My head appeared to have stopped bleeding but my left knee, which was humming show tunes by the treeline, had graduated to full operatic arias by the time I hobbled past the cable car station three miles down the track. I stopped on the Moos to give myself another breather and to watch the sun creep over the top of the mountain – to see another dawn on the earth. The day will come when you will not, I thought to myself. But not today. On reflection, I decided I was quite pleased about that. Then I limped the final leg of the journey back to the hotel.

It had gone 7am by the time I got there so the front door was open. As I shambled across the lobby, I could see Hanny bustling about, setting tables for breakfast. Her back was to me, she didn't see me, and she was humming happily to herself as she worked. I swear I felt genuine love for her then – for her industry and her fortitude and her small but noble ambitions in life. No shortcuts for her, no screwing people over to get ahead. Just build it up by yourself, step by step, brick by brick, and maybe at the end you have something you can look back on and be proud of. That was the kind of person you wanted on your side.

I made my way upstairs and let myself into Caulfield's room. I found the laptop bag stashed under the bed. It took me a few minutes to figure out how to pop the hard drive from Wall's machine but I managed it. Then I went back to my room, threw it on the bed, stripped naked, cranked the shower as high as I thought I could stand, and just lay on the stall floor, letting my mind go blank as the near scalding water washed everything away.

CHAPTER FORTY-TWO

About an hour later, I got dressed. I phoned Neumann and told him I had all the answers he needed, but that he would have to come to me because the walk was beyond me. He said he would be there in twenty minutes. I said I would be sitting on the bench by the war memorial. I went there and waited for him.

He was right on time. He got out of his car, and came over, sitting down next to me.

"What happened to your head?" he asked.

"It's a long story," I said. "I'll start at the beginning."

I told him a version of events that was as close to the truth as I could manage, leaving Abby out of it: Caulfield had killed Wall to steal his laptop and its contents, Harvey had beaten him to it, he had then killed Harvey. I had found the medallion out by the woods, thought nothing of it, and he had lured me up the mountains when he realised I had it, and that I had given it to him. He had murdered his co-conspirator and tried to shoot me, but his gun had exploded and he had gone over the side, taking the medallion with him. I told him where the body would be found and that he would probably find the laptops in Caulfield's room.

Werner sat through all of this until I finished, then said, "You're lying to me, aren't you? I figured some things out myself. Ms Guerin killed Mr Wall. Because she holds Wall responsible for the death of her sister and in turn, both her parents."

"You figured it out," I said softly. "Well done you."

"Brandt told me that you asked to see the iPod in storage. That you got him to scroll down the playlist then you stopped at one song. Edith Piaf. The song that Marianne Tate was listening to as she died. About halfway through it changes to the anguished voice of a young woman, crying hysterically and saying how used and stupid and worthless she was. I had been in contact with a policeman in England who investigated her death. He had made a note of the song on the record player. That was Ms Guerin's sister. She put the noose around Wall's neck and murdered him."

"She didn't murder him," I countered.

"She engineered the circumstances that resulted in his death. What's the difference?" He was stern.

"So what are you going to do now?" I asked.

"What am I going to do? I am going to arrest her and charge her. After that, the courts can decide."

I sighed.

"OK, Werner. Double or quits."

"I don't understand."

"You will," I said. Then I threw the last card I had on the table.

CHAPTER FORTY-THREE

It was raining when I left the Southern Cemetery in Manchester and caught the bus back into town. When I got off at the town centre just after noon I went into the WH Smiths near the station and bought a map of the city. I sat in the same café as I had before, drinking a cup of tea and studying it. The same man behind the counter asked me had I found the cemetery okay, and I said I had.

He then asked what I was looking for on the map. I said I was looking for Maine Road, the stadium of Manchester City. It was the only thing I could think that an eighteen-year-old might want to see in Manchester.

"Not Old Trafford?" he asked.

"Maine Road," I said.

"Good lad," he said and left me to it.

What I was really looking for was Kensington Street, which was about a ten-minute walk from Maine Road. That was the address I had to work with.

It took me forty minutes to walk there. Red brick terrace rows on both sides. There was a pedestrian alley at one end and I hovered there waiting for any signs of life in number eleven. I'd had the foresight to buy a sandwich and a can of coke at the cafe, and I ate as I waited. Eventually, at 2pm, a man came out, got into the tatty looking Vauxhall Viva parked outside, and drove off. I stepped back as he drove past. I thought about my original plan. A revision had come into my head based on the car. I thought it through and thought it better. I left then, scoured the neighbouring area for shops that might sell the things I would need. Three stops got me what I wanted. The man came back at around 5pm. By then I was back in my original post in the pedestrian alley. I was patient. I had waited this long, I could wait a little more.

Eventually, around 7pm, the man came out again, and this time he forsook the car to walk down the road. I trailed him at a distance of about fifty metres. I guessed correctly where he was going. The pub was called the Turing Tap. Further than I expected – the best part of a mile, across Whitworth Park. I hovered, walking up and down the road in a loop, never letting the pub entrance out of my sight. A couple of local lads gave me a bit of hassle in passing but I ignored them and they moved on.

It was about 10.30pm when he came out. He'd been in there three hours, so I guessed he was maybe four or five pints in, but his walk was steady enough. Not long now. I followed him at a distance and when he was within fifty yards of his house, I sped up to close the gap between us. I timed it just right, five feet behind him, just as he was reaching into his pocket to get out his house keys, opposite his car. I looked around. It was a Tuesday night in outer Manchester in 1978. There was no one else on the streets. I called out.

"Excuse me."

The man turned. I took a step forward and he looked at me. Ten years had aged him twice that. I had grown since he last saw me and it took him a while, but he got there.

"Danny?' he said. "Is that you?"

"Hello, Charlie," I said, producing the revolver that my father had taken from the corpse of a French officer, nearly forty years before. "Get in the car."

For a moment, he looked nonplussed.

"What are you playing at?" he asked, more confused than angry. "Where's your dad?"

Where's my dad? Not my mum.

I took a step forward. "I'm not messing about, Charlie. Get in the car, or I'll shoot you right now."

This was the dangerous part. If he didn't do it, I was sunk. But he did. He carefully unlocked the driver's side and I got in the back seat behind him. We were off the street now, so I felt a bit safer.

"What's going on?" he asked. "What's got into you?"

He was acting confused but there was something cagey in his demeanour that hinted he'd always known that it would eventually come to this – sitting in a car with a gun pointed at him. Maybe he just had not expected that it would be me.

"We're going for a drive," I said.

"I've been drinking," he said plaintively.

"You seem sober enough to me. I think you'll be okay." I jammed the gun into the base of his neck.

"Okay, okay," he said. "Where are we going?"

"Salford Docks," I said.

He twitched. "Not sure I know how to get there."

"You found it six years ago," I said. "You'll find it again."

He knew then. Why I was there. But in the end, he started driving.

It took us a half an hour. I had memorised the route that afternoon, so I was keeping an eye out to see if he tried anything. I also kept an eye on the speed limit and the traffic signals, but he behaved.

We got there and I told him to find a quiet spot to pull over and he did. The Irwell River was to our left, and we were surrounded by nothing but derelict storage buildings and heaps of ballast overgrown with weeds. It was dark and there was no one in sight. I had expected this. It was where they had found my mother. If it was quiet enough to dig a shallow grave and hide a body, it would be quiet enough for our business. I told him to take the keys out of the ignition and he did that too. I pocketed them. Then I carefully got out of the back seat and moved to the front passenger seat, next to him. Another place where I had to be careful.

By now, he had sobered up a bit and was trying to assert his authority.

"Is that your dad's old gun? That probably doesn't even work, you know."

"I wasted a bullet on that bit of old land near Northwall," I said. "Just to make sure. It worked fine and I've got five rounds left."

He was silent for a minute.

"OK," he said at last. "What now?"

I reached into my rucksack and removed the bottle of cheap vodka that I had purchased that day. "Now," I said, "You have a drink and you tell me what happened with my mother."

He protested at first. He had no idea what happened to my mother, what I was talking about, but he stopped when I hit him in the bridge of the nose with the gun barrel. He yelled in pain but stopped protesting.

"Why do you think she came here?" He whined.

"A letter you sent my father. There was a corner neatly cut out of it where the return address was. The only people who would have seen it were my parents. My dad would never have come here. But my mother? She didn't write very well, so if she needed the address – to show other people, to get directions? I remember the way she used to neatly cut out coupons from newspapers with scissors. It was her. You put the address on the letter as well, so I found you."

"That's it?" he asked. "That's nothing…it…"

"Stop, Charlie," I said. "I know roughly what happened. I just want the details. It's your only chance of staying alive. Just have a drink and tell me."

He looked at me for a long time, then he unscrewed the lid of the vodka, had a swig, and started talking.

My mother had originally planned to come to Manchester in the two weeks that James and I had been with the Frasers on the south coast. She hadn't counted on my dad hitting her hard enough to break her ribs and make her immobile for the best part of a month. Charlie had come north the year before. Ronnie's fate had confirmed that the good times in London were over. He had some problems with some gambling debts and owed about five grand he didn't have to people he couldn't pay. So he just skipped out one day, heading north, eventually settling in Manchester, where he got a job in a bookies and started running a few side hustles.

When my mother arrived, he was surprised to see her. He had only written one letter to my father telling him where he was, to let him know if any opportunities came up down south, and he would do the same in return. He had not expected a reply.

My mother told him that she was leaving for good, taking us with her, and she wanted help getting set up in a new town. Charlie had helped her in the past, maybe he could help her now. Help her find a job and a flat, then she would come and get us.

Charlie had no idea what to say about any of this, but he invited her in. They had a few drinks and as she sat there and vented, Charlie formed a thought. It involved my mother's engagement ring, the one my father had given her all those years ago.

"Your dad always said it was worth a fortune back in the day," said Charlie. "I said to your mother that I could flog it for her, get some cash, get her set up. She said no, she needed that for your education. She said you and James were smart enough to go to college, to live better lives and she wanted that for both of you."

He was drunk now, about halfway down the bottle.

"She fell asleep on the couch. I think she was very tired and a bit drunk. I thought maybe I could pawn it – we could take that money, work it up a bit at the dog track then get the ring back. Your mum would have cash to really set you up and I'd have a bit to get me back on my feet again."

He stopped, maybe realising that this was the same story as always. Work it up a bit. How many times had that worked out?

As my mother lay there sleeping, Charlie had tried to coax the ring off her finger.

"I wasn't going to steal it," he said. "I was just going to get it valued so I had a number to convince your mother with."

But she woke up just as he had it off her finger and she had launched herself at him in a rage, hitting him around the neck and head, shouting that she must have been mad to come to one of my father's ne'er do well friends, expecting anything different than had gone before.

"She was screaming blue murder and hitting me, so I grabbed her around the shoulders and put my hand over her mouth and told her to calm down and stop shouting. She was still trying to scream and only fought me harder, kicking now, and trying to claw my face. I kept holding on then suddenly she just went still."

I said nothing.

"I didn't know what to do," he sobbed. "So I waited until the middle of the night, then put her in the car and drove out here."

"You stripped her naked, Charlie. And dumped her body in a shallow grave on waste ground."

"I only did it because I thought if Old Bill found her, they might think she was the victim of some nonce. That's what they did think when they did find her. I didn't enjoy looking at her. I swear I didn't. It made me feel sick. I'm so sorry, Danny. I loved your Mum. Not like that, but she was always good to Ronnie and me, to you and Jimmy, and the times sitting around your kitchen drinking and singing were the best times of my life. It felt like family."

He sobbed a little to himself and had another swig of vodka without me prompting him.

"It's all right, Charlie," I said. "I just needed to know."

We sat there in silence, and he kept drinking. He finally passed out with about a finger of vodka left in the bottom of the bottle. Right at the end he offered one more piece of information.

"Danny," he said. "The ring. I took it to three different pawn shops and they all said the same. The diamond was just paste. Only worth about a three quid, and that was because the setting was nice. The rock was worth nothing."

Thinking about it, that didn't surprise me.

He passed out, snoring loudly. I got out of the car. It was about one in the morning. I rummaged in my rucksack, took out a length of garden hose – another of my purchases that day – fed one end into the tailpipe, the other through the passenger window and sealed it all up with masking tape. Then I started the engine and sat down on a nearby slag heap to wait. I think it was all over in about half an hour, but I waited three times that just to be sure. Then I walked back to Manchester Piccadilly and caught the train home to deal with my father.

CHAPTER FORTY-FOUR

For a long time, Werner said nothing. When he finally spoke he sounded flummoxed.

"You're confessing murder to me? That you killed someone when you were eighteen years old?"

"Nearly thirty-five years ago. For much the same reasons that Abby killed Wall. All just little bits of history repeating."

"You could have gone to the authorities."

"What was my evidence? A cut-up envelope? Charlie would have known the law couldn't touch him if he held tight and kept schtum. He was never going to face justice. He killed my mother, Werner, and I couldn't live with that. So I did what I did. It didn't make me feel any better. If anything, it made me feel worse. Then I went and became a policeman. Maybe not a very good one at the start, but I got better. I did some good. I loved a woman, married her. I lived and shared a life."

"No, you didn't," he said aghast.

"I'm pretty sure I did."

"It was all a lie. How can you say you shared a life with someone if you kept that secret?"

"I didn't," I said plainly.

"What?"

"I told my wife what I just told you now on our first date. On a bench in Hyde Park, near the Serpentine, in 1985."

For a long time, Werner struggled to speak. Eventually he said, "You took that chance? Why?"

"Because sometimes it's very, very important to give people a chance to reject who you really are." I stood up. "You think about what you want to do. Like I said, two for one. If you come to arrest Abby, I will confess to the murder of one Charles Turner in 1978 in Manchester. We won't run. Our train leaves for Innsbruck at 2.30pm. Come and find us there if you have to. It was nice to meet you. You're a good man, and I think you're a great cop, and no matter what, I hope we're still friends. You do what you think is right."

I started to walk off, then one last thought occurred to me, and I turned back. "Oh, and seriously mate, no messing. If you like Melanie, just ask her out. Life is short and there's always less time than you think. Take care of yourself. One way or another, I'll see you around."

CHAPTER FORTY-FIVE

There's not much to tell after that. I went to find Abby in her hotel room and got her up to speed. While mortal danger had passed, we weren't completely out of the woods yet. We went to our rooms, packed up, said our goodbyes to those of the group who had not already left. Bryce, Margaret and the Smiths. I got a hug from all the women and a handshake from George. I wished them all well, then Abby and I caught a taxi to the train station a half-hour early.

We sat on a bench enjoying the sunshine, both of us waiting for the howl of sirens that never came.

The train arrived and we climbed on board. Five minutes later it trundled off, leaving Ehrwald behind. As we passed the town limits, I glanced out of the window and saw Werner and Brandt. Their car was parked on a layby overlooking the tracks, and they were leaning on the bonnet, watching the train pull away. Brandt saw me and waved. Neumann sat there with his hands in his pockets, watching me go. But since that was exactly what I had asked him to do, I didn't figure I could complain about it.

I left Abby at the airport in Innsbruck to catch a flight back to London. At the departure gate she gave me a hug.

"Thank you," she said. "For saving my life. For keeping me out of prison."

I didn't have the heart to tell her that living with your past, living with what you have done, was a prison that you made for yourself. And that, in my experience, you needed someone else to show you the way out. I hoped she found that person, but I also knew it would not be me.

She kissed me softly on the cheek, then turned and walked to the security gate. I waited until she had gone from sight, then I went to find the train station.

It took me two days to make it back to Wiltshire. Fred was happy to see me.

A couple of days after I got back, I went to a local computer recycling company and bought a laptop compatible with Wall's hard drive. It took a bit of effort but I finally got a look at what all the fuss was about.

I assume that Wall's coding genius was like the space behind the curtains where a little man worked the levers of Oz the Great and Powerful, because what I could see looked like a fairly intuitive dashboard tracking live stock prices of a few sample companies against a target. From what I could gather, there was a company called Paradigm who manufactured digital twin software. Their stock was currently at 16 quid a share, but pending changes in EU law, a potential competitor buyout, and a few other feeds, it was predicted to shortly top out at twice that.

The red line seemed to be forty-five quid a share. So I phoned Helen and asked her to buy me 20K of Paradigm stock and to sell it at 44.90. Then I gathered up the hard-drive and the pendant and put it in a jiffy bag addressed to Wall's company.

I got it weighed and stamped and asked Jon to drop it in the post box at Paddington station next time he went to town.

Around the first of December, Helen phoned to advise that Paradigm stock had topped out at 45.20 and had levelled off at thirty-seven quid, and that my ill-gotten gains were in my account. I took a trip into the bank, got a banker's draft made out for twenty thousand Euros and mailed it to Hannah Szabo, care of the Vorsehungberg Hotel, Ehrwald. I took the other 15k and mailed it locally.

A few days after that we were all having Christmas drinks in the pub and Peter came in, very excited. He had just received an anonymous donation that covered the cost of the cinema equipment, with the only caveat being that the donor wanted a specific film shown as the premiere. He was hoping to get the installation done in time for a grand opening on Boxing Day.

"It's sort of a Christmassy film anyway," he said, "so all good."

"*Die Hard*?" guessed Jon.

"*The Great Escape*?" said Bruce.

I got up to get a round in and didn't guess anything.

I received two communications that I didn't expect. Both were on Christmas Eve. The first was a text from a number I recognised, with a photo attachment. It was a picture of Werner and Melanie – at a party, judging by the hats they were wearing and the streamers obscuring the shot. They were both smiling at the camera, hugging cheek to cheek, and I guessed they both had a few drinks on board.

The text simply said 'Fröhliche Weihnachten'.

I assumed it was just a scattergun to everyone in Werner's phone, so my number must still have been on it. I hesitated to reply, but only briefly.

Fröhliche Weihnachten to you and Melanie too, mate.

The second was an A4 envelope that Jean handed me at the post office, along with the usual mountain of junk and bills. It was the brochure of a charity company that was working to build community health centres in Namibia. There was a flyer with the charity's logo and two words scrawled on it in a sloping feminine hand:

'Rise again.'

It also contained an eight-by-ten photo of two teenage girls. From the clothes and the hairstyles I guessed it was from the late 80s. I recognised one of them. Hugging each other on a park bench, laughing at the camera, with their whole lives ahead of them. I took it home and carefully set it on the one small bookshelf I had on the boat. Next to my favourite picture of Emery.

On Christmas Day, I had no plans, but it was clear and crisp, cold but with not a breath of wind, so I took Fred for a really long walk along the Ridgeway. I got home to my boat, lit the stove, and started reading *Life After Life* with the dog snoring on the couch next to me. It was a good day.

The following morning, I met Peter on the street and he reminded me that it was the inaugural night of the village hall cinema. I told him that I was really sorry but I wouldn't be able to make it, as I had a prior engagement.

That evening, I made a flask of coffee and, for once in my life, remembered to grab a head torch. I wrapped up well, marched up the frosty hill and deep into the forest, off the beaten path, until I found the oak sapling that I was looking for. It looked like it was doing well.

"Hi Rock," I said sitting down. "Thought I'd come and say hello, as it's been a while."

I poured myself a mug of coffee and started talking.

On one hand I knew this was stupid, that I was a grown man sitting on the cold hard ground talking to a tree, but on the other hand I figured it had to stand for something, because if it didn't then nothing did.

I told her everything, and when I got to the end, I just sat there. I listened very carefully, and I could just about hear the strains of *Edelweiss* drifting out from the village hall, across the canal, up the hill through the forest, to the stars, and the darkness beyond.

This book is dedicated to the memory of my father,
John Joseph Sheerin, and my friend, Sandra Collins
– both of whom walked the same hard road to Iowa.

ACKNOWLEDGEMENTS

I need to offer huge thanks to a number of people for getting *Marley's Ghosts* over the line. First and foremost, Charlotte Fleming, who did as much work on this novel as I did. I hope Katherine Vile would be proud of both of us.

Thanks go to Rebecca Varley-Winter for a brilliant line edit. Dominic LeHair at PaperRhino for the interior design and Marija Džafo for the cover.

Jon Stock provided invaluable early guidance. Thanks to Professor Susan Anderson and Bruce Mason for medical advice. Gary Crisp for a steer on London policing in the 70s and 80s. Peter Angus for advice on ballistics and a handy map of the Ehrwald region. Any mistakes are mine and not theirs.

Pauline Fleming for the best birthday present ever. Also to Fiona Lund, Tegan Day, Bruce White, Matt Melly, Angie White, Prue Saunders, Helen Angus and Adrian O'Reilly who all read early drafts and provided much needed feedback – be glad the Parisian swingers bar scene never saw the light of day.

I should also apologise to the good folk of the Tyrol for those times when I got a bit liberal with the geography of their environs as the story demanded.

I would also like to give special thanks to my mother who is the epitome of the valour of women.

And above all Karen who has been the Pole Star in my night sky for more years than I can remember.

Printed in Great Britain
by Amazon

56947585R10219